THE BRIDGE OVER THE NEROCH
AND OTHER WORKS

Also by Leonid Tsypkin

SUMMER IN BADEN-BADEN (FABER EDITIONS)

Leonid Tsypkin

—

THE BRIDGE
OVER THE NEROCH
And Other Works

Translated from the Russian by
JAMEY GAMBRELL

faber

First published in 2013 by New Directions
This edition first published in 2024
by Faber & Faber Ltd.
The Bindery, 51 Hatton Garden
London ECIN 8HN

Typeset by Typo•glyphix, Burton-on-Trent DE14 3HE
Printed and bound in the UK by CPI Group (UK) Ltd, Croydon CRO 4YY

The story 'The Last Few Kilometers' originally appeared in *The New Yorker*. The story 'The Cockroaches' was translated by Ann Frydman and is used here with permission of Stephen Dixon.

This book is a work of fiction. Any references to historical events, real people, or real places are used fictitiously. Other names, characters, places, and events are products of the author's imagination, and any resemblance to actual events or places or persons, living or dead, is entirely coincidental.

Note to reader: The language in these pages is a reflection of the historical period in which the book was originally written.

A CIP record for this book
is available from the British Library

ISBN 978–0571–38691–8

2 4 6 8 10 9 7 5 3 1

Contents

Foreword
by Jon McGregor

The Bridge Over the Neroch opens in 1972, with one of Leonid
Tsypkin's narrators, who are all versions of one of Leonid Tsypkin's selves, emerging from the Moscow Metro into the 'blinding
July sun' and noting that the Moscow Metro smelt the same in
1936 – a smell that he doesn't describe but which I imagine as
some combination of warm, damp air, a metallic odour like the
taste of pennies, with a vague underlying sense of soot and
grime – preoccupied by the thought of all the people in the metro
carriage he has just left growing older, marrying, arranging
meetings and hurrying home with their purchases in a shopping
bag before disappearing from the memory of those who have
seen them, disappearing altogether, the 'crowds sauntering along
the wide streets during holidays' also all disappearing, this idea
of sudden or eventual disappearance underpinning Tsypkin's
personal history and understanding of the world at large, haunting his thoughts and his writing, the writing to which he
dedicated all the spare time of his tightly constrained life, writing
that would be discovered two decades later by Susan Sontag,
emerging from the warm, damp, sooty air of the London
Underground at Charing Cross and picking up from outside a
second-hand bookshop a slim paperback by a little-known
Russian writer, finding herself blinded by the light of what she
will later come to call one of 'the most beautiful, exalting, and
original achievements of a century's worth of fiction and para-
fiction', in an essay that accompanies the 2001 reissue of that
short novel, *Summer in Baden-Baden,* a novel written in

dizzyingly long and digressive sentences that seem to represent something of the mental state of this most twentieth-century of writers, trapped as he was by his family's experience of the Holocaust and by the anti-Semitic repression of the Soviet empire, a novel whose reissue Sontag was largely responsible for and that she championed, a copy of which this writer reads in a hectic daze while crossing Poland and Belarus and Russia by train, emerging from the Moscow Metro one bright July evening in 2004 to fall into conversation with an elderly man both well-dressed and obviously down on his luck, a man who is not Leonid Tsypkin but carries somehow a Tsypkinian air, who has many things to discuss and an elegantly accented, almost professorial way of discussing them, including the writings of George Orwell, the woeful state of Russian literature, the best restaurants in the neighbourhood and the restaurants one should avoid, the numerous benefits that could be made of any delicious pennies that might possibly be spared, and the idiots who had refused to read the manuscript he was lugging around in a white plastic carrier bag, an almost fantastical final detail given that the image of the unread manuscript is so central to the story of Leonid Tsypkin, a man who spent his entire life writing only for the drawer, dedicating – according to his son, Mikhail – every evening after work to a dogged writing and rewriting of his sentences, anxiously striving for the achievement that Sontag and others would eventually recognise without ever daring to show those sentences to anyone, such was the threat posed by the Soviet authorities to writers and especially to Jewish writers, not daring even to circulate his work as underground samizdat, waiting to smuggle those manuscripts out of the country until his son and daughter-in-law emigrated in 1977, this emigration being both the vehicle for his eventual publication and one of the two great personal losses in his life, as described in the closing scene of the second novella in this collection, *Norartakir*, with the haunting image of the parents watching from their balcony as the son walks across the boulevard and into the piercing autumn wind, 'a stooped figure wearing a nylon jacket and carrying his suitcase', disappearing behind a tree and then reappearing, and then disappearing again behind a trolley bus which carries him away and out of their lives, this loss appearing almost as a foot-note to the recounting of a couple's visit – riven with bureaucratic humiliations and paranoias – to Norartakir, in Armenia, while the other loss, the slow death of his father, is threaded through the background and occasional foreground of *The Bridge Over the Neroch*, the title novella in this collection, which is both a memoir of that slow death and of the era of war and anti-Semitic persecution his family narrowly lived through (which is to say that some of his family narrowly lived through it, the fifteen-year-old Leonid and his parents smuggled out of Minsk at the last moment in a lorry full of pickle barrels), these greater and almost unfathomable losses running beneath everything in these stories, happening in Tsypkin's telling almost in passing, out of frame, coming briefly into focus in parenthetical asides made all the more striking by dropping unannounced into the middle of a long description of a stamp album, or a pair of binoculars, this being Tsypkin's central technique, and his gift, and his com-pulsion, the thing he laboured over during all those long evenings that his son Mikhail has described: to digress, endlessly, anxiously, as though rushing – as his narrator does in *Norartakir* – 'from one side of the lane to the other', incidents blooming one from the other as though all things were now and forever happening, the trains always pulling up in the sidings at the camps, the card-playing guards getting up one more time to adjust the dials on the pipes before returning to their games, and Jesus, as in the astonishing sequence that makes up the third chapter of *Norartakir*, 'God Is With Us', still and forever looking down from his cross through fly-encrusted eyes at the disciples in their fishing boats, the marching crusaders crossing the hills, the priests at the head of the torchlit pogroms, the careful stepping down from the trains of the patient Jewish families with their well-packed suitcases and bags, a sequence that will stop your breath each time you read it and which is only one among the many that are layered upon each other in this collection of stories and novellas that have only by a series of chances made it from Leonid Tsypkin's drawer and out into the world, into the typescript that this writer now finds himself reading on Line 4 of the Paris Métro towards Montparnasse, worrying about missing his connection and wondering if the smell of the Paris Métro in 2024 is identical to the smell of the Moscow Metro in 1972 or 1936, or the smell of the London Underground in 1991, when Susan Sontag was first reading Tsypkin's work, or of the New York Subway in 1982, when Mikhail Tsypkin – who would settle into a long American career and can now be found on Instagram, posting mostly photos of his dog, Toby, and occasionally his son, Leo, both of whom have large, puppyish eyes – first took the smuggled manuscript pages of his father's work to the offices of *Novaya Gazeta*, the Russian émigré magazine who would publish Leonid's work for the first time on 13 March of that year, the news of the publication reaching Leonid and his wife Natalya just seven days before Leonid Tsypkin died of a heart attack at his writing desk, a death that his son can have no way of foretelling as he inhales those identical metallic and sooty smells of the metro, clutching on his lap his father's manuscript, wrapped carefully in a white plastic carrier bag.

THE BRIDGE OVER THE NEROCH

1

The smell of the metro in 1972 is identical to that of the metro in 1936, and for a second I experience the same feeling of irrational, trenchant joy that I did then, in 1936; it seems to me that right now, when I rise to the surface, I'll be under the same blinding July sun near the Sokol metro station. I don't remember why I was there, I only remember the blinding sun, the tall, new buildings I'd never seen before, and the burning, cold taste of an Eskimo Bar—Moscow is the only place they have Eskimo Bars, nowhere else, they're almost synonymous with Moscow. However, for some reason, I can't remember the faces of the people who sat in my train car, rode up the escalator, and walked down the streets: What did they look like? Who did they look like? Like heroes from the films *Circus* or *Jolly Fellows* in overly wide ties (back in fashion again now) and baggy trousers, their naïve, good-natured faces filled with belief in a happy future, or like Natalya Rozenel, in a long dress with short hair, and wide-open eyes spinning in amazement? I exert my memory, but in vain: there are no faces, no suits, no people. What is it—my forgetfulness or the forgetfulness of history? And will my neighbors in the subway train of 1972 and I disappear in the same way from the memory of the schoolboy in a nylon jacket sitting right across from me now? He already has an almost fashionable haircut, and I can make out the features of a youthful student in him, tall and thin, sweeping their hair out of their eyes with a casual movement of the head like this entire generation—I see his features when he is no longer a student, but a husband, a newlywed with a wedding ring and a string bag in hand, hurrying home with his purchases; and just like me, he will disappear from the memory of those who will see him, and for a moment I imagine all the people filling this car—worried, carefree, having just left a woman or traveling to a rendezvous, discussing the morning planning meeting, riding with sketches, folders, synopses, with lawyer's briefs typed on twenty-two pages—the lawyers' pencils follow the lines and underline particularly important places that should be emphasized during the hearing. For a moment, I imagine all of them lying in identical poses: their arms crossed on their chests, their heads arched back, their faces yellow, wax-like. All of them, as though on command—some sooner, others later—will disappear, leaving nothing behind, and the crowds sauntering along the wide streets during holidays will disappear in the very same way, and sometimes I imagine that they are all riding with me in one car—bipeds dressed in suits, with briefcases and purses in hand.

2

The hunchbacked road of lustrous cobblestones descended steeply to the river. A pudgy, short-legged adolescent boy with unhealthy circles under his eyes rode a bicycle along the very edge of the pavement, hugging the sidewalk. His heart pounded in his ears like a hammer, and he touched the brakes with his foot; rumbling wagons passed him, but he felt that he was racing along at incredible speed, passing everything and everyone, and that's the way it would seem to him his whole life, because his pride would never allow him to acknowledge his weakness. Descending safely, he rode on to the wooden bridge with a victorious expression. Below him flowed the Neroch, a narrow little river unmarked on any map, even the large-scale ones; the boy found this a bit insulting, because, even though by summer's end, rusty tin cans and broken bottles covered with algae jutted out of a trickle of water, in the spring, the river flooded, inundating the municipal park and even the little houses behind it; the current became powerful, and the dark water almost reached the bridge; large chunks of ice crashed against its piles, causing the bridge to shudder. Trees torn out by the roots floated down the Neroch, as did beams and boards. At that time of year only the Volga—which the boy had never seen—could compete with the Neroch. Having crossed the bridge, he turned left and, pushing the pedals, drove up the street to the incongruous building, resembling an ancient castle, that housed the Opera Theater— just a few days ago on the square, in front of the theater, where the local fops rode bicycles, sometimes "no hands," with only a barely noticeable movement of the torso—just a few days ago, his mother's first cousin, Tusik, had taught him to ride the bicycle. Tusik ran, holding the bike with one hand on the seat and the other on the handlebars, pouring sweat, because it wasn't so easy to keep a bicycle with a pudgy boy in a state of balance—he had to take on his weight and push him straight, so that the boy and the bicycle didn't crash into him; and he kept on repeating the same thing: "Pedal, Gavrila," though the boy wasn't called Gavrila at all; but the boy heard something rakish in this cry, something that put him on equal footing with Tusik—like men understanding each other—and he pedaled industriously. The bicycle began to acquire more independence so his teacher was no longer supporting the vehicle, but simply holding it by the seat, and occasionally the boy even felt like this was a hindrance, so he turned the pedals even harder, and for a short moment he completely escaped all oversight—the teacher was just running alongside, and the boy couldn't believe that he was riding by himself, without anyone's help, as though he'd suddenly flapped his wings, risen up, and taken off—and he felt a combination of terror and sweetness at this scalding, sudden independence, which threatened to end in a crash. He looked back—Tusik wasn't running or even walking, he just stood there, his figure grew smaller and smaller every second, and with his arm he made a movement that meant "turn faster!" Losing his balance, the boy flew onto the asphalt, scraping his knees, which bled, and Tusik ran over, helped him get up, and it started all over again. Tusik was tall—at least he was the tallest in the family—with straight dark hair that easily strayed over his forehead, and calm, deep-set gray eyes in which something reckless occasionally appeared: his grandfather had been a Don Cossack, whose photograph was preserved in a gold locket that Tusik had inherited from his mother; the boy loved to open it and look at the photograph: the Don Cossack had a long, bony

6

face, and mustaches like Taras Bulba, and his light eyes were even deeper set than Tusik's. The boy was very proud of this kinship, although no one in the boy's family had ever seen the grandfather—his daughter, Tusik's mother, had been obliged to convert to Judaism in order to marry, and the Don Cossack, not very happy about this fact, never visited. Tusik's parents had died when he was two or three years old, and since then he'd lived with the family of his aunt, the boy's grandmother: she loved Tusik more than her own daughters, at least she said so, maybe because of his calm, agreeable disposition, or maybe because, since he was an orphan, he gave her the opportunity to feel that she was a benefactress . . . Riding on to the little square in front of the Opera Theater, the boy merged into the stream of other riders—less than a year later, the German headquarters would be located in the building of the Opera Theater, and the boy's family, already evacuated, and seized by a premonition of the winter of '41, received a postcard from Tusik on just such a clear, late-summer day—the only postcard they ever got, written in his careful handwriting, which leaned left. Tusik begged them not to worry, everything was fine, but how are they, how is Mama?—that's what he called the boy's grandmother—and on the other side of the postcard, written in his own hand as well, was the return address: "247 A. S. B." After asking around among friends, the boy realized that A.S.B. was the "Aerodrome Service Battalion," and he kept trying to imagine Tusik's duties—for some reason he thought that Tusik carried crates of ammunition or cleared the airfield, but by then Tusik was a commanding officer, although a junior one; during the Polish events he was in the army and was awarded one square for his service. The boy remembered quite well the photo of Tusik in his field cap pushed back at a jaunty angle, and the square pinned to his lapel; they managed to get that photo later from some distant relatives, then enlarged it, almost made it into a kind of portrait—and now it's on my mother's desk, under glass, next to other photographs and a group family portrait, where the boy is still a little boy: thin, wearing a sailor's uniform, his ears sticking out. And when the knee-high autumn mud on the outskirts of the Ural town began to freeze and hoarfrost began to appear on the walls of the room where the boy's family lived after evacuating, and the presentiment of an early winter actually turned into an unprecedentedly early winter—but maybe that's the way it always was in the Urals—and all the streets, and roofs of the one-story wooden houses with carved window frames were covered with snow and the brushwood bought at the market could easily be brought home on a child's sled, and milk was sold in the form of semi-transparent ice chunks—a whole bundle of letters and postcards arrived with the stamp: "Addressee left," but the thought of Tusik's death didn't gain a foothold in the family immediately, and even after the war was over, they kept on hoping and asking, and then they found out that one night German tanks had suddenly burst into the place where Tusik's unit was staying. Tusik and the other soldiers were quartered in barns on the outskirts of a village, and the boy tried to imagine the expression on Tusik's face in the last minutes of his life, when the tank drove over the shed and, turning right and left, it began to crush everyone there with its caterpillar treads; then they probably took him away to be shot because he was a commander, a communist, and a Jew, and they couldn't take him prisoner; but the boy could never imagine the expression on Tusik's face just before dying, because Tusik could pin him flat on his back with one finger—he was the tallest person not only in the boy's family, but in the whole building. When the boy's classmates came over, he left the door to his room open on purpose so they could see Tusik when he walked down the hall. Tusik couldn't die by someone else's hand—he was stronger than everyone! The boy smiled sadly at these thoughts, because by that time, when the circumstances of Tusik's death had become known, the boy was no longer a boy. I dream of him often even now, and my dream is almost always the same: I know that Tusik has died and at the same time he's with us—he lives in our pre-war apartment, but he isn't quite living, he sort of inhabits the place; he appears only at night, alien and elusive. I can never manage to talk to him or even see him—but he sleeps in his usual place, on the squashed sofa with protruding springs, in a huge room— bigger than whole two-bedroom apartments are these days—partitioned by screens, behind which grandmother and grandfather live. On this very couch Tusik used to demonstrate various fighting tricks to the boy, pinning him down with one hand and then squeezing and pummeling him, giving off hideous sounds at the same time. In the dream, I walk into this room, but the couch is empty—there are only wrinkled sheets and protruding springs, and I have a feeling, no, I know for sure, that Tusik is at his girlfriend's, that's where he really lives, that's where he talks and acts like himself. Grandmother was very proud that as a sign of obedience, Tusik didn't marry the girl-friend after all; he went out with her for several years, but grandmother didn't care for her: she thought that the girl didn't love Tusik and had her own, selfish designs on him. She had short hair and glasses, but even wearing glasses, she squinted a little. Sometimes Tusik would go see her with the boy—the boy was secretly jealous of her and perhaps precisely for this reason, he revered her; after all, if Tusik loved her, then there was defin-itely something extraordinary about her. Grandmother talked with pride about her own views on life—the family considered her very liberal and inclined to philosophical generalization— she loved to make philosophically edifying remarks: for example, "he who honors not his mother and father is undeserving of God's kingdom," or "c'est la vie," or other things of that sort. Sometimes she'd sit down at the upright piano and play a love song with her gout-disfigured fingers: the only piece left from what she referred to as her formerly extensive repertoire was a ballad about a fairy who lived on the bank of a river, and someone named Mark in whose arms she writhed ardently; the boy couldn't understand—why did the fairy have to writhe in his arms? Grandmother didn't exactly sing, she recited, but in the musical passages accompanying the recitation, and which were supposed to represent the full depth of either Mark's or the fairy's feelings, or perhaps of them both, grandmother would play the wrong notes; her crooked fingers couldn't keep up with the development of the ballad's musical thought and fell on the wrong keys. Grandmother's parents, considered ahead of their time, had taught their children to play the piano, and when grandmother was eighteen years old, they sent her to Paris, where she completed dental courses and learned to smoke. Sometimes after dinner, she would send the boy to her room for a *papirosa* and matches—so as not to carry the matches, the boy would return to the dining room with a lit *papirosa*—my wife still can't forgive my mother for letting me do this. Grandmother valued the independence she had acquired more than anything else in the world—it allowed her to be condescendingly philo-sophical toward grandfather, whom the family thought stingy, and who threw plates at grandmother for her extravagance, to the accompaniment of superb curses in the Jewish language; but he also exhibited the occasional inclination toward didactic aph-orisms, of which his favorite was: "This is how small children drown, bathing in the summer season." That phrase pops up in our family to this very day. Grandfather wore a mustache and was an obstetrician and gynecologist, and he often took the boy with him on his visits. While grandfather examined the patient, the boy sat in the lacquered-top carriage with puffy tires, looking at the coachman's wide back, and waited patiently near some wooden house on the edge of an unpaved street: there was the prospect of the return trip, when they would pass all the dray carts and even a lot of carters. In the evenings, grandfather sometimes took him on walks, and his high, laceless boots, which knew little wear, squeaked cozily; the two of them walked along the main street of town, and almost everyone they met, especially women, greeted grandfather, and the boy was pleased that the whole town knew his grandfather. When grandfather was buried, his head, with its sparse strands of gray hair fluttering in the December wind, bumped around, occasionally hitting the side of the open coffin, because the hearse drove over cobble-stones; it seemed strange to the boy that it didn't hurt grandfather and that he wasn't cold in the freezing weather, since he was dressed only in his suit; the boy walked just behind the hearse—which had black, twining columns supporting a canopy—but in front of the band and the funeral procession that probably stretched for several blocks. From the doorways of houses and from behind front gates women came out wringing their hands—they sighed and lamented: "Lord almighty, it's the doctor who delivered me!"—and the boy was pleased that he was walking to the sounds of the band at the head of such an enormous procession, and that the entire town was saying fare-well to his grandfather. However, he knew about the women mostly from family stories, because he doesn't actually remember them himself; nonetheless, I can still see these sighing and lamenting women clearly; they lined up along the sidewalk as though waiting for a cosmonaut to pass in a parade. Just before his death, grandfather asked to be given morphine to hasten the end, and while everyone had gone to the pharmacy, he called his grandson to him to say good-bye—the boy leaned over him and for his whole life he remembered the touch of his grandfather's prickly mustache. (Exactly one year later, on the very same day, their dog disappeared, a little white dog with black spots, which sometimes left puddles that looked like figure eights on the linoleum.) Returning home after the funeral, they ate dinner, because after spending so long in the cold, everyone was starving—the boy remembered they had meat patties for the second course, and that he ate a lot—however, it's entirely possible that his aunt told him about the dinner later on. She and her husband arrived from Moscow early in the morning not long after grandfather died, on the train that passed through their town as it made its way between borders. The boy never did manage to see this Trans-Siberian Express, but for some reason he thought that it was made up of yellow wooden cars with mirrored windows. Grandfather had died at night when the boy was asleep, right after he was given a shot of morphine, and when the boy awoke, his aunt was already in their apartment as though she lived there. On one of her visits, she had brought the boy a canary in a cage; when the canary died, they cut open its stomach for some reason, and it turned out that the bird was teeming with worms. The boy would make his aunt draw—he would lie in wait for her, and besiege her with sketch books or pieces of paper; while drawing, she chewed on her tongue, putting it in her cheek, and it was rather lovely. While doing his lessons, the boy also stuck out the end of his tongue, especially when he was working hard, and his aunt told him that he got that from her, and he was proud of this, because she could draw vases or a glass with a flower very precisely, sometimes even using paints, but when the boy asked her just to draw something, she would say that she only knew how to copy—later he found out that her specialty was called "art history"; when he had grown up, he would go to Moscow and she often took him with her to openings, anniversary evenings, or artistic discussions, because he thought that his true calling was painting, and she supported him in this thought. Introducing him to some of her colleagues, she imagined him as her spiritual son, although she would clap him on the shoulder condescendingly even though she was much shorter than he, and tell the story about the time he was mistaken for her chauffeur—he was still wearing an overcoat bought during the evacuation at the time. When they looked out of a taxi and saw people hurrying somewhere, scurrying about, or standing in line, she would say things like—just think, each of these people has his very own, specific personal life, probably someone has just buried his mother, someone else is late for a rendezvous . . . Remember, in Cezanne, or Chekhov? And there you have it, don't you, this is life in the full spectrum of its colors, and only the two of us can understand, because of our spiritual kinship. Sitting in the taxi, they pitied people walking on foot or standing in line, but this pity was very abstract, contemplative, Tolstoyan—and sometimes she would then make a very expressive gesture, as though weighing a round of cheese on her palm, or even an entire cone of sugar—and her fingers were deformed, like grandmother's, although at the time she couldn't have had gout yet—in short, this gesture was meant to indicate the presence of some very subtle philosophy accessible only to the two of them, apparently some more profound version of grandmother's "c'est la vie," and when an acquaintance was sick or dying and she was getting ready for a dress rehearsal or a banquet, she would say: "Remember the meat patties?" raising her eyebrows meaningfully and weighing the invisible round of cheese on her palm—just like grandmother, she liked to emphasize the breadth of her views on life, turning to her relations with her husband as an example: when some young female graduate student would come to see him, she would leave the house on purpose. Her husband was Armenian, but in the first post-war years, he was often taken for a Jew, and he bore this silently, possibly because he wore a hearing aid and couldn't make out what was being said to him; in the morning, on waking up, he snuffled loudly for a long time, as though he were doing something indecent . . . Soon after receiving a packet of letters from the front, grandmother began to lose her memory, and she coughed from smoking, and snored at night, and the boy, who was an adolescent by then, began to pick on her and tease her—he'd shout "Sura-Bura!" at her nonsensically, although she had her own, quite melodious Biblical name; several times she chased after him with a brush, but she never managed to catch him, and once, unable to stand it, she burst into tears and ran out into the street undressed, into the bitter cold of the Ural winter—through her tears she repeated that she'd leave home, because she couldn't stand living there anymore, she was sufficiently independent and could earn enough to eat; the boy's mother had a great deal of difficulty returning her to her room. Her illness progressed, but over a long time: after the war, returning with the boy's family to their home town, she would pour cold water on herself to the waist and go for walks near the house—sometimes she even went to the baker's and signed for her miserable pension, which did, however, allow her to feel independent; she chatted with old acquaintances whom she no longer recognized, always trying to direct the conversation to abstract, philosophical questions; and she called her daughter, the boy's mother, Mama. Actually, that was only later when she spent most of her time lying down and soiled herself, and the boy's mother braided her hair into a thin braid, changed her sheets, held the bedpan under her, and resorted to the Jewish language, in hopes that grandmother would understand her directions better, but she still wet herself. She asked when Tusik would be home from work, and thought father and I were her brothers, who had not been among the living for some years. She died in the spring, the day I moved away from my home town—Mama fell asleep after dinner, and through her sleep she heard grandmother snoring, but didn't ascribe any significance to it. That evening, I was already on my way, and learning of grandmother's death, I immediately saw her running out into the snowy Ural night—she was only wearing a robe and she was sobbing violently and Mama was trying to calm her. I don't remember that the adolescent got in trouble, but I remember that grandmother, whom he had pushed to the point of despair, had more than once threatened that he'd get his comeuppance. She was probably religious deep down, but I didn't get any comeuppance—at least not during her lifetime, and the person has to see it for it to really be retribution—anyway, I'm quite certain that it was only words. Now, in the evenings, I walk into Mama's room—after my father's death, she moved in with us—and I sit down heavily in the armchair that she brought from our post-war apartment. There were two of them, and both had been in the dining room; guests loved to sit in them, and so did I when I visited my parents, but now only a fragment of our apartment remains, only in Mama's room, but it's a deceptive little island, because my wife can't stand the smell that comes from the top drawer of the chest, where Mama keeps her medicines—even the ones that father was treated with when he was sick—my wife claims that the medicines smell like urine and that she can tell two rooms away when Mama has opened the little drawer—though truthfully, she's wrong sometimes, but then she assures me that I simply didn't notice Mama opening the drawer. I sit down in the armchair, cross my legs, and look at myself in the mirror—I see a man who's put on weight, and is no longer young but wants to seem young. With my face in this position it seems to work; and Mama lies on the small sofa in her colorful dark blue zigzag-patterned flannel bathrobe, her legs also crossed; they're bow-shaped for some reason, like a horseback rider's—and she jiggles her right foot rhythmically while making a fan-like movement with her toes, as though she had positive signs of Babinski's syndrome. I want to tell her to stop it, but notice that I myself am jiggling one of my legs as well—it's inherited—Mama herself once caught me doing it. I look in the mirror—I really do have a noble facial features—and I catch myself flaring my nostrils exactly like my father did: before leaving for work he would go to the mirror and, raising his head a bit, like I just did, nobly flare his nostrils, and at that moment he probably thought his features evidenced high breeding, and he would not have seen himself as a sick old man with jowls resulting from the strict diet Mama kept him on; he was a fine young fellow, still fully capable of a great deal—he never did let a single young woman pass without his eyes following her, and I, too, increasingly find myself doing this. Once, Mama told me on the phone that when he was taking his walk near the house in the evening, a drunk tagged along with him, followed him right up to the entrance and then pushed him, and father fell; I imagine how this drunk began to harass him at the intersection near our building—there are traffic lights, but often they don't work, which, by the way, never affects traffic, because at that time of day trams and cars pass by no more that once a minute, and even during the daytime they don't come much more often; arriving home, I stand on the balcony for a long time, looking by turns at the clock and the intersection, which is nothing like Moscow, where I couldn't visually grasp, much less count, all the vehicles passing along the Garden Ring Road at a given moment—when the drunk began to pester him at the empty intersection, father probably quickened his pace, but he couldn't walk very fast, and the drunk ran on ahead, blocking his path, brazenly smirking and winking, as if they had known each other for a long time, but now father was just putting on airs and was pretending not to recognize him. Father retreated into the raised collar of his new fur coat—in the last few years he had developed a strong interest in fashion, and he ordered a Persian lamb's wool coat in Moscow, one with a high black collar like artistes and performers wear; his son tried on the fur coat, which looked good on him, and he thought it was a shame he had to send it off to his father— but the drunk wouldn't leave father alone; he grimaced, aggressively demanding acknowledgment of their old friendship, and then, near the entrance door itself, cursed effusively and shoved father—father sat down softly in the snow drift in his new fur coat with the Persian-lamb collar as though he'd decided to have a rest; grunting and groaning, it took him a long time to get up. Mother brushed the snow off his coat. In the mornings when he operated at his clinic, he was irritable and shouted at the assistants and the operating nurse, as one expects of surgeons. One evening in the tram, when I still lived in our city, a drunk also began pestering me—I got off at the intersection, but he followed me, continuing to bother me, so then I walked straight over to the booth of the duty policeman, who managed the work of the traffic lights, and demanded that he take some measures—the drunk went his own way, and I kept demanding that the policeman do something—he came out of his booth and listened to me with an indifferent, indulgent expression until the drunk was out of sight. Mama was lying on the sofa, jiggling her leg, her mouth was slightly open, you could see the gums in the black trough—she only puts on the dentures she keeps in a cup on the table next to the sofa to eat or when guests come—and so her cheeks are sunken like most old ladies. Maybe I'm just protecting myself, preparing for the inevitable? But when she kicks my son and me out of her room—this happens after he notices that she has been looking through his class notes in order to expose him as a lazy ne'er-do-well, and reveal my connivance, and in reply we accuse her of moralizing and a penchant for reading newspaper essays and editorials on moral themes. When she pushes us out of her room, you can feel that there's still plenty of strength in her arms, her movements are decisive and sharp, like those of a soldier acting on the command "Forward thrust!" She rushes back and forth in the room in search of a suitably heavy object, grabs the stool, brandishes it at us—she's shaking all over, her lower lip trembles—just like mine does in moments of rage, and my aunt's, too, and my grandfather's, I seem to remember now, when he threw plates at grandmother—apparently this is a trait we inherited from him. When we are already on the threshold of the room, mother pushes us out into the hallway with the aid of the door, after which she turns the key twice. "My old lady's made of iron . . ." declares my son, quoting Zabolotsky; he goes into his room and returns with a pencil and a piece of paper. He sticks the paper under the door of Mama's room, and inserts the pencil in the keyhole, pushing the key out of it—he devised this method a long time ago; after a few seconds he pulls the paper with the key lying on it from under the door. When we enter the room, Mama is lying on the sofa, her face turned to the wall, her shoulders shaking soundlessly; the room smells like the sedative Validol— we hesitate in the doorway, I try to say something conciliatory, but as soon as I open my mouth, she jumps up with the same trembling lower jaw and shouts: "Get out of here!!!" in a voice that can probably be heard a block away. We leave, quietly pulling the door shut, as though there were a corpse in the room, and stand in the hallway hanging our heads, avoiding each other's eyes; but my wife, coming out of the kitchen, reprimands us. "You don't have to make so much noise, it is quite possible to express your point of view calmly." Her reprimand is a mere formality because she immediately calls our son to eat, though I still want time to tell him that she is my mama, after all, she's old and anything could happen; but he's already heading toward my wife in the kitchen or calling his friends on the phone and I put off the conversation for another time. Mama doesn't come out of her room—a courageous garrison, dug in the middle of the enemy camp—for the rest of the day. In the evening, when I run into her near the toilet, I again try to speak with her, and without looking at me, she tosses off the phrase: "You'll reap what you've sown!" and again disappears into her room, holding the chamber pot. It's probably a family thing from grandmother—belief in the ultimate triumph of justice, because I am also afraid that I will indeed reap what I have sown, and I anxiously get regular annual checkups.

3

Reflections of flames dance on the wall, snatching a sinuous crack in the wallpaper out of the dark again and again—when the boy was sick, he would gaze at that crack until it turned into a rooster, or an acrobat, or the figure of a stooped old man. The binoculars in the leather case should definitely be taken along; Tusik got these binoculars from his father, who had served in the tsar's army during the recent imperialist war, and, although he was a doctor, he was issued a pair of binoculars for some reason—they were kept in the wardrobe at grandmother's together with two stamp albums—Tusik had a rich collection of stamps, the largest in the entire town—at least that's what the boy thought. Occasionally, he was allowed to take out the binoculars and the stamp albums—the boy would go out on the balcony, focus the binoculars on the window of the next building—where the Sovtorg Employees Club was—the boy wasn't quite sure what this meant, but one time they brought the first secretary of the Party to that club—grandfather had treated his wife and had been at his house—this first secretary, the most important boss in the town, shot himself because they were going to come and take him away, but they didn't get there in time and so he wasn't officially an enemy of the people, but still, no big solemn funeral was held; instead, they brought him to this club, rather furtively, and they only let people in for two hours to say farewell; the boy, who lived right across the way, managed to get in—the coffin was set up in a small room on the second floor—that was probably where the Sovtorg employees had their meetings—and when the boy, proceeding in line with the other attendees, made the turn around the head of the coffin, he noticed a small round wound on the dead man's temple: that was precisely how he had imagined a bullethole. He focused the binoculars on the window of the Sovtorg Employees Club, a squat, two-story stone building, and the window became so huge that it didn't even fit into the viewfinder; then he moved the binoculars toward the far roofs: brick pipes and dark dormer windows that seemed dangerous, but enticing, moved toward him swiftly; near and far all seemed equally close. He sometimes showed the stamp album to his classmates—they knew it was Tusik's album, and when he carried it into his room, they grew reverently quiet; when, carefully turning the album pages, he got to the stamps, each of which was almost the size of a post card—amazing how they could stay attached to the thin paper strips!—when he got to the stamps, his classmates were transformed into nobodies—at that moment he felt stronger than all of them, though it was a shame that he couldn't manage to lure Shlema Mozovsky to his house; Shlema would stick his pen in the crack of the slanted part of the school desk, which was meant for writing, and its flat top; with the tip of his pen upward, he'd pull the pen back and let go—spraying ink onto the nape of the boy's neck and onto his suit, leaving the gray cloth covered with violet stains that wouldn't come out: the boy's mother even decided to complain to Shlema's family, but it turned out that he was an orphan, he lived with an aunt or something. When Shlema tired of spraying ink, he would quietly poke the boy in the back or the arm with his pen. Tusik would have pinned Shlema down with one hand, but Shlema ignored the boy's invitations to come to his place; tall, skinny and stooped, always dressed in the same khaki colored shirt, Shlema would poke the boy with his pen and splatter the back of his neck with ink spots—and all the while his expression remained absolutely impassive. The day after grandfather's funeral, when the boy returned to school following a three-day break, secretly hoping that now Shlema wouldn't bother him, but at the first recess Shlema came over—the boy straightened up, was certain that now he'd hear words of contrition—stuck the boy in the buttock with his pen and asked him if his grandfather had begun to rot in his coffin yet.

A strange half-gloom reigns in the apartment: the light of the not-yet extinguished day—the longest of the year—and the flickering reflections of flames, because the House of Scientists is burning, it's on the same side of the street as the Sovtorg Employees Club—not right next to it but off to the side; in order to see it, you have to go out on the balcony—and the reflections of the fire reach the farthest corners of the room, playing across the walls and on the ceiling; someone just came in and said that the flames had already jumped to this side and the Tunikov house had burned—the third, no, the fourth building from here; in the boy's family the building was referred to by the name of the former owner of the bakery on the first floor of the house; Tunikov had been liquidated long ago, but the bakery remained, and they sold delicious rolls with scallions baked into them, and poppy seeds sprinkled on top. No, no, the reflections of the flames snatching the crack in the wallpaper from the dark came later of course, when everything had already been decided, but now all the members of the boy's family: father, mother, grandmother, and he himself, were loitering oddly in the apartment, like when you're getting ready to move to the dacha for the summer, when everything is packed and you're just waiting for two carts and the drivers. In fact, it's no different: now they're waiting for Tusik— that morning he said he'd come by for them in a truck; but by now, all possible deadlines have long since passed, and father says that there's no point in waiting anymore, and grandmother listens closely and glances out the window to see whether Tusik has arrived. Stefanida is the only one who isn't waiting for anything—she prays quietly in her little room between the kitchen and the toilet, crossing herself first in the Russian Orthodox way and then in the Catholic way; she went to both churches and often took the boy there with her—in the Catholic church painted wax figures of the saints stood in niches—I always think of them when I see a bride in a white dress, frozen in a deathly pallor, between two bodyguards, girdled in colored "Volga ribbons." In the Orthodox church there was the flickering of candles and icon lamps, the smell of incense, and the mysterious gilding that one always had an overwhelming urge to touch, though it was strictly forbidden. Once, when the boy forgot to take off his cap, some devout old ladies dressed in black hissed at him, and he decided to take his revenge—to come next time wearing the Budenny helmet with a five-pointed red star that his apartment neighbor, a Civil War veteran, had given him; but he never got around to doing this, and then the church was blown up, because they were planning on building something else in that spot but didn't; because churches were believed to be a remnant of the past. Stefanida said that she didn't believe in God, but that she went to the Catholic and Orthodox churches just for something to do—in the corner of her little room over the bed hung a dusty, flyblown icon, and next to it a photograph of her niece Sonya with a scarf covering her head, shoulders, and chest; her forehead bulged, and her sleepy eyes strangely resembled those of the female face depicted on the icon, though the icon face was leaning toward the infant. In the evenings, sitting in the little room, he played the card game Sixty-six with Stefanida. For tallying points, the 8 covered any other card; as the game progressed and you won, this card moved, opening up the points you'd won. Stefanida wet her fingers with spit before taking a new card from the deck, and the boy covered the deck and got three points straight off, then another three, and another two—Stefanida shook her head and feigned a sigh; she called two open cards a "pince-nez," three, a "side table missing a leg," four, simply a "side table," and seven was something totally obscene, but for some reason Stefanida wasn't embarrassed to say it out loud in front of the boy; by this time she rarely came out of her room and another woman worked for the boy's family, Marya Antonovna. Everyone in the house called her formally by her name and patronymic, and grandmother would say to her: "Help yourself to a little soup," because Marya Antonovna adored soup and could eat two full bowls in a row; everyone in the house played around with grandmother's phrase. Stefanida became the honorary housekeeper—on Marya Antonovna's days off, Stefanida sometimes did the cooking, and then the boy felt that everything was just like it always had been, because Stefanida had been working for them for twenty years! None of his friends had a housekeeper like this, and no one cooked like Stefanida— in her hands a little flour and water acquired the consistency of dough, and smelled particularly delicious when it had almost risen—the top of the pot lifted all by itself under the pressure of this living, breathing mass. Stefanida would take it from the pot—it still stretched out in sticky strings, but was already sweet—and turning out the dough onto a board covered with flour, she began to knead it, adding a bit of flour, until it became stiff; then she'd roll it out; she'd slap it, beat it, and squish it, muttering: "We're gonna spank your papa's behind." The boy also set about slapping and kneading with a certain zeal, all the time imagining his father's fat rear end, although, when he thought about it many years later, he realized his father's buttocks were scrawny; by that time Stefanida already had the dropsy, and had trouble breathing, and before that she had a cyst—the boy imagined how her entire stomach was filled with this cyst, which contained liquid—grandfather arranged for Stefanida to go to the hospital, and they removed the cyst for her there, but, in Mama's words, until his very death grandfather could not forgive

Stefanida that the night I was born she refused to light the samovar to warm water for my first bath, and once she told grandfather that they were sucking the blood out of her, and Mama still can't forgive her for that. Stefanida was praying quietly in her maid's room, and at the same time there was a knock at the door and everyone rushed to open it, but it wasn't Tusik, just our friends who lived a block away. Their building was on fire and they came to us—each of them with a small suitcase in hand. At their house they had always set the table in the old fashioned way: next to each plate lay a starched, white serviette in a silver ring inlaid with the family's initials.

The third day of the war was coming to a close.

4

On Sunday morning, the boy was woken by the factory horn. It blew long and steadily on one note, like it did on weekday mornings—the sound was nothing like the alarming howl of sirens. The town wasn't far from the border and there were often practice alarms—everyone was informed in advance, everyone took their khaki-colored bag, worn over the shoulder; in the course of ten seconds you had to open the bag, unfold the mask inside, and pull it over your head; but the stiff rubber was hard to stretch, and your glasses fogged up immediately, and then everybody looked like elephants with long, corrugated trunks that you always felt like squeezing to cut off someone's air flow. Having put on the gas mask, you had to take shelter in the lobby of the nearest building; otherwise they'd grab you, lay you out on a stretcher, and take you off to an underground room somewhere with a sign: "Gas Shelter." The siren blew long and evenly; and now you could tell clearly that it wasn't just one factory, but several at the same time—maybe even all the factories in town—and you could also hear some short blasts coming from the direction of the train station—that was the steam engines blowing their horns. The boy's mother was talking on the phone at that moment with a girlfriend who had called her. She had the same name as Mama, and the boy thought it was unbelievable that there was another woman on earth who had the exact same name as Mama; he felt that this woman's existence was an encroachment on his rights and his Mama's; once, his heart beating hard, he took the woman's purse out of the foyer, locked himself in the toilet, extracted a brown wallet, which smelled of leather and powder, and removed a crisp threeruble note—the hardest part was to put the purse back in its place without being noticed. This woman was a head taller than Mama, she smoked and always spoke with an authoritative voice; she and the boy's mama worked in the same hospital, but she was a neurologist, and Mama said that she knew how to hypnotize people. When the two of them returned late in the evening from the hospital, the boy wasn't worried—if anyone got any ideas about attacking his mother, her friend would hypnotize him in an instant. Mama's friend said this wasn't a regular drill. Someone had called her early in the morning to say that the Germans had crossed the border, though they weren't saying anything on the radio. Tusik had once managed to get Berlin on the airwaves. A shrill, hysterical voice, verging on falsetto, threatened, appealed, cursed, and in this mad cascade of German phrases only two words could be clearly distinguished, paired, like twins: *Juden und kommunisten*. "It's war," grandmother exclaimed, and burst into tears. They were all sitting around the radio, but not too close, sort of in the middle of the room, that is, the part of the room where Tusik lived; the radio stood at the head of Tusik's couch, because he knew how to work the radio better than any of them, and before the purchase of this factory-made one, he once made his own radio, an awkward construction of lamps, wires and connections fed by batteries, but suddenly a human voice came right out of it, it was unfathomable. Now they were sitting in the middle of the room like shipwrecked people in a lifeboat in the midst of the raging sea. Grandmother burst into tears quite unexpectedly—that was how she had cried in the first few months after grandfather died: she'd be dusting off the fireplace or taking something out of the closet. At first the boy was surprised, and then he understood that the objects were the reason why she started crying; but grandmother cried like a hurt child, she completely dissolved into the crying, real tears ran down her face, which also seemed unbelievable to him—only children had the right to cry. What he discovered about the relations between men and women seemed just as unnatural to him—children might do things like that, but grown-ups? When he and Mama once ran into an acquaintance, and then Mama told someone else that she was pregnant, the boy couldn't imagine that this grown-up, a serious woman who lived on the next street in the basement apartment, that this woman just two or three months ago had done that, and over several days he worked up the courage to tell Tusik that he knew a certain word—Tusik bent down to him, and the boy, putting his palm up to his mouth so no one could hear, whispered the word almost inaudibly—he thought it was terrible that he knew this word, he felt guilty and dirty and was afraid that Tusik would stop talking to him after that, but nothing showed on Tusik's face—he listened to the word calmly—apparently he'd known all about it for a long time, or perhaps he didn't want the boy to pay too much attention to it. In the same calm way, the head doctor of the hospital where I worked and where we lived—he was very kind to me and my wife, he even fancied her a bit, and she liked him too—took me into his office, even though I couldn't bring myself to ring his bell, sat me down in an armchair near his desk, and remained sitting in his usual place, leaning forward slightly in an anticipatory pose. He was thin, not very tall, and had gray hair; he walked home from his hospital office along the main boulevard—it was called "Doctor's Alley"—in the black hat that he wore even in the hottest weather, with a smoking pipe in his hand—he never parted with that hat, and no one had ever seen him at a meal, he only smoked and drank strong tea. Responding to greetings, he would lift his hat and make a slight bow. His wife suffered from sclerosis and smiled at everyone with an Ophelia-like smile—people said that when her condition worsened, he himself held her bedpan. Not looking at him, my eyes wandering all around the room, I asked him to give me a different apartment, because on the other side of the wall lived a woman with whom . . . and at this point I faltered, but well, you understand, this is all very unpleasant for my wife. He kept looking at me expectantly, as though I hadn't yet come to the most important point, and when I was completely mixed up and fell silent, he told me that things like this happen, you know; it wasn't out of the ordinary; he offered me a glass of strong tea, and shook my hand firmly when I left, so that I even began to doubt whether I had acted all that badly in regard to my wife.

The main street was crowded, as it was every Sunday. Tusik and the boy bought kefir, and when they left the store, there, under a large black loudspeaker attached to the corner of the building, at the place where the tram turned with a squeak from the main street and hurried down along a narrow lane that crossed the street where the boy lived—he always thought that the brakes would fail and the tram would run into the three-story, barracks-like building called the Union House—a crowd of people stood listening quietly: usually they didn't talk like this on the radio. The person speaking paused in unexpected places and sometimes stuttered, especially on words beginning with "p" and "t"—the boy caught on to this immediately because he stuttered too, especially in physical education class when you were lined up and had to count off by numbers: "first," "second," "third"—he always looked out at the line, trying to count in advance which number he was—if he was second, he would wait calmly. Not long ago, he had seen a photograph in the newspaper: the man now speaking on the radio, his pince-nez shining, was looking somewhat askance at a man with black hair, bug eyes, and a lock of hair that fell across his low forehead at an angle—they said that one of his arms was paralyzed or even completely missing, but no one dared say it out loud because he was now considered

29

our friend and ally—he stood there like he was reviewing a parade; it was impossible to see his hands, and his bulging eyes gazed off somewhere into space.

. . . And again the bicycle. The boy pedaled for all he was worth, the real way now. Sweat poured off him, his heart pounded—he had left home, taking advantage of his parents having gone to work—his mother categorically forbade him to do this. He passed by the small building of the local electricity station that had disproportionately tall chimneys, and was called "Elvod" for some reason, and now he was riding along the main street of town, beside the tram tracks—he'd never ridden this far before—and the cobblestones ended and the bicycle now rode along the unpaved part of the street, raising a cloud of dust: to the right behind a fence stretched the local botanical gardens where the trees that grew were the same as everywhere else; on the left was the five-story Publishing House, built not long ago, a blindingly white building with black rectangular windows divided by white crosses, and now came the end of the tram line and the turnaround, and further on, the Moscow highway. To the right was the beginning of Vetryakovsky Forest—on their days off, the townspeople came out here to relax, there were pine trees, and the smell of pine, and this especially attracted the Jewish population of the town, because it's always dry where pines grow—my Mama still likes to repeat this—and between the trees, on special hooks, they would hang rented hammocks, the canvas kind, because the string ones cut into your body—the children or the older members of the family would rock in them like cradles, and everyone else settled nearby on mats; egg shells and scraps of oily paper appeared all over the trampled grass, children ran through the forest, the sound of balls being kicked was muffled by the calls of women's voices: "Monya! Come to Mama, have some strawberries!" Tusik called them all "coconegglings" from the words "cocoa" and "eggs"—and on days off, the boy and his mama would also go out there with hard boiled eggs and cocoa in a thermos. The boy passed the tram turnaround and rode along the asphalt of the Moscow highway toward Vetryakovsky Forest, and if I were now in the boy's shoes or he were in mine, we would almost certainly recite to ourselves, "Here crossed the rails of the city trams/further on the pines stand guard, further they cannot go," but at the time I didn't know Pasternak existed—although there can't be any doubt that the boy could have recited these lines or at least thought about them, because to this day, when Mama hears the word "frost," she always says: "Frost and sun, a marvelous day . . ." And, if looking at the first snowfall, you say the word "winter" around her, she'll immediately respond with Pushkin's line: "Winter, the peasant celebrates . . ." and so on, and when I once asked someone who had just come from Bulgaria: "Well, and how is Bulgaria?" Mama immediately quoted: "Bulgaria is a beautiful land, but Russia is best of all." She probably got this habit from grandmother, and I got it from her. The boy rode through Vetryakovsky Forest, paying no attention to the road, straining hard, the bicycle tires crushing egg shells, and rustling over greasy pieces of paper that remained from the previous morning, and pedaled past the pines with lonely, rusty hammock hooks sticking out. Near the green-plank booth where they usually rented the hammocks, bicycles stood in neat rows at a hastily erected railing—to this day I can't understand how they stayed up, because there weren't any special stands or even any posts there—perhaps they held each other up? A private in a field cap took the boy's bicycle and wrote out a receipt. The boy carefully folded it and hid it in the inner pocket of his jacket. The receipt indicated the factory serial number of the bicycle, so that after the war he could get it back. When he got to the tram turnabout, the wind picked up. Dust got in the eyes, crunched between the teeth, and simultaneously the boy heard the howl of factory horns and whistles—not monotonous and steady like yesterday

31

morning, but alarming, first soaring upward, then unexpectedly falling into a deep bass. A horde of boys ran across the road and clambered up onto the roof of a barn with a joyous whoop. On the opposite side of town, just about where the train station was, brownish-black, pear-shaped patches of smoke began to appear one after the other—they arose out of nowhere and hung in the air a long time, and only the dull thud of weapons from afar, a kind of rumbling, explained their origin; the boy also got up on the fence in order to see better—it seemed like all these bits of smoke and this firing were for no reason at all—just entertainment or training, but suddenly, amid the smoke, in the shimmering pale blue of the sky, he saw airplanes. They flew in an even formation like at an air show—three silvery spots in each chain, paying no heed to the cloud of explosions, as though they had nothing to do with them, and at that moment the air shook with another blast—at the opposite end of town, somewhere in the vicinity of the train station, an oily, black fountain of earth shot up toward the sky, and settled slowly—just like in movie pictures about Spain.

People crowded around the doors leading out into the courtyard of the Specialists' House—among the crowd, the boy immediately recognized a girl with two long, golden braids tied with blue ribbons. She stood next to her mother, and the boy pushed his way over to them—they were either setting off somewhere or just coming home. The girl smiled joyfully at him, as if he were her savior, and he felt like a hero—having turned in his bicycle, disdaining all danger, he was returning home through the city, while they were huddled in the entrance of their building. She smiled, baring her teeth. They were sprinkled with small spots that looked like fly droppings. Actually, the spots were what started it: their fathers worked together—the girl's father ran the clinic where the boy's father worked, and they were both invited as consultants to a sanatorium that had been opened in a resort town—the town used to belong to Poland but after the reunification, it became ours. She sat on the terrace in a chaise longue, it seems, or maybe the boy was sitting there and she walked by and smiled or said something, and he saw those tiny black spots on her teeth—exactly like the ones he had—dental deposits, which wouldn't go away, although he brushed his teeth meticulously. At first this made an unpleasant impression on him—a girl he'd been afraid even to speak to, and it turned out she had the same defect that he did! This was so incredible that for a few days she ceased to seem such an unattainable creature to him, and it's possible that precisely because of this, she noticed him, or maybe she simply felt her own vulnerability. By the middle of the summer, the boy began to feel that he had lived in this resort town his whole life. In the evenings, from the two-story villas (the boy heard the word "villa" for the first time here) which had been given to the sanatorium and rest home—from the villas, densely overgrown with greenery, came the sounds of the tango—not the usual tango recorded on gramophone records, but a fashionable Polish tango performed by live musicians. The boy was afraid to even peek in to see how things were done, and had only the vaguest idea of what went on from a classmate who spent the summer there also, a tall boy who seemed almost a grown man to him at the time; the classmate told him how he danced the tango with the formerly Polish maids, and even hinted that he didn't just dance with them, which made the boy's heart flip-flop with a sweet terror. In the middle of that summer, he and the girl went out on a rowboat. They left the house without saying where they were going—at that point the boy was still capable of decisive action, because he hadn't learned to reason—but as it turned out, everyone at home had been quite worried, especially the boy's mother; when they returned, she reprimanded him and explained that the boat could have capsized, and he could have drowned because he didn't know how to swim. Since then I've been afraid of water, and all my attempts to learn to swim have come to naught because I keep having to check whether my legs can reach the bottom; but back then, at that noontime hour, the blinding, smooth, mirror-like surface of the lake was empty; far off in the distance, on the shore, you could see the green grove of a cemetery with a white stone arch crowned with a Catholic cross. The rowboat slipped easily across the water, and the boy, who had never set foot in a boat before, handled the oars effortlessly. He handled the oars like a regular racer—at least, that's how it seems to me now when I see some sports update on television—and the girl sat across from the boy, facing him in such a way that he could see her brightly colored cotton panties with two wet spots in the most shameful place; possibly these were traces of the water that he sometimes splashed with the oar. He tried not to look at her panties and those spots, and this made her even more vulnerable in his eyes—at that moment he even felt sorry for her, and this feeling probably resembled what we like to call tenderness. Once, in the evening, when he was wandering around the garden of the building where they lived, hoping that perhaps she hadn't gone to sleep and would come out, he saw a blindingly white statue in her lighted window. It was all very fleeting, because the light in the room was turned off the next moment—but the vision of that pinkish white body with the even more blinding, white, small half-circles of her breasts, which seemed to glow from within like an altar or the Joconda, visits me more and more often—the boy caught his breath for a second; now he knew everything, her most important secret belonged to him now, and when, a few days later in the evening, on the eve of her departure they sat on the sofa in a half-dark room and she asked him if he had ever loved anyone before and had he done anything disgusting, he lied to her because he wanted to seem like a man and make her jealous, so he said that there had been something with a girl who came to clean their apartment; then the girl cut off a

34

piece of her braid and gave him the knot of golden hair and he wrapped it in a piece of paper and hid it in his wallet; then he often took the hair out and put it to his lips, although they lived in the same town—could that really be the very same woman I walked around Leningrad with recently? She told me about tourist sites in the well-rehearsed voice of a professional guide, and showed me the buildings where it's thought the characters from Dostoevsky's novels lived; she had a foxlike face with thinning hair—I don't even remember what kind of hairdo she had, but she did have the same fly spots on her teeth—mine disappeared a long time ago, it was just plaque; she had disproportionately small hands and withered fingers, on one of which she somehow managed to keep a wedding ring. She wasn't showing it off anymore, but just after she married, she tried to hold her hand so that the ring couldn't fail to be noticed, and kept saying: "My husband, my husband . . ." According to her, he was an extraordinary man and adored her, and she adored him as well, of course, and their life was filled with extremely subtle intellectual interests and similar friends, but at the same time she appraised me with a knowing look, as though all this was not supposed to have any effect on our relationship—which actually hadn't even existed for quite some time. After the war, when she returned from Germany, where she had ended up with her father, I often accompanied her to the outskirts of town, where she and her father had moved into a wooden house with some Old Believer friend of hers—they said that it wasn't entirely safe to walk in that neighborhood. I would stare carefully at every post and bush and keep count in my head how many houses remained to her garden gate, and all that time she would carry on an endless conversation about German art of the Renaissance and religious mysticism, to which she'd been drawn, living with her girlfriend . . . One morning, when the boy got up, it was overcast and drizzling in the resort town, and the girl's window was shuttered—she had already left, but he clung to hope and wandered around the garden, and then, when the shutters were opened, he climbed up on the wooden cornice, slippery from the rain, and, grabbing on to the window casing, he looked inside, but only saw his own reflection. He jumped down on the ground and began walking around the wet garden again—clouds crawled across the sky, touching the tops of the trees, and probably this was what was called longing. When he returned to the city, the boy began to frequent the four-room apartment in the Specialists' House, which was actually right across the street from the building where Tusik's girlfriend lived—now the boy had his own girl, and he dreamed about how he and Tusik would travel together on the tram to one and the same stop and silently, like real men, shaking hands, go their separate ways—each to his building. The girl's mother, a dark-haired, talkative woman, usually opened the door for the boy; in the boy's family they called her an unpleasant sort, probably because she loved to dress up and she always smelled of perfume—the Germans killed her because she was a Jew. She would take the boy along the brightly lit rooms with red carpets on the floors and on the walls, too, and he tried to pass through rooms as quickly as possible so as not to run in to the girl's father—even when he wasn't home, his spirit was present, he was probably born a member of the academy—a large man, with a large, pedigreed face thrown back, his chin buttressed by his stiff, starched collar. He seemed created to look in the mirror—was my father imagining himself to be this man when he flared his nostrils nobly in front of the mirror? When the girl's father spoke at scientific meetings, he sprinkled his speeches with Latin terms like *summa summarum*, or *nolens-volens*, or things of that sort; not long ago, we were at the same conference and he again pretended that he didn't see me, although we had met numerous times over the years, but this time I pretended that I didn't see him either, I even think I raised my chin a bit, but I'm

36

not sure that he noticed. The dark-haired talkative woman who smelled pleasantly of perfume led the flabby, chubby boy with unhealthy circles under his eyes to see the girl with the long golden braids that were plaited with blue ribbons; her room had a secretary with a table lamp, a narrow, polished cupboard, and a fold-out couch covered with a carpet that flowed down the wall over the couch and then onto the floor. All this created an intimate setting—the boy sat on the couch, and the girl sat on the chair, or sometimes it was the other way around—but I can't remember what they talked about, I can say only one thing for sure: the boy felt quite grown-up, because at this moment Tusik was probably in the building across the way. The boy had been there with Tusik one time: it was a small, dark apartment with rugs, and a platform bed for some reason, from which Tusik would get something, and in the half-light there was a shorthaired woman in glasses with a myopic squint and, it seems, freckles on her face and hands—even in dreams she still takes me away from Tusik. All in all the boy and the girl behaved very decorously, like genuinely well-mannered children, but one time, arriving at the girl's apartment, he found Lyova Zaits there—his chin not only jutted out straight ahead, it also pointed up somehow, meeting the end of his flat nose, like Plyushkin or Judas, and he breathed heavily through his nose, as though he had a chronic cold or adenoids; but Lyova Zaits could jump straight into the water, feet first, hands at his sides—in his red bathing trunks, dark skinned, with a rubber cap on his head, he also swam well, he could even do the butterfly, raising his swarthy body out of the water up to his waist. During the summer, Lyova Zaits lived in the same resort town, where there was a special swimming pool, the boy went there to learn how to swim, they even taught him specially, and theoretically he knew all the movements—lying on his bed he had swum more than one kilometer doing the crawl, the breaststroke, and even the butterfly, but in the swimming pool he immediately pulled his legs up under him as though he were protecting his stomach from a mortal blow—which means he was already suffering from fear of water at that time. I just feel like blaming everything on Mama; it's easier to live with things when it's someone else's fault. But Lyova Zaits could jump in feet first, sometimes he even bent his arms back as though he were a gliding bird, and he'd swim under the water a long time, flattened out like a frog in his red swimming trunks, under transparent green glass, and the girl swam well also, but of course she wasn't anywhere near as good as Lyova Zaits, and the boy often imagined the girl and Lyova Zaits swimming together—they were already far from the shore, and her strength gave out, and Lyova Zaits would save her; the boy tried not to think about this in great detail, because Lyova Zaits would have to hold her with one arm, but the uncertainty was even more awful, and sometimes the boy imagined that he was Tom Sawyer, and she was Becky Thatcher—they had gotten lost in the cave, it was pitch dark, so he lit a candle—they were together and there was no one around, she was trembling with fear, she was completely in his power, and her helplessness and the knowledge of his power over her sparked a feeling of pity in him—of tenderness toward her, and yet another feeling, indistinct, but overwhelmingly sweet and for that reason forbidden—why didn't Tom Sawyer take advantage of his opportunity? The boy had felt more or less the same feeling when he was still very little: it was a hot noon in an evergreen forest not far from the dacha they were renting; for some reason he was alone—maybe for a few minutes, or maybe for longer—and under a large, spreading fir, or perhaps on its lower branches, he saw a green frog, not a frog, but a baby frog, because when he got up closer, it didn't even try to run away from him. Was it dead? He picked up a stick and touched it—the frog didn't move, though it was probably alive all the same, only sick, but then the grown-ups came and called him. He thought about that frog all day long, he thought he could have done something with it, what exactly, he didn't know; the smell of hot, dry pine mixed with this forbidden, sweet thought, and when he came there the next day, the frog wasn't there any more—although he wasn't sure it was the same fir tree; he went back to the same place several times, and even the next summer when they were living at the dacha again—subsequently he felt the very same feeling when he saw a crying baby left unattended, and sometimes he even dreamt about a foundling. I experience something similar now when I'm left alone with unguarded state property.

"Good-bye," he said to the girl with the long golden braids, standing with her mother among the crowd in the entryway to the Specialists' House. She probably smiled at him, and one of them, perhaps even both, said: "We'll see each other again."

5

Outside, it was light as day, and the boy didn't even glance back at the two unpretentious iron posts holding up the canopy over the front steps of his building's entrance. From above, from the balcony, you could see that the canopy was covered with rusty iron, exactly the same as the roofs of buildings—later in the snow-covered wooden house how many times did he remember the entrance to his building. The landlady only gave them two iron beds and one chair, and from the kitchen came the smell of potatoes being fried in pork fat—once, when the landlady wasn't home, the boy's mother opened the little hanging lock the land-lady used to lock them out of the kitchen—but the boy's mother and grandmother and he himself knew where she hid the little key. He and Mama went into the kitchen and she, directed by some unerring sense, or maybe she'd already noticed the loca-tion, stuck her hand through a little curtain and retrieved several potatoes, rosy and firm, not frozen, and the boy also grabbed a couple of potatoes, and he wanted to take more, but he imagined he heard the landlady's steps and that she was already standing in the kitchen door—it was like expecting to be shot in the back—and the little lock for some reason took a long time to click, and the key got stuck in it, and they probably left some traces, or maybe the landlady counted her potatoes: that evening she let out a scream in the kitchen, and then she burst into their room, screeching: "You people come and take over the place, you're all sinners, you haul in your gold and then you go and steal!"—but the boy's mother kept repeating the same thing in response: "What's wrong, are you out of your mind?"—and at that moment he realized that his mama could lie, and the last word, "steal," which referred to what the two of them had done the day before, he was afraid to even pronounce it in his head, so discordant was it with his view of his mother; but as for "sinners" and "gold," the landlady had shouted the same thing before this incident and now she said it again and threatened to throw them out on the street. At nighttime the boy covered himself with his father's rustling rust-colored raincoat—it was particularly unpleasant when it touched his bare skin—because at that time his father was being treated in a psychiatric hospital. How often the boy recalled the canopy held up by two iron posts at the entrance to his house, and the wide stone staircase inside that smelled of cats—he dreamed of that staircase more than once: he'd be walking up it, but for some reason he would miss the second floor and end up on the landing of the third, top floor— he had always been a bit envious of the people who lived there because from their balcony, you could see more buildings than from his balcony, and besides, they could see the boy's balcony clear as the palm of their hand; and he could only guess what was happening up at their place—so he would end up on the landing of the third floor and ring the bell, but for a long time no one would open the door, and then they'd open it, and he'd wander around the apartment—the rooms were arranged exactly like his apartment, but a different family lived in each room—it was a genuine communal apartment, while only two families had been moved into theirs, but still, these people lived one floor higher, and he dreamed of getting to their balcony and it even seemed that he went out on the balcony. Once, in the evening newspaper, he saw a photo of his town—which by then was deep in the German rear—taken from a bird's-eye view, by our airplanes—he tried to find the block where they had lived, though he already knew that his house had burned down, and

41

for that matter the entire block as well, but he continued examining the photo, trying to recognize at least the neighboring blocks or some other familiar place—it seemed to him that the whole problem was the dimness of the oil lamp, so he brought the photograph right up to his eyes until it consisted of alternating dark and light dots—traces of the printer's plate. Then, after the war, when they returned to their town, he went to the place where their street had been, and amid the piles of bricks, he tried to find the remains of the iron posts that supported the canopy over the entrance to their house—but the entire center of the town was a pile of bricks with the occasional empty frame or a Dutch oven attached to a wall and wallpaper blowing in the wind. Then the piles of bricks were removed, and right where their block and the neighboring blocks had been, the central square of the town was constructed—a huge, open space covered in asphalt with a wooden dais erected for members of the government, and right in the middle, a bronze statue of Stalin. It was liquidated one night, but it's base had been dug so deep into the ground that for the next few nights explosions could be heard—it had to be taken out in pieces, like the roots of a broken tooth . . . The boy forgot to look back at the entrance to his house, but for some reason I still remember the darkened street with its shiny cobblestones and the dancing shadows of the fires that were moving closer, and the silent, dark three-story house awaiting its fate, with its attic window facing the courtyard and therefore not visible from the street, where Stefanida, sitting on the bed, prayed softly either to the icon of the Virgin and Child, or to the photograph of her niece, and in the darkened dining room, on the massive tall chairs with caning on the back, sat our neighbors from International Street, who had placed neat leather rucksacks on the floor next to them—the tall, old, bald man with the aquiline nose, his wife, an intelligent woman who was not yet old, but whose features I can't recall, and their daughter, an overly developed girl with a narrow face like her father's, who wore a pince-nez and had the German name Elsa—they were all murdered in the ghetto. Maybe Stefanida was already wandering like a silent shadow around the apartment, opening the closets and suitcases—after the war, someone told us that she took some things and left for the countryside to stay with relatives, and by then she could barely walk because of her swelling, and she soon died. Mama still can't forgive her—is it possible that some of our things could still be out there somewhere? The plaid blanket Tusik used, or the binoculars, which the boy didn't end up taking with him after all? Finding them was just as improbable as suddenly discovering the corpse of Homer or Alexander the Great. But why was it light as day? Probably because we were near Getsov's house, which was engulfed in flames; the house was at the corner of two streets where the tram turned around, across the street from where he and Tusik, standing in a crowd of people the day before yesterday, had listened to the stuttering voice coming from the black loudspeaker. Getsov had been dead a long time, but in the boy's family this house, just like the Tunik house, was called by the name of its former owner—Doctor Mints had lived in Getsov's house and in the boy's family everyone always told the same story about Doctor Mints: a woman came to see him for an appointment, and when he asked her "What is your complaint?" she told him that it hurt when she breathed, to which he replied: "Then don't breathe." This story apparently came from grandfather, who knew Mints, and then after grandfather's death, grandmother told it, then my Mama and aunt, and now when someone says that it hurts to bend over or walk, Mama or my aunt retort: "Then don't bend over or don't walk, as Doctor Mints would say," and I have repeated this story to my son more than once, and he will probably do the same with his children, if he has any—a genuine passing of the torch from generation to generation. The Getsov house, where

Doctor Mints once lived, was burning, embraced by flames from all sides. It was a four-story house, and stood on a high place—the highest on the block—so it was visible from the dormer window of the house where the boy lived; he would go up to the attic with Stefanida when she went there to hang out the clothes, and, clambering onto some old furniture, grabbing on to the rough iron warmed by the sun, he'd look out the dormer window—well, this window was placed exactly to the left of the Getsov house's fourth floor, and all the other roofs on their block were so much lower you didn't even have to pay attention to them, but the Getsov house was something! At the same time, the boy reassured himself that the Getsov house stood on a rise, and if it had stood next to their house, then it might very well have been the same height, especially since the boy's house had very tall ceilings, so that three of their floors might very well be the same as four of the Getsov's—when I meet successful people, I comfort myself with the thought that I am still smarter and more talented than they are—and now the Getsov house was burning, a mere skeleton embraced by flames, and probably about to collapse. The boy's family was walking in the middle of the street because the building opposite the Getsov house, the one with the loudspeakers attached to its corner, was also burning, but it was only two stories; red hot, smoldering beams of wood fell on the pavement with a dry crack, splintered into shards, and erupted in a sheaf of sparks. It was hot, as though someone had opened the little door of a locomotive furnace, and the smoke made your eyes tear; further, on Rosa Luxemburg Street, houses were also burning, shooting out blazing embers; it was only on Ostrovsky Street near the home of Professor Oizerman that it was dark and cool. The family stopped right under Professor Oizerman's balcony, and the boy suddenly realized that it was a late summer night, but the Oizermans weren't home—most likely they had left too. Then someone they knew, who happened to be walking along the sidewalk under the Oizermans' balcony, called out to them, and they also recognized some other people and exchanged a few words. They all walked together, descending a similarly dark and silent street toward the river, and crossed the wooden bridge; reflected in the black Neroch, which had not had time to dry up, were the flames of fires blazing somewhere up on the hill—on holidays, the Moscow River reflects the lights of fireworks in exactly the same way, because water doesn't care what it reflects. Along the main alley of the municipal park, someone's feet could be heard shuffling in the darkness; from the side lanes, dark figures appeared unexpectedly, and other figures moved down the main walkway and then along the silent, unpaved streets beyond the park, past tall wood fences and one-story houses with black windows that also trembled with flares of crimson. It was only when they had reached the highway—not the one toward Moscow, because it was likely to be the most dangerous, but the other one that also led east—only then did the meaning of the shuffling, dark figures appearing out of the side lanes and streets become completely clear to the boy; along the shoulders of the highway, on the right and on the left, was an endless string of people leaving town—with briefcases, with small suitcases and bags in hand, with bicycles loaded down with belongings (the boy could have held on to his bicycle—how useful it would have been now!), with baby carriages in which people carried either babies or their possessions, or perhaps both; there were many carrying children or leading them by the hand. The boy had never realized that so many people lived in their town, and he was even seized by a feeling of pride for his hometown—you might have thought that people were out for a stroll, or a May Day rally or a demonstration—only it was strange, why under the cover of night? Many called out to one another in recognition, and asked about someone in particular. The main thing was not to lose each

45

other—the boy's mother and the boy himself served as a kind of link between father and grandmother, because father kept breaking away and running off ahead. Subsequently, the situation became clear; the boy's father lay on the floor of a room teeming with bedbugs, which the inhabitants of a provincial mid-Russian town had let them have, and where they ended up during the hot days of July; father lay on the floor and rustled the rust-colored raincoat covering him; he shook the bed that the boy and his mother and grandmother slept on in a heap at nighttime; he ate cucumber peelings during the day, kept running to the window, and, when he saw soldiers, he paced the room shouting: "They're coming to get me!"; father thought that Tatanov, the head of the local Municipal Health Department was looking for him, and "Tatanov" became the name for a non-existent danger in the boy's family. When this was all clear, the boy's mother said that his father's urge to go on ahead, his impulsive running off, were the first symptoms of psychosis. Grandmother walked behind at a normal pace. In the boy's family it was known that grandmother liked to walk; later, grandmother said proudly more than once that she was able to walk those thirty-six kilometers at age seventy only because of this, and everyone confirmed it; moreover, the speed of her step perhaps kept back the thought that Tusik hadn't come by for them, and that meant he'd stayed in town; and all of them, except for the boy's father, looked intently at the trucks that passed them—could Tusik be in there? The days were the longest of the year and the nights the shortest—at their back was the crimson glow of the burning town, and ahead, in the east, it was already growing light; the smell of smoke, which occasionally reached them, blended with the smell of early morning at the dacha, and even though the boy had never gotten up that early, he guessed that it must be like this. Along the sides of the road a line of people moved single file, and between them, on the road itself, passing them, came the trucks—dark, immobile figures in peaked caps sat on benches in the back. Among the crowd on the side of the road, the rumor spread that this was either the police or units of the NKVD. The boy kept on catching up with his father, and while they stood to the side, waiting for grandmother and Mama, it seemed to the boy that the line of people was about to come to an end and he was seized by the fear that they would be the last ones, and his father kept shouting impatiently: "Hurry, hurry!," and Mama shouted back to him that grandmother couldn't walk that fast, but without waiting for them, he ran ahead again. The trucks passed between the two lines of walking people; a two-wheeled cart, hitched to horses, rumbled along the asphalt, either carrying weapons or a field kitchen, driven by the silent, slumped figures of soldiers in field caps, dark figures against the bright sky—by word of mouth people began to repeat someone's idea that these were our troops retreating, but they talked about this almost in a whisper, because our borders were supposed to be inviolable. Some old lady with disheveled gray hair ran after the horse cart—she gesticulated desperately, pleading with them about something, but they just sat there silent and immobile—then she ran after some other cart and even tried to climb up on it, but the people in it just sat there silently, slightly hunched over; then she began to throw herself from one vehicle to another, so it even seemed that she was being deliberately dramatic, but then she stopped in the middle of the road between the carts that drove around her impassively and, raising her hands to the sky, began a loud lament—her matted gray locks were blown by a slight dawn breeze—someone said that she was probably insane, and it was only later that the boy realized that she was a Jewess. And when the sky had become completely bright and it was obvious that the day would be hot and cloudless, and the troops had almost finished passing—only stray carts passed by now with a rumble, catching up with their fellows, as though they'd fallen behind in a parade—airplanes appeared above the road. They flew low, on a flyby, glinting silver in the rays of the as yet unseen sun; in the cutout of the fuselage, the figures of pilots in helmets were distinctly drawn. They swept over the road, veered off to the side, then again returned—short machine gun rounds could be heard and many of the people walking on the road rushed to the side and the boy's family also ran for a little patch of forest. There were several other people with them, acquaintances it seems, whom they'd met on the road at the beginning, then become separated from, and then met up again, because along the way you kept meeting friends and other people you knew, just like during a demonstration or a public holiday, and when the boy heard a short, whistling sound "whit" right near his ear in the forest, as though someone were gently cracking a whip or calling a dog, he wasn't surprised, because he had heard it many times watching *Seven Brave Men*, or *The Thirteen*, and that was exactly how he imagined it, so he just shouted: "Lie down!," because he knew from books and films that that's what you're supposed to do in such situations; and the adults, following his command, fell to the ground, dropping their traveling bags nearby, and for the first time the boy understood what morning dew really was. In the half-dark, still pre-dawn of the forest, somewhere far away, between the trunks of trees, a few gray figures flashed by— maybe soldiers, or policemen—and then everything grew quiet and when they came back out on to the highway, someone told them that they had been in a skirmish between border guards and German parachutists dressed up as policemen—could the parachutists have been dropped in by the same airplanes that flew over the highway? Later on, the boy found out that this was called an airborne landing, and that the Germans used this tactic widely—so that meant that they had come face to face with real Germans—interesting, he wondered, what kind of faces did

Germans have? How could they fall into the Germans' hands so easily—but this vanguard group apparently wasn't interested in the civilian population, although, as he later learned, the very next day the Germans rounded up people and returned them to the town, which they had occupied by that time; later the boy often imagined his family, along with the rest of those who fell into the Germans' hands, being returned under guard to the town; the German soldiers, in helmets, with massive, protruding chins and colorless Aryan eyes, drove them behind barbed wire with the butts of machine guns with bayonets attached, sewed yellow stars on them—and further was too frightening to think about, because Professor Oizerman hadn't left town—a very stout man with a bald patch that cut slantwise through strands of hair carefully combed down, which only emphasized his bald-ness—he'd been called to grandfather on the eve of his death and felt his pulse silently and everyone awaited his conclusion—and the Germans had forced Professor Oizerman to clean the toilets with his bare hands and he was probably suffocating, and then they did things with him that no one even talked about out loud, and only then did they kill him, and they could have done the same thing with the boy's father, although he probably would have committed suicide, because he had already tried to when the boy was still quite small—that time, father had been brought in and placed on the bed with the large spring mattress—his spine was injured from throwing himself over a staircase either when he was being brought back from interrogation or was being taken to be interrogated; apparently he gave such fantastical evidence that even there it seemed suspicious—his psychosis was already beginning—so they let him go, and he lay on the bed, oblivious to anyone around him, and kept repeating that he would never get up again. The sun had already risen some time ago and now it was hot, and the boy was thirsty, when columns of people in worn gray clothes began to appear on the highway;

their hair was cut short but their gray faces hadn't been shaved for a long time. Each column was accompanied by several soldiers with rifles on their shoulders—passing the people walking on the side, the column then went beyond the turn, and when the sun had already risen high in the sky, almost right over your head, and was mercilessly scorching, and the mouth had dried up from thirst, and the boy had learned how to sleep as he walked, the first sleepers began to appear on the side of the road—people in worn gray clothes, their gray faces long unshaven—they lay on their sides, their legs slightly bent at the knees, and a small, round, dry wound on their temples, with congealed blood that had trickled down into their beards. People walking along the road skirted them silently, but as they passed by, they didn't take their eyes off them and then for a long time afterward they kept looking back, as though trying to imprint their features in their memory—just like the people who had passed the coffin of the first secretary in the Sovtorg Employees Club. At first, everyone thought that the bodies were German, but the sky was clear, and no skirmishes could be heard, and then a rumor circled that convoy guards were shooting anyone in the column who couldn't walk fast enough and was falling behind.

6

In early spring, a stocky man of medium height with a face that looked half flabby, half rumpled, strolled out of the gates of a building on Kropotkinskaya Street, stopped for a moment, and surveyed the street with the gaze of someone new born. Along with the folders and books in his briefcase was a phial of pure alcohol—like hell the guy'd get it—he'd done the right thing after all not giving it to that drunken handyman—you can't give anything to that sort, the guy would forget by the next day—and besides which he had had to write down his own name, patronymic and the time of the appointment on a dirty piece of paper covering the table where there stood a drained half-liter bottle, a cloudy vodka glass, the remains of an onion, and black bread crusts; he wrote down his own given name, and then when the drunkard asked him "What's your handle?" he was flustered for a moment—he wrote down the first patronymic that came to mind, and it turned out to be derived from the name of the drunkard, who gave him a nasty smirk and said "Oh, so you're my son?"—they were about the same age—and, nodding meaningfully at the briefcase without turning his head because the guy was in bed drunk as a skunk and also had the flu—he asked "Whatcha got in that briefcase there?"; but the man was damned if he'd give that drunk the phial, and when the guy saw the exact time the visitor had put down, even with minutes, he smiled with the same smirky distaste and said "just like an ambulance"; but out of professional habit the visitor placed his fingertips on the drunk's heavy, muscular wrist anyway—his wrist was hot, he probably had a fever, and his pulse was hard, vibrating like a tautly pulled string—the pulse of a person with heart disease and high blood pressure. However, it could have been the next day when what he desired had finally happened— the woman left a bit earlier, so they wouldn't be seen leaving together, and he dropped into the boiler room where the handy-man, who was well by then but already tipsy, was fixing something, or pretending to fix something, and gave the visitor a heavy, inquisitive look. While they were there, the handyman kept going over to a door, and even tried it one time. He gave him the phial, and the guy began bugging him to treat his friend; however, the visit could have happened a day or so later, too, because why would he have been looking around with the eyes of a newborn, although, on the other hand, when you leave a room and go out on the street, or even enter the tram, or just go from one state to another, you always look around that way.

Entering the metro, the man merged into the stream—people were going down the escalator in several rows, pressed tightly against one another as though they had been convicted and were being taken to the place of execution on a conveyor belt; among them, was the man, wearing a no longer new, but well-made sheepskin coat with a Persian-lamb collar like artistes wear, and a Persian-lamb fur hat with lowered ear flaps which, despite his Jewish face, gave him a strange resemblance to a German pris-oner of war. From the very top of the escalator, he could see the expanse of the station's underground lobby, teeming with people; its heavy chandeliers also came into view, swaying slightly from the movement of the air, and coming closer and closer, as if he were an airplane coming in for a landing. It was probably the "Auto Factory" station, "Avtozavodskaya," because that was the only place where the arches were high enough for the whole plat-form to be seen at once. Spring hadn't arrived yet—winter was in full swing, there was a snowstorm outside—and the man was simply returning home from work. Once he reached the bottom of the escalator, he entered the human whirl—the oncoming stream of people kept pulling his briefcase, and he had a hard time jerking it back. Crossing the underground vestibule, the man climbed the steps leading to another metro line, probably to the Taganskaya or to Sverdlov Square station—which meant that he had actually already traveled part of the way, or maybe he had entered in one entrance to the metro and immediately transferred to the other line—and as he climbed, he was met by descending briefcases, cloth bags, string bags with oranges and loaves of bread, trousers that were very, or not very, narrow, frayed bell-bottoms, women's boots of all types and designs, legs covered in stockings, and mini-skirts. Among the people descending, he saw a slender, fashionably dressed girl with a purse across her shoulder, wearing a very short fur coat, pants that had a zipper on the side, and short suede boots, which also had zippers; the man slowed down a little, watching her—in another minute she would disappear. Pushing everyone aside, he caught up with her, and whispered something in her ear; she laughed, he took her by the elbow, and here they were now, in a dimly lit room: she was sitting in an armchair in her outfit, her stylized overalls emphasized her figure, and he had settled on the rug at her feet—he'd already removed the suede boots, and now he began to unzip the zipper, going from the bottom up—the higher his hand holding the clasp went, the slower his movement became, and when he reached her thighs, he leaned toward the opening and his lips reached for her body, and he felt he was plunging into a warm bath, when someone pushed him and said something in an irritable voice: he was standing on the steps, blocking the passage. Now he was walking over the little bridge with railings, and below, the roofs of train cars swam past—the trains, quickly gaining speed, disappeared into the tunnel with a rumble, and in the tunnel you could still see the red signal light; the man went over to the railing

53

on the other side of the bridge, and leaning on it, looked down at the black tracks with their gleaming steel rails—the lights still trembled uncertainly on them; from the blackness of the tunnel, two headlights approached, but the train stood there, far from the end of the platform, and it seemed strange: the train had stopped and there was a long, open piece of track ... near one of the train's cars, he saw a small crowd gathering—people hurried from every direction—the crowd grew right before his eyes; the man also ran over, and when he elbowed his way through the crowd, he saw a man lying on the platform in a pool of dark blood—his legs had been cut off and bits of cloth were embedded in the flesh, but his hand was still convulsively squeezing the handle of a briefcase; the corpse's face was black—he was probably killed by the electricity—but wait, that's not when it happened, it was in summer, because it was so easy for him to run, and now he was walking downstairs in his good, heavy coat, with a briefcase in hand, just a small particle amid a huge stream of others like him. Along the edge of the platform, several rows of people were waiting for the train, and he merged into this new stream, which had stopped for a moment. His eyes couldn't help but fall on the station wall, white marble intersected horizontally by a black ribbon of tile—a bus adorned with funeral bands moved slowly along the main street of the city, and behind it an entire motorcade of cars, and at one crossing, a policeman even closed off the traffic to let the funeral procession pass.

7

"What soft hands he has . . . just like the living," some woman said, adjusting father's hands—the funeral procession stopped across from the gray building and from the bus, the windows of their apartment could be seen quite well: four windows and a balcony with plump, rounded columns of porous lime-stone—"They say it's only when a person has lived a very pure life . . ." another woman said. A third person knocked on the driver's cabin.

There was still a lot of snow at the cemetery—it had already melted on the city streets, under the rays of the spring sun; but here people were plunged up to their knees in snow. At the freshly dug grave, the mourners were arranged in a dense ring around the mound of earth. Some tried to climb up it, but unable to keep their footing, they slipped backwards; some tried to perch on neighboring fences and railings, and the rest stood a ways off, alone or in small bunches, carrying on business conversations in lowered voices. One after another, people spoke near the grave; they spoke in loud voices—you could tell they were talking by the movement of their mouths and their gestures, but you couldn't hear a word; between speakers, Chopin's funeral march was per-formed at high volume and off-key; the man stood next to his mother right near the grave and held her arm, though rather unnaturally—you could tell this wasn't normal for him. Others who had been close to the deceased—the man's wife, relatives, friends—were there, too; however, there was a certain unseen distance dividing them from the man and his mother, silently emphasizing the particular closeness of these two to the deceased and their right to a special status. The sky was cloudy and a fine snow fell—it settled on the deceased's face and his suit—father was always afraid of the cold—when he went outside in the winter he turned up the collar of his old-fashioned fur coat, and mother was also afraid that he'd catch cold too. During father's illness, they would open the vent window in the next room, and from that room, the door into the room where father lay. Father had worn the new fur coat with the extra-high Persian-lamb collar—the kind actors and opera singers wear—for only a few months; it looked good on his son, and today he'd put it on—glancing at himself in the foyer mirror on the sly—using the cemetery wind as a pretext. He kept looking around anxiously for someone, occasionally even craning his neck or rising up on tippy toe—he tried to be discreet, because in this situation such things weren't done—until he located the tall girl with slightly slanted eyes and luxuriant black hair showing from under her hat. She stood back behind the crowd surrounding the grave, and when her eyes caught his, she lowered them, and then turned away completely, as though they weren't even acquainted.

8

A low morning sun came through the car windshield, blinding him so that he lowered the visor—normally his father sat next to the driver. Disappearing into the coat with the raised collar, father would sit turned slightly toward his son, listening, or not listening to him, because he was always occupied with his own thoughts, or maybe it was simply that the raised collar got in his way. He kept wiping his steamy spectacles without taking them off; when he did take them off, you could see that his eyes bulged slightly, moreover an expression of helplessness shot through them, and two flabby folds of skin hung from his chin, like Boxers have—his face had diminished in the last few years and it was completely hidden by the raised collar; his son would tell him the news of the capital, casually mentioning the scientists whose lectures he'd attended or whom he'd met at conferences; he told his father about the opening of a new metro station or some theatrical premiere with the same feeling of superiority, as though these were his own accomplishment; father wiped his glasses and nodded distractedly, partly in time to his son's voice, partly in time to his own thoughts, sinking into the raised collar—the back was quilted—of his Persian-lamb coat. Now, riding the bus at this early hour on a winter Sunday, the streets of the city were almost empty . . . On Sundays, mother usually hadn't risen yet, and Nastya, who had already been at the market, was busy in the kitchen, preparing the midday meal, the menu of which had been meticulously discussed the evening before; he and father would go out—father had acquaintances in all the shops, probably because one or another of the counter workers had been his patients; the son carried the bag of groceries because father wasn't supposed to carry heavy things, although the brief-case he took to and from work, filled on the way back with bottles of kefir or large jars of stewed fruit, was no doubt a good deal heavier than this bag; but the son considered it his duty to carry it, because there was nothing else he could do to help his father. Entering the shops, father wiped his glasses—even when he came home, he looked like a man who had just gotten on the tram—and on the way back the son crossed, jaywalking, because, after all, what was this street compared to even the most outlying street in Moscow, but his father made a loop and waited at the crosswalk for the green light; then they climbed up to the fifth floor together, his father stopping on every landing to rest, and at these moments the son felt especially young, healthy, and strong—he could barely keep himself from racing up to the fifth floor—but he stopped on one or two of the landings, panting loudly to show his father that he, too, was tired. Through the shade of the visor, which he had lowered, the sky looked dense and dark blue, like just before a storm or somewhere in the south; once he'd seen the exact same sky—part stormy, part southern, through the glass sun-roof of a trolley. Now, father's illness was full blown, and he was returning home with diabetic bread and medicines for him; a cloudless sky heralded spring when winter was still at its height; there were buildings that seemed unnaturally dark, as though the sun had disappeared abruptly behind a cloud; and there were new, alien buildings that had grown up here without him, in his own city.

The car stopped opposite the gray building; before entering the lobby, he stood on the sidewalk for a moment, staring at the dark windows of the fifth floor—three square windows and one narrow window with a stone balcony tacked on—and it was only when he found himself on the landing in front of the familiar door that he heard his heart beating; the door was locked, which calmed him a bit, because in those circumstances he knew that doors were usually left open so people could freely enter the apartment. Barely coping with his thumping heart, he carefully rang the doorbell. His mother opened the door—she was wearing her soft flannel robe, as she always did in the morning, and from behind her back Nastya peered out of the kitchen, Nastya with her gloomy, broad-cheekboned face—like a figure straight out of Fedotov's painting *The Major's Marriage Proposal*, or Repin's *The Arrest of the Propagandist*. In the foyer everything was the same— the "trophy" coat rack with the mirror in the middle, expropriated from the Germans, the tall, awkward wardrobe, which held an old dress, a refrigerator, a step ladder, a wall cabinet where there the jars of stewed fruit that father bought in endless quantities probably lined the shelf, along with two or three bottles of wine— father wasn't allowed to drink wine, but he got very angry when he found out that his son, on arrival, uncorked a bottle without him. "How is he?" he wanted to ask, but his mother, forewarning him, said, "He had a calm night, just arrhythmia," and added just as calmly, the way doctors speak about a patient: "You may see him now." He realized that since this was expected of him he had to do it, and he also felt that he was vested with some special right, and this feeling of his privileged position stayed with him all through his father's illness and through the funeral. Cautiously opening the door, he entered the room. Over the dining table, uncharacteristically strewn with medicines, was a lamp with an orange shade. Daylight shone through the curtains, which weren't closed tightly, and this double light created a strange sensation of deepest night continuing while day had already dawned; the room smelled of camphor, and on the daybed which had been pushed away from the wall so it could be reached from both sides, father lay in a white nightshirt on whose left side, where the heart is, a large, spreading splotch of blood darkened—they'd bled father with leeches the day before. He lay on his back, breathing heavily and irregularly like a wounded animal; his son went right up close to him, and the figure of a nurse in a white coat separated from the bed—she moved away somewhere into a corner of the room, probably so as not to interfere with the son's visit to his father; and he once again sensed his special rights, which were fully recognized by all and even underscored. His father's bulging eyes were focused upward, as though he were trying to make out something on the ceiling; on his cheeks, under his eyes, a net of red capillaries had popped out—similar capillaries had recently begun to appear in the same places on the son, but for the moment there weren't many of them. Now, when father had no glasses on, you could see that his nose was aquiline, one might even say handsome. The son silently took his father's hand and began to feel his pulse, which was fast and weak; father kept on making an effort to pick out something on the ceiling—he wasn't at all surprised by his son's appearance, it was as though they'd parted only yesterday, or perhaps he simply didn't recognize him. "Gotcha," he said unexpectedly. He said this into the air, still paying no attention to his son. "That's all right, everything will be just fine," said the son, because he knew that in such situations one is supposed to say things like that; on the dining table amid the medicines, ampoules and syringes, lay father's eyeglasses and his flat pocket watch.

9

They came and went every day, several times a day—morning, daytime, evening, changing shifts—in their light, semi-transparent bags, which they set carelessly on the floor, under their coats, you could see textbooks, pussy willow, various colors of knitting yarn, and some unnecessary female things whose purpose he couldn't understand; rolling up fur coats and fur hats or fluffy head scarves, they pulled white robes out of their bags and put them on, glancing in the mirror as they passed—a farewell glance before entering the room where the patient lay—birds with clipped wings, falsely meek; they changed the patient's sheets, turned him over, gave him shots in his emaciated buttocks, yellow from iodine, touched his body; the smell of camphor mingled with the barely perceptible smell of perfume, and before leaving they became particularly zealous so as to hide their barely contained joy at approaching liberation; even after the arrival of the next shift worker, they stayed for a little while in the patient's room, as if they were in no hurry: the most important thing for them was what was happening here, and everything else outside the walls of this building had no meaning for them—they put on their fur hat or headscarf in front of the mirror, taking their time, the way people take their time to raise the first toast and down the first vodka at a holiday table, but from the window he saw that once outside, they ran for the trolley or the tram grace-fully, with a light step.

10

As was his habit, he was sketching with a pencil or perhaps just sitting, his chin on his hands, when she entered the room—tall, wearing a white robe, a starched cap affixed to her luxuriant black hair—there was no place for all the medicine in father's room any longer, and she came in here to get a syringe for an injection.

"Eat something," he said to her, because the dining room had now been shifted to this room and because he really wanted to offer her something; but she refused—then he pushed a little bowl of candies toward her, but she shook her head. Breaking off the tip of the ampoule, she filled the syringe—and when part of the liquid had entered the syringe, she turned it upside down in one movement, and continued to draw the liquid from the ampoule, not even holding it—it was amazing how she managed it!

"Are you watching your figure?" he asked her with affected irony.

"Goodness, what are you talking about?" She said it so simply and with such surprise, that he felt awkward about the vulgar platitude. She was already standing near the door with the syringe in her hand—another second, and she'd leave the room.

"How about some sunflower seeds?" He suddenly remembered that the night before he'd bought them out of boredom, and they now lay in his pocket.

"With pleasure," she smiled and unexpectedly blushed, probably because of the alacrity with which she'd agreed.

He walked over and held out a handful of seeds.

"I'm sterile" she said, nodding toward the syringe, and then he carefully put the seeds in the pocket of her robe—as he let them fall through his fingers, she stood without stirring, as though anticipating something, and at the same time fearing it.

11

She was walking down the street leading to the river, and he was standing near the bridge—he'd been standing there for a long time, impatiently checking his watch. She walked down—her eyes were slightly slanted, and her hair was teased up high—and he walked to meet her—she came nearer, as though descending from somewhere high above—he no longer saw any buildings, or streets, or people—only her figure and face in a halo of tall, teased, dark hair. They stopped opposite one another in an awkward silence—and he thought she could hear his heart beating.

"... I kept waiting and ..." he slipped into the familiar form— "I've been waiting for you."

They walked toward the small river where he'd been waiting for her, then across the narrow wooden bridge, where they stopped at the railing ... The small, narrow river, not much more than a stream, had been taut with ice, but suddenly it had grown wide and swift; the dark water, carrying chunks of ice, nearly reached the underside of the bridge, and schoolboys ran down the street that led to the river, knocking each other's book bags off, a whole horde of them; and he was one of them. They ran, their joyous shouts announcing to all around: "The river's back inside its banks! It's ba, baa, baa, Baaaaanks!" and they said this even though the flood was still at its height—the entire park on the other side of the river was flooded, and the trees seemed to grow straight out of the water, and it was only beyond the park, between the little wooden houses, that little lakes shone—evidence that the water had begun to recede. Running onto the bridge, the school-boys spread out, hanging over its wooden railings—large blocks of ice floated by on its swift black water, they banged against the pilings, making the bridge shudder—and the boy, also hanging on the railings, felt that the water wasn't moving, rather, the bridge was sailing, slicing through icebergs, and the bridge was no longer a bridge, but the icebreaker Sedov or Krasin, and he was the captain.

"It's amazing," he said, "almost everything in town burned, but this bridge survived." After a short silence, he looked at the girl: "How old are you?"

"I was born in 1940."

"So you're pre-war issue, then," he caught himself being trite again, but for some reason he was pleased at the thought that she was born before the war, and then, when they were walking in the park, he asked her about her childhood. During the war, she and her mother lived in a tiny town, and she didn't remember the Germans, but what could she remember at three or four years old anyway? He kept trying to imagine her mother carrying her and managing to get a hold of potatoes somewhere in the next village, carrying them back herself, and how cold it was in their house—a window covered with hoarfrost, not a soul on the street and it was dark—only the marching German patrols, but still nothing really threatened them—the Germans walked past and even came by the house several times just to make sure they weren't hiding Jews. On the lawns, the snow was powdery and in some places the earth had blackened under the rays of the spring sun; the pathways were slippery, little streams flowed, forming small lakes in some places—he took her by the arm and she stepped carefully in her open-toe suede shoes, choosing the dry places and at the same time trying to walk in step with him, though he could feel a sort of caution in her whole figure and her movements. He gave her a candy, and she twisted the wrapper for a long time, unsure whether or not to throw it away, until he took it out of her cold hand. Now, they were passing by the summer pavilions with their peeling paint and snow from which icicles dripped like fringe; he snuck glances at her profile—her slightly ruddy cheeks, and the dark hair that rose out from under her hat—then at her legs, which were sheathed in transparent stockings—she continued to step carefully, walking in time with him, and there wasn't a single wet spot on her shoes; for a moment he imagined moving to this city and living with her: they would stroll down the main street of the town, and she would study at the institute, and in the evenings he would explain anatomy to her, because he knew all about it . . . From the cycle track the sounds of a waltz, "The Waves of the Danube," could be heard—probably through a loudspeaker—and teenagers—both boys and girls—slid their skates across an ice-covered field; the girls wore tall white lace-up skates that fit tight to their ankles . . . bicyclers raced along the surrounding steep hills . . . no, there wasn't any ice, and this was simply a smooth square of packed earth sprinkled with yellow sand, and the bicyclers raced along sloping tracks. Back then, "The Waves of the Danube" waltz played as well—and he remembered the unfulfilled evening with the girl after those long summer days; steering the bicycle by the handles, he approached the people watching the skating; and among them was a girl in a calico dress that outlined the small bulge of her budding breasts; her bulging, watery eyes—she'd been standing there for a long time—saw him and she made her way over to him; he took her by the hand and his other hand steered the bicycle, holding it by the seat. They walked through the park in the swiftly thickening twilight— there was a chill coming up from the river and a scummy smell of sludge, but they headed for the farthest corner of the park where high grass had overgrown everything, and it probably even smelled of warm pine—no, it wasn't then, of course, because the first real date had been the first evening of the war. That time,

66

they walked along the street, holding hands, her palm hot and rough, and she asked: "Are you going to marry me?"—or maybe she said: "You'll end up marrying me anyway," yes, that's right, they were coming back from the movies: when the lights went down in the theater, he had placed his hand cautiously on her knee, and then inched it upward . . . he'd already overcome the taut elastic and the girl sat without moving—it almost seemed she wasn't breathing, and he wasn't breathing either, their hearts were just beating like crazy and he didn't even remember what film they saw. But no, the beating hearts were actually earlier: another girl was cleaning their apartment because her mother was sick that day, and he followed her relentlessly from one room to the other. She was wearing a red sweater made of cheap wool; it had probably been remade from something old, or at least dyed, because the boy had never smelled that acrid, almost poisonous smell before—how many times since then had that smell haunted him?—his breathing would even stop occasionally . . . One time, later, he decided that when he returned to his town, he would immediately look for the girl who had cleaned their apartment . . . He followed her from room to room—the poisonous red sweater was stretched around two bulges on her chest—and when they were alone in the room he went right up to her and took her by the hand—she looked at him with frightened, colorless goggle eyes; stupefied by the smell of the red sweater, he dragged her to the sofa, saying: "You see, I'm stronger than you." He didn't recognize his own voice, it was as though someone else were speaking—he grabbed the dust rag from her hand and tossed it aside, and they struggled on the sofa, flattening its protruding springs, and "You see, I'm stronger than you"—his voice cracked; they lay still, and her bulging colorless eyes looked at him with an expression of numb submission. "Don't," she said softly, but she didn't tear herself away, she just lay immobile, breathing irregularly, their hearts pounding . . . The cycle track remained behind, and now "The Waves of the Danube" came from somewhere far away; they came to a large round pavilion covered in snow, its door half open—he offered the young woman his hand, and, crossing an icy snow drift, they found themselves inside the pavilion; it was an abandoned fun house, with piles of garbage on the floor, and many broken mirrors on the walls. They walked along the wall, stopping at the mirrors as if viewing an exhibition of paintings, metamorphosing first into Don Quixotes, then into a fat, bloated married couple; near one of the mirrors she took out a brush and began to fix her hair—he tried to draw her to him, but she slipped out of his hands. In the mirror, he saw the reflection of a midget with hands hanging helplessly in the air . . . the skirmish between the boy and girl resumed, but he ended up on top once again—she breathed heavily, her mouth half open, an inane expression in her bulging, watery eyes—the eyes of a dying person, and the two of them lay immobile, and then only the beating of their hearts could be heard—at first fast and even, then gradually losing all rhythm, disordered, galloping. And the son, standing over his father's bed, listened to the rhythm of his father's heart.

12

Placing a stethoscope on father's chest, he listened to his heart—
it was the middle of the night and he had just awoken, and a
slight shiver passed through him; his mother stood nearby—she
was counting father's pulse. The nurse sat near the head of the
bed, wiping sweat from the patient's face—it appeared to be the
nurse who had been on duty the day the son arrived, a plump
young woman of medium height. "What is it?" "Sixty-two."
"Mine is ninety." "A large discrepancy." The mother and son
talked in low voices, almost whispering, though it was unnecessary—the patient's bulging, near-sighted eyes were fixed on the
ceiling, just as they had been on the day the son arrived, as
though the patient kept making an effort to read something
there. Occasionally he tried to turn on his side, but he wasn't
allowed to do this, so he would start shouting: "I'm the captain of
the guard!," and sometimes he screamed the phrase, lying on his
back and still looking at the ceiling. He shouted as though he
wanted to tease someone, but the nurse patiently explained to
him that he was a professor and that she worked for him in the
clinic and she even told him her name—for a few minutes he
would quiet down, but then with even greater excitement he'd
begin doing it all over again; there was something housewifely
and practical about this woman, and he remembered that
someone had told him that she was married. His mother went to
her own room, because it was quite late and she always felt bad
when she didn't get enough sleep; remaining alone, they began
to change the sheets—when he saw father's yellow legs and his

emaciated, needle-punctured hips, he became embarrassed that she was seeing them in his presence, as if they were his own legs, and he tried not to look at them, and when they lifted father in order to spread out a fresh sheet, their fingers touched for a moment under the patient's body, and he remembered that someone told him that she'd recently gotten divorced. He settled in the armchair, placing a book on his lap, and she again sat at the head of father's bed—father was calmer now, for minutes at a time he even appeared to be falling asleep—and she started knitting something, but the wool fell out of her hands several times; he read his book mechanically, without understanding the meaning of the sentences—even when he wasn't looking at her he saw her: under her white coat was a thin top—it would have been no trouble to unbutton it—and her neck was the neck of a young woman; her thick, chestnut hair was pulled back in a heavy bun at the nape of her neck and he imagined how, standing in front of the mirror, she let her hair down lazily, holding the hair pins in her teeth—somewhere he had even seen a painting like that—a woman unplaiting her hair in front of a mirror, and somewhere there, in the depths of the room, was a rumpled bed. A slight shiver coursed through his body—in the entire house, and perhaps even in the entire town, they may have been the only people who weren't asleep.

"You should lie down," he said to her, "my bed is made up." When she left, the thought that she was now lying in his bed, still warm from the heat of his body, took hold of him, and he remembered that he'd left his cigarettes in his room. He walked out into the dark foyer—from the kitchen he could hear Nastya snoring—and he quietly opened the door into his room: something white showed on the back of the chair, probably her coat or clothes, and he heard the calm, even breathing of a young, sleeping woman . . . Without taking off his pajamas, he lay down next to her, covering himself with the same blanket, while she moaned quietly in her sleep and turned toward him, and his hand already felt her hot, lithe body, which pressed against him, because she had been waiting for this moment so long and he continued to stand in the doorway; reflections from the street lamps played on the ceiling and on something dimly white, carelessly thrown on the chair; the boy and the girl lay motionless—her watery, bug eyes looked at him with numb submission, their hearts beat insanely, deafening him, and from the patient's room, the mischievous phrase could once again be heard: "I'm the captain of the guard! I'm the captain of the guard!"

13

He would wait for her in the dark wasteland opposite the hospital building. The lamp hanging near the entry booth swayed in the wind. He thought every female figure that appeared in the wavering cone of light was the tall girl, and even ran out of his hiding place, but when she appeared, he felt it immediately because his heart first plunged and then rebounded. Keeping her within sight, he walked along his side of the street then at the corner he crossed to her side and walked along next to her—she wasn't even surprised, it was as though they'd been walking together from the very start. They turned into a side street—there were fewer street lights—and he stopped and kissed her on the cheek but it seemed to him that he kissed the fluffy collar of her coat; and then, when they stopped once more and he kissed her on the cheek or maybe on the neck, his face sank again into that collar, which smelled of fur and perfume so strongly that he could hardly breathe; she stopped when he wanted to, like a sensitive dance partner, but still, she was walking her own way, and at a populated intersection, they separated without discussion—he turned onto the town's main street, merging with the crowd of people sauntering along the sidewalk, trolleys and cars slipped silently along the asphalt, store windows were brightly lit, and the ice of a March evening crunched underfoot—walking on a little, he turned into another side street and they met again and walked together, along the same poorly lit street. Neither of them was surprised by this encounter, it seemed completely natural; then they turned into unfamiliar streets, and while kissing her, he thought: here I am, kissing her, and this is probably what happiness is, because he'd dreamed of it for so long—but, on the other hand, what sort of happiness was it if he didn't actually feel it, but understood it with his intellect? Could this really be the same girl who'd asked him: "Your voice sounds so anxious—did something happen?" That was a few days ago; he had called her to find out when she was going to be on duty at their house, but he didn't remember leaving the telephone booth or how he ended up in the middle of the sidewalk; he could still hear her voice, faintly melodious—she was worried about him and his father; and though he understood how totally unthinkable the idea was—which only intoxicated him more—he began to think of her as his wife: his father had recovered, she had moved in with them, he got a job in the city he had once left and had the legitimate right to enjoy the new buildings and stores because he was now an inhabitant of the town; he could see himself hurrying home from work, where he thought of her constantly—and there he was, standing in the middle of the sidewalk, obstructing the passersby, the sky above the city was blue and cloudless; and he had forgotten what he was supposed to buy at the drugstore. Now he was actually kissing her, and she allowed him to, and it really was her—it was her voice he had heard on the telephone—but why did he have to remember all this to understand that he was happy? Wasn't this windy March evening and her stifling fur collar enough for him? They stood under the street lamp on an empty street near some red brick building—perhaps a factory or school of some sort—and he suddenly realized that she would leave now, because, even though they hadn't been paying attention to the streets and had walked randomly, she was still going her own way, and maybe he should have just stopped a cab, taken her home and stayed with her; and suddenly he felt light-hearted and pleased at the idea that they would soon part—he imagined returning home now, and how he would think about her and about the fact that he had kissed her—his palms probably still smelled of her perfume and he would put them to his lips and to his nose, and sink into his memories, which at present were still a reality. This very moment had to be savored, right now, when he kissed her again, and her slightly slanted eyes and luxurious hair tumbling out from under her fur hat, and the color in her cheeks—she allowed herself to be kissed, she was standing silently, as though completely uninterested, sometimes even glancing distractedly to the side—she was a female who had to be taken—and now he was in the tram and smelling his palms, which had retained the scent of her perfumed fur collar; getting off the tram, he ran home, because he always thought that it might happen in his absence.

14

"All the same, it's outrageous to stay so long," said his mother; she and her son were in the small room that had now been converted into the dining room, while their neighbor, who was the son's age, sat with father. She lived on the floor above them, right over their apartment, in fact—she had a pretty face, framed by a heavy, dark blonde braid, and a tiny bit of lipstick, which she and father talked about. Even the nurse had left father's room and the son tried not to look at his mother, but she didn't seem to feel awkward about the neighbor—"you have to realize that there's a limit to everything—it's bad for him to talk and get excited, doesn't she understand that?"—and he felt the same way he did when father's gaze followed young girls. The neighbor taught French, but she had graduated from the conservatory also, and for some time now father had been buying records obsessively and often put them on, but almost always forgot to turn them off, so they continued to turn idly, irritating the son when he visited. The son heard her heels clicking on the floor in the mornings when she was hurrying to work, and sometimes she played short passages or musical pieces, and two times a week she came down to their apartment to teach music to the grandson, who lived with them because his grandmother believed that a child should live wherever the most could be provided—coming home from work, father was interested first and foremost in finding out whether there had been a music lesson that day, and sometimes right after work, without going home, he went straight to the sixth floor; he was constantly presenting her with vases or cups or things like that, supposedly in gratitude for the lessons that she gave the grandson—but mother said that you have to know where to stop and that he had simply lost his senses and that it was shameful. Before falling asleep, the son heard her heels clicking again—his room was right under her room—and then everything grew quiet. Her bed stood right over his couch—she was going to bed, and he often dreamed that the ceiling collapsed during the night—after all they were the same age—and he wondered, had she allowed father to kiss her even once? One time, settling into the armchair in his son's room—father liked to drop in to see him for a chat before bedtime, the son was usually already in bed and waited impatiently for him to go because he actually wanted to sleep—settling in the armchair, father sat silently for a long time, and then said that if he were a different person he might have been able to make a certain decision to do something; but the son was really very sleepy, and besides which, he felt like he was reading someone else's letters, and now, during his illness, father was no longer embarrassed, and repeated her name, often calling her by all sorts of affectionate nicknames, and he asked for her to come see him, and so here she sat in father's room and perhaps caressed his hand or even held it in hers—after her departure, for the first time during his entire illness, the father asked the son how his dissertation was coming along.

15

"You and I will still drink champagne together," Professor Zaitsevich said to father—the professor still hadn't caught his breath after walking up five flights; sitting in the armchair, one leg crossed over the other, rocking the pointed tip of one of his unseasonably light, short black boots—sinking into the armchair, from which only his shiny bald head was visible. He kept jerking as though he were stubbornly refusing something or wanted to shoo a bothersome fly away—his wife was half his age and worked as his assistant, a frail blonde who wore a fur coat; they occupied a separate cottage which he surrounded with a tall fence, though people said that there were always a lot of soldiers who visited her at home, sometimes even in his presence, but he was considered the best specialist in the city. His head continued to twitch and the glass of his pince-nez gleamed; he had just listened to father's chest, moving the stethoscope's flat metal disc, steamed up from the cold, with surprising facility over father's back, which was covered in large red spots from cupping glasses, and meticulously guarded from the cold; he did this as though he were playing checkers, nonchalantly capturing pieces one after the other—there was one smart move that was supposed to get him a king. They had pulled up father's shirt and were holding him in a sitting position because he could no longer sit by himself—he couldn't get enough air, and was overtaken by coughing spells. At first it seemed that he was simply coughing things up, and that was perfectly natural, so that if you were in the next room you might well have thought that father had simply caught a cold and that his cough was intentionally loud, as if he deliberately wanted to annoy someone; and then the coughing turned into a bark, but this bark too seemed unnatural, a forced cough; father barked as though he were teasing a dog and was not quite succeeding; gradually, however, he got into the role, working himself up more and more until he could no longer stop, and had become the victim of his own mischief—possessed by a dry, cracking coughing fit, as though he'd strewn the room with peas or lead pellets, and in the breaks between the attacks of coughing, he spasmodically gulped the air like a fish thrown out of the water—his near-sighted, bulging eyes gave him an even greater resemblance to a fish, but when Zaitsevich began to listen to him, he almost stopped coughing—which meant he could control it after all; so Zaitsevich, putting the stethoscope in various places, even told him several times: "Cough," and he coughed—Zaitsevich's sweating metal checker was clearly demanding a queen, and the son, standing right there, felt the touch of that cold metal on himself, but since Zaitsevich was doing it, that meant it was all right—perhaps father had simply been taken a bit ill, and Zaitsevich had been called in, and he was having a look at his patient. Sitting in the armchair, holding his pince-nez, tapping the pointed tip of his boot, not yet having gotten his breath back from the steep climb, Zaitsevich dictated prescriptions, and father, who had been laid down again, was overtaken by a coughing fit, but no attention was paid to this, because the main thing now were the prescriptions, and father's cough was just a distraction. "You and I will still drink a bottle of champagne together," Zaitsevich said to father as he put on his pince-nez, with a nod, shooing an imaginary fly away. He outlived father by three months and was buried near him, but a bit closer to the central alley; when all that was left at father's grave were the rusted remains of wreaths and rotting ribbons, a veritable hut of wreaths wound with red and white ribbons still rose over Zaitsevich, and this hut was a bit fancier and brighter than father's because it was already summer and because Zaitsevich had treated all the high officials in the city.

16

It was the middle of the night. He stood near the window, and his mother lay on his bed because the doctors from father's clinic were now spending the night in her room. They were there in shifts. They came straight from surgery and knew nothing about father's illness, but mother thought that because the patient's condition was deteriorating, doctors should keep watch at his bedside, so they came: blond men, young residents, who diligently wiped their feet clean, and stomped around the foyer for a long time before going into father's room with an exaggerated willingness, which made them clumsy when they helped carry the oxygen tanks in and out; when they went out to smoke on the stairway landing, clutching the cigarettes in their fists like school boys, and at night they slept the deep sleep of doctors on call. Mother was in her soft, blue cotton robe dappled with colors. She wasn't lying down, but half-sitting, resting her elbows on a pillow; from the room came a cough—now it wasn't even coughing spells, but a continuous cough, so that it wasn't clear how father managed to inhale in order to store up the air required to support such a cough. His mischievousness now turned to tragedy: the cough filled his entire chest, the whole apartment, to such an extent that when it stopped for even a moment, the son went into his father's room to find out whether something had happened; now father was half-sitting all the time, supported by nurses or the doctors, and no one worried about it now, though earlier he'd been forbidden to even turn over—so that meant that it didn't even matter anymore. Mother was the first to say the word "pneumonia": In his mind the son pictured the grayish-blue infiltration spreading higher and higher, only the very top of the lungs was still clear, but it too awaited its fate; these were the lungs of his father, and he and his mother were together in the farthest room, as though sparing themselves father's cough, leaving it to the others—somewhere down below, chains of streetlamps could be seen, and the black, empty street seemed to be varnished—opening the vent window a tiny bit, the son listened to footsteps on the sidewalk; an hour earlier, mother had called a friend and asked her to come—this friend was a pediatrician, but mother thought that she was a very good doctor in general, and had literally cured her own husband who had recently had the very same illness as father, true, in a significantly lighter form—but now they were awaiting her arrival as though it could change something—sometimes the son even kneeled at the window sill and stuck his head out the vent window to look for her—at such moments it seemed to him that father's cough subsided.

"He's going under," said mother. She sat on the bed in her cotton robe, no longer leaning back on a pillow, but hugging her knees, which were covered with a blanket—on her finger the gold ring with the small diamond shone dimly—she had put it on when they left the burning city and hadn't taken it off since. She stated this the way people talk about strangers or as though father were doing this on purpose—it was entirely possible that at this minute, she somehow resembled a figure on Martos's tomb; later on, it often seemed to the son that his mother hadn't been sitting, but standing—the sheets unwound at her feet, white as clouds, and she rose up from them like an unyielding patriot in the Gestapo's torture chambers, or a rocket taking off into space.

17

The oxygen tent was eliminated, but the end of the rubber hose, which stretched through the whole room, was placed near the patient's mouth—at first, the end of the hose was wrapped in damp cheese cloth so that the oxygen wouldn't burn the patient's lips and mouth, but later they stopped putting on the cheese cloth in order to increase the oxygen flow—father lay on his side, he was no longer turned around, and the end of the hose was only lightly attached so that it was near his mouth—his lips had grown swollen and charred from the oxygen, and the oxygen flow was now regulated with the help of a metallic clamp placed over the hose because the oxygen couldn't be given without a break—the son, sitting in an armchair, opened and closed the clamp, and when he closed it, father began to convulsively gasp for air, his lips and his face turning blue—the days had long ago turned into nights, and the nights turned into days; the curtains in father's room weren't opened, weren't closed, the light bulb under the orange shade wasn't turned off, even the lamp on father's desk was on; and from the son's room, where the telephone had been moved, endless calls could be heard—the Chinese bowl with the dry Kiev cookies that all visitors were offered was still on his table—everyone ran to answer telephone calls, as though they were all waiting for some important news to arrive and change the course of events, and everyone rushed just as hurriedly to the foyer when the doorbell rang. Father was constantly given shots, but he no longer reacted to them; and then Professor Zalmanzon came—he was also a surgeon—he used to visit them frequently and he and father would discuss the latest medical news. Zalmanzon would depict his conversations with patients and other doctors with facial expressions, and everyone laughed because he did it quite wittily, but he always talked about his operations, thumbing through papers lying on father's desk, he would take the needle off the record playing Handel's mass right in the middle—and continue to talk about his last operation on a urethra, getting into the spirit of his role deeper and deeper, pacing the room back and forth, opening and slamming books, moving crystal vases around—the glasses that he wore didn't distort the expression of his radiant gray eyes, which always remained serious, he almost never laughed for that matter—he only allowed himself the occasional smile in passing, but even then, he would immediately banish the smile, vouchsafing it to no one, not even himself. Now his large hands, overgrown with hair, which were accustomed to the most difficult operations, were trying to puncture father's breast bone in order to remove the liquid that had collected in the pleural cavity—this could provide a little relief for two or three hours, but for some reason, everyone had high hopes for the procedure, and surrounded the patient's bed as though a miracle were about to take place. He attempted the puncture, but apparently unsuccessfully, because the cannula contained two or three drops of bloody liquid; removing the needle, he tried the puncture in another place—father didn't even groan, and really, what did this punctured body, with bluish hands, lips charred from oxygen, and a dark gray face that no longer reacted to anything, have to do with father? But this was his father after all, it was he who had given the son life by embracing his mother—father's own wife—and now he was dying and the son and his mother stood among the group at his bedside like mere observers, as though nothing that happened had any connection to them— Zalmanzon finally hit the pleural cavity, because a stream of liquid, directed by his own hairy hand, poured into the liter bottle positioned by the nurse. Everyone immediately exhaled with relief and stepped back from the bed—either amazed by Zalmanzon's magic or simply afraid of being sprayed—and Zalmanzon handed the cannula through which the fluid flowed to one of the doctors, as he did during an operation when the most complicated and crucial part was behind him and all that remained was to suture the incision. He, too, stepped away; placing his hands behind his back, he watched—like an artist might look at a recently finished painting—the liquid flowing into the liter jar that had originally held conserved fruit—it seemed to foam up, like beer, and it almost reached the brim. Someone held the jar up and looked at it through the light, and mother said that the liquid should be sent to the laboratory for testing.

18

The face of the young woman with slightly slanted eyes and thick black hair under her snow-white nurse's cap with the red cross, appeared before him against a white tile wall—it appeared and then disappeared again—she always gave father injections carefully, boiled the syringe, and like a magician turned it up with the ampoule already set and, without holding it, and no liquid dripped out—she rubbed father's emaciated, needle-tracked buttocks with alcohol so she wouldn't introduce any infection, and then, with the artful movement of a javelin thrower, stuck the needle in his insensate body—father didn't even move and didn't moan—she was a very good nurse who conscientiously followed the doctor's orders, and she would probably be just as good a wife; her shift was coming to an end, and the rubber hose was stretched through the entire room to the bluish body with the swollen, charred lips; the doctors never left the room, both lamps burned, and as it turned out, it really was nighttime. In two hours his wife was supposed to fly in from Moscow, they had decided that she should come, and he had just spoken with her on the phone; he had stubbornly tried to get a call through to her in Moscow, and mother kept coming into the room to find out whether he had; and when he spoke with his wife on the telephone, mother stood nearby, as if father weren't here, but there, in the other city, and his wife could provide information on the situation, and he, too, expected some news of father; and then he called his aunt, his mother's sister, to come, and then his cousin, and he and his mother felt the same thing, as if someone would give them some comforting news—but there was no news—everyone on the other side of the line was asking them or was afraid to ask, but still it seemed that the arrival of relatives could change something, and the son stubbornly kept trying to call the train station and the airport to find out the schedule of trains and planes—he really wanted to see his wife—and they would all gather together here in the apartment like they used to when they visited—the whole family—and father would be feeling better, he'd be improving, and the son and his wife would occupy the small room from which he was calling that had now been turned into the dining room, as they had on earlier visits, or as they did when they still lived here; in the morning when they were still asleep, father would carefully open the door a crack—carefully, but with the idea of waking them up—he had just shaved and his cheeks were as smooth as a new born baby's—the son's wife loved to stroke father's cheeks when they were smooth, and even liked to fluff up the hair on his head, laughing melodiously—he'd already had breakfast, was getting ready to go to work and smelled of eau de cologne, and its fragrance blended with the smell of the oatmeal mixed with kefir he ate every morning, in accordance with mother's diet. They would wake up, and father would finally enter the room with a guilty smile, and, engulfing his son in a wave of eau de cologne and oatmeal, inform him that Yakovlev didn't work there anymore and would the son like to drop by for a chat? Father still hadn't lost the hope that the son would take a job nearby, and they would move here to live with them—and this irritated the son because he himself had wanted to return to his hometown for a long time, and moreover, he disliked the fact that father saw him and his wife in bed—was it really necessary to start a conversation on this topic right now? Father would have a guilty, sad expression on his face and slowly withdraw from the room, and then the lock of the front door clicked—father had gone to work. The last day of father's life was approaching, and the tall young woman with slightly slanted eyes was supposed to leave soon—at first he kept watch for her to appear in the foyer—she was walking back and forth to the bathroom holding bowls, pouring and rinsing something out—he deliberately tried to catch her eye, but she hardly noticed him, and besides, strangers kept coming in, so he went into the bathroom and stayed there while she came and went—her shift was nearing its end, time had passed, and it was probably hard for her to understand why he was staying in the bathroom when his father was dying in the next room. She came into the bathroom with yet another container, a bedpan it seemed, in which there was a tiny bit of dark, concentrated urine—she held this clear-glass bedpan, and he, taking advantage of this, placed his palms on the white tile wall as though he wanted to leave his fingerprints on it; he placed his hands on either side of the young woman, so that she ended up in a sort of trap, her face began to swing to and fro, and there was an expression of bewilderment and horror in her eyes, but he pressed her face to the white tile and kissed her on the lips several times—her lips were hard, but she didn't resist.

19

The champagne was taken from the wall cabinet in the foyer—
for some reason the bottle had already been uncorked and wasn't
full, probably father had treated someone, or maybe he had just
tried it himself—and when the wine was poured into a table-
spoon there weren't any bubbles, but one of the doctors said that
was good, because the formation of gas could have a negative
effect on the heart. Father got along without oxygen now, he lay
on his back, breathing calmly and smoothly as though he were
sleeping; wine was recommended to raise the vascular tone,
because the injections weren't working—he breathed peacefully,
regularly and not very often—a doctor, no longer a young
woman, sat at the head of the bed, holding father's watch; she
took his pulse and said that the patient's condition wasn't as poor
as she expected, judging by what she'd been told. They tried to
pour champagne into father's mouth, but it ran down his chin
onto the pillow, forming a spot. Father's lips and mouth had
finally recovered from the oxygen and this was very important;
plans for the patient's treatment tomorrow were already being
discussed—they had probably been too quick in making all those
telephone calls. Many people went home—the last day of father's
life was coming to an end, but the middle-aged doctor sitting at
the head of his bed was an experienced physician, she had probably seen people die more than once, and when he heard his
wife's voice in the foyer, he ran out to greet her, embraced her,
and kissed her—her lips softly gave way to his kiss—they hadn't
seen each other for over a month—and while she was taking off

her things and he was hanging up her coat, for a minute it seemed to him that everything was as it had been; she had flown in at night to spend two or three days, and they might even fly back together—the airplane had arrived in the evening, and now they would sit down to dinner at the round table in father's room and the son, as always, would devour spoonfuls of sour cream, and father would say: "How much sour cream can one person eat?," because father wasn't allowed to have any, and his wife would laugh sonorously, tousling the fluff on father's head. Only the desk lamp was lit in father's room now, and his wife stood near father's bed; she carefully touched his fingers and said that they were as thick and soft as ever, and that he recognized her—she was absolutely certain!—just a little longer, and she would stroke the fuzz on his head, or touch the hair growing out of his ears, and maybe she'd even laugh, and he, too, thought that father had actually recognized her, and a lump rose in his throat, because his father and his wife loved to go to secondhand shops together and buy things, for which father always got in trouble with mother, and because father called his son's wife a "white slave" because she drew his son's bath and even helped him bathe—maybe he was even a little jealous of his son, and he called his son's wife affectionate names. Sometimes, father spoke to his own wife affectionately, refashioning her name in the Jewish style and shaking his head sadly, as though afraid that his wife, the mother of his son, would die before him, and maybe she was sick already and he would bury her first, and sometimes he talked about what would have happened to them if they had ended up in the ghetto; it was unpleasant for everyone to hear, because it was the truth. Over the last few days, the son had grown a terribly bristly beard—he couldn't go to bed with that kind of bristle so he went into the bathroom to shave while his mother and wife shared their own news, and father, thank God, was sleeping—and when he had shaved one cheek, and the other was still soapy, he suddenly heard his mother's voice calling him: "Papa stopped breathing!"—she said it as if she were telling him that the phone was for him, or the soup was on the table. He ran into the dining room: two figures were leaning over the head of father's bed—the residents from the clinic—they were trying to do something with father: one of them inserted a rubber tube in his mouth, pushing it deeper and deeper, and the other breathed into this tube with all his might, as if he wanted to start up a samovar that had gone out. "Exactly twelve," said his mother, looking at father's watch, and she and her son left his room like people leaving an overly long performance, while the others continued to fuss with the rubber tube, and his wife started comforting the nurse—the woman who was working the day the son had arrived and the night father cried out: "I'm the captain of the guard!" Mother and son joined her—they sat her down on the couch in the son's room—the nurse undid the top hooks of her sweater because it was stuffy, and they clustered around her—mother gave her valerian drops, and she and her son explained that as a medical worker she must not be afraid of what had happened just now, it was a completely natural outcome of the illness, and was to be expected, and the son even opened the vent window so that she would compose herself more quickly, but apparently nothing terrible had happened to her because she started fanning herself with a handkerchief, though she was a bit pale; they urged her to stay the night, because she couldn't just go out on the street right away, and then everyone began to hurry to bed, but for a long time they couldn't figure out who should sleep where, because everyone had been sleeping in different places recently, and switching beds constantly, and the son was worried that he and his wife would end up in different beds and maybe even in different rooms, though in the end, they were able to sleep in his room after all, on the couch where they usually slept when they visited, and when they were alone, he embraced her and said: "I wanted you so much." These weren't his words—he had heard them from someone or taken them out of a book, but they seemed natural and enflamed his desire even more.

20

The tunnel's lamps were probably forty or even fifty meters apart, and just below them along the porous tunnel walls stretched two or three rows of black cable cords. The lights resembled lamps of blue light, only they weren't blue, they were regular bulbs and very bright. A light would float away toward the next train car, shine through its windows, and disappear, and at almost the same moment, perhaps even a bit earlier, a new one appeared somewhere ahead; the lights floated by the windows, replacing earlier ones and once again disappearing behind the next car—the black door between the cars wouldn't allow you to follow its path, cutting the light off forever, but as soon as the train sped up, the lights began to flicker quicker and quicker— as though some invisible person were throwing them, like snowballs, harder and harder—until finally their flight turned into a continuous fiery line that pierced the blackness of the windows and the figures of people, as if a flame thrower had joined the action. A man with a good-quality, but worn, fur coat with a high Persian-lamb collar and a Persian-lamb hat with the ear flaps down, sat slightly hunched, his head lowered, a good-quality briefcase on his knees—he walked like that, too, a bit stooped, his head and shoulders pulled down in the collar as though he wanted to hide his face from someone or was afraid of being hit.

On the station platform where he got off, just at the foot of a marble column, a woman was selling lottery tickets at a low table hung with brightly colored posters all the way to the ground.

There was no one nearby, but she turned her wheel like an organ grinder—he slowed down and even reached into his pocket for coins, but then changed his mind. On the square near the metro, the streetlamps were lit, a wet snow was falling, and women with baskets, pressed against the wall of the nearest building, were doing a brisk business selling flowers—snowdrops, violets, and some yellow flowers that he'd never seen, or maybe he'd seen them and forgotten what they were called. He decided to buy just a bouquet, but some old lady lowered the price a half a ruble and handed him two bouquets right away; and he put them in his case, because he didn't like to carry flowers in his hand. Near the front door of the building where he lived, children were finishing a snowman, patting it with shovels on the torso and head. His wife opened the door. He reached out and handed her the flowers; she looked at them uncertainly and asked whether they were from the cemetery.

21

For a whole week, he couldn't get through on the phone—either no one answered, or it was busy, or they said there was no such person there. Finally, a woman answered the phone, and by her voice he knew that it was the cleaning lady of the dormitory where that drunk worked.

"What Aleksei Tikhonovich?" she asked again—she always asked two times and he had to explain things to her, but he stubbornly continued to call the guy by his name and patronymic. "The one who works there . . . the handyman."

As expected, a pause followed—the cleaning lady was apparently correlating the facts. "Alyoshka the repairman?" she said joyfully, having realized who it was about. "You should have said so." "Yes, yes, that's him," he answered even more joyfully because for several days now, waking up in the morning, in his mind he saw the narrow room with the wide bed and a feather mattress, the clean towel that the drunk left for his guests; next to him, he saw the woman on the feather bed with a blissfully tormented expression on her face, and the lightness in her whole body, with which she subsequently walked along the street, almost jumping up on the trolley as it passed.

"Yeah, they're bringing him out right now," said the woman, as though informing him that the repairman had moved to another apartment.

"What? What do you mean, they're bringing him out?" the caller asked, although he'd already understood the situation.

"He croaked," the woman on the other end of the line

94

explained. "Three days ago, he kicked the bucket, right before the holiday"—and the man immediately remembered the hard pulse of the figure lying on the bed, and the dirty paper covering the table with the empty half-liter bottle of vodka, a grimy vodka glass, and the remains of an onion—when it happened he was probably lying alone in the room just like that, dead drunk—and the man imagined that a vein in the drunk's brain just couldn't hold out any longer—it burst and the blood rushed into the brain's soft, supple substance, transforming it into mush, and then convulsions began and the drunk began to wheeze, and his heavy arm flopped over and hung off the bed all the way to the floor, and he lay there dressed and dead until evening, when his girlfriend came by—she worked as a cleaning lady at a hospital and sometimes came to spend the night . . .

That evening, the man rested on the couch, a soft pillow under his head—in the glass of the bookcase across from the couch, right near his feet, he saw his reflection: he saw his face, lifted by the pillow, the torso, which was very short for some reason, and the disproportionately long, immobile feet—as if they weren't his, but someone else's—his feet covered the face and torso giving the impression that he was being carried out feet first. Pulling the cord on the floor lamp, he turned off the light.

22

I stand in the middle of the kitchen wearing nothing but a night-shirt and eating halva. At night I crave sweets and I can eat enormous amounts of them, which is extremely undesirable given my tendency to gain weight. I bought a little lock myself and attached loops and every evening, when my last bedtime preparations are finished—I've rubbed fish oil on the crack on my lip because it needs vitamin A to heal; I've inserted the hemorrhoid suppository; I've taken a liter bottle of water from the kitchen; I've laid an apple and two candies on my desk like they do on graves in rural cemeteries, because you have to have at least something to eat at night; and I've taken a sleeping pill—when all this has been done, I click the lock to the kitchen. My wife hides the key somewhere in the hallway, and while she does this, I voluntarily close myself in our bedroom, just like we did in childhood, when we played at hiding things. I even plug my ears so I won't hear what part of the hallway she's in. Several times, directed by an unerring sense probably possessed only by lunatics, I have found the little key at night—and, hands trembling with impatience, I've opened the lock as though I were a treasure seeker discovering a hidden treasure chest. Tonight, I just jerk the lock and it opens, because for several days it hasn't worked quite right; I haven't exactly informed my wife of this, but I have given her a number of loud hints so that my conscience would be clear. Although it's almost night, it's totally light on the street, and in the kitchen, too, it's the beginning of summer now—the longest days and the shortest nights; exactly thirty-six years ago this very day, or, more precisely, this very night, I traveled to Moscow with grandmother—I remembered as soon as I was in the kitchen. In the blackness of the window, only a dark, blue light could be seen—actually a reflection—and this light, untiringly covered a huge distance for two or three hours—the boy wouldn't have lasted even a minute in this sort of race. The compartment was illuminated by the transparent-blue light, and because of the clank of the wheels, even grandmother's snoring was drowned out. The boy pressed his face to the cold glass, but outside the window he couldn't see anything anyway—only his own face when he moved back from the glass a little bit, and the transparent-blue compartment with its light-blue piqué blankets, under which two strangers and grandmother were sleeping; one covered him, but he wasn't asleep—the compartment rushed along, cutting through the black of the night, tossing back invisible kilometer signs like balls, and he rushed along with this transparent-blue compartment through the darkness without any effort, yielding to this inconceivable speed. The mirrored door reflected the black window, and again in this reflection, the mirrored door could be seen again with the blue sphere, and on, and on, until it was impossible to follow the mutual reflections, which became smaller and smaller, but didn't disappear—apparently all this had something to do with infinity, but at the time the boy didn't understand—and when he awoke, it was light, the lamp was no longer on, and outside the window there were spruce trees planted along the embankment in order to protect the rails from snow drifts; it was foggy in the hollows, and a fiery orange ball rolled along just over the horizon, keeping up with the train—the boy lay on his stomach on the top bunk, sticking his head between the edge of the bunk and the window frame, and holding the curtain back as though he were looking into another world, striving to grasp it all with a single glance: from the oncoming tracks running backward with their tarred, black crossties, and the kilometer posts whizzing by (more than half the distance lay behind) to the fiery, flaming ball floating along with the train, always keeping up with it—the night was behind, he didn't have to sleep anymore, and not some time later, not tomorrow, but today, he would arrive in Moscow. Our courtyard and the streets the kitchen window overlooks are deserted at night, but the windows of the two-story wood house across the way are open wide, as though its inhabitants can't get enough air, but the window openings themselves are dark—this house has been on the list to be razed for ages, though people are still living in it; not long ago a truck ran smack into its corner, smashing through the wall of the house and even driving into a room, they say, but no one was there at the time; the damaged wall was fixed at government expense, very quickly, and therefore the corner of the house looks newer than the rest of it, although the house is painted every year; the lane running up from this house is equally deserted, and sort of pours into our courtyard; along it are old stone houses of different heights—beginning on the second story, all the windows are wide open, but on the first floor, only the vent windows are open—open all the way so they look like fingers pointing; it rained overnight, or perhaps, the streets have already been hosed down—it looks like they're covered with lacquer. Right now is the best time for people who didn't sleep at home to leave the buildings where they stayed; the streets are empty and light; but there are crumbs of halva on the floor next to my bare feet, the kitchen table where I unwrapped the halva is also strewn with crumbs, and my hands are sticky as well. From the hallway, a familiar sound can be heard, something like the rattle of castanets—it's our dog shaking himself after crawl-ing out of the wall cabinet, where the lower shelf was fixed up as his living space, according to my design. The doors of the cabinet were cut horizontally, so that the lower part covers the dog's bed, and the shelves are separate. I'm very proud of this idea, and always demand that everyone in the household acknowledge that this was my invention and that it's quite clever; the dog is a bit cramped in there, however, and several times a night he comes out to stretch and shake himself: he's a boxer who grew old quite early. His back is bowed and he has ulcers—every evening I walk him, and our path is always the same: to the right, out the downstairs door, around the courtyard, keeping close to the edge of the building, and ending up at the bank of earth, which in summer is overgrown with dusty thistle and discarded bits of newspaper and cigarette packs; in winter it's covered with snow that has reddish-yellow, honeycombed indentations—the traces of dog urine; in spring and autumn it all turns into slippery, clayey mush. Halfway there, the dog begins to pull me, so that I have to run after him—he puts all the power of his back legs into this, and I try in every possible way to resist, sometimes I lean back with my entire body, like a horseback rider trying to make a horse rear—someone told me that this strengthens the back muscles of the dog's limbs, and besides, I believe that I'm developing strength of character in him. In the mornings, after I do my exercises, I feel the muscles of my arms, and, crossing them, I pat myself on the shoulders like an athlete who has successfully completed his program and is now calmly awaiting the jury's decision—similarly, sometimes, on seeing the open doors of the subway car I refrain from running on purpose. Making it to the bank of dirt, the dog lifts his back leg as though it weren't really necessary, just an empty formality, a tribute to an aging tradition, and he lets loose a stream of urine—in the winter it pierces the snow, leaving a yellow funnel; the rest of the year the stream hits the earth with a splash—part of it runs down the pavement, part of it sprays in droplets so I try to stand far away, but in the end I always squat down to look at the color of the urine, because several times now there has been a touch of blood in it and we were all worried—could he possibly have a tumor? Walking from the bathroom to my room just in my nightshirt, I try to avoid meeting the dog because I'm afraid I'll get a tumor from him, and in order to hide the depth of my concern from my family, because no one has yet proved that tumors are contagious, I try to turn it all into a joke: with exaggerated caution, as if he weren't a dog but a ticking time bomb, I pass him on tiptoe, holding the hem of my nightshirt all the while so that it covers my body as tightly as possible; passing the danger zone, I run away shrieking, and dive into my bed as though it were a dugout, and cover my head with the blanket. Only the director of our institute has such a strong stream of urine—after he's used the toilet, the foam stays a long time, as though someone had poured a bucket of beer in it; he never closes the cubicle door, because his right hand is paralyzed—from an illness he contracted in his youth during an expedition when he got infected by a microbe he was looking for—so it's stuck in his pocket; sometimes he takes it out with his healthy left hand and puts it on the table like an alien object, half withered with crooked fingers that don't bend, it somehow resembles a premature infant; in his left hand, he holds his briefcase, because he usually goes to the bathroom on the way to his office or when he leaves to go somewhere—his left hand is huge, though it's quite pale. Once during a banquet I myself saw him use that hand to pinch the breast of a new co-worker who was walking by; he did it in passing, casually, but at the same time rather mischievously, as though he'd tightened some prohibited screw; the co-worker continued sitting at the table as if nothing had happened—perhaps that's the secret of his success with women?—by that time, saliva was already trickling out the corner of his mouth, the result of his illness and the onset of intoxication; he danced, but not in time to the music, thrusting his chest out, pressing his partner to him with his left hand, cocking his head in a lopsided sort of way, drooling, and in the breaks between dances he would go up to a group of colleagues, pushing through with his shoulders like an icebreaker—they immediately and respectfully parted, and he would give some command, because colleagues would begin running around from one group to the other, and sometimes the music even stopped: tall, straight, somehow resembling Peter the Great, he used his left hand to take the cognac that one of our colleagues had obligingly brought to him, even though by this time there was none left on the tables; the music quieted down and he would propose a toast in honor of one of the foreign guests, his face shining with bliss and kindness. He went to each table, leaning toward our colleagues, and he'd say something to each of them as he clapped them on the shoulder and sometimes even stroked their hair—in '52, he refused to fire doctors that were considered suspect and he was supposed to be expelled from the Party, but he didn't stop fighting with high-placed persons and even with a minister, and in the end he was removed as director and made assistant director. Even now, when I end up in the bathroom stall after him, I experience a feeling of communion with certain higher spheres and I don't flush, imagining the foam bubbling below as our joint creation or even my own personal one. He usually greets me with a short, barely noticeable nod of the head, but the last time we met, he drew me into the bathroom, as I was on my way out and he had just entered, and suddenly he began talking to me about a promotion—the heavy briefcase pulled his shoulder down, and therefore his other shoulder, pointing at me, was higher than usual; he looked at me from above, but slightly tilting his head to the side, as though examining some unknown insect that he was seeing for the first time. I mumbled words of gratitude and nodded my head, too early, without listening to all his arguments; he drew me in farther and farther and even began to unzip his fly, holding his briefcase in the same hand, and I thanked him, but now he's no longer director . . . I walk down along the pavement and the dog sprinkles every few steps and smells the bushes as though he'd lost something there, in other places he lets go an equally strong, but now shorter stream, in a sense showing that he's completed his search for what he's lost and is no longer interested in it—his attention is already entirely focused on the next bush. We're connected only by the leash and it isn't taut, it drags along the ground, but the dog feels the distance quite accurately, and if the leash catches on a bush, he doesn't try to go ahead, but goes around the bush to my side—my wife insists that our dog is very smart and kind, and unfortunately this is true, because dogs usually resemble their owners; however, I'm not completely certain about how smart I am, if by that is meant the ability to understand people and what's going on around you correctly—but I do have an intellect. I have no doubt about that, and after all, the mind and the intellect coincide with each other at some point, that is, the mind is inconceivable without intellect, and consequently I have doubts once again, this time about my intelligence, though in fact I'm really being coquettish, because I'm actually convinced of my superior intellectuality and demand that my wife acknowledge it, especially since it was she who long, long ago, when we'd just gotten married and had been fighting, said in a burst of anger that I wasn't very smart: I remember quite well, we were walking down the street and just at that moment we passed by a hole in front of a basement window—at the bottom of the hole, it was dark, and there were bars on the window so thieves wouldn't get in—at that time they hadn't begun to resettle the inhabitants of basement apartments—and I was ready to throw myself into that ditch. "What do you mean, I'm an idiot?" I asked her, and I was ready for anything because at that moment I had nothing to lose, and then she explained to me that what she meant was that I wasn't smart in a practical sense; but when we crossed the street

I was able to get her to admit that she'd only said all this "out of spite," and in subsequent years that expression would calm me right down; but at the time, when she called me that, I'd began to tear at my robe or nightshirt because even if it was "out of spite," it meant that at that moment she really believed it; and now, she is even ready to acknowledge I am like Lev Tolstoy or Miklukho-Maklai, but when I say anything she doesn't like about the household, especially in my mother's presence, she can't refrain. "Up yours!" she shouts from the bathroom: she works in an architectural institute—when I telephone, I politely ask them to call her, and one of her colleagues asks me just as politely and respectfully what message to give her because she's in the director's office at the moment. "So I'm a piece of shit?" I shout, bursting into the bathroom—when I walk down the halls of the institute where I work, almost all the employees say hello to me, mainly because I'm on the staff-review commission—when they drop in to see me, they sit down cautiously on the very edge of the sofa, and apologizing, I move my briefcase so that they will be more comfortable and so the breakfast my wife gives me in the morning won't get squashed—she stands there naked, getting ready to take a shower, bending slightly, covering her breasts with her arms as naked women do—they probably stood exactly that way in Auschwitz or Maidanek before they were shot. "So that means I'm just crap?" I shout, because what else could there be in that place besides crap, and at that moment it's obvious to me that she thinks I'm a good-for-nothing piece of crap, and I even see its form, and I am that crap, and all because of her. She's getting ready to turn on the water like nothing happened, she has a deliberately distant expression on her face—how could she possibly fail to understand the harm she's just done? Now I won't even be able to read a book before bedtime because what joy can reading bring, if you're aware of thinking that you're just a piece of shit?—I could strangle her with my own

hands, and wouldn't feel the least bit sorry for her—I hate her
face, covered with yet another kind of cream, as though a whole
cake had been wiped on it, and her body, which arouses me but
is therefore all the more hateful. "So that means I'm a piece of
shit?" I shout—by now I even want her to say it so I'll have a
justifiable right to be overcome by anger and strangle her, and I
even lift my right fist up as though I was chanting "Rot Front,"
adjuring her to give me a final answer—her whole body cringes,
as if to avoid a blow, there's an expression of animal fear in her
eyes, and suddenly I realize that I really did raise my hand; she
has a lot of gray hair and wrinkles on her face, which she tries to
get rid of with the help of various creams, but she does this
irregularly because when she gets home from work she starts
making dinner and because I can't stand the look and smell of
these creams, and so she does this secretly, away from me. I go to
my room, sit down at the desk, and try to do something, but
what do all my pursuits matter if I'm just a load of crap—this
thought gets in the way of me understanding the meaning of the
sentences that I'm reading, and of course the idea of taking up a
pencil or a paint brush isn't even thinkable. I go into the bathroom again—she's taking a shower, her back is under the
showerhead in such a way that it looks like it's being scratched.
"So, you think that I'm a piece of shit?" I ask her, ready to flare
up again. "You're talking nonsense," she answers. This response
suits me, because it has long been part of my wife's armory—this
was exactly what I wanted to hear from her, but all the same, she
was the one who said *that sentence*—I wonder how she'll get out
of the situation, although I can see some possibilities already, and
maybe for this reason I decide to ask the last, decisive question:
"Why exactly up my rear end?"—"Well, shit comes out of the
rear end, not anywhere else,"—this, the logical conclusion I was
expecting, calms me down completely, but in the end, just in
case, I ask again: "And who am I in that case?" "You're talented,"

she answers, scrubbing her back with a long-handled loofah; and I run out of the bathroom the way a customer who has gotten a double portion of something in short supply runs out of a store . . . The mound of earth ends, we turn left, and walk along the high, incongruous building—it's called "the Sculptor's House"—its central section was built before the war. In the middle of what is now a horseshoe-shaped building there's a huge arc which an entire barge could easily float through, there's always wind in the arc; there are almost no sculptors left in the building, but they added two side wings onto the central part after the war—they're lower than the central section—and the staff of a certain very important ministry were given apartments there. The inside of the horseshoe faces the embankment, and from there the building resembles a man standing with his legs set wide, holding back two teenagers with all his might, who are trying to tear themselves away from him. On the empty plaza in front of the building, the dog begins to turn around and around while keeping his nose glued to the ground—and I follow him submissively, because even prisoners are allowed to take a walk and relieve themselves—he's already hunched his back and squeezed his rear several times, and I've even stopped, but no! he absolutely has to climb the little hill, which is even lit by a lamp, and although people are always walking their dogs on this wasteland and it's covered with dog excrement, which you keep stepping on, officially one isn't supposed to walk dogs here— they erected a playground for children in the middle of this wasteland, and at New Year's, next to the playground in the tamped-down snow, they stick up a tree with lights, and each spring they plant twigs there, which are probably supposed to turn into trees, but they remain bare until the end of the summer, and then they completely disappear. The dog clambered up on the tallest and most brightly illuminated point so he could probably be seen even from the other side of the river—the inhabitants of the building for whose children this square was intended have every right to make a remark to me or even say something rude, because in our country children have a special status—at parent meetings, the teachers and parents talk about "our children"— both sides use the word "our" in order to place themselves in an invulnerable position and at the same time demonstrate the commonality of their interests, and you can't argue with that. Once, when I was walking the dog on the other side of the Sculptor's House, where green grass grows in an indisputably civilized fashion, one of the inhabitants of the side wings rebuked me when the dog urinated on a cement telegraph pole that stood at the very edge of the lawn: "Children play here," he said; since then, seeing an oncoming figure, especially if it's a man, I hold the dog on a short leash, and he tries to pull me to the pole which we're always passing precisely at this moment, and I jerk his leash angrily so that it hurts him, and I do it with a kind of joyous hardheartedness, because after all, it's because of him that I could get into trouble, and I'm ready to kick him because I'm allowed to, and then I can vent my anger, but I still try not to do this in front of strangers, because they might intervene on the dog's behalf, so I do it secretively. He empties his bowels at the very top of the hillock almost at the intersection of two shafts of light, from two spotlights shining over the children's playground, and I stand down below, almost dropping the leash and looking off to the side with an aloof expression, as though the dog has no relationship to me and I bear no responsibility for what he does—I would be glad to yank him down from the hillock so hard that he'd break two legs—I feel just about the same way toward the Israelis when they undertake any action. I avoid the growing crowd of dogs who are being walked by their owners— we've been skirting them for a long time because my dog retreats in fear when a certain little dog sees him from far away, barks and rushes over to him and gets underfoot; my dog leaps back like a coward, instead of grabbing the little dog by the throat; the owner of this little dog, whose face I haven't had a good look at because it always takes place at night and it's already dark, calls his dog back and even shouts at it, but this is only a formality, deep down in his soul I'm sure he is exulting. I experience a feeling of animosity toward him—for some reason, I think that he's a former arctic pilot, probably because in the winter he wears very high fur boots that resemble the boots of northern indigenous peoples. Recently, spying us, he leashed his dog and this seemed even more insulting to me; several times, I've grabbed a lash that we got in order to train our dog, although it usually hangs uselessly over his bed because it's enough to say the word "lash" for him to obediently back out of the room into the hallway—hiding it under my coat, I think of ways to lure the arctic pilot's dog over and whip it, but the pilot is always nearby. Moving away from the other dogs, I jerk our dog's leash, trying to hurt him or to step on his paw, and I call him the most insulting names, and he looks at me with bewilderment and fear—he probably thinks that he's not walking the right way—his ears lie back guiltily, and he walks by my side in a cowardly jog; and by the time that my stream of insults reaches its apogee and I begin to kick him, he's nearly crawling on his belly. My wife claims that our dog's behavior is the result of nobility, combined with a sense of self-esteem, and that with dogs who are his equals or larger than him, he would definitely start a fight, and that she herself has even had to pull him off some large, ferocious dogs to stop him from fighting with them—vaguely hoping this might happen, I began to walk him closer to large dogs and even deliberately, but discreetly, set him on them, but he would just pass them by without noticing them, and they didn't pay any attention to him—until my son said that I shouldn't ask for trouble because our dog doesn't know how to fight and the others would chew him to bits; at that moment the three of us were out walking—my son, the dog, and I—and we happened to turn the corner of the Sculptor's House, passing a German shepherd and its owner; the dogs lamely sniffed each other. I decided that this was just another one of my son's obsessive fears about our dog, and walked even faster, having seen a black terrier up ahead who it wouldn't be bad to fight, but I felt that something inside me had broken, because my son is much more realistic than I am, and while we were going around the corner of the building, lit by the lamps on wooden posts which for some reason hadn't yet been replaced with cement, he told me that they hadn't wanted to tell me this, but recently, when my wife was walking the dog across from our building near the two-story wood house—the one that the truck had crashed into, and which I can see this very moment from the window of our kitchen—they ran into the Armenian boxer—we started to call him that because his owners are Armenians—a very large dog with unclipped, floppy ears that look strange with his powerful chest and give him a kind of puppyish look, and the Armenian boxer attacked our dog and grabbed him by the neck and our dog didn't even try to resist, and finally the Armenian managed to pull his dog off, and then my wife cleaned his wounds with iodine, but they decided to hide all this from me so that I wouldn't come to hate our dog once and for all. For a moment I stopped and closed my eyes . . . in a far-off town in the Ural mountains, on the high, white limestone banks of a river, a boy, almost a teen, walked along; he wasn't alone, but with his father's boss and his young son—the boss was the head of the hospital, a tall, hefty man with a large, meaty face and similarly meaty hands, and a kind smile that displayed two rows of blindingly white teeth, both of which remained with him until his very death; his father had been a merchant on Hunters' Row, who chopped up meat and bones with one swing of the axe and the man himself was the best surgeon in the country, though it was hard to figure out how his enormous hands could manage such delicate maneuvers. The sun was blinding, reflecting off a wide, unfamiliar river flowing down below at the foot of white limestone cliffs; there was a group of boys sitting on a pile of limestone, and one in particular stood out—he was smaller than the teenager, but he walked up to him calmly as if to ask a question, and then slapped him in the face, also quite calmly, as though he had wanted to kill a fly that had settled on the teenager's cheek, and just as calmly called him two of the most insulting words possible, words that the teenager had almost never encountered before; he then returned to the group of boys with the obvious sense of a duty accomplished. The father's boss and his son were walking a bit ahead of him, but maybe it was just so that the teenager would think they hadn't seen anything; he walked on, his cheek burning, pulling his head into his shoulders, afraid to even glance back in the event this might all happen again; he was gradually suffused by a feeling of guilt—that boy couldn't have slapped him out of the blue, and with such an air of calm . . . Every time someone reminds me of this on the bus or the commuter train, I experience the same feeling of guilt, and it's only later, when there's no longer any opportunity to respond, I fire up my imagination with images of revenge—each more refined than the last—perhaps feeling guilty is a saving grace, because it's unbearable to live with the awareness of unavenged insults, and therefore you invent some sort of guilt for yourself; or perhaps it's simply a trait handed down from generation to generation. In 1952, with the very same blindingly good-natured smile on his meaty face, the best surgeon of the country—who had become the director of the institute by that time—tried to relieve himself of doctors who could be seen as "unreliable," and the surgeon's son, an adolescent by that time, drew words on the walls of the building where they lived, words in consonance with his father's actions; he followed in his father's path, became a doctor, and in that capacity made on extraordinarily exotic journey, decisively glorifying his father; but on his photograph, printed in the newspapers, I couldn't find even the slightest resemblance the fair-haired little boy who walked ahead of me with his father under the blinding spring sun along the high bank of limestone rock above an unfamiliar, wide river flowing far below . . . Opening my eyes I saw my own son; we were still standing under the lamp light, with the dog looking at us in bewilderment: why had we stopped? My son is taller than me, he stoops and is slender, with untidy hair down to his shoulders and curls in little rings at the ends, and he has thin, delicate, almost childlike hands. For a moment his face turned into a soccer ball—that's what he looked like the day I came home from work and he was lying in his room, his eyes swollen shut, and his teeth broken, unrecognizable and strange: "They beat you up!" my wife exclaimed in the morning when she saw him; he'd come in late at night when everyone was asleep, and in the morning he said he'd fallen and hurt himself—later, he had a hard time remembering what had happened. The host, a tall, thin kid in jeans and a muffler thrown casually over his shoulder and hanging down to his ribs, had given him a sly, conspiratorial wink, as if wanting to tell him some interesting piece of news; they got up from the table, leaving the guests—a number of young people wearing the same casually wrapped scarves around their necks as though they all had sore throats, and there were two or three girls in jeans with hair flowing down to their waists, in addition to an entire battery of dry wine; in the foyer the voices of the people at the table were muffled by the sound of a tape recorder; then a dry fist with bony knuckles advanced from far away, as if from another world, and it all seemed unbelievable to him, as though he were looking at the scene through the small end of binoculars—it couldn't have anything to do with him—until the fist grew to gigantic proportions, obstructing his view of the owner's face, on which a malicious smirk had appeared for some reason—the chandelier in the other room swayed with the sounds of music and hoarse voices singing, plunging him into a strange darkness and deafness, as though the electricity had been turned off and his ears had been plugged with cotton—several times he managed to float out of this darkness, but his ears were still plugged with cotton—he lay on something, a fold-up cot it seems, and above him faces kept appearing—sometimes he recognized them—he thought they were the ones who had been sitting at the table; they were afraid he might kick the bucket, and kept coming back to check—at this point, the young guy whose house it was, was talking on the phone with grandmother, who had called to tell my son it was time to come home and that it wasn't decent to stay so long at someone's house drinking vodka . . . Modulating his voice—the host had studied acting—he told grandmother in restrained and noble tones that they had given him a bit too much to drink and were now getting him back in shape, but that she shouldn't worry, if necessary they would accompany him home; someone took off his turtleneck and then his undershirt, because they were covered in blood, and one of the girls even tried to wash them—practically all the guests had left—they pulled the undershirt and turtleneck on him—and he stood in the foyer; the chandelier swayed again though the music was gone, and the girlfriend of the host—one of the girls with flowing hair—tried to convince him to leave, but for some reason he didn't want to leave. His face was already swollen, but hadn't yet turned blue; there was a trickle of dried blood at the corner of his mouth, and the girl rubbed it off with her handkerchief so no blood would show and, since he so stubbornly didn't want to leave, she threatened that her boyfriend might show up any minute, and she put a ruble in his hand for a taxi. It was already very late, and he walked along some wide, dark street—it must have been the Garden Ring Road—that looked like a nocturnal river with the occasional red light floating on it, and he had to swim across this river; that night he lost the medallion with the crucifix that he wore on a thin chain, but he later replaced it with another. His school globe, standing on the bookshelf in his room is always turned now so that Africa seems the largest continent on the entire earth . . . Going around the Sculptor's House from the back, the building also looks like a giant with his legs spread apart and two disobedient adolescents at his sides—only from this vantage point they aren't trying to get away, rather he appears to be dragging them along and they're digging their heels in with all their might—going around the building, the dog and I find ourselves in the courtyard of our building. The elevator ladies walk back and forth on the paved path that runs along the edge of the grass, jealously guarding the entrances to our building from incursions of knife sharpeners, women with bags of potatoes, or milk cans, and boys from neighboring build-ings; however, when drunks or tipsy guys appear in the courtyard, the ladies immediately disappear, as though the wind had blown them away; when I leave the entrance or return home, these ladies follow me with respectful looks as if I occupied some important position or, at least, had a scandalous reputation and were temporarily in disgrace; for a moment I really am infused with a feeling of my significance. However, so as not to trample their self-esteem and to demonstrate my democratic convictions, I always greet them first—true, after a little pause, so that I don't seem fawning—and their respectful attitude even extends to the dog: "Ay ay ay, his little paws are all scrunched up," one of them says, holding the door open for the dog, who is tearing at the leash to get home—it even seems a bit insulting to me, because they should have let me in first. While I'm still walking across the courtyard, I can see the three lit windows of our apartment and in the middle window, the figure of my mother—she's looking out—although it might not be her, but a Chinese vase that stands on her window sill—I frequently confuse them; she often looks out the window, waiting for me or my son, but then on seeing that we've noticed her, she immediately disappears so we won't think that she's waiting for us or is at all concerned about us because my son didn't put on his long johns before he left and he might catch a cold—she called him an idiot and he replied by throwing a slipper at her—she ducked the slipper, but shouted that he was an ingrate, and slammed the door to her room so hard that plaster fell from the ceiling, and when I defended him she jumped out of her room again and, standing in the door with her lower jaw trembling and her hands shaking, maybe from old age or perhaps from powerless anger, trying to but not finding some object that she could throw at me, she called me an ingrate as well, and slammed the door for good, so hard that the key fell out of it; and moreover, ever since the globe in my son's room has been in the same position, she has become an orthodox Marxist and explains that the shortage of oranges is due to the growing prosperity of the masses . . . Each evening before bed, I give her injections for her high blood pressure—lowering her underwear, she lies down on her couch like an experienced swimmer floating on the water; her buttocks, unusually white for her age, are covered with dots—traces of the injections—and have lost a considerable amount of their elasticity; they're too narrow to accommodate so many shots, so every night, lying on her stomach, she checks out her buttocks with her hand, showing me where, from her point of view, the best place is; on her ring finger, which feels her buttock with particular meticulousness, she wears a gold ring with a small diamond—she never takes it off, but it doesn't fit as tightly on her finger as it once did, and I think it could even be turned around because her hands have gotten thinner and her finger joints stick out like an old person's. Her heart has been working for almost eight decades now, and it's some sort of miracle—after all, it was contracting the very same way in the last century; I try to imagine it—a little hypertrophic from working so many years, laced with sclerotic blood vessels like tourniquets, in some way resembling the plaster replicas they give students for lessons in anatomy—even now it beats during her sleep, and close by, near the head of her bed, on a low stool, just in case, so she doesn't have to reach up to the bedside table, her medicines are laid out, sorted according to their function: sleeping pills are separate, heart drugs are separate, blood-pressure medicine separate, and next to them is a little bowl of water, and a packet of mustard plasters whose expiration date is three months, otherwise they won't be sufficiently effective, and right there, a small glass of water to swallow pills. Across her room, on the desk, under glass, illuminated by a strip of early-morning light breaking through a crack in the two tightly drawn curtains, family photographs are laid out in several rows, as if they were from the lives of the saints. They comprise a general picture: there's a young lieutenant with one square fastened in his buttonhole, his field cap cocked dashingly, and with serious eyes that have a touch of wildness; a young woman in a high fur hat and fur coat like they wore in the last century and still wear now, photographed with the Eiffel Tower in the background— her entire figure expresses an unreserved *emancipée*; she's wearing a long dress that emphasizes her stately figure, and is sitting on a chair with a high, old-fashioned back, her elbow leaning slightly on an open book that lies on an inlaid table: posed like Kramskoi's *Unknown Woman*, thinking about the meaning of life. Then there's a lean but very proper, solid man, with a pointed, Bunin-like beard and mustache that scratched his grandson when he said good-bye to him before being given morphine; and then there's a large, short woman, hiding her droopy lower lip in an epicurean smile—behind her in the back-ground, photographed deliberately out of focus, is a section of the Artists' House; when her husband, having become a well-known member of the Academy, traveled abroad, she would move in with us, because since her retirement she'd fallen into psychological depression—she could no longer write articles on art history and thought that she had fallen hopelessly behind in contemporary Soviet painting—a fold-out bed was placed in her sister's room for her next to the desk with the photographs, and she would lie on it like a pile of rags until dinner, rising only to go to the bathroom, and coming out, would turn off the light uncertainly, looking back as though she'd forgotten something, but was resigned to it because now she didn't care; by the end of the day she was usually a bit more lively, and shuffling along, her hands behind her back, she would enter my room—trying not to notice the sketchbooks and pencil drawings lying in front of me on the desk, she would ask how things were going with my scientific paper, and turn the conversation to the frailty of existence—sometimes she tried to weigh an invisible head of cheese or sugar on her palms with crooked fingers, but somewhere in the middle she would drop it. Waving her hand she would run it across her throat, making a characteristic wheezing sound, but she'd do it very softly, winking at me conspiratorially, because only she and I could understand each other. Next to this photograph is one of a middle-aged, almost old man wearing a heavy coat and a professor's cap, taken against the background of the hospital building—the photograph captures only his face and the upper part of his torso, and by the angle of the building, you can tell that he is going somewhere but was stopped and forced to be photographed—he smiles sarcastically, as though he's about to joke at some one's expense, though there is really more sadness than derision in his smile, so it seems that the sarcasm is addressed to himself; he's also the one in the pre-operation ward, wearing a white cap with his white coat sleeves rolled up to the elbow; in his hands he is holding something like a cheesecloth napkin, or maybe a mask; on the lapel of his coat there's a dressing forceps, which may be replacing a missing button—flaccid folds hang from his chin, and the expression on his face, directed somewhere toward the top of the photograph, is mournful, almost tragic, as though he sees and guesses what the others don't see. There's another photo, of a black-haired woman doctor, no longer young, but not yet old, in a white coat and cap, sitting at the table in her office—her hands lie on an open case history, there's a stethoscope lying next to her, the one on her desk right now, next to the photographs—and on the ring finger of her left hand is the ring with the little diamond that she always wears, though you can't see it in the photograph. Her expression is calm and sober—she is the competent medical professional in her office; she never abuses her position and is distinguished by extraordinary objectivity in regard to the personnel who work for her, a quality that has brought her well-deserved respect and authority. She is the visible and invisible mistress of her home—her son, who lives just outside of Moscow, always calls her to find out whether the insignificant pain he occasionally experiences in his left gastrocnemius muscle was dangerous, or whether the feeling of an alien object in his right eye—could that be a tumor? It was enough for him to hear her voice to calm down, and she was categorically against him driving a car himself, because he might have an accident; though her husband suffers from diabetes, he doesn't always come right home after work but climbs one flight higher—but he more or less holds to the diet prescribed for him, which his wife observed strictly; their grandson lives with them because their living conditions are better than those of the son and daughter-in-law, and, besides which, here he has the opportunity to study in music school, where Nastya takes him and then picks him up. Grandmother meticulously followed his progress and regularly chatted on the phone with the director of the class, and the grandson worshipped his grandmother—between the woman doctor who sits at her desk in her office and the old woman now asleep with her half-opened mouth, her toothless gums visible in its black depths, there is an extremely distant resemblance which, however, becomes more noticeable when the old woman occasionally goes to see friends, putting on her false teeth and dark-blue wool suit with a small gold brooch—in those moments I want to tell her that I don't like my job, but with silent disapproval she keeps track of the wine I drink, and after the fourth small glass, she leaves the table so as not to witness this licentiousness and see me destroying myself and my son with my own hands, setting a pernicious example; and absolutely no resemblance can be found between the old woman and the flirtatious short-haired student whose photograph lies next to that of the woman doctor in the white coat. In the next photograph there's a painfully fat boy with bangs and unhealthy circles under his eyes—he stands, leaning against a bicycle; and in the center of all this is a large family photograph, like the apostles in a cathedral—here the boy is still quite a little boy in a sailor suit, his ears stick out, and he is hugging his grandfather around the neck, and there's grandmother with her gray hair—that's how the boy remembered her his whole life—sitting in the first row next to grandfather, she sitting so straight that it seems she doesn't have anything to do with him and she stretches out her neck so that two tendons clearly stand out like strings; there's a young lieutenant in uniform with parted hair combed smooth—he sits on the back of a chair in the second row so as not to be taller than all the rest, and therefore it looks like he's shorter; and a little ways over, the boy's aunt and her husband in huge round eyeglasses—he looks something like a falcon blinded by the flash of the camera—press idyllically against one another. A woman with short, black hair who still resembles the student in some ways stands next to them, but separated from her husband, because this family picture was made just when her affair with the doctor-bacteriologist was in full swing—in the boy's family, he was called Bey-Mey, for the first letters of his name and patronymic—this abbreviation implied some kind of forbidden knowledge which was allowed for some reason; Bey-Mey had a luxuriant, gray *chevelure*, wide, slightly turned-out nostrils from which hairs sprouted, and he breathed heavily through his nose as if he had adenoids. He was sent somewhere north, beyond the Arctic Circle, and the boy's mother even went to see him there—the boy tried to imagine the room in which he lived, a small room in a wooden house with a window covered in hoarfrost, a sweeping blizzard outside, a place where it was night even during the day . . . his mother had been there twice, both times during the winter—when Bey-Mey went out to work she would cook dinner on the kerosene stove and listen carefully—was that him coming? . . . and at night when the two of them were alone in pure darkness, his mother and the strange man with hair growing out of his nostrils, she saw the northern lights—and told everyone about it, even in front of father. But in the boy's family everyone thought that she had the right to do this because her husband was mentally ill, and if she didn't divorce him, it was only because he threatened to kill himself and she had to think of her son. Father sits in the first row near grandfather, crossing his hands, with their short, fat fingers on his stomach—just as he did in the photograph in the pre-op ward when he held either a mask or a cheesecloth bandage—looking through his glasses, somewhere past the photographer, his tall brow already balding, but it still had wavy hair combed a bit to the side—he had a lot more hair than the man with a solid bald spot and a paunch standing in his nightshirt, who has now finished off the halva. Having carefully searched the buffet and the refrigerator for something sweet, and washed his sticky hands, he lies on his couch perpendicular to the couch where his wife sleeps—she sleeps, covering her head, and sometimes even hiding it under the pillow, sleeping without dreams, rising like a bulky mountain—she is a stout woman beginning to grow old, with a once beautiful face, and these are the only hours in her life when she isn't tormented by the thought that she isn't the mistress of her home and that the elevator ladies say all kinds of things about her to each other and to the tenants of the building, while her colleagues at work deliberately foist all the hardest papers on her just to reveal her ignorance. He lies on his sofa on his right side because he can't sleep on his back or on his left side. Exactly thirty-six years ago at the same time—the same sort of early morning, still indistinguishable from the light summer night—the sun's red hot sphere, hanging over the saw-toothed edge of the distant, bluish forest, raced along with him. The train had already traveled more than half of the distance; and pressing his face to the glass, the boy tried to capture all the space opening up within a single glance: from the oncoming tracks running backward through hollows filled with fog—which he imagined as streams—to the ever bluer forest on the horizon with the blinding hot sphere hanging over it, he could smell mugwort mixed with locomotive smoke through invisible cracks in the window frames—soon they would both fall asleep—the middle-aged man with the bald spot lying on his right side on his sofa, and the boy, traveling to Moscow—the boy would fall into a deep, dreamless sleep, and when he awoke, the high, wood platforms of Moscow dacha villages he'd never seen before would flash by. The aging man, on the other hand, did dream: he was on a platform among people who had come to see others off; and everyone, the travelers, sticking their heads out the windows, and the people seeing them off, were cheery—smiling, joking, laughing, because this was some kind of entertainment, just a train trip, they were parting only for a few days; but he's not seeing anyone off, and everyone can tell, and it's very unpleasant for him, he feels uncomfortable, like a man who accidentally ends up at someone else's party—the train moves; the travelers and the people who came to say goodbye wave back and forth, shouting and laughing—then, so that no one notices anything, he also waves and smiles and follows the train, and because he does, he really feels quite happy and cheerful inside, but still, he never forgets for a moment that everyone knows he's not seeing anyone off; and therefore, even though he really is running, waving, and shouting, he can't shake the feeling of his own inferiority. The train has pulled out of the station, and everyone is walking back along the platform—now, after the train has left, they are all in the same position, and he walks calmly among them, because he doesn't need to pretend—he is an equal among equals.

August 19, 1973

NORARTAKIR

And the ark rested . . . upon the mountains of Ararat.
Genesis: 8, 4

I
THE TERRORIST

Norartakir was the highest part of the city, the part open to winds from all sides, including those blowing from the Ararat valley, and although it remained unclear how wind could blow from bottom to top, nonetheless when the guides said so it sounded impressive and professional; even more convincing was their claim that the mountainous location of the city gave rise to differences in temperature and various microclimates—when it rained in the lower, central part of the city, snow fell higher up, and Norartakir was one of the first areas to feel the blow. However, at the moment, this was all very difficult to imagine: the endlessly long, hot, almost shadeless streets were flanked by four- and five-story buildings fashioned from stone blocks that for some reason were called tufa; this tufa was supposed to be colorful, but it was gray like ordinary building cement. Still, Boris Lvovich imagined that inside these buildings, inside the thick stone walls, it was cool. The streets climbed upward—no doubt to the highest, invisible point of Norartakir which was probably impossible to get to: from dawn to dusk cars sped along the streets, the most important of which directly connected the city's lower part to the highest, unattainable, point of Norartakir. Buses and trolleys stretched out in an endless line and trams rumbled along rails that more closely resembled railroad tracks because the pavement between them had been dug up, or, perhaps, on the contrary, it hadn't been put in yet; when crossing the street, you had to jump across the ties, and the wind raised the dust and blew grit in your teeth, but the sky toward which the street rushed remained hopelessly blue. The hotel where they were staying was called the "Artakir"—the prefix "nor" meant "new," so the area was new Artakir; one of the locals or guides explained that this neighborhood had been built fairly recently and was inhabited by returnees from the west. "That's why there's almost no laundry hanging from the buildings in this area," guessed Tanya immediately. In the morning, on awaking, Boris Lvovich ran out on the balcony in his white underwear—the balcony looked out over the courtyard, which was piled with boxes, barrels, and rusty iron. Sheets and cotton-stuffed blankets hung from a metal cable stretched between the blind walls of neighboring buildings, facing the hotel court-yard—you could wrap an entire family in each of those blankets, including the swarthy, dark-skinned children who ran through the courtyard or down the street with warlike whoops. Boris Lvovich rushed out on the balcony dressed like that to tease Tanya, especially because the next room also had a door leading to the balcony, though the curtains were always drawn. "Are you out of your mind?" she would shout after him—he pressed right against the balcony railing, even leaned slightly over it, which caused a nauseating, sweet weakness in his knees—"Can you see him?" Tanya asked, pulling on her robe, as if they were talking about a living thing. And indeed, he was visible. Boris Lvovich found this comforting, because if their room had overlooked the street they wouldn't have been able to see it, no matter how far they leaned over the railing the hotel wall wouldn't get in the way. "Look, look!" they exclaimed to each other, standing on the balcony and gazing to the left, toward the south. "Come closer over here, you can't see anything from there," said Boris Lvovich, grabbing her hand, trying to pull her toward the railing, but she had been afraid of heights since childhood—that is, at least for the twenty odd years they had been married. "Look, look!" They stood with their heads turned to the left: Norartakir and all its houses, courtyards, and streets dropped off and disappeared somewhere below, lost in the haze clouding the lower part of the city and the plateau, which was probably called the Ararat valley; and beyond the plateau, above the horizon and the haze, high up in the sky, hung an immobile, transparent cloud that looked like two snowy summits—one was closer and taller, the other was smaller and hid behind the larger, but still visible nonetheless; and as the sun rose higher the clouds melted before your eyes, changing into a ghost—in a half-hour there would be only sky, whitish-blue, hazy. "Give me the telephoto lens!" he shouted at her, and she obediently ran back to fetch it, and the next morning, with the inevitability of the dawn, of night, or of death, the silvery, double-peaked cloud appeared high in the sky again— the two snowy peaks of Ararat. Tanya and Boris Lvovich had arrived only a few days ago—three, or perhaps four. Having completed a farewell circle over the shore of the resort town where they had vacationed, the airplane set course for the southeast; you couldn't see the sun from either the right or the left—that meant they were flying toward the sun, which had only just come up, because it was early morning. Opening the curtain as far as possible, craning his neck and pressing his face to the cold glass of the window, he could still just see the sea and the meandering strip of shoreline heading south to the state border—dozens of kilometers of endless beach over which ran a similarly endless long wave, and it even seemed to Boris Lvovich that at the end of this wave, at the place where it touched the shore, a lacy foam boiled up; he was struck by the emptiness of these endless beaches, until he suddenly realized that from this height it was impossible to discern figures, or even houses—it was almost a geographical map outlining the mainland. The sea and the shoreline drowned in a bluish gray haze because the human eye couldn't see further than one hundred kilometers, and through the window of the opposite side, especially when the airplane banked left and the shore and sea disappeared and in their place, sky with an unnatural hue appeared—probably the cosmic blue—through the window of the opposite side, mountains suddenly appeared—probably the entire Caucasus mountain range. Boris Lvovich really wanted to see the shore and the mountains at the same time—he even rose from his seat a bit to look through the window behind him, but the luggage netting above the seatback got in the way; on the other hand, the mountains could be seen particularly well—"Tanya, Elbrus!" he shouted in his wife's ear, trying to override the sound of the engine. She was always afraid she'd get sick to her stomach in airplanes, so she sat back against the seat, her eyes shut tight, looking like she was about to be operated on; nevertheless, she did open her eyes for a moment and turned her head, trying to see. A few years ago, they'd vacationed at a resort in the Caucasus, and when the weather was clear, the snowy, two-headed summit of Elbrus was visible—Tanya spoke of it as if it were alive, calling it "that guy." Now, from high above, at this height, the mountain seemed strangely accessible, and you could see the central, snow-less part of the mountain and even its green foothills—it was just a mountain with two snow-covered summits, and nearby, more mountains, a bit smaller, many of them also snow-covered, or at least *snowmen* as the mountain climbers like to call them or even plain tourists or the people vacationing in the sanatorium, who were taken in buses to be shown the fissures and mountains— and Boris Lvovich also caught himself using this word when he told people in Moscow about their trip. You could still see Elbrus, and ahead, if you leaned against the window or looked out the very first window of the opposite side, Kazbek had come into view—Boris Lvovich recognized it immediately although he'd never really seen it before, only on cigarette packages. On one tour, he and Tanya were supposed to be able to see it from the bus window, and they avidly scoured the distance beyond the horizon where the tour guide pointed, but there was only sky, and then the tour guide told them that specific atmospheric conditions were required in order to see it; but right now, from the airplane, Boris Lvovich saw it—"Tanya, Kazbek!"—and it was just the way he had imagined it: sort of unfinished, with a defective, corroded summit, as though someone had chewed on it; through the back windows, Elbrus could still be seen, in front, Kazbek—the two highest peaks of the Caucasian range and he, Boris Lvovich, was much higher up, as if he were looking at them from Mount Everest like Tenzing, whose name Boris Lvovich suddenly remembered, although he'd never been interested in mountain-climbing, but he was higher than Tenzing had been, because the airplane was still flying at a height of nine thousand meters, and Mount Everest was eight thousand meters, and somehow no one was surprised by this—the passengers dozed placidly in their seats, sometimes glancing distractedly out the window, or, just as distractedly, leafing through a magazine as though they were riding to work on the commuter train. The shore and the sea were no longer visible no matter what the position of his head, even if he stuck it between the window and the seat in front of him. On the right, as far as the eye could see, unpopulated hills spread out—they were probably mountains too, although not as high as those on the left, to the east, but from that height they looked like hills, only sort of ribbed, with shadows between them—not even hills and not mountains, but simply folds of the earth's crust which had formed hundreds of thousands or even millions of years ago, when neither people, nor even animals existed, frozen in their primordial state; they were just as deserted now as then. The airplane's tiny shadow, resembling a cross, slipped along the folds, constantly diving into their shadows—the sun was somewhere to the left of the plane—so that meant they'd turned south, and those gray, deserted hills turned into Turkey somewhere, or maybe this already was

Turkey, and the plane's shadow was slipping over Turkish land—only why was the land so empty and unpopulated? Somewhere, past those hills, unfamiliar foreign towns hid: noisy, full of bright advertisements in an unknown language—towns that Boris Lvovich had never seen and probably never would; towns where you could stand in the middle of the street and shout out things you were afraid to say in a whisper, even when you were at home in your own apartment, and where you could stand at the busiest intersection and tear a newspaper into tiny pieces, stamp on them, and no one would pay any attention to you; you could shout as loud as you liked about the lie shrouding that small country that carried on an unequal battle with an enormous caliphate; where you could just buy a ticket, go to the airport, and fly to any city in the world you saw fit, and that land was close as close could be—maybe fifteen or twenty kilometers away, and he actually saw the shadow of their airplane slipping over that land, and he felt a kind of bittersweet lump in his throat. "Tanya, it's Turkey," he said to his wife almost in a whisper after looking around carefully, but she heard him and then they both looked out the window, pressing their foreheads to the cold glass, flattening their noses; in order to reach the window, she had to sit up a bit and lean over, her hands pressing on his legs—for a moment it even seemed that the airplane would bank to their side. "The Anatolian plateau," said Tanya— in school she had loved history and would say things like "Patchwork Empire," or "appanage princes" instead of "princes"; and instead of "Disraeli" she'd say "Lord Disraeli," and she particularly liked to say "Lord Beaconsfield." Boris Lvovich had never quite understood his historical role and whether Lord Beaconsfield and Disraeli were one and the same individual. "Why plateau? Those are mountains," asked Boris Lvovich. "A large part of Turkey's territory is located on the Anatolian plateau," Tanya stated—her hands were making his legs burn.

"Alright, alright," he said. "Well, of course, since it's me saying it . . ." she said, freeing his legs and flopping back in her seat in a fit of pique, though she couldn't manage to produce the look of expecting to be operated on this time. "What do you think, is he a terrorist?" Tanya asked him in a whisper, nodding toward a young man sitting in front of them on the aisle leading to the pilot's cabin. He had a broad back and long, black hair that covered his neck all the way down to his jacket, which was very well cut and made of some shiny material; the whole trip he'd been sitting immobile, as though glued in place, without reading anything, without exhibiting any interest in what was going on beyond the window. Tanya and Boris Lvovich had noticed him earlier, in the airport, when their luggage was being checked—because for this border-zone flight, a uniformed guard stood next to the metal partition, squeamishly and unwillingly sticking her hand into the partly opened suitcases, which were then impossible to latch shut because various outfits and pajamas stuck out. The tall young man with a swarthy face and suit made of shiny material wasn't carrying anything at all. He stood with his arms crossed over his chest, as though feeling the muscles of his rib cage, and he lightly tapped the ground with his patent-leather shoes in a condescendingly expectant mood while all the fuss and bother of checking suitcases went on around him. "I'm sure he's a terrorist," Tanya said again. "I don't know," Boris Lvovich replied indifferently, but his heart skipped a beat, and for a moment he imagined the broad-shouldered young man in the shiny suit jumping up suddenly and pulling a sawed-off shotgun and a hand grenade from the hem of his jacket, aiming the shotgun at the passengers and threatening the plane crew—the terrorist's swarthy face was fierce—he stood in the doorway leading to the pilot's cabin keeping an eye on the passengers while dictating his demands to the pilot—the airplane changes course abruptly: "We'll land in Turkey," Boris Lvovich whispered to Tanya, half joking, half-serious. "Would you stay?" asked Tanya with not much more than her lips, and, since he only shrugged his shoulders in reply, as if he'd forgotten her conspiratorial tone, she repeated the question: "Don't tell me you'd stay?" And it wasn't clear what prevailed in her voice: admiration for his courage or disdain for what he was planning to do. "Of course," he said, so as not to disappoint her. The windows of their Moscow apartment looked out over the boulevard, and standing at the window and looking out at the passersby or the people strolling along the boulevard, it was easier to think—phrases just came to him—and he barely had time to get to the desk to jot them down, and when speaking at a meeting at which he'd work himself into a frenzy, occasionally putting aside a prepared text and choosing the face of a young woman—a relative of his client or just someone present in the courtroom—the woman couldn't take her eyes off him, they followed him with hope and admiration—the wide open eyes of a school girl . . . Actually, the Turkish authorities could turn them over . . . "He's probably just a guard," Tanya said, either with relief or disappointment, and since Boris Lvovich didn't answer, she repeated: "I'm sure of it," and even though he understood that the young man sitting in front of them was most likely an ordinary passenger—he probably had a meeting today and would fly back this evening or tomorrow morning. Nevertheless, Boris Lvovich began to think of him as a guard and was even filled with a feeling of trust and gratitude toward him because he was protecting him, Tanya, and all the other passengers from all manner of bandits and terrorists; he probably had a small Browning in his right pocket or maybe even a large pistol, and if anyone even moved a muscle, he'd pull it out of his pocket—only it was hard to understand why he sat with his back to everyone and hadn't turned around once, although his broad back extended a peaceful confidence and knowledge of his business.

Boris Lvovich sucked on a candy that he'd automatically taken from the stewardess and only then noticed that his ears were popping—the airplane was beginning its descent—and when it banked right, he could see city blocks rushing by, squares and rectangles of white and gray houses with flat roofs like you usually see in a model, and between them, for a few moments, he saw streets straight as an arrow, then the whirling, narrowing funnel of a stadium, then again blocks of the model city, all faster and faster, growing larger with catastrophic speed—now you could make out trams and even people—it seemed that the plane wouldn't make it to the landing strip and would crash into the blocks of houses. Boris Lvovich's heart sank along with the airplane, his whole body filled with lead, his hands clutched the arms of the seat as though they were his last support, falling out from under him; his ears were plugged up, and to make sure the engine hadn't stalled, he swallowed furiously, because he'd already eaten the candy—the nose of the plane came down and the whitish-gray blocks gradually receded into the distance—the plane tilted to the left and in place of the rushing squares that had just been there, Boris Lvovich saw two snow-covered cones against the sky: one closer, taller, the other farther away and smaller. The plane was probably making its last circle before landing. "Excuse me, do you know what mountain that is?" he asked the young man with the long hair and the shiny suit, leaning over right to his ear, because his work day was probably over and besides which, Boris Lvovich felt an ever-growing trust in him. Most likely, he was returning home after a night spent in the seaside town. "That's Ararat," he replied almost without deigning to turn his head toward Boris Lvovich. "Tanya, it's Ararat!" he shouted to his wife, but she was sitting pressed into the back of the seat, her eyes closed in a martyred expression, as though the operation had already begun but she was still expecting the worst. "Do you know whether they have excursions to see it?" he asked the young man, leaning all the way forward as though he wanted to put his head on the fellow's shoulder. "Ararat is in Turkey," the man answered without turning his head in the least, he simply moved his shoulder as though he were shooing a bothersome fly. For a second, Boris Lvovich was ashamed that he didn't know such simple things: "Tanya! The real Turkey. Look!" He even tugged on her sleeve, because she still had her eyes closed. Then, the airplane landed and the passengers descended onto the summer tarmac, standing somewhere between the plane's wing and its fuselage waiting to see what would happen to them next; somewhere from the side, a bus with connecting sections drove out, the kind that usually transports air passengers, and everyone decided that in a minute they'd be driven to the air terminal; one person even started off toward the bus, but it didn't stop and drove off empty. Amid the people standing near the fuselage, Boris Lvovich saw their neighbor from the front seat—the young man with the well-fitting suit of shiny material. Boris Lvovich was amazed to see him standing among all the others, awaiting his fate, just like all the rest—perhaps he would even wait for the luggage to be unloaded. He, too, headed toward the disappearing bus with the others: "Everything is always topsy-turvy here," he said. Since his words elicited no response, his eyes turned toward Boris Lvovich and Tanya, and Boris Lvovich suddenly realized that the young man was simply a Georgian.

II
THE MARK OF KING DAVID

The square next to the gray one-story building of the air terminal wasn't terribly clean—in the middle of the square was a bed of withered flowers, and the pavement was strewn with pieces of newspaper and cigarette butts; further on, there was a kind of wood fence, and someone had told them that there was another airport, the main one, for long-distance flights. They stood and waited for a taxi: Boris Lvovich had decided that this was where the taxi stand should be. Several families with suitcases stood near a post dug into the ground: on the post was a peeling, tin, stenciled sign with faded checkers, over which something was written in letters resembling hairpins and fish hooks. Boris Lvovich and Tanya joined the line as well, but stood back from the rest; Boris Lvovich kept checking the suitcases—were they all there?—he kept his right hand in his pocket, clutching a three-ruble note in his fist as if it were already time to pay the driver; and he kept sticking his left hand into the inside-jacket pocket, nervously fingering a piece of paper folded in quarters—the hotel reservation confirmation that he'd been given in Moscow at the central travel bureau. Sometimes he thought that he'd lost it or that this wasn't really it, and then he pulled it out of his pocket in order to reassure himself that it was indeed the reservation; several times, the used plane tickets turned up in his hand and his heart sank. Tanya walked over to the other end of the square and tried to get one of the empty taxis, but after driving around the flowerbed they either drove off or reluctantly pulled up to the people waiting near the stenciled signpost.

"Come here! It's pointless! This is the line," he shouted to her, waving furiously, touching the suitcases with his leg to make sure they were still there; she always put him in awkward situations, and someone might well make a comment. "What a lousy city," said Tanya returning, "I knew it." They got a taxi after everyone else had already gone their way—a worn Volga with a faded checkered sign stopped right at the post, although they were the only ones left, they had to run over a bit so the car wouldn't leave; the driver continued sitting at the wheel like a stone until Boris Lvovich asked him to open the trunk. He took his time getting out—he was sure of himself, heavy set, swarthy, gray hair, gray eyes—he probably had his own house here, a garden, children, maybe even grandchildren, his grandfathers and great-grandfathers had lived here, and he probably wondered why all these people came on trains and airplanes from far away, standing around in the hotel lobbies for hours to get their beds. For that matter, it was almost dinner time, and these two tourists probably needed to go in a totally different direction than he did, and opening the trunk was also a pain, all their junk could have fit on the lap of this bald guy who was fussing about like he was late for a soccer game. Still, he opened the trunk; inside, there was a spare tire smeared with lime, a dirty tarp, some rusty tools. It didn't even occur to him to take the suitcases out of Boris Lvovich's and Tanya's hands to put them in. "They won't get dirty, will they?" Boris Lvovich asked, carefully arranging the suitcases near the tire—Tanya helped him—while the driver watched silently as though none of this had anything to do with him. Tanya sat in the back seat with a grim face; Boris Lvovich sat next to the driver. "Hotel Artakir," said Boris Lvovich, taking out the reservation receipt for the hundredth time just to check, although he'd known the name of the hotel by heart for quite some time. "It's rather far, is that right?" Boris Lvovich asked cautiously, even though in Moscow he had already found out that the hotel was not in the center of town. "Artakir. Don't worry, we get there," the driver said in a conciliatory voice—it was probably on his way home or maybe the distance suited him. They turned onto the highway, or a large street, they were on the outskirts; on both sides, unsightly stone buildings appeared here and there, sometimes with a crumbling stone wall made of flagstone or crushed rock—then came what were clearly streets, lined with four- and five-story modular apartment buildings, white and gray—that was probably what Boris Lvovich had seen from the airplane. "And from where you are?" the driver asked. "From Moscow," said Boris Lvovich, but for some reason he didn't experience the feeling of superiority over the provincials that he always did when he went somewhere on vacation or a business trip. "I was in Moscow, I was vun time," the driver said slowly, with deliberation, as if he were counting money—when he said "one," he raised his hand slightly from the steering wheel and lifted his fat, hairy index finger, as though he weren't entirely certain of the intellectual capabilities of the passenger who sat next to him—thick and swarthy, he seemed to have merged with his seat, just as he'd no doubt merged with his land and his people, and Boris Lvovich realized that his gesture, and his sentence, and what he was planning to say: all of it had been prepared in advance and had probably been said more than once, and that he, Boris Lvovich, just represented an opportunity for the driver to express himself—"von time," he said, lifting his short hairy finger once again. "No good there," he said, sighing, as though it upset him that it was no good in Moscow. "Two peoples wants drink, yes?" and he showed Boris Lvovich two fingers, his index and middle finger, also covered in hair, "why want three peoples—why half litter for three—you get it?" and he showed Boris Lvovich three fingers, the index, middle finger, and thumb—his ring finger probably didn't bend very well, and, besides which, he was holding the wheel with his ring finger and pinky. "I got a friend, he's got brother, yes? What for stranger guy? I invite friend home, I get wine, food on table, right? How come stranger? . . . Lotta bad peoples there," he added after a short pause, "you walking, you scared—maybe they hit you. I was in car—policeman stop, I scared too . . ." They crossed a bridge; somewhere way down below, a thin stream sparkled in the sun—it was probably a mountain stream, flowing at the bottom of the crevasse; the city was above them, and on the stony slopes of the crevasse descending to the stream, small stone houses were sculpted into the rock; it seemed they had been cut from the same stratum, and even farther below, the ruins of a stone wall, probably the remains of some fortress rampart, descended sharply. "What is that, an ancient part of the city?" Boris Lvovich asked, because there had been modern buildings the whole way and he couldn't wait to see something ancient. The driver glanced briefly at the houses and stone wall, sort of in passing, as though they were all trivial, hardly worthy of notice, and he glanced just as briefly at Boris Lvovich, as if deciding whether it was worth being open with him. "Everybody still crawlink on fours, we have culture," he said after a slight pause, and Boris Lvovich couldn't decide whether he should be insulted by this or not. In his mind, he imagined tribes of Scythians or Polovtsians roaming across the vast expanses; dismounting, they sat down around the campfire, the light of the flames flickering across their high cheekbones, while a mammoth or some kind of fossil roasts on the fire—they pull off pieces of meat with their hands—the silver chain mail that Boris Lvovich saw in the Historical Museum jingles on these warriors—grease flows down their hands and chins; but behind the walls of a monastery in this small, stony country, on whose territory he was now driving, dozens of philosophers and poets who understood the wisdom of life and truth, sat at thick volumes or wrote, dipping cleansed eagle feathers into pomegranate wine; scanty light came in from the narrow slits in the stone arches, but by night, reflections from candle flames, stirred by the wind, fell on their faces and fingers, while close to the monastery wall the driver's distant ancestor worked his barren plot of stony soil; he was stocky and thickset like his descendant, and around him were the very same swarthy, noisy children and grandchildren—but who were these people in comparison to Boris Lvovich's people and Tanya's, although Tanya had wide cheekbones and could easily pass as a descendant of the Scythians or even Tatars? Boris Lvovich not only had the characteristic face, but a kind of strange scar behind his ear and on his neck which appeared when he was an adult, as though it had waited for its time to come—the scar resembled a scar from the blow of a sabre, and someone told him that it was a sign of belonging to the line of King David. What were these people in comparison to his, Boris Lvovich's people? When the driver's ancestors were digging in the stony earth, and the monks penning their church books full of everyday wisdom, his people had already been dispersed, because they had long ago achieved wisdom and truth; in his mind's eye, Boris Lvovich imagined the wiry gray-bearded elders, clothed in chitons, sitting on rocks, in deep contemplation and sorrow, holding their heads in their hands—their age was difficult to determine—maybe eighty, or perhaps six hundred, and these elders, who resembled mighty, thousand-year-old trees, were none other than the Biblical prophets or patriarchs: from temple to temple, from century to century, parchment scrolls were handed down, the fruit of their mournful reflections; cities burned, temples were destroyed, and slender, black-bearded people in sandals, wrapped in blue, gold-bordered cloaks, blackened by fire and smoke, who looked like Flavius Josephus, pulled these brown scrolls out of the fires and ruins, hiding them under their cloaks, against the left side of their breast. They ran from one burning building to another under a hail of arrows with poisoned tips, loosed by the hands of invading foreigners—jumping onto stallions galloping away, wrapped in swirls of gray, stony dust, their blue-black cloaks flying above the horse's lathered croups; they raced, illumined by the setting sun or the reflections of the fire, and the poisoned arrows chased after them. Sitting on the stone floor of temples, spreading the rescued scrolls out in front of them, the black-bearded old men rocked rhythmically back and forth, just like Boris Lvovich rocked in the chair at his desk when he couldn't find the precise word that would allow him to cast a proud and victorious eye at the courtroom or when he thought that he was getting seriously ill; and the strange man who prophesied in the temple with tortured, sunken eyes, a fiery gaze, and supple fingers, like a pianist's, belonged to that people, too. There he is, on the wooden cross that looks like a television antenna, his body hangs against his will, the delicate wrists of his outstretched arms are nailed to the horizontal cross piece, and his narrow feet to the vertical post—they're stretched to the very limit as though he were doing some gymnastic exercise or trying to stand en pointe. The streams of blood running down his body are somehow unnatural—they look more like paint or varnish—and it's not clear how his body stays up there anyway. His ribs protrude because his stomach is sucked in, like an athlete taking a deep breath before jumping into the water—but under the ribs, on the right side, he has a deep wound, and bright red varnish blood flows out of it; his head hangs helplessly on his chest, his deeply sunken eyes are outlined with black circles, and flies already hover about him. Fleshless elders wearing long garments, carrying canes in one hand and the Holy scriptures in the other—his tribesmen and students—straggle along the dusty roads, golden halos around their heads, their faces are impassive. Each church and monastery argues for the right to name themselves after one or another of these elders, but the name of the strange man himself isn't even considered, it is such a high honor; and in awe, the ancient poets and philosophers of the country across whose land he had just traveled leafed through pages of thick tomes with heavy silver crosses on the covers. At symposiums, historians with microphones and graceful translations discussed the question of when exactly Byzantium accepted Christianity; and the man pursued by gloomy visions, restlessly walked the foggy streets of Petersburg—a resentful man with a high forehead, who felt an unhealthy hatred for people of the same blood as Boris Lvovich (the almost internalized class hatred of such a guy for others like him)—this man couldn't even speak the name of the one who had preached in the temple, but referred to him as "He," with a capital letter, and, in bursts of feverish argument and prophecy kept turning to the texts of the parchment scrolls that the black-bearded men once carried out of the fire. Old men and women, yawning, crossed their mouths; the black soccer player, a reserve player from a Latin American all-star team, quickly crossed himself before going out on the field; little crosses hung on thin chains glint gold on hairy chests, and in the open collars of young people hurrying to the store at the end of summer on a Sunday to get there before the wine section closes—similar little crosses, only far more elegant and with more elegant chains, are worn by young women—the chains are short and sit tight around their long, slightly curved necks, the crosses fall just below the bulge of the thyroid gland, helping to emphasize the swanlike curve of the female neck, though it seems that the cross makes it difficult to swallow. Like the young men, they don't notice Boris Lvovich, who has stopped to watch them for some time . . . The very same crosses, only huge—probably about two or three times the height of a man—glinted gold on the church and cathedral domes—they were so clean, their reflection hurt your eyes; they seemed so highly polished, that even scratches from the sand used to polish them should be visible. Just as painful to the eyes the cleaned, gilded cupolas, and the towers and bell towers, constantly freshened and restored, blinded you with an unnatural white. Upon entering one of these churches, Boris Lvovich carefully made his way over to the side, in order to remain unnoticed. He felt the unfriendly looks of churchgoers on him—moving their lips, they repeated after the priest words from the sermons the strange man with a martyr's sunken eyes had spoken in the temple two thousand years ago. Boris Lvovich's distant ancestors spoke his language, but the priest here spoke Russian or maybe even Church Slavonic. Boris Lvovich understood everything or almost everything that the priest said, and the people repeating the words after the priest understood as well. Why was it, though, that all of them—the people in the church, the priest, the young men and women who wore gilded crosses around their necks and didn't notice Boris Lvovich, the black soccer player from the Latin American team, the man with the high forehead who bore an abnormal hatred for Boris Lvovich's tribesmen, the historians discussing the development of early Christianity, the insomniac monk, the poets and philosophers of the country upon whose earth Boris Lvovich now rode—why had they all forgotten who the strange man preaching in the temple really was, and who the powerful, ancient elders sitting on stones in mournful thought or raising their hands to the heavens were, and who the lithe, black-bearded people that carried the parchment scrolls out of the fire were, scrolls whose texts the man preaching in the temple invoked; and who the incorporeal elders with halos "round their heads and staffs in their hands" were? They had all forgotten, or didn't know, or didn't want to know; they only knew that the man with the sunken eyes of a martyr was betrayed by one of his students. But in what country, amid what people, where, and when, haven't there been traitors who turned people over to the authorities; and hasn't there always been an indifferent or enraged crowd, a common mob from which Boris Lvovich hid his face? When this war began, he was glad to leave Moscow for the south, hoping to blend in among total strangers who were also swarthy and dark-haired, going about their own strange business, spending days on end standing in one place near the piers counting amber beads, or making arrangements for nocturnal pleasures, but they'd left these people behind, and he and Tanya had gone further south, and now they were driving through the southernmost city, and the driver—a stocky, olive-skinned fellow who had the crooked legs of a cavalryman, as though he'd spent his whole life in the saddle, and had short, hairy fingers—didn't look anything like Boris Lvovich, just like the people who stood around the piers counting their beads hadn't. "Now we pass stadium," he said as though they were approaching Kilimanjaro or Niagara Falls—"Number one size of Europe," he added, raising the index finger of his right hand so that it seemed that it wasn't Europe he had in mind, but the entire expanse of the cosmos; "I already saw it from the airplane," Boris Lvovich said drily, trying to turn toward the driver so he'd notice the scar on his neck. Passing the stadium, they turned onto the street connecting the lower part of the city with the upper—Norartakir, though Boris Lvovich didn't know this at the time—a hot street that led somewhere up higher, a street with an endless stream of cars and a tram rumbling through the middle of it. The street was lined with buildings made of stone slabs that were supposedly called "colored tufa," but Boris Lvovich wasn't sure of this—"Tanya! Look, colored tufa"; she was sitting with a sullen look on her face. "It's a gloomy city," she said, "I knew it right away." Boris Lvovich wanted to object—he tried to think of what to say to her—but suddenly he realized that she was right—the city was truly gloomy and he had already realized it, but just couldn't find the right words, and there wasn't any colored tufa either—just regular old gray stone, and later in Moscow he talked about how colored tufa was a legend.

He was already groping in the inside pocket of his jacket for the receipt folded in four—the reservation for the hotel—but instead he kept pulling out either the airplane tickets, or a ten-ruble bill, which made his heart sink, and having driven along the street which never ended, they turned onto a side street. "We arrived at hotel," said the driver, slowly getting out of the car and unwillingly opening the trunk, as though it were all the same to him whether his passengers took their belongings or not. Boris Lvovich and Tanya got their things muddled up, bumped into each other, and burst into the lobby of the hotel, afraid that there wouldn't be any rooms left or that they'd be turned away and what would they do then in this unfamiliar, hot city? In the far corner, behind a polished wood desk, sat a lean, tidy man sporting a mustache and a tie—Boris Lvovich handed him the paper, his hands shaking. "How long will you be staying?" the tidy man asked without rising or looking directly at them; he spoke with such an unbelievable accent that Boris Lvovich even imagined for a moment that it was a trick question: "It's all there," he said, nodding at the piece of paper, because the paper was given to them in Moscow, they were required to obey the regulations, and the money had been paid in advance for six days; Boris Lvovich began to tap on the desk impatiently and with a certain defiance, while the tidy man, still not looking at Boris Lvovich, handed him two forms to fill out—his neat black mustache drooped slightly, and he was wearing a tie and dark suit: in the lobby it was semi-dark and cool, he was at work, and he was probably used to the heat, so it wasn't surprising that he was wearing a suit, for that matter a dark one; and he was thin; but Boris Lvovich kept on sweating, especially since he was nervous, his shirt stuck to his body and sweat dripped onto the form he was filling out. Next to the line "specialty," he wrote "Associate Professor," although he only had a PhD, but Associate Professor made more sense to people and sounded good—the administrator, taking their passports, still not looking Boris Lvovich in the eyes or at the forms that Boris Lvovich placed in front of him, gave him some sort of chit and said: "Third floor, Room 306." The sum of the numbers, thank God, wasn't 13, but if you added in the three of the third floor you'd have twelve—the number just before 13—so some unpleasantness might be in store, but Boris Lvovich suddenly felt such an unusual sensation of peace and lightness—he almost had the key to the room in his hands, and soon he'd change his clothes, take a shower, Tanya would unpack their belongings, and then they'd eat and set out to look at the city. They walked up the stairs, weighed down by their bags, panting from the ascent and the joy that suddenly overtook them—"Just like in the West!" Boris Lvovich said as he stepped onto the soft rug covering the staircase; "Did you notice that he's a Turk?" said Tanya, but Boris Lvovich didn't understand right away who she was talking about. "A real, genuine Turk," she repeated insistently, "I knew it right away," and Boris Lvovich suddenly realized that the tidy administrator with the drooping black mustaches was indeed a Turk—why hadn't he noticed that immediately? It even seemed to Boris Lvovich that the administrator was wearing a fez on his head.

III
GOD IS WITH US

In the mornings, when the asphalt on the shady street near the hotel and the earth in the square across the way were still damp—whether from nighttime rain or from watering—Boris Lvovich and Tanya headed for the tram or trolley stop; the driver wouldn't turn on the engine, but just braked at the stops. Settling on the bench next to the open window, they experienced a strange lightheadedness from the movement downhill in public transportation that hadn't warmed up yet; gradually, the car filled with people, and the endless street, connecting the upper part of the city with the lower, threaded, spiral-like toward the city center as if it were the funnel-shaped stadium that Boris Lvovich had seen from the airplane; and now it seemed to him that the entire city was a huge funnel. People stood densely packed in a solid wall, exchanging pleasantries and phrases consisting of guttural sounds, and Boris Lvovich thought that they were doing this on purpose, hiding the true meaning of what they were saying from him, or simply teasing him. Behind the high, patterned cast-iron fence, silverish firs, paths strewn with gravelly sand, and bushes with red flowers were visible; and the driver finally had to start the engine because the slope had ended and it wasn't easy to get a tram or trolley packed with people going—it wasn't far to the center now. In the depths of the park, hidden among the silvery firs and some other unfamiliar, probably decorative, trees, stood a bulky, yet light, white building with mirrored windows and columns; in the nearly empty alleys, people occasionally appeared, wearing dark suits and carrying black folders, walking briskly in a businesslike manner—the local authorities were located here; the bosses, sitting in separate offices with telephones and secretaries, were the same kind of dark-skinned people as those riding in the car with Boris and Tanya; their speech probably consisted of the same guttural sounds, and at such moments, Boris Lvovich wanted to live and work in this city and converse in this incomprehensible language, to go to the white building hiding behind the decorative trees and silvery firs, and, strolling into the office of a thickset, dark-skinned guy with the legs of a cavalry officer—who looked like the taxi driver that picked them up at the airport, only this one was wearing a black suit and pacing back and forth on the waxed floor—and on entering his office, he would exchange a firm, almost friendly handshake with him, and at the gracious nod of the man's head, Boris Lvovich would sit down in an armchair, pushed slightly back from the desk, meant for semi-official chats. After the iron fence, they had to get up to have time to push their way to the exit. Boris Lvovich made the path through, protecting Tanya because she couldn't stand it when someone touched her, and once she'd reproached Boris Lvovich on this score, but for the life of him he couldn't remember whether it was the front or back which was more insulting—though both seemed equally offensive to him, and so he sometimes walked ahead and sometimes walked close behind her, anxiously watching her face and the expression of estranged disgust that never left it, and as a result Boris Lvovich always felt guilty, as if he should have jumped the culprit. "Are you getting off at the next stop?" he asked, playing intelligently with his voice and trying to speak in the Moscow fashion, but no one answered him; they simply moved aside, pressing against one another more closely, instead of being quick to answer "Yes, yes, of course," as Boris Lvovich did in Moscow when asking if the person in front of him was getting off: "No manners," said Tanya when they got off the tram. She said the same thing in Moscow when, all sweaty, they pushed their way out of any form of public transportation. Boris Lvovich also said "No manners," although somewhere in the depths of his soul he allowed himself to maintain his own opinion both about the people riding in public transportation, and about Tanya: here he could allow himself to bump someone's shoulder because the faces around him were almost the same as his—even more black-haired and olive-skinned for that matter—but no one noticed this similarity—they just moved aside for him, and only once did someone behind him ask him something in their incomprehensible language. "Yes, yes, I'm getting off," Boris Lvovich nodded readily, scrunching his head down and at the same time feeling the superiority of the big city dweller over provincials, but behind him, everyone had already understood and gone back to explaining things to the person who asked, or discussing some problem. Boris Lvovich felt like he was on the very edge of the sea, floundering in the water at the shore—on the horizon and beyond was the dark, blue bulge of the sea, and ships floated on it, who knows how, it was frightening to think about how deep it was—and Boris Lvovich squatted, turning his back to the waves, and when the waves ran over him he began to row with his arms, pretending to swim. "What a lousy city," said Tanya, when they got out of a bus or tram and headed off to some travel bureau or to the post office. Boris Lvovich kept approaching passersby for directions; choosing their words with difficulty, they would say something to him, pointing their fingers at first in one direction, then in the opposite, while Tanya moved away, with an indifferent look, as though she weren't even acquainted with Boris Lvovich, and unfolded a map of the city. "Forget about the map! People are giving us directions. You'd be better off listening!" Boris Lvovich shouted at her, not putting much store in his ability to understand what they said, and fearing that someone would shove her or bump into her and he would feel guilty or even ashamed. They wandered down some hot streets whose tall buildings were hung from top to bottom with laundry left out to dry, as though the inhabitants had been trying to protect themselves from the scorching sun; and at the intersection of three streets, at the turn, trams screeched, there was the supermarket, which occupied the entire first floor of some long building and smelled of coffee and meat left out too long. The locals bantered with the saleswomen behind the counters as though they were old friends, probably finding out when some scarce item would be delivered, or discussing recent soccer news or a cousin's illness; one fat cashier with a sweaty, shiny face and huge earrings was shouting at a gypsy—who also wore earrings, only hers looked like coins—and the gypsy was shouting back, or maybe it was the other way around; for a second, Boris Lvovich almost felt he was Aryan, but the woman and the gypsy stopped arguing unexpectedly and began chatting like bosom buddies. They always ended up at the grocery store in the long building, and the post office or the travel agency was somewhere off to the side . . . Tanya examined the street signs—most of the inscriptions consisted of hairpins and fishhooks—and she opened the map. Boris Lvovich stopped passersby and they gestured to him as though he were a deaf-mute, and in reply he also gestured and spoke loudly, as though they, too, were deaf, and once in a while a wind rose and rustled pieces of newspaper on the pavement. "It's a lousy city," said Tanya, walking next to him. "They don't understand Russian," Boris Lvovich tried to defend them. "Don't you worry," said Tanya, strangely angry. "They understand perfectly well, when they want to." Boris Lvovich tried to remember a similar episode, but he couldn't. "A linguistic void," said Tanya unexpectedly, repeating a phrase that they read recently in a letter from "over there," and her face took on a thoughtful, even poetic, expression, as if she were reciting Pushkin, whom she still remembered quite well from her school years: "That's how it is over there, can you imagine?" She said it almost in a whisper, narrowing her already narrow, almost Tatar eyes, as if seeing something through the far, foggy distance, "No, I don't care, no matter what, I love my old lady Moscow, damn it!" she added, as though she were about to start a folk dance. At those moments there was almost something of the merchant in her full figure and light-eyed, broad-cheeked face—hands on your hips and dance, oopla! To the devil with all of you!! At moments like these, Boris Lvovich himself began to believe in her Scythian origins, and her imagined genealogy even included him—on entering a church with her, he'd cast aside the unfriendly looks accompanying him, with dignity, even indignation, and he felt the very same way with her in public transportation or in a store. Eventually, they would finally find the travel agency or the post office or the airlines, then they went sightseeing: Tanya would stand a ways off while burying herself in another tourist map or travel guide, Boris Lvovich, carrying two cameras—one for color film and one for black-and-white—tripped over the ruins of the fortress, and rushed back and forth between Tanya and the groups crowding around the tour guides. Tanya had the extra lenses in her bag; and he wanted her to hear what the tour guide said, because she was good at remembering things like that. The tour guide, a slender, young fellow with a dark face, probably new at this, spoke enthusiastically, pinching the fingers of his right hand together as though he were salting or peppering something; when he spiraled that pinch upward toward the heavens, the whites of his eyes became yellowish, like a gypsy's. He recounted the story of how, under the leadership of some tsar or other, his people's cavalry routed the Romans—valiant riders, with their crooked legs digging into the horse's belly as though they wanted to pierce its sides, raced along the Appian Way, bending low, splitting the air with their curved sabers; among them raced a dark, well-built warrior, the whites of his eyes yellowish—with one hand he pulled his saber from its scabbard and raised it, and his other hand was pinched to the heavens—it was probably a warrior's gesture—and the rest of the riders followed his example, so, wrapped in clouds of dust, sweeping away everything in their path, the Armenian cavalry burst into the ancient city and streamed down its streets, flowing into them through the white triumphal arch erected in honor of the victory over Boris Lvovich's ancestors—it was under this arch, in a shameful procession, his head bent low, that Flavius Josephus passed silently, and now the valiant riders with their bare, curved sabers poured through these stone gates, blindingly white in the sun. The young tour guide was telling this story for the second time; he'd told it first in the bus, and even then, Tanya had whispered to Boris Lvovich: "What kind of nonsense is that? It was the Armenian king who was taken prisoner—remember, in Feuchtwanger?" Boris Lvovich had taken a liking to Feuchtwanger of late, and would read out loud to Tanya before they turned out the lights—at first, Tanya would cover her ears, shake her head, or start to read the newspaper aloud (curiosities about the lives of great people or something about someone discovering a treasure, or a painting) and Boris Lvovich would stop reading—but then, quite unexpectedly, she began to listen to Feuchtwanger and Boris Lvovich tried to read as much as possible before she fell asleep, he hurried and swallowed his words, and Tanya lay there with her eyes open; his voice became raspy and gruff, and she still wasn't asleep—"Well, go on," she'd say, when he stopped for a moment to rest. "I think it was the Parthian king, not the Armenian," said Boris Lvovich, remembering how they brought the imprisoned Parthian king before the emperor's box, the king carrying a gold saber, which he set at the emperor's feet. "No, it was definitely the Armenian king," Tanya said with certainty, "that's what happened and the tour guide is a bald-faced liar, and who knows, it might be on purpose." Boris Lvovich tried to imagine himself as the imprisoned Armenian tsar, but for some reason he didn't care whether it was the Parthian one or for that matter even an Iranian, however, his trust in the guide wavered a bit; even though for some reason he really wanted the king to be Armenian . . . Tanya stood to the side, aloof, studying the guide book; the ruins of the fortress they were viewing at the moment were truly ancient—gray, sun-baked, fuzzy stones, some with half-erased cuneiform, and similarly gray columns with the tops broken off that resembled old gravestones, and between them, a blue sky, almost like in a Leonardo da Vinci painting. "Tanya! 500 B.C.! Just imagine!" Boris Lvovich shouted to Tanya, torn back and forth between his wife and the tourists, who followed the guide along the stony ledges of the ancient church, he was trying not to miss what the guide said and at the same time to find the most advantageous point for taking pictures. "It's almost a Biblical landscape, look!" he cried, going down on one knee and leaning so far back that he almost lost his balance in order to get two columns into the frame close-up, and in the rest in receding perspective, with the deep, blue sky and the two silvery summits that accompanied the group the entire way, like the moon or the orb of the sun, and which hadn't melted, even though it was afternoon. The light was probably different here, and besides, according to the map that showed everything beyond the state borders as blank, that is, like a clean sheet of paper or the Antarctic, with only the most important geographical points sketched in, the ones you couldn't do without, the summits themselves were much closer than at the hotel where they were staying, and if you stared at them intently, you could see clearly that they were cone-shaped and that these cones were covered with untouched snow, and that the shadow of the nearer, larger cone fell on the smaller cone, and that part of the larger cone facing you was also in shadow, and that further on it wasn't visible at all, like the dark side of the moon, and you could tell that these cones weren't hanging in the air like they seemed to be from the balcony of the hotel, but were in fact the tips of a mountain whose contours peeped through the rippling, blue-gray haze, and through this very same haze you could see the mountain's foothills, which eased into a plain—you only had to cross the plain, and though the plain was also drowned in the haze, it appeared that the mountains were very close—you only had to cross the plain—which he imagined as black, ploughed earth—to reach them; and he thought it strange and improbable that this mountain and part of the plain were on foreign land—and that somewhere over there, in the haze, was hidden barbed wire, barbed wire that marked the state border, and that all this was a convention, because the land on both sides of the barbed wire was identical—black, ploughed soil, consisting of the same molecules and atoms, but for some reason over there, beyond the invisible wire stretched between posts, you could say and do what you couldn't say and do here; though perhaps the barbed wire existed only in his imagination and it was actually possible to walk calmly, without looking over your shoulder, across the black, ploughed field that dissolved in a hazy cloud; the snow covering the mountain top being pristine seemed even more improbable. Boris Lvovich imagined that somewhere over there, on the very summit of the large cone, or on its invisible side, were observers and artillery crews, perhaps even rocket launchers—powerful, broad-shouldered, bearded men with faces covered in a golden tan from the mountain sun, resembling the characters of Jules Verne in some way, vigilantly observed day and night everything that happened on this side of the barbed wire—they reached their hands out to Boris Lvovich and Tanya, who were clambering up the icy stones and ledges, and now they found themselves among these bearded people—who warmed them, gave them food and drink, as though they'd survived a shipwreck—these people came here on airplanes from somewhere far away, like explorers at some polar station—Boris Lvovich wants to tell them everything about himself, how he conceals his face and how he's afraid to say things out loud, he can't even bring himself to whisper them at home, but they already know it all—they have open, energetic faces, reddish-golden beards, and light-colored eyes; a bittersweet lump rises in Boris Lvovich's throat, the kind of thing that only happens when he listens to Beethoven's music and thinks about Beethoven being deaf and street urchins running after him because his hearing horn stuck out of his pocket. They were in the bus again, accompanied by the two silvery cones; and the dark-skinned young tour guide—standing next to the driver's cabin with a microphone in one hand and the fingers of the other forming that pinch and pointing at the ceiling—told them that the mountain had been climbed only twice. An American expedition searched for the remains of Noah's Ark, and Boris Lvovich remembered that many years ago there was an article about that expedition, which, as indicated in the newspaper, was actually a spy mission against the country that Boris Lvovich lived in, but they were covering themselves with biblical fairy-tales, and this point was played up in all sorts of ways, so that the article was constructed something like a feuilleton, and Boris Lvovich even thought it was witty; when he read it, he automatically recalled the phrase: "On the slopes of Ararat, great grapes are grown," which he'd heard in childhood and then later, during the war—the r's in this phrase were all rolled: *r-r-r*, but in some instances the rolling could turn into guttural r's, and when he read the article, Boris Lvovich recalled being told that during the war the Germans forced children to recite this phrase in order to determine whether they were hiding their ethnic origin (but in his case the r's rolled beautifully, although if he wanted to, he could pronounce them gutturally, so that he ended up with a kind of parody of guttural "r"s). Just the same, the Germans wouldn't have spared him because it was enough to take one look at his face . . . Someone asked the tour guide about the result of the expedition, and he replied that they didn't find anything, and no one was surprised by his answer, but it was as if they'd been talking about the excavation of some ancient city whose existence was known to be a certainty. The road the bus traveled, the low stone houses and fences flitting by outside the window, the plateau that stretched out on either side, the city, visible in the distance on a rise, drowning in a haze that dissipated only on the upper, green slopes where white sculptures rose (the sculptures might have been mourning mothers, or warriors, or space ships)—he saw it all covered with water pouring in from somewhere, only the tops of the two silvery cones were visible, but they, too, were swallowed—first the smaller one, then the larger cone, and now everything was covered with water to the very horizon and even beyond the horizon—the ocean covered the whole earth, and on its boundless, desertlike surface, a small crate that looked like a trunk slowly rocked upon the waves— the man sitting inside stood up, and his head broke through the top as though he were the Tsarevich from *The Tale of the Tsar Saltan*. The man was naked. Water flowed from his gray beard which resembled icicles stuck together; water flowed—streams of green water—and he himself seemed to consist of water green as glass. Through the broken top of the box, wild birds resembling archaeopteryx spread their wings and took off beyond the horizon. The gray-bearded giant emerged from the green water; he stood on the shore near a mighty oak, and next to him stood his three sons: the eldest, the middle, and the youngest, who obediently followed him; but when the weary old man fell asleep in the shade of the tree's spreading branches, one of the sons— the middle one—didn't cover his father's nakedness and laughed about this to his brothers . . . The mountain was first climbed in the previous century by a local scientist and researcher after whom one of the city's streets was named; sometime after climbing the mountain, the scientist disappeared without a trace—he left his home and never returned, and his disappearance was surrounded by mysterious circumstances: "He probably tried to climb the mountain a second time," said Tanya, unexpectedly displaying interest in the guide's story, "I'm absolutely certain of it," and squinting in the direction of the mountains, relentlessly following them, she added: "And of course, his disappearance was no accident." Boris Lvovich was surprised that he hadn't thought of that himself and he even began to think that he had thought of it before Tanya said anything. Boris Lvovich imagined: carefully opening the door of a two-story wooden house at the very edge of the city, in the middle of the night, a man in traveling clothes with a rucksack over his shoulder and a walking stick in hand—the man was blind because once he had already tried to climb the mountain, or perhaps it was simply dark as pitch; walking as far as the stone fence surrounding the house, he groped his way along it, his stick in front—and making it to the gate, he turned, casting a last look at the sleeping house merged with the darkness. Throwing his stick ahead of him, he stepped quickly along a narrow, well-known path melting into this darkness. The bus stopped near gates made of the same rough gray stone as the long, squat, two-story buildings stretching along the monastery courtyard—they'd reached the residence of the local church authorities; the church, visible at the end of a long lane, was just as gray—they couldn't see the church itself, but its silhouette, because the sun was about to set on its other side, backlighting it, so that both its bell tower and cupola appeared to be surrounded by a golden halo; but in a photograph, you would only see the silhouette of the church. The tourists were far ahead, but Boris Lvovich kept unscrewing and changing his lenses, dropping them on the ground as he knelt first on one knee and then on the other, calling out to Tanya who was walking down a side street; he rushed from one edge of the lane to the other, because it wasn't clear whether they would get as far as the side of the church that could be photographed in normal light before the sun completely set, although the silhouette of the church with a halo was interesting in and of itself . . . the small figure of a man in traveling clothes, leaning on a stick, his hand outstretched as though groping the air, clambered up the steep slope of the mountain—above him, the untouched snow of the large cone was just as unattainably close and white as ever, as if he didn't have many days of climbing those cliffs overgrown with scraggy bushes and moss—behind him. The large cone still shone silvery and the man stretched his hand out to it. On a bench near a flowerbed a bit to the side of the lane, three or four priests with gray beards and pink faces were chatting in black garments, and, for some reason it looked to Boris Lvovich, like they wore black top hats. "Please, please get a picture of that!" Tanya said, running up to him. In fact, that was how he noticed them—it was the same way she stopped near every dog they met: "Please just look!" she'd say. If the dog was small, she'd take it in her arms and start petting and playing with it; she was more cautious with big dogs, and would just say: "Oh my, just look at us!"—and you could feel that she was resisting the urge to hug the dog and scratch it around the ears. Boris Lvovich tried to lead Tanya away or stand to the side with a nonchalant look, because there could be problems with dog owners, and besides which, the dog could bite Tanya and then they'd have to wait thirty or even forty days in order to find out whether the dog had rabies or not, and some dogs that Tanya petted were strays, and in a strange city to boot. "Nothing will come out against the sun," he said, although the sun wasn't behind the priests' backs, it was behind the church; but he was afraid of trouble. "The one over there," said Tanya, nodding in the direction of the priests—"he's probably the most important one. I'm absolutely sure of it. The Catholicos of the Armenian Church," she added, in the same tone of voice she'd say "Lord Beaconsfield" or "patchwork empire." Children ran through the side streets, and near one of the monastery buildings sat an artist with an easel, and Boris Lvovich took a picture of him from the back together with the canvas where the contours of the monastery building were already sketched in . . . In Moscow, Boris Lvovich assiduously skirted an empty, crooked lane that rose slightly, connecting two old, busy Moscow streets; on the left side of the lane, if you were going up it, just at the point where it bent like a knee, was a building with columns and a triangular-shaped roof—wide steps led up to the columns, almost like at the Bolshoi theater—and there was something about the building itself that recalled the opera—but Boris Lvovich couldn't remember its color or any other details; he couldn't remember because he'd only rushed up that lane a couple of times, having found himself there accidently and only later realizing what lane it was, but it was already too late to turn back. He had walked briskly, almost running, staying close to the walls of the houses on the other side, with his eyes almost closed, holding his head down so he wouldn't happen to look at the building with the columns—the empty lane could be seen clearly from one end to the other, and policemen stood on the busy streets that it connected and they could also turn up here, so Boris Lvovich hadn't raised his eyes until he'd darted out onto the busy street and merged with the crowd. Once, soon after the death of his father—who knew the language of his people but only spoke it with old men, distant relatives, or with the drivers who delivered firewood, so that Boris Lvovich thought that his father only used the language to bargain or settle old family scores—once, on an autumn evening, when the streetlights shone through a veil of rain and fog without dispelling the darkness of the street, he and Tanya slipped through the doors behind the columns: inside it was light; in two or three rooms off the hallway, old men sat at long empty tables; they resembled his father's distant relatives, in black yarmulkes and beards—some sat, others walked about, some of them jotted notes in accountant ledgers. The old men clustered in small groups and chatted and, just like when his father and his father's distant relations gathered, among the incomprehensible expressions, individual familiar words burst out, even whole phrases, but to Boris Lvovich it seemed that they were negotiating some deal. He and Tanya went upstairs, because women were not supposed to be downstairs: upstairs there were rows of armchairs, like in a theater, and they sat close to the handrails; below, people stood, and somewhere ahead, as might be expected in a theater, was a platform—like a stage or a tribune—and there were people there, too, and on the balcony across from them, almost right over the stage, sat a woman in a white dress and a tall hairdo—everyone stole glances at her and whispered—it was either the Ambassador's wife or the Ambassador herself, Tanya informed him, but he never could remember who the lady was. "Look at the dress she's wearing," Tanya whispered with admiration. It was some holiday, maybe the New Year, or maybe some other exodus—chandeliers burned brightly below the ceiling, the choir was singing, and in the choir one voice stood out, a tenor, and this also increased the resemblance to a theater; but neither the choir, nor the owner of the tenor voice could be seen, so it wasn't clear who was singing. The music was melodic like Italian opera. "Almost like church," Tanya said, and Boris Lvovich had also noticed this and was surprised, because he had thought that there would be howling in the eastern style, after all, he'd come here to honor the memory of his father—Tanya told him that that's what you had to do. Both men and women sat around them: "There are a lot of Russians here," Tanya informed him, "especially women, they come just to listen." The choir and the tenor continued their Italian aria, and on leaving the place Boris Lvovich inhaled the damp autumn air with pleasure—it was a long time ago . . . A small human figure climbed higher and higher, clambering up the cliffs, slipping on the icy ledges, stretching his arms out toward the unseen snowy summit—the man was blind—and from the summit, from above, hands stretched out to him, but the man didn't see them—the arctic explorers had reddish beards, faces golden from the sun, and their calm Scandinavian eyes were fixed upon the blind man—he had dropped his stick along the path, and it now slid slowly down, catching for a moment on gentle inclines, and then continuing its steady fall—the arctic explorers grasped the exhausted man under the arms, and this man was Boris Lvovich. Meanwhile, the naked, gray-bearded old man with his three sons, the eldest, the middle, and youngest, continued on their way into the depths of the stony country; the birds they had released flew over their heads and disappeared, then reappeared, it wasn't clear who was showing the way to whom; the middle son who hadn't covered his father's nakedness when he slept walked in front—was he the one leading the others? . . . In the half-dark church-turned-museum, sightseers craned their necks and their mouths opened slightly from the tension of looking up at the ancient murals on the cupola—the darkened frescos were barely illuminated by the pre-crepuscular light entering through the narrow slits, it was particularly hard to see the images under the very top of the cupola: angels with trumpets floating in the clouds, the dark faces of saints encircled by dim halos, the image of the mother of God, the Virgin Mary, holding a disproportionately small infant, as though he were still an embryo or had been born prematurely. You had to photograph with a long, handheld exposure, and Boris Lvovich took careful aim and tried to maintain an immobile pose, but people kept bumping into him. Almost all the sightseers who had come to view the residence were crowded into the museum, and the city tour leaders, as if by an unspoken gentleman's agreement, yielded to the museum tour guides, and remained somewhere on the street, waiting for the return of their groups with practiced patience; the groups then crowded around the heavy double doors with gold carvings that looked like the royal gates—they let people in there in small groups, but the museum tour guides didn't go in for some reason, they just informed the visitors uncomfortably that one was supposed to give something toward the renovation of the church, as though they themselves, and the tourists, understood each other perfectly well, what can you do?—you have to take the believers' traditions into account. Sticking his hand in his pocket, Boris Lvovich clutched several coins in his fist as if they were his entry ticket and he was getting ready to show it. Tanya also dipped into her purse, but it wasn't clear whether they should pay separately or whether if one person donated, it would be understood that it was for two. Beyond the doors everything was brightly illuminated: there were chandeliers, and it was stuffy—it smelled something like wax from the polished parquet floor, or perhaps it was incense. People moved in a slow line past the incrusted tables and glass cases that filled both rooms; under double glass, reflecting with silver, gold, and mother of pearl, lay, stood, and hung, pearls, bracelets, brooches, icons, crosses, some kind of ancient weapon—either a poleaxe or halberd—brocaded garments, raspberry red miters studded with precious stones, and ancient books in heavy silver covers. People leaned over the tables, their hands behind their backs as though they were tied; they brought their faces right up to the cabinet glass, almost squashing their noses, while keeping their hands behind their backs. An acolyte in a long garment walked among the tourists holding a wood box, and people dropped their coins into the slot shyly, as though they were doing something illegal—Boris Lvovich and Tanya dropped their coins in, and when they did, the acolyte holding the box lowered his eyelids for a second, to express either embarrassment or gratitude. Most of the tourists crowded around a tall, black-bearded man with jet-black eyes and an aquiline nose that gave his face a haughty look: holding a pointer, he was explaining things, while continuing to look somewhere over people's heads—he was positioned so he could see everything that happened in the second room where the visitors were moving in the same kind of line among tables and cabinets filled with treasures. With the end of his pointer, he touched the glass briefly as though he weren't counting on his audience understanding anything. He wore a black suit, and Boris Lvovich for some reason thought that it was a tuxedo or a smoking jacket with tails; the tuxedo was actually more like the long black vestment worn by an individual of the highest holy orders, and the man's well-groomed hands in white lace cuffs, like some archduke's, were covered by this attire. He held the pointer casually in his left hand, and with the long fingers of his right he fingered the links of the silver chain and cross hanging on his breast—during a pause designed for visitors to look at the object he'd been speaking about, people climbed silently over each other, loosing a stream of hot breath on the necks of those in front of them, standing on tiptoe, stretching their necks in order to see better. "Noah's Ark" was heard among the viewers who had just moved away from the cabinet—the phrase was conveyed mouth to mouth; Boris Lvovich, standing on tiptoe, tried to see at least something, but people were packed in a dense wall. Then the crowd broke up, moving on to another object; Boris Lvovich, who still hadn't seen anything, opened his camera, his heart pounding. "You can't, it's not allowed," he heard all around, and one tourist even pulled on his sleeve, pointing at the tall bearded man in the black soutane who, removing his hand from the cross on his breast, used it to make a powerful, forbidding gesture, and that gesture was directed at him, Boris Lvovich.

Boris Lvovich stood in front of a piece of a wooden board, tarred and cracked; it was in a large gilded frame as if it were a painting by Leonardo da Vinci or Raphael. That was precisely how he'd imagined it: a piece of smoke-darkened oak, a tiny fragment left from an enormous shipwreck . . . The naked old man with a long gray beard looking like icicles or streams of water, and his three sons, the eldest, the middle, and the youngest, continued their journey into the depths of an unknown country, stopping for the night under spreading, green oaks; during the day they walked across a plain scantily covered with undergrowth, scorched by the hot sun. The middle son, who hadn't covered his father's nakedness, now walked behind all of them—the sons were naked, just like their father, and these people were Boris Lvovich's ancestors—really everyone's, but Boris Lvovich's ancestors were the first to tell the story in their sacred books. The bearded man with the raven-black eyes, dressed in a long, black mantle—for whom Boris Lvovich was just one of thousands of faceless visitors arriving here daily on tour buses in order to satisfy their idle curiosity—this stern man who looked over people's heads had also learned the story from sacred books handwritten by Boris Lvovich's ancestors—these books, bound in thick leather, stood in his holiness's office; once in a while he would walk over, choose one of them, and, slowly, unhurriedly, flip through the yellowed pages, losing himself in sections that were particularly impressive in their profundity and wisdom, occasionally straightening the silver cross that hung on his chest . . . For some reason the naked old man and his three sons remained fleshless—the old man consisted entirely of green sea water and his beard looked like seaweed; his sons' bodies were transparent and had no contours, and the small figure of the blind man who had left his home at night, kept on clambering upward to the main silver cone, stumbling and slipping, his hands clutching at the icy outcroppings. There weren't any arctic explorers, there was nothing but untouched snow, blinding in the sunlight, receding to heights that took one's breath away. The man's shoulders were pulled back by his travel bag, which looked like a backpack, and the clothes he wore resembled a mountain climber's outfit; the stick that had slipped out of his hand continued its slow slide downward, while a middle-aged woman bundled up in a black shawl came out of the gate of the two-story house on the outskirts of the city, took several steps along the path, stopped, reached toward the snowy cone hanging in the air, and then, falling to her knees, began to pray, intermittently placing her palms on her forehead as though checking for a fever; she moved her lips and whispered in a language Boris Lvovich couldn't understand. A bit higher and to the left of the wooden fragment preserved from the enormous shipwreck, also under glass and in a wide, gilded frame, was a rusty spear blade—actually not even a blade, but just the tip of it—one of the Roman legionnaires poked the crucified man with it under the ribs to ascertain whether he was alive or not. The soldiers standing in a solid wall around the place of execution, they wore armor, and helmets that looked German, and when they reported to their superiors or greeted one another, they thrust an arm out, palm up, as though shielding themselves from the sun. The man on the cross was still alive because a spasm ran though his stomach muscles in the place where the spear tip touched him, just as it would when a scalpel touches the body of someone on the operating table; he slowly opened his sunken, black-circled eyes, and several horseflies rose lazily from his swollen eyelids but didn't fly away, they just buzzed around his face because they knew that the man would soon close his eyes again—he no longer saw what was happening around him on the square atop the high, bare hill, and his body hung limp as a sack, held up by his hands which were nailed to the crossbeam, and on his right side under his ribs there was a wound that looked like a sponge oozing blood—the rusty spear had probably pierced his muscles and reached the liver, and for some reason the wound itself looked like a sponge. His gaze barely distinguished the contours of the temple or the city that spread out over the hills, wrapped in a bluish gray smoke; but the farther his vision reached, the clearer the distances became: somewhere out there, through the pre-storm veil covering the hills and valleys, loomed the sandy shore of the sea—slow heavy waves ran up onto it and retreated reluctantly, drawing with them a long, tarred boat with an oar lying under the seat, and at the bottom of the boat dark water collected dangerously—on that day, too, the sea was calm; he stood in the middle of the boat pulling the oar first on the right, then on the left, so the boat remained in the same place; bearded people stood on the shore in a dense wall—fishermen with ragged pants rolled up above the knee, and the setting sun illuminated their faces with scarlet light; the man standing in the boat was also barefoot, but his ankles were delicate. The people standing on the shore were shouting, their arms outstretched, probably in warning: an enormous foamy swell approached him, blocking the sun, so it was dark as night, but the man standing in the boat rowed calmly, and coming within several arms' length of the boat, the foaming swell suddenly subsided—the figure of the man standing in the boat was clearly drawn against the setting sun, a gold aura flared for a few seconds around him. Now the empty, tarred boat with an abandoned oar and black water pooling in the bottom was carried farther and farther from the shore; the shore was also empty, there were only sand, stones, and a storm cloud approaching the shore like a dark wall, and further on—beyond the cloud and beyond the blinding blue of the sea freed from the cloud—stretched vast lands totally unlike the country that the man now hanging on the cross had traversed. From clouds of steam or smoke covering those lands, chariots carrying warriors burst forth unexpectedly, and similar

warriors, clad in mail, holding spears and swords, and wearing
heavy helmets with lowered visors hiding their stern, grim faces,
also burst forth from clouds of smoke, riding horses and followed
by squires who could barely keep up. Crosses were engraved on
their shields, and the same black cross was on the flags, flapping
in the wind, under which the warriors marched. Coming from
different parts of the vast lands, spreading north from the blue
sea, the chariots and riders collided, striking and destroying one
another, piercing the enemy with their swords; and shouting the
name of the man whose hands were now nailed to the crossbeam,
while his body hung slackly—the man probably could have been
saved if his body had been taken down and the best Roman
healers had been called—and then, under the flags with the
black crosses, in elegant sailing vessels that looked like the ones
Boris Lvovich had seen in Leningrad in the Army-Navy
museum, the warriors sailed across the blue sea and stepped onto
the land that the man hanging on the wood stake with the crossbeam had walked, sowing devastation and death all around
them. The man's eyes dimmed like the eyes of all the dying, but
through the even whitish film pierced only by dancing black
horseflies, he saw the bright flares of campfires in the night—the
same people, only arrayed in long black garments with heavy
silver crosses on their breasts, stood on a rise, and pointed
authoritatively at the crowd below, which strangely resembled
the group of fishermen on the seashore who had stretched their
arms out to him—they were dragged to a stake, tied to it with a
metal chain, and burning logs were thrown at their feet, while in
an entirely different part of the huge continent extending north
from the blue sea, a dark crowd of people moved along streets
paved with cobblestone and lined with flowering acacias—the
priests in long garments who led the procession wore the same
silver crosses on their chests as those who stood on the rise at
night, illuminated by the crimson reflections of the fires, and

carried white banners with images of the man with the martyred, black-circled sunken eyes, and other cloths bore the figures
of saints with faces strangely recalling the faces of the people on
the shore who stretched their arms out to the man in the boat.
The people carrying the banners sang something in low voices
and a language that the dying man on the cross didn't understand; behind them, someone in the crowd threw rocks at the
houses—panes of glass smashed to smithereens on the cobblestones, and when the priests with the banners and the crosses on
their chests turned the corner, the stone throwers broke into the
houses and dragged out old people who had the same mournful
eyes as the people depicted on the banners, and the same curly
beards, only gray and knotted because they were dragged out by
their beards; and others grabbed the children and women: black-
eyed women with disheveled hair, pressing their screaming
children to their breasts, fell to their knees and begged the ones
who had dragged them out, who reeked of alcohol; and from the
broken windows above drifted white tufts of cotton and goose
down, covering the sidewalks and the cobblestones like snow—
now even the hovering horseflies didn't cut through the film
covering the eyes of the dying man, but through that veil he
suddenly saw clearly the black smoke emitted by chimneys built
tall in order not to foul the air, and this smoke seemed glued to
the chimneys like black flags, slightly rippling in the wind.
People with yellow appliqués on their chests disembarked silently from the silent trains arriving in the night, and were blinded
by the criss-cross of searchlight beams; they carried good-quality
leather suitcases and travel bags carefully packed with blankets,
suits, warm underclothes smelling pleasantly of soap, and toothbrushes in plastic cases. Leading carefully dressed children by
the hand, they quietly passed the soldiers holding bayonets, who
wore heavy helmets and black overcoats, and stood in tight ranks
on either side of the paved road as though they were an honor

guard greeting important guests. Of course, the law on resettlement probably provided for safeguarding the citizens' personal belongings; behind each column was a man wearing the same black overcoat, though instead of a helmet, he wore a tall, peaked cap with a coat of arms, a patent leather visor, a shoulder holster, and a pistol at his side; standing back from the columns of people he barked several short, staccato words at the soldiers—two or three of them stepped forward, thrusting their right arms out with the palm turned upward, just like the soldiers in helmets who surrounded the place of the hanging man's execution. The officer in the peaked cap and visor responded with the same short, staccato gesture, as though he were doing exercises; then, standing to the side, he let the soldiers pass. Catching up with the column, they pushed the people at the back with the butts of their automatics—they were probably supposed to, because many people had arrived and everyone had to be placed in their lodgings before the morning so that the soldiers could also rest; and the people in the column walked faster, many picking up their children because the children couldn't keep up. In anticipation of receiving orders for their lodging, the new arrivals were taken to a spacious area that resembled a barracks, where families grouped together on long, wooden benches that stood along the walls—some of them retrieved thermoses with coffee still warm from their travel bags and poured it into plastic cups for the children; one woman, taking out a pocket mirror, looked at herself on the sly and fixed her hair; right under the ceiling, on cables just like in the circus, electric lamps covered in grills shone brightly. An officer accompanied by several soldiers appeared, but no one noticed them come in: they were probably bringing the papers for the lodgings and so the officer and the soldiers stood in the middle of the room, the soldiers a bit behind in their long black overcoats and helmets, automatics at the ready, and this surprised everyone, because no one was planning on running away—people were only thinking about quickly settling in for the night, and acquainted, or newly acquainted, families were even ready to spend the first night together in one room. The officer stood there, his feet planted firmly in his calf-skin boots, swaying ever so slightly on his heels, a belt with a metal buckle pulled tight at the waist on which some words were engraved— the same words were engraved on the badges of the soldiers standing in the rear, but it was difficult to decipher the letters at such a distance, and the children decided later that they would find out. With a high, staccato voice, in a language that the man now dying on the cross didn't understand, the officer said something to the hundreds of people gazing at him in tense anticipation; this was their native language, they had spoken it since childhood, their parents had spoken it, their favorite poems were written in this language, and for this reason they didn't understand right off what the fit man in the polished calf boots had ordered them to do—but of course, why didn't they guess right away themselves? You have to bathe after a trip, and they'd probably be taken to the bathhouse now: opening suitcases and traveling bags, they began to take out fragrant soaps and a change of underwear, but they must not have understood the officer's order after all, he had to repeat what he'd already said, and they began to undress right there, in front of each other; it was probably simpler and faster that way, and the clothes and soap weren't to be brought with them either—taking off their shirts, the men folded them neatly in the suitcases, and the women undressed the children, and then, turning to the wall, began to unbutton buttons and unzip zippers—the officer with the pistol at his side continued swaying on his heels just as impatiently; the encaged electric bulbs burned brightly right under the ceiling. The men and women stood in their underclothes, turning away from one another, and slowed down for some reason; a round pocket mirror fell on the cement floor and rolled off, but the woman found it—fortunately it hadn't broken, and she put it in her suitcase so she wouldn't drop it again, and only the children were completely undressed now, or in under-shirts and hanging garters, pressed against their mothers' legs, looking at the grownups with curiosity—the officer standing in the middle of the room once again gave commands in a high, strained voice, as though splitting the air with the crack of a whip, like animal trainers in a circus do to raise the horses who've lain down. Tangled in suspenders and ribbons, the men and women began to take off their underclothes, still averting their gaze, and for some reason their bodies were suddenly overtaken by an uncontrollable shiver. They stood naked, whereas just an hour ago in the train the men would apologize to ladies if they bumped into them near the toilet, and the women, sliding past them, would wrap the flaps of their robes tighter; now they stood naked, no longer ashamed, as if it were all entirely natural, but their bodies shivered because the flesh understood the meaning of what was happening before their reason did. The women stood slightly hunched with their arms crossed over their chests, as they did when they stood under the shower, and the men held their hands below their stomachs, but it was still clear that they were all circumcised, just like Boris Lvovich and the dying man now nailed to the cross, whose ears caught the sharp, high-pitched voice of the Roman centurion commanding the guards to remain on the hill after the execution—he knew that out there, at the foot of the hill, kept back by the guards' spears, their hands shading their eyes from the scorching sun, bearded people in tattered clothing squinted at the top of the hill; but the three wooden crosses with bodies hanging on them, rising over the square, dotted with legionnaires, resembled garden scarecrows. The dying man realized that this displeased him—he wanted to be seen and distinguished from the two others: in conversations he had often spoken of "temptation"; more than once he had said that alms should even be given secretly, so that the recipient wouldn't know who gave them, and the giver wouldn't be tempted in his heart; but why did he allow them to admire his mastery when standing in the boat and watch with secret gladness as they stretched out their arms to warn him of the danger that threatened? Once, in the evening, they came to the city after a long journey, and the starving people sat down near the city gates, spread out their victuals, and began to eat, although it was the evening of the Judgment Day and it would have been better not to—they might be driven away—but he couldn't bring himself to tell them, lest they think that his words diverged from his deeds. At that moment, men in turbans and long white robes belted with blue ribbon appeared—someone probably brought them since they always seemed to come out of nowhere. He leaned against the stone wall, looking at them with feigned calm—the hungry laid their food aside, and looked back and forth at the approaching group and at him—they should have gone on about their business: how could they not understand? He was angry at them and at himself; the approaching group surrounded him and began to talk in high, querulous voices, interrupting one another, and shouting; only one of them, a tall, thin man with faded blue eyes and two flabby folds hanging from his chin, which gave his face a peevish, doleful expression, stood silently to the side; he was surely the leader, because as they shouted and quarreled, they kept looking back at him, but he remained silent, and the barefoot man was also silent, leaning against the stone wall, tracing something in the sand with his narrow foot, as though deep in thought—he knew that in such situations it was best to remain silent. The tall man with the flabby hanging folds—he'd probably had some serious ailment and lost weight and that's why the two folds formed, hanging loosely like two curtains on either side of his neck—silenced the talkers with an abrupt movement of his hand; his voice had cracked and he spoke very softly, quoting someone whom the barefoot man with the delicate ankles also quoted, and it was hard to object to the words right away—you had to think like a chess player does when an opponent makes an unexpected move. The black-bearded men in tattered clothes looked expectantly at the barefoot man with bared ankles, as though he were about to walk into the sea. "He who is not with me, is against me," he said softly, looking off in the distance, his foot continuing to draw in the sand automatically. The men surrounding them didn't shout—they guffawed, laughed, bellowed, and grasped their bellies, which jiggled under their white garments. "Aren't you our king?" asked a short fat man with a round face and narrow slits for eyes, and he reached out with an unexpectedly long arm as though wanting to grab the barefoot man by his chin. They were already leaving, still laughing, holding their stomachs, as if they'd just seen an uproarious comedy, but the tall, thin man wasn't laughing—departing with the others, he stopped for a moment and looked at the barefoot man as if he wanted to tell him something, but changed his mind . . . The soldiers standing behind the officers seemed to have been waiting for this moment: using the butts of their guns, they began to drive the naked people closer to the door into one group; the metal buckles on their belts were now eye-level with the children, who already knew how to read and finally made out the familiar Gothic letters: *Gott mit uns*. The heartbeat of the man nailed to the crossbeam was rapid, irregular, and stopped occasionally; even the most skillful Roman healers probably could not have done anything, because the dying man had lost a great deal of blood. The naked people were now driven along a narrow lane between two high stone walls with several rows of barbed wire on top—a sparse December snow melted on their shoulders and backs and the crossed shafts of spotlights shone on them. The narrow lane ended in the stone wall of the building with two tall chimneys from which black smoke poured—even against the night sky you could see that it was black. Well of course, they were taking them to the bathhouse, it was important to get through this passage as quickly as possible and get out of the cold—women and men picked up children and held them tight so they wouldn't catch cold; the entire procession resembled an exodus, the way they're depicted in paintings, but on canvas the men and the women were usually dressed in some sort of garments and only the children were naked. A soldier stood next to a dark, narrow slit in the stone wall where the lane ended, and as people entered the door, he counted them, shining a blinding flashlight on their faces; holding back each person with his gunstock because people were in a hurry to get inside and warm up; in the basement room, two corporals had removed their black jackets, hung them neatly on the backs of chairs, and were singing a Christmas song softly while decorating a fir branch they'd chopped off the evening before and placed in a zinc bucket; they adorned it with silver candy wrappers and gold stars obtained from who knows where. In the opposite corner of the room gleamed nickel gauges of some sort—they were connected to a system of pipes leading away into the wall. The men and women were separated now, the men walked with their sons and the women with their daughters along two narrow white-tile corridors and brightly lit by light bulbs enclosed in grates—at the end of each corridor there was a sign: "Bathhouse and Clothing Disinfection," with a red arrow pointing at the door—after bathing they would receive their clothes; during wartime, quarantine was often necessary, of course, only why that whole business with them having to undress together? And how would they find each other? They'd have to pretend that they weren't acquainted. The two low-ranking officers in freshly starched shirts, having torn themselves away from the fresh evergreen fragrance of the branch and continuing to hum something, walked over to the opposite end of the room; and one of them turned the shining, nickel-plated handle, and the arrow of the gauge reached the necessary number: they both watched it carefully, because one person alone could make a mistake and moreover, they were supposed to watch each other. The gas pressure was normal and they returned to their modest Christmas dinner; they clapped each other on the shoulder in a friendly manner and laughed. In another room, also located underground, an entire brigade of people dressed in gray peasant clothes and seated at a long zinc table as though awaiting the beginning of a banquet, readied themselves for another batch of hair . . . By now a cloud covered almost the whole sky, it was dark like twilight, and hard to make out the three crossbeams with the bodies hanging on them; many of the people in tattered clothing who had besieged the foot of the hill had dispersed because a thunderstorm was clearly coming. The wind that usually preceded a storm had risen, and the first warm drops were already falling on people's faces and arms, on the shoulders, arms, and chest of the crucified man, and he suddenly realized how long he had been thirsty . . . A stream of clear water flowed from a tipped white pitcher held carefully by one of the slaves, and another slave held a similar white basin, though it could easily have been placed on the marble-tiled ledge. Two narrow, white hands with long fingers, one of the fingers bearing an amethyst set in gold, reluctantly washed each other, letting the stream of water flow over them as was necessary; the water filling the basin was clear and cool— you could plunge your face and mouth in it, open your eyes, and see the basin's white, unsullied bottom through the rippling water. The face of this man, to whom they'd brought him this morning, vaguely reminded the dying man of someone else, but he couldn't remember who; but he thought that if he could remember right this minute, his thirst would be quenched. Flinging a towel to one of the slaves, the tall man in white robes headed for the court, and as he walked, unhurried and slightly hunched, the red lining of his cloak was revealed for a moment. He didn't ascend the judge's podium, but leaned against it, as people entered, he looked at no one: the man brought to him with his hands tied behind his back tried to catch his eye, but the Roman dignitary looked away. Perhaps, the dying man thought, he should have fallen to his knees and lifted his hands to the heavens as his predecessors did; then he would again be walking from town to town followed by fishermen at a respectful distance, and townsfolk and villagers catching sight of him would stop, whisper to one another, and follow him with rapturous gazes until he turned a corner, and he would pretend that he hadn't noticed because it didn't become him to pay attention to earthly honors. The Roman dignitary was still staring off to the side—through the wide-open window there was a blue, cloudless sky, and grape vines could be seen growing on terraces; whosoever begged forgiveness had already admitted his guilt—the more ardent and humble the supplication, the greater the guilt acknowledged—no, he shouldn't fall to his knees, and he stood with his hands tied behind his back, trying to catch the dignitary's eye—he shouldn't have done that either—and yes, he saw it now, this was the thin man with two mournful folds hanging from his chin who had wanted to say something in parting to him earlier; however, his thirst didn't abate when he recognized him, and perhaps his memory deceived him . . . He felt something fuzzy and wet being thrust between his lips, as if to wipe his lips—he drew in the moisture, but it burned his tongue and throat, like a lit torch—and then the Roman legionnaire nonchalantly tossed the long spike with its vinegar-drenched sponge to the side . . . The cloud covered the whole sky now, though it wasn't a cloud anymore, but dense, black billows of smoke, nor was it in the distance, but right here in front of him and the dying man saw the huge vaulted alcoves filled with naked bodies—writhing men and women embraced each other as though in the last convulsions of love—many families were reunited and many might be created over again—and in the square rooms behind the double metal doors, which had been shut tight and bolted from the outside so that there wouldn't be the slightest chance of gas leaking, behind these doors the new group of people stood in anticipation of hot water, and when they felt that there was no air to breathe and understood what it all meant, they began to scream, tearing at their mouths, and the cry of the man dying on the cross was drowned in their cry . . . When Boris Lvovich and Tanya left the church, the sun was already setting and the church could have been photographed quite well—its cupola and crosses would have come out in relief against the sky, but Boris Lvovich couldn't make up his mind to take the picture. Tanya had managed to buy yet another little book at the museum store kiosk and was now looking through it, standing aloof from the tourists who were returning to their tour guide—their whole group walked leisurely along the monastery enclosure toward the bus, because the tour was over; the tour guide again twisted his right hand in a pinch toward the sky—he was pointing up somewhere, the yellowish whites of his eyes gleaming—pointing to the place where, on the heights surrounding the city, presently illuminated by the setting sun, an enormous arrow of white stone that narrowed toward the top could be seen rising against a background of dark green. It was a memorial to the victims of the genocide: armed with yataghans and pistols, the Turks had poured in at night from beyond the mountains, flooded the whole valley, burst into sleeping auls, and slaughtered nearly a fourth of the country's population. Several years ago, on the street where he and Tanya were now living, young people held a demonstration and demanded that a memorial be erected, and visiting this memorial was now officially included in the tour, which surprised no one. The tour guide himself had probably walked among them, screwing his fist into the sky, the yellowish whites of his eyes gleaming, passionate as he demanded that a memorial be built . . . On the outskirts of a large, ancient city with ancient churches and acacia-lined streets, a huge ditch was dug in the clay soil of a ravine on the shores of a wide river—soldiers in long, black overcoats stood in a chain, aiming their automatics at a line of undressed people trembling in the morning cold; after each round of gunfire, people fell as if by command into the brown water that had seeped into the bottom of the ditch and which was gradually becoming rusty-red. New people were brought to replace them, their arms flapped and their bodies twitched just as awkwardly, like marionettes in a puppet show, and they also fell to the bottom of the ditch after a round of gunfire; they were driven to this place in vans that followed the same acacia-lined streets that the processions of church banners had—these undressed people were the sons and grandsons of the people dragged by their beards from their homes and stores when the windows were smashed with cobblestones by the stragglers at the end of the processions . . . A few years ago, Boris Lvovich and Tanya visited the Baltics and were returning to their lodging slowly, buying things for supper; it was the first day of their vacation and many other peaceful, carefree days stood before them, so that even on the street Boris Lvovich felt like he was standing in the warm sea, his back to the oncoming waves: "I would shoot them all and dump them in a ditch," Boris Lvovich heard. Two workers returning from their jobs, black work jackets flung over their shoulders, had caught up with Boris Lvovich and Tanya. One of them—a huge guy with broad shoulders, a flat white face, and a broken nose—glanced at Boris Lvovich as he passed; he spoke to his pal in a loud voice, as if it had nothing to do with Boris Lvovich, and for a moment Boris Lvovich thought that it was all a dream. Tanya was walking

behind him and didn't hear anything, and when Boris Lvovich—
who no longer felt like he was in the warm sea but on the shore
without his underwear and everyone was looking at him—told
Tanya about it, she tried to calm him down saying maybe they
were talking about speculators; but for some reason she immediately added that mixed marriages really irritated them, and that
in this little resort town there were vacationers on union tour
packages. Boris Lvovich recognized them again from afar by
their untucked shirts, and their slow, waddling gait; they resembled bus drivers punching their cards at the last stop where a
huge crowd has already gathered in anticipation of the next bus
and everyone is waiting for the driver to open the door; he recognized them by their idle, wandering gaze, as if they were looking
for something to do. In this same town, after the morning news
which was broadcast through a speaker on the little plot between
the pharmacy, the liquor store, and the post office, these same
vacationers said the word "circumcised" and named the country
in which circumcised people live, also in loud voices. Boris
Lvovich and Tanya began to avoid this spot and walked to the
sea by a roundabout path, but even there, when they only wore
swimsuits, Boris Lvovich recognized them with an infallible
sense, like a wild animal senses the hunter . . . On the clay soil
long settled and overgrown with grass, on the banks of the wide
river on the outskirts of the large city known for its ancient
churches and acacia-lined streets, a crowd of several hundred
gathered—the children and younger brothers of the people who
had jumped awkwardly and fallen into the ditch under rounds
of gunfire; no one said a word, but it was the anniversary of the
day that their fathers and brothers were brought here in covered
trucks. Vans appeared on the highway leading here; they drove
up to the people standing silently, and slammed on their brakes:
policemen in peaked caps with five-pointed stars representing
the unity of the earth's five continents jumped out and formed a

ring around the standing people, as if they were about to lead a folk dance; they crowded them toward the vans, one common group divided into smaller ones, and those divided into even smaller ones, and then people were pushed into the vehicles. One after another, the vans sped silently along the highway toward the city . . . In the evenings after sightseeing, Boris Lvovich and Tanya would eat in a restaurant with the same name as the mountain whose snow-covered summits melted by noon—the local soccer team had the same name as this mountain, as did a brand of cigarettes, and a consumer-services center that was always closed for repairs. In a cellar with a low ceiling, they occupied one of the far tables, closer to the exit. According to Tanya's observations, only local residents went here—obviously nationalists—and in the depths of the cellar, there was an invisible stage that Boris Lvovich never saw because in order to glimpse it you had to go a little further into the restaurant than where they usually sat; from the stage came the sounds of a strange wind instrument making plaintive music with unexpected pauses, so that it seemed the instrument wasn't being played, but only tried out. Tanya was convinced that it was a zurna; Boris Lvovich wasn't sure, but he couldn't come up with the name of any other instrument and Tanya had lived in Central Asia for a few years. Thickset, swarthy well-dressed men sat at the tables pinching their fingers like the guide had done; the same gesture was directed down at some dish in the middle of the table—they might have been peppering it, or dipping their food in sauce, or grabbing some sort of greens—their tables were covered with bottles of wine and unknown dishes. For the remainder of this trip, no matter how hard Boris Lvovich and Tanya tried to choose among the exotic names, they always ended up with some form of ground beef. The waitress passed by them with a blank look and the only local thing they'd receive was bread—Boris Lvovich and Tanya called it "lavash" although it had a different name, but they both forgot the name each time and asked for lavash, and then the waitress looked at them even more blankly. In revenge, Boris Lvovich always tried to take the remainder of the bread with him after they finished their meal, but Tanya gave him a scathing look—once she wrapped a piece of it in a napkin herself and put it in her purse, but she thought that Boris Lvovich wouldn't know how to do it without being noticed. In his mind, he sat down with one or another group of men, imagining himself in their place; he'd be chewing something slowly, dipping his food in sauce, making deals, discussing the latest news or the death of some mutual acquaintance named Huren, but the awareness that he was pretending never left him; and then they rode home to the hotel in a packed bus or trolley that crawled up the endlessly long street, the one that connected the central part of the city with the upper, invisible part called Norartakir. People were going home after work with briefcases and purchases, they got on and off at unfamiliar stops; it was already completely dark like autumn in Moscow when Boris Lvovich returned home from work, although here, in the south, it got dark even earlier—and they stared tensely out into the darkness so as not to miss their stop. Boris Lvovich stood on one foot because there was nowhere to place his other, as he tried to protect Tanya from behind or from the front; he didn't dare ask anyone where their stop was or Tanya would get mad—they also carried bags with provisions for dinner and breakfast, so it looked like they might live and work here. Everyone in the bus or trolley, however, was going home—setting down their purchases they would share the latest news with their family, and then they would all sit down to eat at a round table under a family lampshade, but for some reason Boris Lvovich and Tanya were supposed to go back to the hotel, get the key to their room, and walk silently along the hallway so as not to wake the neighbors, and in the daytime, holding their breath, to look at churches and museums that the locals passed by without noticing, as if they were lampposts. Arriving at their room, they got ready for bed—each on his own bed, and Boris Lvovich, putting on his glasses, began examining a wart on his stomach. It was located a bit above and to the right of his belly button, and he had noticed it for the first time on the day of their arrival; it couldn't have popped up in just one day, he must have missed its appearance. It protruded a tiny bit above the skin and he touched its fuzzy surface with his finger—Tanya assured him that it was nothing and he also thought so, but still, each evening, he examined and touched it, his heart pounding, to make sure it hadn't grown; it seemed not. Then, turning out the light, he placed the transistor radio with an extended antenna, like Sputnik, on his chest; the radio was heavy and his heart beat irregularly, but it was easier to hear that way. "Tanya, do you hear what they're saying? How do you like that? Do you hear? Are you already asleep?" he said; stretching his arm across the narrow space dividing their beds, Boris Lvovich tugged Tanya by the hand, by the hair, and shook her shoulder, because how could you fall asleep with that noise? Tanya mumbled, covered herself with her blanket from head to toe and snored lightly; and Boris Lvovich, turning off the radio and setting it on the throw rug next to his bed so he could turn it on at any moment, listened to the distant hum of motors that rose and fell somewhere high above the city and above the hotel, military planes flying in the fathomless night sky, heavily loaded, in regular intervals, one after the other, group after group, and therefore their hum increased, or diminished, though maybe it was just the wind carrying the sound to one side. The planes flew with their wing lights turned off, so it was pointless to stare into the sky—the hum of their motors sometimes changed to a whine, like during the war. The direction of their movement was obvious—southward. By the time the sound from the first flights reached Boris Lvovich's ears, they were nearly over a foreign country, having left behind the sleeping city that spread out like a wide pit, twinkling with innumerable lights, and the incredibly tall mountain with snowcovered summits that was invisible now in the dark. Pilots in helmets, with impassive white faces, verified their course by the plane's instruments—everything was correct, southwest—and in an hour, or perhaps even less, the airplanes would land in a foreign airport, also plunged into darkness, and from their bellies, weapons and tanks with five-pointed stars would roll out and crates with guided missiles would be unloaded, and swarthy, curly-haired people who looked something like Boris Lvovich, would use these missiles to kill people who looked exactly like Boris Lvovich. The continual hum of invisible aircrafts came and went, moving off to the side, and Boris Lvovich didn't feel like he was lying in a hotel on a soft bed, but that he was lying on his back under a scorching sun on the hot, dusty earth of that small country; he was visible from above and could be strafed by machine-gun fire, but he didn't have the strength to move a muscle, as happens in dreams.

IV
EXILE

That day they were particularly lucky. When they arrived at the
tour office the bus was already there, freshly washed and completely empty; the driver let them in, and they almost choked
from the abundance of empty seats. Pushing and bickering with
each other—Tanya kept nodding meaningfully in the direction
of the driver who had his nose in a newspaper—and changing
seats two or three times, they settled on the shady side, and that
side remained shady during the whole trip. The window was
lowered slightly, so that there wasn't a draft, but at the same time
they could breathe fresh air. When they left the city, low mountains stretched out on their side, overgrown with grass or small
bushes; probably nothing grew at that height because even
though the city where they were staying was in a basin, the basin
itself was much higher than sea level, and now they were driving
to some very high, mountainous place, and the highway was
supposedly rising slowly and steadily, although to the eye it
wasn't really noticeable. The valleys and plateaus stretching out
between the bus and the mountains were strewn with rocks—
round and polished, ranging in size from a cobblestone to a
boulder—sometimes the rocks also lay on the mountains,
especially on the foothills, and the tour guide, a young guy who
was also olive-skinned, told them that according to legend, when
God created the world, he began to throw rocks, but he didn't
simply throw them one at a time, he strewed them like a farmer
sowing seeds or a card dealer tossing cards—that is, a few at a
time, with an expansive gesture, turning around as he did it. As

a result, the small rocks, including these boulders, fell here, because here was where he threw them from, and the larger ones fell on the territory of the neighboring republic, which is why huge mountains formed there; but this contradicted the laws of physics, and so perhaps Boris Lvovich hadn't understood correctly and it was the other way around, but anyway, nature in the neighboring republic turned out to be more fruitful and beautiful, while here it was starker, but grander. The tour guide mentioned this as if in passing, as though he didn't really expect anyone to understand, or didn't want to profane his own feelings. During one of the stops, Boris Lvovich walked over to him—the guide stood next to the open bus door, shading himself from the sun while the tourists wandered a bit from the bus, for some reason testing the soil with their feet; yes, of course he knew the works of that filmmaker very well, and even named one of his films that Boris Lvovich hadn't heard of; the director wasn't allowed to work in Moscow, and now he was going to move here, to his home town. "You hear that, Tanya?" She stood nearby. "I told you from the start that he understands everything," Tanya said, when they walked off a bit. "I'm even certain that he studied in Moscow," she continued, "he even looks like one of our acquaintances. Don't tell me you can't figure out who?" Boris Lvovich shrugged his shoulders uncertainly, but his heart skipped a beat, because in these sorts of situations Tanya's eyes flashed with a spark Boris Lvovich didn't recognize, there was even a hint of contempt for him, as though he didn't notice things that everyone else noticed, things that affected Tanya and him. He couldn't actually remember who the tour guide looked like, but the rest of the way he thought of him as someone who understands everything, someone who maybe studied in Moscow; and he tried to catch Tanya's eyes, but she was listening to the tour guide the way she listened to Boris Lvovich when he read Feuchtwanger to her at night before going to sleep, and in her intense attention there was something unrelated to him, which he found insulting, especially since the tour guide was just like all the other tour guides, and repeated the same old hackneyed things. The bus stopped a few hundred meters from the mountain that was their destination; a nature preserve started here and vehicles weren't allowed through. The tour group stretched out in a long chain, walking along the banks of a lake toward the mountain: a ways in front of them was another such chain, crowded together at the very approach to the mountain, and on the mountain itself one could see a group of people dispersing, separate couples wandering about, some people lingering by themselves, and then these groups returned to the parking lot in a disorderly fashion, having already lost interest in the tour guides. Boris Lvovich, slipping on the rocks beneath his feet, walked down to the very shore of the lake, kneeled, and then leaned over, to get the smooth surface of the water at almost eye level; he photographed the lake with a large rough boulder in the foreground to make the distance perceptible in the picture, and then, moving ahead of the tour group so that no one would be in front of the lens, he began to climb the mountain and shoot pictures of the lake from above; then he entered the two churches known to be very ancient—first one, then the other, and back to the first one again; and inside the churches, it was dark and empty except for sleepy guards: in each church, the earth floor and stone walls exuded damp and the stucco was crumbling, so the saints depicted on the walls were missing noses or arms, or parts of their torsos; but all of this could really only be surmised, because almost no light entered—the tour guide said that restoration work was supposed to start soon. Boris Lvovich climbed to the highest point of the mountain—it was even higher than the cross on the main church—and from this point he could see mountain slopes and the lake stretching out like a sea with a faintly perceptible far shore; there, in the haze, should be the mountain with two snow-covered summits that Boris Lvovich and Tanya saw every morning from the balcony of their hotel, though the mountain was closer to the hotel so it wasn't surprising that it was visible, but here it was at least a hundred kilometers away—which meant that it was very big indeed—Boris Lvovich didn't see it, but he thought that its contours could be glimpsed through the haze. He was on the highest point of the mountain—no one had come up this far—the tourists walked around the churches, wandered about the slopes and he began to wave his arms wildly at Tanya, come up here! She would never see anything like this again! They struck a bargain somewhere midway between the church and the highest point, where Boris Lvovich stood. Tanya was breathing heavily after the climb— she was portly, and lately she'd been getting out of breath, sometimes even when standing still. Boris Lvovich put the camera to her eyes so she could see what the photo would look like, but she didn't like to look through the viewfinder while he was holding the camera and wanted to do it herself, though Boris Lvovich always thought that she'd do something wrong and miss seeing the exact frame he had chosen. On the return trip, there was a stream on their side, now shady because the sun had moved; the stream stretched along the highway, twisting as streams do—it wasn't too wide, and stones stuck up in the middle, so you could probably wade across it. It was the same stream that Boris Lvovich saw in the city when they were riding from the airport to the hotel; all the guides maintained that it was a mountain stream, with the treacherous current typical of mountain streams; it had a loud name that was easy to remember, but for some reason Boris Lvovich always forgot it. "I'd like a dacha like that," Tanya said, looking somewhere off in to the distance. When they had just married she loved to stop in the evening opposite a large building catty-corner from their courtyard—in the curtainless window of one of the top floors a lampshade could be seen. "That's my dream," she'd say, sighing; later she dreamed of winning a car or buying a little house somewhere far from the city, and living there year round. In the place they lived right after marrying, he often came home by way of alleys and courtyards rather than streets; they lived in a communal apartment with a multitude of residents, and someone was always frying something in the kitchen and washing clothes till late at night and a light bulb burned under the smoke-covered ceiling—it was winter and they would turn the light on early. He'd see his building two or three courtyards ahead—the back of the building which eventually turned into an ordinary brick chimney, actually a row of them, but from that perspective it seemed to be one pipe—and if you looked carefully you could see that there was always smoke billowing out against the starry January night—the building was always overheated and the stars were slightly veiled by smoke. He knew Tanya was waiting for him; taking off his gloves, he'd sniff his palms, she always smelled of her "White Lilac" perfume, and he tried to retain the fragrance until evening; at work or in the metro he would remember the building's brick wall with snow hanging from the roof and smoke rising from the pipes, but by the time he returned home he had usually forgotten about it and it arose unexpectedly; the moment when he should have remembered the wall with smoke rising cozily from the pipes was lost, and then he suddenly realized that he'd already been married several years and had simply lost track of time, like one does at parties when all of a sudden it's almost morning and time to go home—or after a train has been racing along with mind-boggling speed, you only notice after it slows down—all of this was probably what was called happiness. The "dacha" that thrilled Tanya turned out to be a burial vault surrounded by a wrought-iron fence: on a hillock across the river was a spacious cemetery that looked like a village with streets and houses—probably family vaults—and both of them laughed a long time about that dacha, and Tanya kept saying "knock on wood" and "cross your fingers," and Boris Lvovich teased her, saying that it wasn't really such a bad dacha. Returning to the city they decided not to go to the restaurant but to have dinner in their room: after they bought a lot of provisions, Boris Lvovich went out into the middle of the street and raised his hand as if he wanted to stop the traffic; a black Volga stopped and they got in. Boris Lvovich sat in front next to the driver as if it were his personal car, and Tanya sat in back after casually tossing their purchases on the seat, like the wives of executives do. They passed trolleys and buses dragging themselves up toward the mountain, and trams that for some reason stood still at the tram stops surrounded by clusters of people, and they arrived at the hotel while it was still light. They casually slammed the doors as they got out of the car right across the street from the hotel entrance—door to door— and Boris Lvovich strolled through the dim, cool lobby with the independent gait of an executive. Tanya followed with their purchases like the wife of a man occupying a high position. Climbing the stairs, he suddenly realized that the woman sitting at the lobby desk had said something to him; she was somewhere down below in the dark. He was walking up the carpeted stairs with the confident step of a man who owns a Volga, and Tanya was just behind him with their purchases—she hadn't had time to get out of breath—when the floor attendant said something in a terrible accent, and what she said had a direct relationship to them: tomorrow they would have been staying in the hotel for six days. Boris Lvovich knew this perfectly well and this morning he'd even wanted to pay for the remaining four days that they would be in the city, after that, they had a plane ticket for the capital of the neighboring republic where they had reserved a hotel room, and then from there they were supposed to return to Moscow—but why had she reminded him that their reservation had expired? And now he remembered that the Turk in the fez, the same one who'd met them the day of their arrival, and who was on duty yesterday, had said something to him about the reservation running out, but he hadn't paid any attention to his words because the Turk had completely mangled them, and besides which, he had been hostile to Boris Lvovich and Tanya from the very beginning. Why did they all get so hot under the collar about it? He was perfectly aware when the six days would run out. "You should go talk to the lobby clerk and pay the money immediately," Tanya said. She stood next to Boris Lvovich on the steps of the staircase, holding their purchases in her arms and breathing heavily—they had stopped somewhere between the second and third floors; Boris Lvovich went back down to the attendant—he said that he had wanted to pay yesterday but didn't get back in time, and when they walked by this morning no one was here. She looked off somewhere past him, as only administrators know how to do, though perhaps she simply didn't understand what he said. He began to take out money— ten, twenty, thirty—how much did he need to pay for the remaining four days? they were flying out on the twenty-ninth . . . She didn't look at him or at the money that he pulled out of his inside pocket, mixing up the paper money with the tickets for tomorrow's excursion to the pagan temple located in a bucolic setting not far from the city—no, she couldn't do anything, it says clearly in the reservation: six days. You want to see the director of the hotel? Be my guest, her office is on the second floor. He ran back to his room where the food was on the window sill and Tanya was setting the table; it all seemed so meaningless now, like brushing your teeth before the death sentence is pronounced. "Well?" Her face paled when he told her. With shaking hands he got out the airplane tickets from the depths of the suit-case—"Take your Bar Association ID card" she shouted when he was almost out the door—he always carried his ID card with him, and felt for it in his back pocket—a hard little booklet with his photograph and the inscription "Moscow Municipal Bar Association"; members of the Moscow Municipal Bar Association didn't stay in crummy little hotels like this very often, and he walked down the stairs, fingering his ID. "Where's the director's office?" Yes, he knew it was on the second floor, and isn't this the second? Oh, that means another floor down—on that floor, several women sat on the sofa in the hallway, and others on chairs nearby; they were chatting about something, the quiet after-lunch banter of people who are not being kicked out of a hotel. "Where's the director?" Boris Lvovich asked, because this *was* the second floor—no one answered, but one of the women sitting on the sofa slowly and unwillingly detached herself from the conversation and looked at him. She wore a sort of inconspicuous dress suit, and her face was grayish and wrinkled as is often the case with middle-aged women burdened with a family and household, and Boris Lvovich realized immediately that she was the director, because an empty space formed around her and he no longer saw anyone but her. "I beg of you," said Boris Lvovich, pulling the booklet out of his pocket and holding the airplane tickets in the other, his hands trembling, "I've been asked to check out of my room, but I have plane tickets, and besides which, I'm a member of the Moscow Bar Association." He handed her first the ID and then the plane tickets, but she, like the on-duty manager, looked past him. "I can't do anything," she said calmly, as if she were just continuing the chat he'd interrupted, "the Znanie Society conference opens tomorrow, and we're booked"; she had almost no accent but her face was the typical face of a middle-aged eastern woman, with graying hair as coarse as wires. "I'm a member of the Znanie Society myself," Boris Lvovich said heatedly, remembering the little blue ID card that they'd foisted on him a few years ago and how he'd been asked to give a lecture, and he barely managed to get out of it, and he even wanted to tell the director all about this, so that she'd understand that he was more important than the Znanie Society. "So ask them to find you a place," she said, just as coolly as if she were talking about irrelevant details that didn't have anything to do with Boris Lvovich, as if he weren't the one being kicked out of the hotel. He suddenly saw himself standing in front of the director in a pleading pose, his hands trembling, and he and Tanya dragging their suitcases out of the hotel, replaced by members of the Znanie Society, who were just a bunch of ignoramuses or maybe even thugs who'd come here to have a good time, and he and Tanya were out in the street under the stars because they had nowhere to go, these kinds of things had even been written about in the newspapers. "So you're throwing us out on the street like dogs, but I bet you find places for your own people!" This was already a direct attack against the authorities, and a case could be brought against him—the director glanced at him, and this time it was with a touch of curiosity; one of the others participating in the conversation also looked at him curiously—he thought that he might be army or former army personnel; he wore a single-breasted jacket and a medal hanging from a ribbon. When Boris Lvovich returned to the room it was almost dark, but they didn't turn on the light, as if their presence here were already illegal—the floor swayed oddly under Boris Lvovich, as though he were on a sailboat, probably a spasm of the brain vessels. "Turn on the light, damn it!" Boris Lvovich shouted, as though this would change their predicament. It was all Tanya's fault because in this city as in many other cities and republics there were managers, or regional offices, under the jurisdiction of the Moscow directorate where Tanya worked, and the people who worked in these local offices depended on Moscow and could set them up at any hotel and would even consider it an honor; one time in a resort town, a hotel like that was arranged for them, the Intourist, the best in the town. Boris

Lvovich couldn't forget the room, and they were even met at the airport in a Volga and driven to the hotel like honored foreigners or VIPs, and the doorman opened the door for them, bowing respectfully, and the people who'd met them walked behind them and carried their suitcases, and they didn't even have to talk to the manager—everything had already been arranged, and they were immediately given the key to the room, and the floor attendant also stood respectfully when they approached Tanya, who was accompanied by the local bigwigs carrying their suitcases; but now Tanya flatly refused to take vacations like this, because her boss had hinted to her that now she would have to pay them off, with train loads of rolling mills or some other machines—it was a joke of course, because everyone in her office vacationed that way, and besides, Boris Lvovich didn't see anything terrible about sending them some extra equipment, after all, it wouldn't go into anyone's pocket, it would benefit the state; but Tanya wouldn't even discuss the subject, and now because of her idiotic stubbornness they were being thrown out on the street—she listened to him silently, her eyes cast down—under the light of the lamp, her face seemed pale to Boris Lvovich, and her voice was considerably lower; she began to persuade him to lie down—she was probably afraid for him—and he imagined being taken to the hospital; Tanya would be out on the street and penniless for that matter, because their letter of credit was in his name. The floor swayed under him again and he lay down, while Tanya went to look for the cleaning lady, a middle-aged woman who spoke good Russian, and who wasn't a local—for some reason Tanya thought that she could help them. Tanya returned to the room with a mysterious look on her face: the cleaning woman had promised to try and help—not quite definitely, but she promised and even said that she'd drop by their room, and the rest of the evening they strained their ears listening for her steps in the hall, but she didn't come, and Tanya again ran to look for her—the cleaning lady was nowhere to be found; maybe she had gone to talk about them with the management, or even with the director herself—Tanya went to look for her again, but the cleaning lady had disappeared without a trace: most likely she simply went to bed. In the next room, which shared a balcony with them, eastern music thumped away like a variety show, and it smelled like shish kebob from the restaurant—probably some of the locals were having an orgy; that evening Boris Lvovich even forgot to look at the wart on his stomach and he didn't turn on the radio.

V
REVENGE

The Aeroflot ticket windows had just opened, and a crowd already stood at each one. Tanya stationed Boris Lvovich to the side, near the posted schedule, and went off somewhere, taking the tickets and passports from him, because Boris Lvovich kept mixing up the tickets with other papers and the letter of credit always flew out of his passport, gliding in the air like a leaflet. That night he had fallen asleep though it wasn't really sleep, rather a forced plunge into sleep, when you can still feel time flowing by—Tanya also tossed and turned as though something was bothering her, though the room next door had grown quiet—probably all the action had moved to the bed and the swarthy, hairy aborigines held the visiting blondes in their embrace, inflaming the unruffled northern girls like Pushkin wrote somewhere, and on the floor in the middle of the room lay the remains of shish kebob like an extinguished campfire, and empty wine bottles, and a cassette player with a torn tape: there were definitely two local guys because it was a room for two, the kind that Boris Lvovich and Tanya had, and besides which, you had to have no fewer than four people for an orgy—the northern girls moaned quietly, digging their fingernails into the hairy, muscular backs of the guys while outside it was growing light. Tanya tossed and turned fitfully; above Boris Lvovich's head-board, his camera hung peacefully on a hook, his shirts and Tanya's dresses hung neatly in the closet, their underclothes were folded just as neatly on the shelves, and he should sleep, because Tanya needed time to put herself together in the morning—maybe they'd be able to change the tickets for today—yes, it was already today, because night was almost over—in which case this evening or tonight they'd be at home in Moscow, though it seemed incredible, almost like flying to another galaxy. Boris Lvovich slept as though having an operation under light anesthesia, when there's no pain, but you are aware of everything and even feel it. In the morning they left, as though hurrying off to yet another tour—up until the very last minute, when Tanya was packing her things, Boris Lvovich was sure the maid would appear and inform them that everything was fine—or the manager, or even the director herself, repenting her actions, and he shivered each time he heard steps outside the door. As they walked through the lobby of the hotel, he fixed a hateful stare on yesterday's manager, whose shift hadn't ended, but she didn't even raise her head from the counter—she was probably ashamed after all. A slight chill overtook Boris Lvovich outside even though the sun was high and it was pleasant like it always was when they left the hotel early—the streets had been washed, or perhaps a light rain had fallen overnight, and they boarded a trolley and rode down the endless street as they did every morning and people got in and out of the trolley as usual, hurrying to work, so for a moment Boris Lvovich thought that nothing had happened and it was all just a dream. Tanya returned with the passports and tickets—nothing could be changed today, only at the airport right before the flight, so they left the Aeroflot agency building and without saying a word, they headed for the street where the regional administrative headquarters under Tanya's jurisdiction was located—Tanya had noticed the sign on the building a few days ago, she even stopped to show it to Boris Lvovich, and for a moment he thought that she wanted to drop in there, but this memory only reopened old wounds and he unleashed another tirade of angry reproaches at Tanya, but now they were on their way to that street and the expression on Tanya's face was both decisive and vacant, it was the sort of expression she had when they went to the seaside and she got ready to swim. Boris Lvovich barely knew how to swim—in deep water he tried to keep close to Tanya and make her stand in one place like a buoy so he'd know where she was, but she started swimming immediately as though Boris Lvovich didn't exist, she didn't even look his way. The same expression appeared when Boris Lvovich kissed her, which scared him because at those moments he thought that she was hiding a secret from him—on occasion, she would glance at Boris Lvovich fleetingly, hinting at anxiety over his health, or the condition of his suit, but in this particular look, rather, on the verge of it, where the pupil turned into the iris, there was something akin to contempt for Boris Lvovich, as though he hadn't been able to protect her from someone who had insulted her honor, or maybe he had pushed her toward the offender himself, and now he was demanding that she acknowledge the correctness of his action, or the courage he had displayed. Ten minutes later Boris Lvovich stood with pounding heart under the sign near the entrance to the local headquarters, waiting for Tanya, who had gone upstairs because each floor housed different organizations. She hadn't shown up yet—he didn't know whether that was a good or bad sign, but he couldn't stand it, so he stepped inside; a young woman, her heels clicking in secretarial fashion, was descending the stairs. "Are you Tatyana Lvovna's husband?" she asked in a friendly, respectful manner. "Forgive us for not coming down right away. They're waiting for you upstairs." He followed her, and a bittersweet lump welled up in his throat, almost the same kind as when in his imagination he and Tanya climbed the snow-capped summit, and calm, suntanned people with clear blue eyes stretched their hands out—for a second he saw himself again standing like a pitiful supplicant in front of the couch where the director sat surrounded by her managers and a few chosen hotel guests—she held court, like a sheikh amid fawning courtiers—he thought that she was knitting something, and he had offered her his papers with trembling hands, but she didn't even look at them or at him, and at this point Tanya had still hoped for something. He'd give that woman with the gray, wrinkled face something to remember him by: on leaving the hotel he'd go to her office with his suitcases, accompanied by local bigwigs whose very names would probably make her tremble—he'd let her know! The small, smoky room was noisy, and Tanya sat at the desk with her back to the window—this was probably the boss's desk, because it was the largest, and was placed at the window so that whoever sat there could see all the employees; two or three men fussed around Tanya; one of them, maybe even the boss himself, or his deputy, was making phone calls from the telephone right there on the desk, probably to find a hotel for them, and another man, also an employee, ran off to another department—probably to make calls as well. They sat Boris Lvovich down on a chair, like an honored guest—the chair had been brought in from a neighboring room—during the intervals between phone calls and running off to the next department, the men joked respectfully with Tanya, who was no longer simply Tanya here, but Tatyana Lvovna, and it all seemed very strange to Boris Lvovich; Tanya apologized for the intrusion, and they asked her about mutual acquaintances—probably Moscow employees—and reproached her just as respectfully for not having asked for their assistance from the very beginning. "He criticized me for that too," said Tanya, nodding toward Boris Lvovich, and he began to recount heatedly how he had begged Tatyana Lvovna, and how she refused, and how they had been kicked out of the hotel, and how scandalous it was, and Tanya was also indignant and they all nodded yes, yes, yes, to him and to Tanya. Somewhere over to the side, others bustled about—someone told somebody something in a low voice, the boss and his deputy kept making phone calls; another person came in from the department next door and someone again left the room silently—it was as though guests had unexpectedly shown up and they had to be taken care of, but there wasn't anything to offer them and somebody had to run to the store to buy something, but the closest stores were closed, and everything had to be arranged, but the guests couldn't be forgotten, and Boris Lvovich suddenly understood why Tanya apologized for the incursion. A half hour later they were driving in a Volga that had been specially freed up for them—one of the local bosses accompanied them, but Boris Lvovich and Tanya entered the hotel on their own, and Boris Lvovich opened the lobby doors in a fury—first the outside ones, then the inner ones; he pushed them with his entire body and deliberately let them slam shut. Loaded down with suitcases, he and Tanya left the door to their room open—just to let everyone see that they had been thrown out, they didn't care, an important local person was waiting for them downstairs in a black Volga, and they would be taken to a good hotel for the elite, not this little rat hole for members of the Znanie Society or for tourists who had put their names on a general reservation list through Mostransagency. Boris Lvovich barged into the director's office, pushing the door open with his suitcase, blind to everything in front of him, but it turned out to be the secretary's office, and the secretary told him that the director was busy now. Inside he was actually pleased to hear it, and anyway Tanya had kept on saying: "What do you need this for?" and continued to walk downstairs with their bags, not waiting for him, and anyway they couldn't keep the car waiting. The hotel they were taken to was named after the republic they were in, and was located right in the city center, a special hotel for people with connections, just as Boris Lvovich had expected, and with old-fashioned lions, a fireplace in the lobby, and even the remains of a fountain. The director of the regional headquarters, who accompanied them, went straight to the registration desk himself and brought them the forms to fill out—just as they had at the resort-town hotel when things had been arranged through Tanya's connections. When Boris Lvovich and Tanya walked into their room which looked like an old-fashioned boudoir, Boris Lvovich gasped at the luxury: a spacious balcony with decorative cast-iron grill work looked out onto one of the city's main streets—a wide, tree-lined street carpeted with yellow leaves; vehicles weren't even allowed on this street; aimless crowds strolled across it, and the best shops and cafes lined its sidewalks. Boris Lvovich and Tanya had walked down this street a few times but the memory was like a dream— it had seemed so inaccessible to them then, but now their balcony looked out right over it, and the rustle of leaves under the pedestrians' feet was audible. It was just a stone's throw to the most central plaza with its famous singing fountains—which had to be seen and heard in the evening because they were illuminated with different colors, but at that hour Boris Lvovich and Tanya were usually heading back to their hotel. Now it was all close, and in the evening they could go out and lose themselves in the crowd; now they could go outside and come back, and then go out again. "Tanya, this is great! Come take a look!" he shouted to her from the balcony, and since she didn't respond he glanced back—she was sitting on their as yet unpacked bags, crying— she had a strange way of crying, squeezing her eyes shut and closing her eyelids tight, as though someone were about to force them open, and for some reason tears ran from her nose, like they do from an infant, and her face wrinkled like an infant's, and her voice was high and plaintive, like an infant's, or maybe she did this deliberately. "Cut it out!" Boris Lvovich said in an irritated voice—because it was so wonderful here, and Tanya was ruining his mood. "Cut it out right this minute!" he almost shouted, but Tanya covered her face with her hands as though to protect herself from any attempts to force her eyelids open—he tried to pull her hands away from her face, but she shook her head, and her voice became even higher and more plaintive. "I beg you, please stop." He stood in front of her, his arms hanging down, not knowing what to do. "This lousy city . . . we never should have come here . . . I don't want anything," burst out through her sobs—his wife, Tanya, was crying because they had been kicked out of the hotel, and because she had to go and ask for favors, which was humiliating, and he, Boris Lvovich, her husband, a respectable man, an associate professor and member of the Moscow Bar Association, a man for whom the doorman respectfully opened the door when he entered the court building, and a policeman tipped his cap, he hadn't been able to do anything: they were put out on the street like dogs, and he had stood there, in front of the director like a pitiful suppliant, handing her his ID booklet and plane tickets, but she hadn't even looked his way, and today he hadn't gone to see her either, to remind her of his existence, and the whole incident had rolled off the director's back and she would go on holding court surrounded by her subordinates, with her ashy exhausted face. On the table between the old-fashioned beds intended for Tanya and him, there was a telephone—also sort of old-fashioned, with a long receiver, like they had in Edison's time: the best thing would be to call the director, saying he was calling from the prosecutor's office—he had even seen the building with the big black plaque next to the door—that's right, we've been informed, and the prosecutor has asked us to look into it—and the director would rush around looking for Boris Lvovich to apologize, and then she wouldn't hold court among her subordinates with such aristocratic calm; red blotches would appear on her face, or maybe she'd turn white as a sheet. That was just wishful thinking because of course she knew people everywhere, and she'd ask immediately who was calling, and say that actually she hadn't violated any law; no, the best thing would be to curse her out, after introducing himself, though given her connection, she'd probably come looking for him and he could be called to account. Several times, when Tanya left the room, he dialed the first two digits—one time he even dialed the whole number, though no one answered, probably because the work day was over—and then Tanya would come back, and his heartbeat drowned out the ring of the telephone, and when he hung up, he perhaps thought that he'd heard someone's voice on the line, though it could have been static, and anyway, he didn't really know what to say. After lunch he and Tanya walked along the street beneath their balcony—everything was close, just a stone's throw away: people in cafes sat at little tables, and shoppers crowded around food stalls, and no one had kicked them out of a hotel, they had a legal right to enjoy all this, but he and Tanya had to appeal to her subordinates to rescue them, and explain that they had been kicked out and lost their tickets to the pagan shrine tour; it was all the fault of that middle-aged woman with the colorless hair, and the local inhabitants who sat in cafes or strolled down the streets as well, and Boris Lvovich thought of stinging remarks he could address to them, but Tanya didn't say anything, because from the very beginning, she had understood what a lousy town this was, and Boris Lvovich only understood it now. That evening, lying in bed, Boris Lvovich remembered his wart, and he touched it: the surface was rough and pale green—but it hadn't grown in the last few days, and had probably been there a long time. Falling asleep, he suddenly saw the director's face— sallow, gray, wrinkled—now he knew what to say to her; he imagined how her face would break out in red splotches or turn a ghastly green, and how the floor would sway beneath her, and how she'd run to the clinic to register for a doctor's appointment. The director's telephone was busy the next morning, so when he and Tanya went to the Aeroflot agency to turn in their tickets, because Tanya no longer wanted to go to any neighboring republics—Boris Lvovich ran to two pay phones, while she stood in line, but neither of them worked. On the way to the train station, he didn't let a single phone booth escape him, and Tanya didn't even ask who he was calling, she had probably guessed, or perhaps she even hoped he would. At the station they managed to get tickets on the international train for a small bribe: they would travel all the way to Moscow in a two-person compartment and they were staying in the best possible hotel in the very center of town—but in order to fully appreciate it all, he needed to call the director, and the more reasons he found to feel happy, the more insistent need desire became. Walking down the street, he only saw telephone booths, occupied or unoccupied, working or not working, and he kept running off and calling, but the line was always busy or no one answered, or the phone itself didn't work; it would be better to call from a phone booth of course, because if he called from the hotel she would immediately be able to find out where he was. But they had already returned to the hotel. Boris Lvovich sat on the bed and dialed the number, his heart thumping wildly: "Yes, Ruta Ivanovna is in her office." His heart fell, and beat even harder, because he had really hoped he'd dialed the wrong number; then he heard the usual "Hello?" and recognized her voice instantly. "It was a pleasure to make your acquaintance the day before yesterday," he began, speaking in a polite, educated voice. "You probably don't remember me," he continued in the same tone, as though chatting with a colleague, "I'm the member of the Moscow Bar Association." "Yes, yes," she said vaguely, so it wasn't clear whether she remembered him or not—it still wasn't too late to hang up the phone. "So, then, you kicked me out of the hotel," he blurted out rudely, and now there was no going back. "I'm an expert in forensic medicine," he began, his voice rising, returning to its previous register, though his heart was beating so hard, he couldn't hear his own words. "I'm an expert in forensic medicine," he repeated, gasping, "and given the nature of my work I often have to deal with corpses." Now he felt like he wasn't the one speaking, it was someone else, as if it were all happening on stage, and he was simply a spectator—"What does this have to do with anything?" she asked. Another second and she would hang up; nonetheless, a strange confusion, even fright, could be heard in her voice, as if she were surrounded by a crowd that had escaped from an insane asylum, but she didn't hang up. "So you see, I can make diagnoses just by looking at people," a voice said hurriedly from the stage, and Boris Lvovich listened, his heart pounding: "You have cancer," someone said from the stage, "and you should get treatment," he added, from himself, Boris Lvovich, in order to soften what had been said from the stage, and to make her feel Boris Lvovich's concern for her, as a specialist from the capital who could help her if he wanted to and as a result, her regret for the fateful mistake she made when she kicked him out of the hotel should be even more acute. A strange silence reigned over the phone line, it was tense, as if the person on the other end were being x-rayed—Boris Lvovich even thought he could hear the breathing of doctors leaning over the screen. "Yes, I know that," said the woman they were examining in a tired, cheerless voice, and Boris Lvovich wanted to say something else, but someone tore the receiver from his hands: it was Tanya, who hung up the phone. She was standing over him with a face so pale it looked like it was dusted with powder. "What have you done, my God!" she shouted, and she covered her face with her hands, and burst into tears, in fact, she almost wailed, pitifully, as though someone had wounded her. "I'd make a good doctor! I made the correct diagnosis!" Boris Lvovich exclaimed triumphantly, jumping up from the bed where he'd been sitting, and trying to tear Tanya's hands from her face. Instead of triumph, however, he was overwhelmed by a strange tremor; he stepped out onto the balcony—down below, on the wide, tree-lined street strewn with yellow leaves, crowds of people strolled by; it was exactly noon, but the sun was covered with haze, because the hotel where they were staying was right in the center of the city, in a funnel, and according to the tour guide, all the exhaust fumes were concentrated there.

That night, he and Tanya went to look at the singing fountains. They left the hotel at dark, and when they walked out onto the square, the spectacle was at its height. Jets of water lit by red, blue, and green lights spouted strong and high, then fell or stopped entirely, and it was all accompanied by music—either some national eastern music, or the Appassionata, which sounded wheezy, probably the record had been played too much—but at the height of the melody, its very crest, the point where it screwed itself right into the heart, the red spray beat ever stronger, while the green and blue subsided and the jets became a pulsating artery; then the colors changed, and voices in a major key were suddenly heard. The plaza around the fountains overflowed with people, and the changing lights illuminated their faces: the dark faces of the natives, for whom this was the regular place to meet, have rendezvous, or simply take a walk—children sat on the ledge of the fountains, their legs dangling—and there were the rare, pale faces, these were soldiers wearing peaked caps with green bands, most likely border guards, out on passes, who had come here to enjoy the fountains; they were strangers here, aliens, but the fountains' lights alternated colors on their faces just as they did on the natives', and they listened to the music just as attentively, even the local, ethnic music, and Boris Lvovich felt a special commonality with the soldiers, who probably spoke Russian as well as he and Tanya. After viewing the fountains, Boris Lvovich lay on his high, old-fashioned bed in the hotel room, and, sitting up a bit and putting on his glasses, he inspected the wart on his stomach: it was a kind of strange, green color and even seemed to have grown a tiny bit over the last two days—no it had obviously grown, and he saw the slow but steady multiplications of cells somewhere in its depths and saw these cells beginning to penetrate normal tissue and spread to other organs through the blood vessels and the process couldn't be stopped, because it was all programmed. Suddenly he saw the gray, wrinkled face of the woman right in front of him; she was wrapped in a gray knit shawl and her stomach—for some reason Boris Lvovich was certain she had stomach cancer—was almost entirely filled with a tumor, yellowish-green, because it resembled a head of cauliflower, and she could eat almost nothing now, because food couldn't get through anymore, and even after eating the most innocuous food she felt nauseous, and she lived with this nausea all the time, even at night; and she ate from dirty, poorly washed dishes, because they didn't wash dishes well here at all. He felt an attack of nausea, as though he himself had the crumbling cauliflower in his stomach—his wart would probably be his punishment for what he had said to the woman. Suddenly the phone rang on the bedside table between the beds—a tall, old-fashioned phone from Edison's time—and the ring was lengthy, a long-distance call. Tanya picked up the receiver—Boris Lvovich's mother was calling from Moscow. Tanya's face immediately became alien like in the trolley or the tram when Boris Lvovich didn't know which side he should protect her from. Andrei is going to get married? He's not spending the night at home? To Inna? Yes, he'd been staying with her, but neither Boris Lvovich nor Tanya had ever met her. "It's all your mother's fault," Tanya said bitterly, replacing the receiver, "she's brought him to this with all her nagging." Tanya sat on her bed across from Boris Lvovich, hanging her head heavily and tapping the floor with one foot. "For that matter, she could have made up the whole thing," said Tanya, and her face took on an even colder, more distant expression. "What do you think, is my wart bad? Is it retribution for the whole business with the director?" "He wants to get married so he can leave," said Tanya, continuing to stare somewhere down at the floor, as if the solution to everything lay there. "That's the only reason," she repeated firmly, "and, if you want my opinion, it *is* retribution," she added, looking straight at Boris Lvovich, the familiar sparks of disdain for him flaring in her eyes for a moment. He couldn't fall asleep for a long time, he kept touching his wart, and for the life of him he couldn't understand what was so horrible about Andrei planning to marry without love, and besides which, the whole thing might be nonsense.

VI
MIRAGE

The train station, built from the same gray tufa as the rest of the
city's buildings, began to drift slowly backward; then the train
depots drifted by—barracks, single sleeping cars adapted to live
in, warehouses, piles of crushed rock and lime—the usual railroad landscape, but for some reason Boris Lvovich took pleasure
in thinking that it was a particular kind of trash, characteristic of
this city, and, thank God, they were saying farewell to it, and
further on, there were probably houses, no doubt hung with
laundry, piled on top of each other on steep slopes overgrown
with greenery that hid tall, white monuments. He would probably never see this city again, and for a moment he was sorry that
they had seen so little, because the city was truly ancient, and
tourists from all over the world visited it. The last two days they
had loafed around the center with nothing to do, making various
unnecessary purchases: Tanya bought some silvery slippers with
oriental designs—they looked like old-fashioned boats—she
wanted to buy some for Inna, which surprised Boris Lvovich at
first, but then he decided it was only natural, why hadn't he
thought of it himself? On the other hand, it meant that Andrei's
marriage wasn't just talk; but Tanya didn't know Inna's size,
although somehow she knew that Inna was small, and even
made a touching comment about the size of her feet. They went
back to the shop, but Tanya hesitated for some reason—should
she buy them or not—no, she didn't know Inna's exact size; and
Boris Lvovich decided that perhaps everything would work out.
In the evenings, they walked along the main street strewn with

yellow leaves where they were now staying, and down the side streets that led to the other central avenues. "Isn't it great to be in the center?" Boris Lvovich kept saying and Tanya automatically answered "Yes, yes," in order to stop him, and then, as if waking up, added in an entirely different tone of voice: "Thank God we don't have much time left in this lousy city." They went to cafés, of which there were many, close to their hotel and on the other busy, nearby streets—young people sat at little tables in the cafés, and one of them, with short hair, stuck in his mind—she was a local, but Boris Lvovich liked that type of woman, with brown hair, slightly broad cheekbones, gray eyes, somehow resembling Tanya when she was young. These people were at home here, laughing and talking and joking; but he was a Jew, Andrei couldn't find work after graduating from the institute, and although he was fairer than Boris Lvovich and even looked more like Tanya, he was already trying to hide his face on the street and on public transportation, though he did it inconspicuously, under the guise of untoward whistling or feigned merriment, or even courage; but inside Andrei, there was a string stretched tight, and Boris Lvovich thought it might snap at any moment. Somewhere, on hot, rocky terrain, armored tanks with five-pointed red stars were shooting at people who looked like Boris Lvovich and Andrei, but those people fought, they stood up to the tanks and blew them up, because it was their country and they didn't need to hide their faces. The city, with its gray and white houses, and monuments drowning in greenery receded: "Look! Look!" Boris Lvovich and Tanya said to each other as the familiar double-peaked summit floated alongside the train, turning imperceptibly so that the smaller cone gradually moved behind the large one, just like it did when they went on the tour of the local patriarch's residence with its ancient monastery made of rough gray stone—the railroad probably ran parallel to the highway they traveled that time. The smaller cone was totally hidden behind the taller one, so only the large, silvery one appeared to melt in the white sky, and the snow on it seemed untouched; but what was that?—close to the very summit of the cone the snow looked pitted, as if someone had been digging, or an expedition had passed through, or maybe the lighting was strange. "Look, look, it looks like a cross," Boris Lvovich said to Tanya—they were sitting opposite one another, staring out the window of their two-person compartment, hidden away from everyone; Tanya hadn't had time to arrange their belongings, and a boiled chicken bought for the trip stuck out of her over-stuffed bag. "That's not a cross, it's a six-pointed star, don't tell me you can't see it?" said Tanya. "That's what it is, I'm absolutely certain." The sled or maybe ski tracks led to the very top and down the other side—they crossed similar tracks encircling the summit—and all those tracks, or maybe it was just loosened snow, sparkled in the sun, and the cone gradually moved behind the train, and Boris Lvovich even switched places with Tanya so he wouldn't get a crick in his neck, but could watch it gradually disappearing—and still, something on the summit gleamed. "Yes, I see, it really does resemble one," Boris Lvovich said uncertainly. "It doesn't look like that's what it is," said Tanya as she began to unpack their things. Boris Lvovich tried to remember the name of the phenomenon when people think they see a sailboat sailing in the sky or when someone dying of thirst sees a caravan of camels or an oasis—a mirage, that was it, although Boris Lvovich thought there was a more precise word; sitting in his previous place, facing the direction the train was moving, so he could see the landscape rush by; he spread out a map of the republic and kept his camera with the telephoto lens close by; the red line indicating the railroad ran close to the state border—beyond the border, which was marked by a thick double line, there were no hills or valleys, no rivers, no railroads, no high-ways; just a continuous white field, as if the whole area were covered in snow, with only a few populated areas marked by neutral circles, as if there were hardly any people in the country— just primitive, isolated settlements. A station flashed by the window and Boris Lvovich barely managed to read the name, rather, he guessed it, because he'd already memorized the names on the map, and from that station, the railroad moved even closer to the state border and then ran parallel to it—beyond the window were monotonous plains, and further on, hills, and even mountains. The area beyond the hills—and maybe even the hills themselves—were shown on the map as white, like the North Pole. In the distance, though, some villages appeared—with barely perceptible toy houses; and suddenly right next to the train, below it, so that Boris Lvovich had to stand up to see, ran barbed wire—two rows, and between them he saw striped columns flash by—"Tanya, Turkey!" shouted Boris Lvovich, lowering the window with one hand and pulling her to the window; she nodded meaningfully at the wall and a hot dry wind burst into the compartment. Boris Lvovich stuck his arm out the window up to his shoulder, and it parted the air, rushing over the barbed wire, and he even thought it extended beyond the wire—that meant that the villages on the plateau and even on the low hills weren't in our country, but why did they look empty? Maybe the white map was right? Although come to think of it, how could you possibly see people at that distance? There were barely distinguishable little houses with flat roofs, and in them were peasants, probably poor, but property owners nonetheless, and they didn't have to join any communal farms, and the laws were completely different, but the land was identical, and the houses also looked the same—the silhouette of a tower resembling a grain-elevator silo rose over the little flat-roofed houses—"A mosque! A minaret!" Tanya and Boris Lvovich exclaimed simultaneously. "Well of course, they're Muslim," Tanya said. "Why didn't I realize that right away?"

thought Boris Lvovich. There, beyond the hills, there were probably a lot of villages, all with minarets, because there a village
without a minaret was just as unthinkable as a village here
without a village soviet, but people didn't have to slink to these
minarets, they walked solemnly, because that was their duty.
Grabbing his camera and focusing the telephoto lens on the
village and the minaret, Boris Lvovich began to take pictures,
frame after frame, even sticking his telephoto lens out the
window a bit as if he were firing round after round at the surrounding territory; he hurried, because the village got smaller
every second and would soon be hidden behind the hill, and
besides, the border guards might notice him and inform the next
station, or talk to the train's engineer by walkie-talkie, and then
two ferocious representatives of the Ministry of Internal Affairs
would burst into the compartment and drag Boris Lvovich out
with his camera, although the territory that he was photograph-
ing was Turkish, but the border is the border. A bit further on
was more barbed wire—two rows at first, then more, this was
probably a neutral zone, the same stunted weeds and the same
prickly bushes grew on both sides of this forbidden zone, and
there were wood towers with vertical wooden ladders leading to
observation platforms covered with awnings; the same kind of
towers stood behind the wire—the awnings were supported by
poles, and the platforms were empty—they probably weren't
our towers, and some immobile figures could be seen on one of
them far-off, probably Turkish guards; Boris Lvovich even
thought they were wearing fezzes and carrying ancient
weapons—he and Tanya were climbing the vertical ladder, Boris
Lvovich in the lead, grasping the crossbeam with one hand and
holding out his and Tanya's passports with the other—olive-
skinned Turkish border guards wearing fezzes set their 1896-era
weapons to the side, leaned over the platform, and reached
down, helping them into the tower, just like those bearded

gold-tanned explorers with clear Scandinavian eyes had reached out to them from the summit of the snowy cone: neither group required passports, they understood everything anyway. A familiar, bittersweet lump rose in Boris Lvovich's throat; retreating into the far corner of the compartment so he wouldn't be noticed, he shot several pictures of the tower with the motionless figures of those guards—they might have been our guards for that matter, or maybe just additional posts supporting the awning, and the minaret in the village with the flat-roofed houses could be a watchtower or simply a silo. The rows of barbed wire gradually receded, and the towers, just as the map showed. The last thing Boris Lvovich saw was a sandy road— most likely never traveled—disappearing in the distance, parallel to the rows of wire, and losing itself amid the distant hills; it grew dark quickly as though evening had fallen: the train was passing through a kind of valley with mountains on both sides. Boris Lvovich took out his transistor radio, but only heard a dry crackling, because the walls of the train didn't let radio waves through, and Boris Lvovich knew this, but decided to check just in case. In the evening they ate chicken—Tanya laid out pieces of white meat for Boris Lvovich, while she herself sucked on the wings; that night Boris Lvovich was tormented by heartburn, because after all it wasn't a hot meal, and the evening of the next day, they arrived in Moscow. The bright lights of the station swam through the rain-streaked windows, but they saw Andrei even before the train stopped—for some reason he had a carry-all, and was standing amid the crowds meeting the train, his neck craned, tensely searching the windows of the cars. Boris Lvovich and Tanya knocked at the window to catch his attention, but he didn't see them right away because he was short-sighted and wore glasses. When he did see them, he waved and followed the car, rather awkwardly, because other people began to crowd him. Boris Lvovich, Tanya, and Andrei stood on the platform under a drizzling autumn rain; Tanya held Andrei close as she always did, afraid that he'd be taken away from her, and, pulling his head toward her, she kissed him on the cheeks and forehead; Boris Lvovich also gave him a peck on the cheek, but had to stand on tiptoes to do it. Andrei had soft skin just like he did when he was a child, and a rough, thin beard. For some reason Boris Lvovich found it very unpleasant that Andrei had a beard, that he didn't shave every day like Boris Lvovich—he could have even shaved every other day—but Andrei was still frail, and he slumped as always. Andrei had brought a coat for Boris Lvovich in his bag, because when they left, it was still summer; they were shoved because they were blocking the platform. Boris Lvovich put the coat on, and then they got all tangled up in their bags—who would take what; Andrei walked ahead, looking back at his parents, either irritated that they were falling behind, or afraid that someone would push them. In the taxi, Tanya and her son sat in the back and Boris Lvovich listened intently to their conversation, but they were talking nonsense, and Boris Lvovich kept turning around to them, trying to joke and pun, as he always did, because his son understood him right away; but all his witticisms hung in the air, running into something insurmountable, as though a glass partition separated him from his wife and son sitting behind him, though they were driving home and Andrei had brought a coat for him, so that meant he was living at home. Tamara Borisovna, Boris Lvovich's mother, met them in the foyer—the table was set for supper, but Boris Lvovich quickly checked all the rooms, turned on the lights everywhere, and tightened the weights on the pendulum clock hanging in the foyer. Everything was in its place: his desk, his books, the armchair in his mother's room, and in Andrei's room, above his couch bed, the damaged plaster with cracks running through it: Andrei used to play ball in his room; it was time to fix that bad spot. Everything was homey, not like a hotel—how good it was to be home, especially after what they'd had to put up with during the trip; in fact, the whole story with the hotel now seemed almost amusing, and Boris Lvovich actually couldn't wait to tell it at the table when they all sat down to dinner, especially the part about how he'd taught a lesson to that sallow-faced administrator wrapped in a shawl. "Taanya! Taaanya!" he called, going from room to room as if he were in the forest. "After wandering long and far, Tanya and I came home in a car; our son Andrei arrived and carried our bags away," Boris Lvovich joked, entering his office—Tanya and Andrei were sitting across from each other at the low round table, where Boris Lvovich usually worked, talking quietly and seriously about something, and when he came in they stopped as if they'd been speaking of some illness Boris Lvovich had but wasn't supposed to know about. Rising from the armchair, Tanya turned to Boris Lvovich, as though protecting her son: "They're getting married, and then they want to leave," she said. Andrei lit a cigarette with an imported lighter, took a drag, and let the smoke out in a picturesque manner, but his fingers were trembling—they had trembled since he was beaten up and had a concussion; he'd been beaten by a group of young people he was hanging out with by chance, beaten for no reason by a tall lunker with long hair, wearing a sweater. Boris Lvovich drove Andrei to the hospital and visited him every day, talked to the doctors, went to see his attorney colleagues, went to the police, to a prosecutor he knew, and to the institute where the lunker was studying. When he saw him, his heart jumped and sank, and the wrong words came out, and the big oaf remained unpunished. On the eve of Boris Lvovich's and Tanya's departure, Andrei broke a crystal vase that Tanya purchased several days before— he'd just thrown it on the floor because Tanya said they wouldn't leave, that they couldn't because of Tamara Borisovna, and Andrei shouldn't count on it. "Then I know what to do!" Andrei shouted. The next day he bought a new vase, exactly the same kind, with his own pocket money. Almost every day he brought home letters from over there that people gave him to read; Boris Lvovich and Tanya read these letters avidly, but Tamara Borisovna demonstratively slammed the door and locked her herself in her room—she thought that Boris Lvovich and Tanya were pandering to Andrei, especially Boris Lvovich, that he was simply corrupting Andrei instead of keeping him in check. There were outright battles between Andrei and Tamara Borisovna—Andrei would call Boris Lvovich at work and ask him to calm Tamara Borisovna down, but she remained implacable and shouted at Andrei that he was an idiot and a milksop mollusk, because he was falling under the influence of provocateurs; he hurled a slipper at his grandmother, and Boris Lvovich was covered in sweat, because Tamara Borisovna couldn't see what was happening, she didn't want to see—she was fine with things the way they were. In a drawer of Boris Lvovich's desk, were papers he wrote about Soviet law in the 1920s, and he was afraid to show the manuscripts even to people he knew, and Andrei wrote stories that couldn't be sent to any publisher, and he couldn't find work, and Boris Lvovich had to hide his face sometimes, and Andrei did too, especially after he was beaten. Even when he was in grammar school, a few kids from the other class once formed a wall in the schoolyard; they stood linked together, their shoulders touching, and when Andrei tried to go around them, the whole wall silently moved either to the right or the left, and one of them, a fat, fair-skinned kid with narrow eyes like a pig shouted "Sarah!" at him, which was particularly humiliating, since it was a girl's name too, and he deliberately mispronounced the "r"s. Andrei rushed from one corner of the yard to the other, while they all hooted, and when they got tired of it, the pale kid kneed him in the backside and Andrei and his book bag tumbled onto the asphalt; the book bag went flying, and Andrei's glasses broke, but at home he didn't say a word, just that he lost his glasses, and only many years later did he blurt it out to Tamara Borisovna during one of their battles. Tamara Borisovna just shrugged her shoulders and said that she'd never experienced this sort of thing herself. "It's the right decision," said Boris Lvovich, looking at his son's face, which was dark-eyed but had cheekbones that were slightly wide like his mother's, and Boris Lvovich even wanted to add that it was high time, but the floor suddenly moved under him like it had in the hotel when he returned from the director's office; the floor, the book shelves, and the chandelier all swayed at the same time, and for a second he even thought that the room had grown dark.

VII
A MINUTE OF SILENCE

Boris Lvovich could see his hairy stomach and greenish wart through the rippling layer of water as though he were looking at a rocky sea bed somewhere near the town of Pitsunda, where the water was always transparent and made the polished stones that tossed about seem bigger than they really were; despite the magnification of the water, it was clear that the wart hadn't grown, it had even dried up a bit, and if Boris Lvovich had wanted to, he could easily have picked it off. The sound of water flowing from the faucet—Boris Lvovich always let it run to compensate for the water leaking down the drain—prevented him from distinguishing the words Tanya was saying to Andrei on the phone, but this made everything even cozier, like in his youth, when he would come home during vacation or for a holiday and take a bath and the flames flared brightly and crackled in the iron stove; from time to time he would toss another piece of coal or chunk of wood in without getting out of the bathtub, only raising himself a little so that the hot water wouldn't run out, and he could hear his parents' voices somewhere in the kitchen or the dining room. Was Tamara Borisovna, his mother, really younger then than he was now? He could hear the voice of their housekeeper, Aunt Shura: the table was laid in the dining room, and his father kept pinching things from the plates, even though Tamara Borisovna forbade him because it was bad for him, and besides, everyone should sit down at the table together, so they waited for Boris Lvovich. Then he got married and Tanya came with him, and she, too, participated in the hustle and bustle of preparing dinner, and her ringing laughter sounded from the kitchen. Now, just as then, he left the hot water running so the water in the tub wouldn't get cold, and submerged himself, leaving only his mouth and nose above the water in order to breathe, and the sounds of voices and the table being set reached his ears through a layer of water, and merged into an underwater hum, and the water flowing from the faucet also joined in with a kind of gurgle, all of which transported him to an even earlier time that he barely remembered—but clearly it was also bath time—when he would be wrapped in a fuzzy towel and allowed to eat in bed; and now in the kitchen, dinner was also waiting for him. Tanya had been clinking dishes and frying something, and Tamara Borisovna had already slammed the refrigerator door several times—she and Tanya almost never spoke now, only when absolutely necessary, and Tamara Borisovna tried to avoid the kitchen when Tanya was there. Tanya's voice on the phone merged with the slamming of the refrigerator door and the shuffling of Tamara Borisovna's feet in Boris Lvovich's cozy underwater hum. "Tanya! Taa-aanya!" he called out, squatting in the bathtub and cracking open the door to the hallway to hear what she and Andrei were talking about. Andrei and Inna hadn't gone to the marriage bureau yet, but Andrei spent the night at her place for some reason, occasionally dropping in for just a minute—Boris Lvovich thought that there must be a misunderstanding; he and Tanya had returned from vacation and were back at home, but Andrei was spending the night somewhere else and calling them at night, not to say that he'd be home late and not to worry, but to tell them that Lushka, Inna's dog, really looked like a cat and even scratched, and its tail curled up. The day after Tanya and Boris Lvovich arrived home, Andrei said that he was going to sleep at Inna's, and in the evening Boris Lvovich and Tanya took a walk; approaching their building on the way home, they gazed at the windows—the window of

Andrei's room, that is, and for a moment they thought they saw a light in the window, the old floor lamp with a faded blue shade; Tanya had meant to throw the lamp out for ages and replace it with a desk lamp so Andrei didn't ruin his eyesight, though Boris Lvovich was against it, because Andrei read lying down anyway and it would only be a senseless waste of money. They slowed their pace, and the same bluish light could be seen in many windows—it was just the reflection of the street lamps—and Andrei's window sparkled coldly, like the windows in darkened rooms; nevertheless, when they got home they peeked into Andrei's room, and Boris Lvovich even turned the overhead light on—the floor lamp really was quite old, even broken, and on the wall over Andrei's couch bed there was still a white spot from the crumbling plaster. Boris Lvovich again submerged his head in the bath water. Tanya's voice, as she talked to Andrei, the sounds in the kitchen, the noise of the running water, again merged into a cozy hum, returning Boris Lvovich to the past, as though he'd placed a giant seashell to his ear as he used to do in childhood. Well, he himself had moved out to Tanya's, although they'd gone to City Hall beforehand, and his pals had told him that it wasn't too late yet, and of course all kinds of passions and pranks are characteristic of youth. "Taa-aanya! Taa-anya!" Boris Lvovich called out, raising himself a bit and looking into the hallway. "I can't come now, can't you hear, I'm on the phone." She was chatting quietly and seriously with Andrei the way she did right when they returned home: when Boris Lvovich went into his office, Tanya and Andrei were sitting at the round table and discussing something, and they talked the same way when Andrei would come home for a minute to eat lunch or change his clothes, as if they were hiding something from Boris Lvovich. During one of those visits, Tanya placed herself between her son and Boris Lvovich—like that first time—and said that Andrei and Inna had decided not to go there, but overseas, because war

217

could flare up again at any time, and Andrei was a man, and even young women served there, and in this respect she and Inna were in complete agreement; Boris Lvovich was surprised that he hadn't thought of this himself, and he only asked one thing of his son: don't work against our people over there, because Andrei should remember that he and Tanya would remain hostages here, and when he said this, the floor swayed under him again, like it did then, the day they arrived home, and also in the hotel. Andrei lit a cigarette and said that he understood perfectly, but the floor swayed under Boris Lvovich nonetheless, and he thought the room grew dark. Tamara Borisovna looked oblig-ingly into the bathroom, "Do you need something?" "Close the door," Boris Lvovich replied rudely, because he didn't like his mother seeing him naked, but she wasn't the least bit embar-rassed—that was her personality in a nutshell—and besides which, she was particularly willing to help him when the least bit of tension arose in his relationship with Tanya—at any rate, that was what Tanya said. Tamara Borisovna shuffled off toward the kitchen in a hurt and pointedly independent way, and still, there must be some misunderstanding, which had nothing to do with Boris Lvovich, especially when he plunged into the bath water up to his head and heard the noise of seashells. "Tell him he's Karla!" Boris Lvovich shouted again, rising to the surface— Karl was Beethoven's nephew, his only attachment in his later years, whose dissolute behavior hastened the great composer's death. Boris Lvovich had been keen on Beethoven at one time, and often told this story at the table, a bittersweet lump rising in his throat, and it seemed to him that only Andrei understood him. The nickname "Karla" softened the whole story a bit and also introduced something humorous, as Boris Lvovich saw it. "Did you hear what I said?" Boris Lvovich shouted, turning off the faucet so he could hear Tanya's telephone conversation better—"Tell him that he's Karla!" Boris Lvovich cried, standing up and looking out into the hallway, but Tanya just waved him away as though shooing an annoying fly, and when he sank back into the underwater hum and was examining his stomach with the greenish benign wart on it, she came in unexpectedly and said that the day after tomorrow Andrei would be moving to Inna's for good.

It was Sunday, and they got up not too early, not too late, as always on a Saturday or Sunday when there were things to be done. Andrei was still asleep—he'd spent that night at home, the last night—and Boris Lvovich and Tanya entered their son's room cautiously, on tiptoe; Tanya quietly opened the wardrobe that held Andrei's clothes and began to take them out and fold them neatly on the chest of drawers and his chair—Andrei was sleeping with his mouth open, with his arm outstretched as he usually did, one hand hanging off the bed with its delicate, almost childlike fingers, and the other tucked under his cheekbones, which were slightly broad like Tanya's, and she usually slept just as serenely and deeply. On the weekends or during the holidays, Andrei could sleep as much as he wanted, and Boris Lvovich even proposed conducting an experiment: if they didn't wake him up, just how long would he sleep—until one or until four?— because Boris Lvovich himself usually slept no later than six in the morning. When Andrei slept, Tanya always walked around on tiptoe and said "Sshhh" to Boris Lvovich, even if he was speaking quietly, and she forbade him to go into his room, although this didn't disturb Andrei; but today they had to pack Andrei's things, and for some reason Tanya wanted to give him as many sheets and blanket covers as possible, as though he were a bride who had to have a dowry. Boris Lvovich stood about awkwardly in the corner near Andrei's bookcase as if he needed to get something from it, and he even slid the glass back—Andrei opened his eyes for a second—dark eyes, like Boris Lvovich's, with slightly blue whites: "milky" as Tanya called them for some reason; then he shut them right away, sinking back into his previous tranquility. "Ssshhh!" Tanya said to Boris Lvovich, placing her palm to her lips, tearing herself away from the sheets and blanket covers for a minute. In childhood, Andrei had lived in another town with Boris Lvovich's parents, and when Tanya and Boris Lvovich came for the holidays, or just for a few days, Andrei ran into their room in a flannel nightshirt down to his ankles— his bare feet slapped across the floor and he crawled up onto their bed. "Papa and Mama are here!" he proudly announced to everyone he knew—it turned out that he, too, had parents like other children, and his were even better because they lived in Moscow, where the Mausoleum and Red Square with its clock towers were; his parents were elusive, rare, and because of this, particularly interesting, and on the day after their arrival Andrei would get up early as though it were his birthday and presents were waiting for him in the next room; but grandmother wouldn't let him go in and wake his parents, though he'd manage to get in nonetheless, his bare feet pattering across the floor, and clambering into his parents' bed, he'd settle down between them with his velvety skin and his long, flannel shirt. Piles of clothes lay on the chest of drawers and the chair, ready to be packed, and Boris Lvovich and Tanya went to get the suitcase out of the storage space between the kitchen and the foyer, and then they all had breakfast in the kitchen: the three of them and Tamara Borisovna, just like on regular weekends, all together as if nothing had happened or would happen, and as usual, Tanya made sandwiches with cheese and sausage for Andrei. These sandwiches always infuriated Boris Lvovich, and Tamara Borisovna, too: couldn't Andrei manage to make his own sandwiches? Boris Lvovich would tell people and everyone would shake their heads judgmentally, but Tanya didn't care and continued to make sandwiches for Andrei, trying to put in as much butter as possible, and Andrei would slowly eat one sandwich after another as if that were the way things should be. An autumn drizzle fell outside, the light in the kitchen was on, and Tanya was fussing around the stove and with the sandwiches, while Tamara Borisovna ate silently; and when Tanya poured herself some tea, her hands shook and the hot water spilled on the table cloth, but Andrei didn't like tea, so Tanya poured him some tomato juice as usual, and while he was drinking the juice she was back in his room packing the suitcase. Then she explained how many sheets and pillow cases she was giving him, and where things were, and that she also had more blanket covers, but they wouldn't fit in the suitcase and he could take them next time. Andrei smoked and in between talking about politics, he mentioned Lushka, who looked like a cat, and when he held the lighter up to his cigarette his delicate fingers trembled slightly.

Andrei began to put on his nylon jacket, but Tanya suddenly had to sew something on to it and took it off him, so as not to sew up his memory or maybe his mind, Boris Lvovich didn't remember exactly how the superstition went; once again, he stood near Andrei's bookcase, and Tamara Borisovna shuffled silently around her room—the door to her room was open slightly; Andrei continued to talk about politics and Lushka and put on his nylon jacket again. Tanya explained one last thing to him and cleaned his jacket, which he was now wearing, with a damp brush, while he looked at himself in the mirror hanging in the foyer. Then she brought the suitcase out of the room and set it down next to him, and Tamara Borisovna appeared, stopping in the doorway of her room, and Boris Lvovich went into the foyer, and a strange silence fell, like the silence before a coffin is hammered shut, and the only sound was the measured ticking of the clock pendulum. Tanya suddenly burst into tears, almost a wail; grabbing her son and hugging him tightly, she covered his face and hair with kisses, and Tamara Borisovna also burst loudly into tears, but Boris Lvovich bit his lips in order to refrain, and Andrei kissed each of them in a row, and then once again, and his eyes were also teary, and for a second the clock could be heard again. Boris Lvovich opened the front door to get the whole thing over with as quickly as possible. Picking up the suitcase, Andrei walked out in the hall and down the stairs; Tanya and Tamara Borisovna walked out almost as far as the landing, listening to Andrei walk downstairs. Boris Lvovich also walked over and stood behind them on tiptoe, stretching his neck, but Andrei's steps could no longer be heard. Tanya ran to the balcony and Boris Lvovich followed her; they stood in the rain in the piercing autumn wind—Andrei appeared in the narrow passage between the building and the boulevard, a stooped figure wearing a nylon jacket and carrying his suitcase. He walked along the boulevard and disappeared for a second time behind the trees with yellow, almost fallen leaves, then appeared once again on the other side of the street, but already quite far away—a small figure with a suitcase. A trolley rolled up and hid the figure, and when it drove off, Andrei was no longer there—the trolley had carried him off, and Boris Lvovich and Tanya, feeling neither the damp nor the wind, watched the wet trolley until it disappeared from sight.

September 15, 1976

TEN MINUTES OF WAITING

When I get out of the metro I always check the time on the electronic clock attached to the lamppost nearby—not my own watch, which is always fast, a fact I accept, believing in the truth of the time it shows because it allows me to feel a pleasant disappointment every time—oh, it's still early, I'll have to wait. Twenty past eight. The line for the city bus starts at the post with the clock. This line stretches along the sidewalk, then turns, blocking the exit from the metro and turns again, so it resembles the letter "L"; the metro exit runs right into the horizontal plane of the "L," and I cut through it, heading in the direction of the institute bus stop, but hesitate: should I take the city bus? If you get on the end of that line, which looks frightfully long but actually moves rather quickly because the buses come every two minutes, then you'll leave in five or six minutes—just as long as you don't try to get on the first bus that comes, since they let everyone on who wants on, you can usually find a seat, sometimes near the window, even after most of the passengers on line have sat down. Then, sitting in the warmth—the city buses are always well heated—you arrive at the "Kilometer #25" stop a few minutes before the institute bus gets there. Crossing the highway and entering through the gates' stone pillars, adorned with cracked glass globes and the half-erased inscription "VIDE," which was supposed to be an acronym for the name of our institute, you can walk along the main road, whose surface is gashed by two deep ruts crusted with ice that mark the tracks of the institute bus; the bus drives in through the gates and unloads everyone halfway to the entrance, because farther on there are potholes and mounds of ice, and, according to the drivers, an overloaded bus could break its axle. Then, rather than being part of a procession resembling either a column of demonstrators or a funeral, you can walk all the way to the main building, enter the lobby in no hurry, because there are still ten minutes left until nine o'clock; you can take your time and, manifestly ignoring the timekeeper, take your card out of the slot, number 2602, examine it carefully on both sides to be sure the timekeeper hasn't played any dirty tricks—just so she knows I'm checking up on her— and only then, almost inadvertently, as though doing her a favor, place the card in the clock, lazily punch in the time, jauntily return the card to its slot, and—casting a contemptuous look at the timekeeper, who of course has sensed the full measure of her humiliation—cross the hall with the proprietary gait of an institute director, and take cover in the hallway. All of this is in theory, however. In practice everything is different—as I know well, because on several occasions I've taken the city bus. First, all kinds of acquaintances, co-workers or just plain tag-along leeches always attach themselves to the head of the line with a cool, calm look about them, as though they'd been standing in one place their whole lives; these leeches crowd around the door of the bus, trying to pass in front of you, and they manage to, even before all the seats are taken and the driver lets in anyone who wants in. When this kind of leech pops up, right by the bus door, waiting for a convenient moment to slip through, an invisible battle of strength arises—we don't push each other, but our muscles are strained to the limit, like two fighters frozen in a motionless stance; we feel the hostile tension even through our coats, the mutual, scorching hatred that awaits only a momentary weakness on the part of the opponent to break him and slip ahead. Sometimes I manage to prevail, and then I enter the bus with a modestly victorious look, like a champion who has won another victory; on those evenings, rubbing down after a shower, I look at myself in the mirror with satisfaction, and ripple my muscles, which seem to bulge like they do in studies by Leonardo da Vinci or in anatomy textbooks; most of the time, however, I give in because my nerves can't take it, since single combat around the bus door is more a matter of psychology than strength. So when I feel that I can't bear it and have capitulated, and the other person pushes ahead, green circles of hatred and impotence begin to swim in front of my eyes, and I feel as though my wife was pawed in my presence and I silently put up with it. Since it's impossible to live with this feeling for long, I start down the path of self-deception, convincing myself that this guy was already on line, that I simply didn't notice him, and that maybe I'm actually the one who wormed my way in and cut in line. Even greater unpleasantness lies in store for me inside the bus. If there aren't many seats free and there's no choice, you sit down wherever, without thinking about it, just to get a seat; but if rows of empty seats greet you—like ten market stands piled high with oranges and no line; or a gathering of beautiful women and you may invite each of them to dance—then you stop, your breath taken away by the possibilities, and most important, by the necessity of adapting to the situation in a flash: where will the sun be (get as far away as possible), which side is heated better or has a curtain, is there a driver's booth so you can watch the road as though you yourself were at the wheel? At the same time one mustn't forget the perils of the very front seats (children, the handicapped, all in all it's better not to get involved), while the back is too hot and reeks of gasoline, and if you're in the middle it's really difficult to exit. So there I stand, gasping, while people bump and bypass me, taking recently empty seats before my very eyes—a crowd, bursts into the store and lines up at the counters, or military academy cadets appear out of the blue and soon all the women are taken for the evening. After that there's the march alone

227

along the road that leads to the main building; the unfamiliar solitude can make even a familiar road frightening, and you catch your breath—what if the clock tricked you and you're late, and everyone's watching you out the windows, it feels as though an invisible barrel were aimed at you alone—and you speed up, almost running, swerving and slipping in the ice-covered rut, and your heart is pounding in your ears, and you calm down a bit only when you see the institute bus catching up to you. You move to the side, sinking up to your knees in snow to let it pass, but then you're almost running again because you can't end up at the end of the column, or, even worse, behind it.

All the same, should I take the city bus?

I stand smack in the middle between the city bus and the institute stop, buffeted by the four winds like the soldier from Eduard Bagritsky's poem, because the metro stop I've just come out of, the last stop of the line, was built according to a general plan long before any residential construction, so the only thing rising above the endless snow-covered fields are four elevated glass metro entrances; if they were connected to one another they'd form an enormous rectangle—four glass entrances, three of which can really only be divined, shrouded as they are in the morning blizzard—at some point there will be a square here with a monument and a department store, but for the moment, when you ride across this field on the bus, especially if the bus is speeding up, it seems like you're in an airplane racing down the runway—just a minute more and you'll lift off the ground and a city will unexpectedly spread out under you, though only a minute ago it was impossible to imagine that there were houses anywhere close by—there is only an endless snowy field, and further, at the side of the road, some boulders; in the summer, when everything's dry, barren strips of soil poke out between them, it feels like you're on the moon, and on the other side of the road are some rectangular cement slabs—probably brought here for construction—standing in endless rows a bit apart from one another, forlorn and identical, like a skyscraper city or a Jewish cemetery.

There's hardly a soul at the institute bus stop, and there almost never is; thanks to my watch and constant fear of being late, I'm always one of the first to get here; there are only two or three women technicians, sheltering from the wind behind a beer kiosk with the sign "Russian Kvass," which was built just when the metro station opened. One of the women has the rubber-ball head of a shrewish fishwife; the other is a former machine gunner with the face of a hussy and drawn cheeks on which, like fallen dough, deep wrinkles have settled—just a bit more and her face will turn into a baked apple. She collects the bus tickets from her co-workers on her own initiative, and she does it so professionally that in the beginning, forgetting that I was on the institute bus, I thought she was the conductor. Both of these women come first or at the same time that I do—and both of them can tell unerringly, just looking at the bus from a distance, perhaps from how it drives or turns, who is driving today—Minya or Grinya; they burst into the bus first and immediately occupy all the convenient seats for their girlfriends and supervisor with shopping bags; they instantly engage in amorous squabbling with the drivers, the meaning of which I have a hard time grasping because they have their own personal affairs and personal accounts to settle, and there may even be some hanky panky going on. I was very surprised when I saw them once at work—what happened to all that bus-ride independence? Once I happened to run into our assistant director outside the institute—where did his bossiness go?—he began sharing some of his thoughts, even his doubts, with me, and gave himself away: I could suddenly read indecision and weakness in his eyes, plain ordinary weakness, and I thought that he probably humiliates himself in front of his wife in the evenings like I do, so that at night he can get his due; and to this very day he can't forgive himself (or maybe me) for his openness, and now he skirts me in the hallway as though he has syphilis and I'm the only one who knows.

I stand between the two bus stops, the city and the institute bus, to show my independence from the junior personnel—the women who have hidden behind the beer stand have now moved over to the institute stop, and a few others have gathered as well, and all of them are crowded in a small area where the snow has been trampled down—and moreover my positioning allows me to comfort myself with the thought that perhaps I will in fact take city transportation, especially since the line there has diminished considerably and its tail-end has shortened, revealing the metro station exit, from which our employees stretch in a doleful line, merging into the waiting groups like a rivulets of ink into a blot. Two young laboratory assistants pass by me.

One of them is a little munchkin, almost a schoolgirl, and wears a mini fur coat open to reveal well-shaped legs shod in raspberry-colored boots with laces, crowned with a coquettish little bow—she hangs on the arm of her taller girlfriend, resembling a circus dog with ribbons and bells walking on its back legs and leaning on the trainer's stick with her front paws. Vitiushkin appears out of the metro. Small, feeble, with a long hooked nose, he looks like a newly hatched chick, especially when he walks in little steps like a character from a cartoon, mincing down the institute halls, the soles of his feet turned out (he suffers from flat-footedness), a grayish-yellow down fluttering above his bald spot, and in his hands a tray of chicken eggs—the object of his experimental research; locking himself away in his laboratory he disappears for a long time—he's probably pecking at the eggs with his beak, having first held them up to the light. In strange contrast to his figure, his face has a derisive, even spiteful expression, which, by the way, disappears the moment talk turns to scientific work; his face then becomes serious and even deeply ceremonious, as though he is listening to the state anthem—at those moments he immediately brushes aside any joking comment, although he also takes it in with a tired closing of his eyelids—as though to say, yes, yes, I get it, I appreciate it, but my God, how inappropriate—and it seems to me that he would close his eyes in the very same way if he was hit in the face. After him, Gauze appears. He's twice as tall as Vitiushkin, and his gaze is full of sorrow, but it's sham sorrow, because both his expression and his forehead are sheeplike and it always seems to me that he might walk over, put his head on my shoulder and ask me for some dried, last-season grass to chew. He and Vitiushkin are inseparable: they work together and together they rush down the halls with chicken eggs in hand—and for that matter Gauze gauges his seven-league steps so he doesn't get too far ahead of Vitiushkin—and precisely at half past one a short but forceful knock comes at the door of the room where I sit—you can set your watch by it—and it's Vitiushkin and Gauze inviting me to go to the cafeteria with them, and though I almost always turn them down, they have done it with enviable persistence for several years now—two heads: one birdlike, at the level of the door handle, the other sheeplike, just under the door jamb, but one common torso, though you can't see it because it remains on the other side of the door. Over there are the Mitrokhins. He is fat, with somewhat dirty nails; she is tall and dry, with a long face, distorted either in surprise or horror. He walks just behind her, carrying her shopping bag—like Sancho Panza behind Don Quixote. In the bus they always read newspapers, whole piles of papers that they pull out of the shopping bag, shuffling them and exchanging them with the silent businesslike manner of professional card players.

It's nine twenty-eight and the crowd waiting at the institute stop is no longer a blot, but a genuine ink spot spreading at the edges, though I don't see this because I myself am standing in the crowd, closer to the edge, where the spot fades out—true, the wind is stronger here and the snow isn't trampled down, but this is a better place—according to my reckoning, this is precisely where the front door of the bus should stop—though I might have miscalculated, because one of the drivers opens the front door only, and the other—the back door only, and who knows which one will come; but even if the front door one comes, it's unlikely I'll get a seat, because a lot of people have gathered and everyone will rush forward at the same time, and indeed, the bus should have already been here a long time ago, and every one is looking hopefully off into the snowy distance, and even the fish-wife and the former machine-gunnist have been deceived several times, mistaking a regular bus for the institute one and needlessly crying out either "Minya!" or "Grinya!" but most remain silent and aren't incensed, although it's clear that there must have been another drinking bout at the garage yesterday, and if necessary, everyone will stand like this until evening, hiding in their collars, turning their back to the wind—like a sculptural ensemble called "Waiting," a monument to obedience, but then I don't say anything either. And the end of the line near the city bus stop is already a lot shorter and before my very eyes it shortens further with cata-strophic speed, the bus swallowing up people who have just walked up as though they were on a retractable measuring tape.

"Ah, to hell with it: better to take the city bus," I say unexpect-edly even for myself, not talking to anyone in particular, and I cautiously work my way out of the crowd and the farther off I get, the more decisive and swift my steps become, and now I'm almost running, and from the crowd behind me, with a cry of "Let's get the city bus!" several people take off, and after them more and more, and among them are Gauze and Vitiushkin, who can barely keep up with his long-legged friend, and the little munchkin in the mini-fur coat, and the Mitrokhins, and they are all smiling at me, and their faces glow with excitement and resolve. Looking back, I wave to them, encouraging them:

"Hurry! Hurry!" and it sounds like "Hurrah!" like "Forward! Follow me!" and I feel like I'm a robber chief, a leader, a commander—after all, I was the one who got them up and moving, and at the same time we're all equal because we're walking in one chain, and we have a common fate, and each of us is ready to die for the other. Out of breath from the running, I get on the end of the line and obediently, after me, like train cars after a halted steam engine, the rest of them line up. Now it seems to me that the line is moving too slowly—what if the bus leaves and doesn't take every one?—how will I look at them then?—after all I was the one who roused them. We're almost up to the door and I notice, proudly, that there are still empty seats in the bus—I was right to bring them here! I step up and look back victoriously, but with surprise and horror I see unfamiliar, foreign faces behind me—the kind of thing that only happens in dreams—but across the snowy field, stretching out in a running chain are the people who were just standing behind me—Vitiushkin—he can barely keep up with Gauze, the munchkin in her mini fur, the Mitrokhins—they are all running, bent, their heads hunched in their shoulders, as though they were afraid they'd be hit by a bullet, they're running to the institute stop, where you can see a bus with a crowd blackening the area around its doors. Unfamiliar, alien faces confront me, their features growing larger—I can already make out the acne on their faces, and their eyes are wild—I'm probably blocking them—and I jump off the step and run across the snowy field—if only I can make it in time, catch up!—no longer a robber chief, leader, or commander, but a soldier left behind.

I stand, pressed between the bodies of co-workers, swaying in time with them. Outside the window a snow-covered field spreads out, the glass entrance to the metro swims by me, the lamppost with the clock, the line. The bus circles around the central part of the field, turns around, and, stopping for a second, quickly gathers speed, like an airplane tearing off down the runway. Ahead the snow-covered boulders come closer, and on the left you can glimpse the rectangular cement slabs—looking like a skyscraper city or a Jewish cemetery. Perhaps the bus will lift off from the ground after all?

March 31, 1971

FELLOW TRAVELER

"I'm after you," I said to the woman standing in line with a little girl, and then I rushed to the phone booth.

In profile my face forms a triangle—lines from the forehead and chin meet at the nose, which forms the tip of a triangle, giving me an expression of driven impetuosity that's basically undermined, however, by the oblique cut of my chin. As I dialed, I kept my eye on the woman with the little girl, and after pressing the third number, the phone gave off a busy signal, so, slamming down the receiver, I rushed back to my previous place.

"No one else showed up?" I asked the woman, but she only shrugged, a bit surprised.

There were two or three cars at the taxi stand, but the drivers apparently didn't want to go anywhere, so a woman lugging a suitcase, begging and cursing them, scuttled back and forth between cars. It was rush hour, somewhere between six and seven, and the twenty-first of the month—peak time, since payday was on the sixteenth and the money hadn't been drunk up yet; the second wave of drinking was in full swing—opposite the taxi stand, from the gates of the market, which was already closing up for the day, tipsy workers emerged with torn cabbage heads in string bags, or empty-handed, smoking, or spitting— and hitting the telegraph pole or the poster advertising Garry Grodberg's concert with sniper-like accuracy. As long as I can remember, I've tried to learn how to do that, but instead of flying like a bullet, my saliva runs listlessly down my chin.

I wasn't surprised when he approached me; I had expected this for some time, and it even seemed strange to me that it didn't happen as soon as I'd arrived at the stand. His hair was tousled, his eyes coated with a foggy film.

"I'm last on line," I said to him. I wanted to say: "You're behind me," but that would have been too provocative.

"Going that way?" he asked familiarly, gesturing in the direction I needed to go—I realized immediately that I wouldn't be able to shake him off. On the other hand, the fact that he had initiated the conversation seemed reassuring—at the very least, he wasn't planning on cutting the line, and besides, I really did need to go that way.

"I'm going to the psychiatric hospital, you know, the place where they treat alcoholics," I answered, saying the second part as though just in passing, but in fact especially for him; I even think I looked meaningfully in his direction. A friend of mine worked at this hospital, I was going to see him on business, but I let the guy think that I worked there; after all, I was carrying a briefcase. For that matter, he might have thought I was going to visit some relative or friend, although my face was supposed to counter that idea, but just in case I turned my profile toward him, so that he wouldn't have any doubts on this score: of course, this was a double-edged sword, but he had probably already given my physiognomy a good once over anyway at the very start.

"I know," he nodded perfunctorily, "the alcoholic hospital, near Semashko. Hospital Number Fifteen. We can share a cab."

"No, I'm going past the bus turnaround and Semashko's in a different place altogether," I tried to object.

"That's just what I'm talking about, they're not far apart."

He didn't understand, or was pretending he didn't.

The Semashko Hospital was located quite some distance from the hospital where I was headed; this guy lived in the area—having had a drink after payday, he was going home—of course he knew the location of the hospitals around here perfectly well. For the life of me, I couldn't remember the number of the hospital where my friend worked, but he knew the number of his. I was in an awkward position, but I still hoped that everything would work out.

The woman with the suitcase who had been running from car to car had disappeared—taxis with green lights were driving up to the stand now and she had probably left.

"Transportation is always bad this time of day," I remarked, in order to win him over somehow. He didn't reply, which I thought was a bad omen.

The woman and the little girl in front of me got a cab and drove off, but a huge line had formed behind us, and everyone else could of course see that he and I were talking and even sort of staying together—they may even have thought that we had business together. In fact, there was nothing unusual about sharing a ride—taxi drivers these days are always taking multiple passengers; they get paid double or even triple this way—the line moves faster, which makes everyone happy, and I would only be holding things up if I refused to ride with him, and yet, when my taxi drove up, I stepped decisively toward it as though it were my own personal car—after all, it was my rightful turn, and why should I have to travel with some drunk who didn't even seem to be going in the same direction? But when I'd settled in next to the driver, placed my briefcase on my lap, glanced at my watch in a professional manner, the driver had turned on the meter and even turned the ignition key, and I felt like I'd been saved, like someone crossing a rickety bridge over an abyss who's finally stepped onto firm ground, he approached the car, cautiously opened the door, and sat down in the back. He sat down sort of sideways, on the very edge of the seat, just like some poor relation or supplicant. It even seemed to me that he hadn't shut the door.

"Let's go," I said, "I'm going to the hospital beyond the bus turnaround, do you know it?" For some reason I was certain that the driver knew where this hospital was, and besides, in the depths of my soul, I hoped my vagueness would dull the vigilance of the guy sitting in back or at least delay any conflict. In short, I put myself in the driver's hands, thought of him as my ally, and in case anything happened, even my defender—after all, he knew that I was the legal passenger, and the other guy was just a moocher, there by my good graces in fact, whereas the driver was an official person and therefore obliged to take the side of the law.

"You know the Semashko Hospital?" said the guy in the back seat, as soon as we'd driven off. He said it as though he were clarifying our common destination.

"Why the Semashko Hospital?" I said, but neither the guy in back nor the driver responded, so my question sort of hung in the air. However, this didn't mean that the driver had altered his position and now considered the guy in the back the main passenger instead of me; for that matter, maybe I was wrong and we were going in the same direction.

The driver turned right just out of the taxi stand, and we took off in the opposite direction to the one both the guy in back and I were headed, and this reassured me a bit: left turns were probably prohibited here and there would be a U-turn further on, but just in case I asked:

"Why did you turn right?"

The driver didn't answer—it was probably a matter of the traffic rules and he just didn't think he needed to explain it—I mean, I don't explain to my patients why I prescribe penicillin rather than valerian drops. Well, of course he could have answered, but he didn't seem to be particularly talkative—he was of an indeterminate age, on the thin side, dark-haired; he hadn't looked at me or at the guy in back even once, and it felt as if you told him you were going to the moon, he would have started the meter and turned the key in the ignition with the same calm, cool attitude.

"He's going the right way," said the guy in back. With this statement, expressing full confidence in the driver, he was in effect making a secret pact against me. I couldn't bring myself to turn around, but I could sense that he was leaning back against the seat as if he were my equal—now the driver had every reason to believe that we had taken the taxi together, as a pair, that we were even going to the same place on common business, just as the people standing in line had thought; the guy in back knew the way and understood all the signs, and I didn't understand much of anything in this regard.

We had already driven a fair distance and it seemed to me we'd even passed the place where the U-turn should have been, and now we were approaching the metro station—this was where I had taken the bus to get to the taxi stand, deliberately, in order to take a taxi, and here I was once again at the beginning, and the meter already showed thirty or forty kopecks; with every passing second I was further and further from my destination, and time was being wasted to no purpose. I should have let the guy in back go ahead of me; by now I would be almost halfway to the bus turnaround—in my mind I could see the whole long street we should have been going down: the part of it that was closer to the bus turnaround had a narrow promenade in the center, and we would be driving along side that promenade; on the right side there would be a technical school dormitory, and on the left, the brick wall of a factory, then a bit further on, a cultural center— and at that point, you'd almost arrived because you could see the bus turnaround, and just to the right of it you could see the hospital—you could even walk from there . . . This would be the right moment to ask the driver to stop and to get out of the car. From here, I could make it to the hospital by bus perfectly well, I'd just have to call my friend in advance so he'd wait for me, and call my wife to tell her I was going to be late, since I haven't been able to come home yet. I'd already begun feeling around my pocket for change so that I'd have the necessary amount ready, but at that moment the car turned right. Most likely there actually hadn't been a U-turn until this point, and now we would turn right again on the first street and we'd be driving parallel to the long street we'd just driven down, but now in the correct direction, and maybe we'd even come out on that street somewhere close to the bus turnaround, and I'd get off near the hospital, and let that other guy go wherever he wanted. But we passed one street without turning right, then another, and each second took us further away from the main street that I continued to see in my mind—the whole street, from the metro station with its life-saving letter "M" to the bus turnaround. Suddenly, the plan of the passenger in back became perfectly obvious to me: he simply wanted to catch a ride at my expense and that's why he stuck with me, having immediately seen from my face that it would work. Not only was I going in the wrong direction on account of him, I was supposed to pay for his ride as well.

"Stop here, pal," I said to the driver, "I think I'll get out," and since such a polite, though overly familiar way of putting it seemed too soft to me, I threw in a couple of curses. I cursed good-naturedly, because I thought that was what was called for, but now the other two had every right to talk to me in the same language, and the guy behind me could even add something about my face, and the driver might join in, because he had clear grounds to think that my cursing was directed at him; but they didn't say anything at all.

The car stopped. I stuck my hand in my pocket—the meter already read 60 kopecks—and I turned my face to the side so that it couldn't be seen by the driver, or the guy in back, even if he'd decided to look at me in the mirror, and so, silently now, in an alliance that was overt and no longer secret, they waited. We had stopped near some movie theater or department store on a street I didn't know, and I was supposed to make it to the main street on foot for my 60 kopecks, and of course by now I wouldn't get to see my friend, and moreover, by forcing the guy sitting behind me to pay for himself and in so doing thwarting his calculation, I was afraid to bring down his wrath, and to hear that choice word thrown at me, when I was getting out of the car.

"All right, all right, let's go on," I said.

A little farther along we did turn right after all, though the street didn't run parallel to the main street, but at an angle to it, so that in the end we were farther away once again. The neighborhood was completely unfamiliar to me—there were white, five-story apartment buildings, small front yards with hanging laundry, and empty lots; sometimes I thought that perhaps I was mistaken after all and that by some miracle we would end up on that main street. One time I even mistook some extremely tall ducts or pipes for the factory located near the bus turnaround; for a moment I even imagined myself getting out of the taxi near the hospital fence, pressing the buzzer, and an orderly in a white robe opening it for me and respectfully leading me to my friend's office on the second floor—everything happening now was over, and I was calling home so my wife wouldn't worry; but the pipes came straight out of the ground, like trees, and steel cables were attached to them—there wasn't even a hint of the factory, and again we passed white five-story buildings and courtyards with laundry and benches where people were sitting: they could go home or to the store, or simply stay put and talk to others, but I was being taken farther and farther away from the place I needed to go. I still placed my hopes on something, like an inexperienced skier, zooming down a steep mountain that ends in a precipice: in order to save yourself the smartest thing to do is to fall on your side, but once on the smoothly packed ski run, you speed faster and faster toward unavoidable catastrophe—you can't see the trees, the sky merges with the snow, and yet you still hope for some kind of miracle. "I think we're going the wrong way," I kept saying, adding the same curse words, but by now they sounded like a pitiful adage or the refrain of a song that no one listens to, and moreover the way I said it made it sound as though I were addressing the traffic rules or even talking to myself.

"What, you don't even know your own neighborhood?" said the guy in the back, and he cursed brutally. He cursed the way people do when they're just about to slug someone, and for a minute I was actually ashamed that I didn't know this neighborhood, and I even imagined that perhaps I lived around here and had just forgotten my address. Even without looking at him, I knew how he was sitting—sprawled out on the seat, his knees spread wide, the full-fledged boss of the car—now he could do anything with me, and I felt the gaze of his murky eyes on the back of my neck, following my every move like he was aiming the barrel of a gun—he was leading me to execution, and I was afraid to move a muscle and get the bullet ahead of time. Leaning over, I lowered my head on my chest in order to hide my face, so that my chin completely disappeared, and as a result my nose became even longer, and my right hand, lying on my briefcase— which now meant no more than the possessions of the people taken off to Majdanek or Auschwitz—my right hand occasionally tugged on my left sleeve in order to check my watch or, rather, to pretend that I was checking it in order to demonstrate a mild degree of worry and a professional manner, but it probably looked more like a nervous tick or the seizure of a dying man.

"We're here," said the guy in back, and the car stopped, "it's your hospital, out you go."

"But this isn't where I'm going, this is a completely different place, I'm going just beyond the bus turnaround, and this . . ."

"Go on, get the hell outta here!" said the driver, and he looked at me for the first time.

I had been put up against the wall; spineless, I went limp in anticipation of the final shot.

"You don't have to pay," he said, seeing that I was groping in my pocket, and the look of malice on his face turned to disgust. He cursed, and the guy sitting in back cursed too.

I didn't care which way I went, but I headed in the opposite direction to get out of their field of vision as quickly as possible. Moving a safe distance away, I looked back, pulled a piece of paper out of my briefcase, and began to write down the number of the cab. I even wanted them to see that I was doing this—just to let that driver know this behavior would not go unpunished— but at the same time I didn't want to draw their attention too much, just in case, who knows, they decided to jump out of the car; therefore I wrote as I walked, slowing down a bit, so that it might look like I was writing poetry or music, but was still in a hurry to get somewhere. I actually experienced something resembling triumph: first of all, I had avoided that particular word, although, when the door slammed after me, they probably said something to each other; but I wasn't obliged to know what they said, so all in all, even though we quarreled, things were still on equal footing, and secondly, the guy in the back didn't get his ride at my expense—let him pay the whole fare himself. Then again, this feeling of triumph was close to the triumph of a man whose wife wasn't raped by thugs who broke into his house only because they didn't like the look of her.

The sun was still high and the whiteness of the new housing units was blinding; they were placed such that it was impossible to distinguish the main street from the alleys running through the courtyards. A few guys gathered up ahead, near one of the buildings. They were a little drunk, but were probably about to have another, and were standing like a bunch of plotters. I walked right up to them, the way a ship in trouble sails straight for an unknown island.

"Guys, anybody know where there's a phone booth around here?"

I asked them as though I was proposing myself as a fellow drinker. They weren't surprised, as if I really could have begun drinking with them, and they moved apart, almost as if they were accepting me into their group, and one of them willingly pointed to a telephone booth—amazing, how could I have missed it?

I rushed to the booth, but at that moment I saw a taxi with a green light in the distance. I ran out in the middle of the road and stuck my hand out. The car braked, and the driver, opening the door, politely inquired where I wanted to go.

November 1, 1972

AVE MARIA

A service was held for her in church. I stood to the left of the iconostasis, near an image of the Virgin and Child, and to the right, cattycorner from me, behind an equally large icon as if behind a shield, was the choir—clerks, master builders, grain merchants, tax collectors, artisans, moonlighting seamstresses—where did they all come from? Moscow's Zamoskvorechye neighborhood? Or Ostrovsky? Chekhov? Vasilevsky Island in Petersburg? With each passing minute the church filled with more and more people—elongated faces, noble profiles, graying and white coiffures, delicate black scarves on women's heads, fastened in front with a clasp of non-darkening ruby, and similar, unobtrusive rings on the fingers, put on as if just a passing thought, and the faintly detectable aroma of subtle perfumes mixed with the smell of incense; the choir had already lined up, the voices, divided in the appropriate thirds and fourths, quite unfathomably staying on key, filled the church, rising to its very cupola: the funeral service had begun. I stood in the most regal place; I chose it deliberately, and made my way there with difficulty—the most royal, because from that spot I could see both the choir and the "Tsar's Gates" or Holy Gates, through which the priest would emerge any minute, as well as the faces of the others in the church, and even the coffin with her body, a bit far away, true, but then I couldn't be right up there in the first row among her near and dear—but, my placement was an adequate indication of a certain involvement with her and her life, although because of the backs of the near and dear I couldn't see

249

her face, only the rising mass of her body, and only in snatches, and her head only once in a while, when the near and dear, or those who considered themselves near and dear, whispered to one another or shifted places; then for a short moment the white cloth tied around her head like a compress was visible—the so-called "conductor to heaven." I first saw that kind of head bandage and discovered its name and meaning not long before Maria Yakovlevna's death, when we buried her older sister. The sister hadn't been a believer, but Maria Yakovlevna buried her according to Christian rites—she couldn't imagine it any other way—and it was strange to see the white kerchief with the images of sacred scenes from the Gospels on a typically Judaic face with curly rings of hair and a long bird-like nose; Maria Yakovlevna herself read the psalm book over the coffin and everyone present at the ceremony stood silently, focusing on the floor, while she kept on reading, standing over the coffin and holding the heavy book with the black cross on its cover open in her hands; she had held the very same book in the very same way at the grave of the famous poet on the anniversary of his death, and everyone listened to her silently, their eyes downcast or concentrating on some point in the sky or the branch of a tree, and a slight cemetery breeze stirred the hem of her long velvet dress and her gray hair, which made her forehead seem even larger and the bumps on her brow more pronounced; and when she walked past our windows, hurrying to the bakery or to church in that very same velvet dress, leaning on her walking stick and carrying her corpulent body with remarkable ease, she was always directed forward, like Peter the Great, or perhaps Beethoven, or a priest in a soutane . . . Out of the corner of my eye, I occasionally looked at the man standing next to me—a tall intellectual with a long, pedigreed face and head of graying hair—he crossed himself, but a bit shamefully, as though he were zipping his fly; they all crossed themselves that way, but they didn't do it all the time, only at certain moments in the liturgy, and I strained my hearing and eyesight in order to detect some pattern to the crossing, but they all apparently knew something I didn't, and their long, white fingers touched their foreheads, chests, and shoulders just like simple, devout old ladies, the way it was probably done a thousand years ago by Alexander Nevsky or the boyars during the coronation of Boris Godunov. Through the Holy Gates a priest emerged, not just one, but a whole three of them or maybe four, dressed in sparkling silver vestments, carrying censers—there was a sudden strong smell of incense and the voices began to ascend, higher and higher, toward the highest point—and the faces of the singers now expressed exultation, and the same exultation and joy sounded in their voices. I even closed my eyes for a minute—now I was just a little particle in all this, and a lump that had been forming for a long time rolled up into my throat—I was a particle of it all, together with the others in the church I had traversed a long and terrible path, the beginning of which was lost somewhere in the twilight of Alexander Nevsky's battles on the ice, the alarming raids of the Pskovian and Kievan princes; I had miraculously survived the street bonfires and burning buildings with them, the roaring, enraged crowd; of course I understood what the choir was singing about—otherwise where would it come from, this lump that was swelling in my throat? The voices ascended higher and higher, and here it was, the highest point, the limit, the crest of the wave, the destination of it all: "For the peace of the soul of Your newly deceased servant, Maria. Forgive her her transgressions . . ." and at this moment everyone began to cross, bow, and even prostrate themselves, and I also put three fingers of my right hand together and timidly touched them to my forehead, as though scratching it, then, to my chest, as though I were straightening my tie, and finally, in order—to my right, and then left shoulders, as though I were removing a bit of fluff from my coat. Behind me I heard movement and felt a draft of cold air; through the side door, which for some reason hadn't been locked—we all entered through the main door, and then spent a great deal of effort to find a good spot—so then, through this side door, a very simple-looking man entered, wearing a worn coat of rough material with a bulging pocket—he probably had vodka in there, and maybe he was already drunk or tipsy—at any rate, from the first it was clear that he didn't have and couldn't have had any relationship to the deceased; he walked the way you walk into a store or a tram, and began looking around at what was happening as if it were a soccer match or something—a lot of people turned around and looked at him disapprovingly, and I, too, threw him a devastating glance, but apparently he didn't care at all, he found a spot next to the icon of the Virgin and Child as though nothing had happened, he even leaned against her a bit, and I could feel his breath on the nape of my neck, and the smell of onion was added to the smell of incense. His presence prevented me from absorbing everything going on in the church in the right way, he prevented me from getting into the right mood, from feeling what one was supposed to feel and which I had already been feeling; but for me to cross myself again simply wasn't possible and I even moved a step or two to one side; but I still felt his breath on me and even, I thought, his eyes; meanwhile the priests, standing near the coffin of the dead woman as though they were an honor guard, took turns reading the requiem, and in the interludes between the reading the choir sang, but a certain thread had already been lost, and one of the priests actually kept swinging the censer in the direction of the churchgoers, as though tossing a paper ball on a piece of elastic.

Learning of Maria Yakovlevna's illness, I ran to see her immediately. The door of her apartment was unlocked as always, but there was no one in the room—there was only a wrinkled bed with stale sheets; from the depths of the apartment some noise and commotion could be heard, and when I called her, two middle-aged women appeared—her friends, it seemed—who looked either tired or perhaps apathetic, and just then I heard her voice, addressing me: "Don't come in, you can't come in here!" and it struck me that her voice was loud and powerful as usual, and I even thought that perhaps she wasn't all that sick, but her friends, as if talking about some tangential event, began explaining slowly that Maria Yakovlevna couldn't get up, nor could they help her, and I was all ready to rush to her aid, when I suddenly realized that she was sitting on the toilet. Her friends returned to her again, and a commotion could be heard once more, and suddenly I heard strange sounds, as if a cornered animal were breathing heavily. The friends appeared and just as indifferently, as though nothing happening concerned them, informed me that everything was in order—Maria Yakovlevna was now in the hallway, but not dressed, and I imagined her standing there, leaning on the wall, breathing heavily, completely naked—her massive body with the stomach hanging over, a body that at age seventy had remained virginal—she had a fiancé once upon a time, but he died, and then she took a vow of chastity and soon after that was baptized. Later, I sat at her desk—her girlfriends had gone; outside it was an autumn night and on the bed behind my back Maria Yakovlevna breathed heavily and rapidly, and even now, despite dozing and semi-hallucinating, she managed to pull the blanket over her, pull it right up to her neck as she always did when I came to see her and found her in bed due to ill health or exhaustion; on the desk, lounging on papers covered with her large, decisive handwriting with its letter "T" that looked like something between a Ѣ[1] and a cross, her cats basked in

1 Translator's note: A pre-revolutionary letter abolished by the new Soviet government, which represented an aspect of the letter "e."

voluptuous languor—she sheltered all the stray cats in the neighborhood—there was an entire herd of cats, and I couldn't stand them because they would jump on my lap, scratching me with their claws, or they'd sycophantically rub against my legs; but now they lay on the desk basking in the light of the lamp, as though soaking up the rays of the springtime sun, and among them, most likely, was her favorite, the one she called John Nightingale the Good Thief for some reason, and whom I particularly disliked because instead of telling stories about Bach, or Stravinsky, whom she had known, as soon as I arrived she would begin to tell long tales about the adventures and accomplishments of Nightingale the Good Thief while constantly moving a dish of milk around the room, and the cats would run after her in a flock, rather, they'd run after the milk, and Nightingale the Good Thief was the leader of the pack. Now an overturned dish lay right here on the desk and the spilt milk had made the letters on one of her manuscript pages run. But even this wasn't enough for them: a few silently left the desk and just as silently jumped up on the piano or on the window sill, and then returned to their former places, and this merry-go-round of cats began to make me dizzy and it began to seem like the entire room was teeming with them—the walls, ceiling, bookshelves, icons—everything was dripping with cats—they swayed, stretched their backs, multiplied on the spot before your eyes—perhaps they'd copulated—and Maria Yakovlevna's wide, ageless palms with their strong, agile fingers—how many times, coming to see her after one of her concerts I'd wanted to nestle against them—they probably still remembered every note of the "Moonlight Sonata"—these palms kept pulling the covers up to her chin, to her eyes even; and when the ambulance came and the indifferent, well-meaning male nurse wearing a uniform that made him look like a train conductor, and the woman who came from the neighboring apartment, lifted her and began to dress her, she had almost given up any attempts to cover her body, but I still tried not to look in her direction. At that moment one of the cats—probably Nightingale the Good Thief—jumped up on the bed with her, stretched his back, and began to rub against her anxiously, flicking his tail in displeasure. The male nurse continued silently on ahead, and we took her by the arms, leading her to the door; she looked back uneasily as though she'd forgotten something, and kept trying to explain something about money that she still owed the concierge—then she suddenly pushed us away and, turning her face toward the room, made a low bow, and slowly crossed herself, just as she had done during the service, and when we resumed walking, her bulky body became really heavy, so that we were no longer leading, but dragging her. When we left the entryway, she said: "I will not return." And I realized that this must be true, because previously she had never lost her spirit; and it meant that as soon as I walked into her room, and later, when I sat at her desk, I had already foreseen her death and the funeral service I was now attending.

Since I'd been in the room for a long time, I greedily inhaled the humid night air and suddenly felt an intense, penetrating joy, because this was not happening to me, because I was healthy and could command my own body as I chose, and because the woman pulling Maria Yakovlevna along with me was young and pretty, and, handing Maria Yakovlevna over to the hospital, we would leave together, and before going to bed I would still have time to read a book, and in order to quash that shameful feeling inside, I apparently began to pull Maria Yakovlevna so zealously that she suddenly stopped and spoke irritably in her former, commanding voice: "Wait, for heavens' sake!"; the male nurse had courteously opened the door of the ambulance and was already waiting for us there, as though we were taking Maria Yakovlevna home after a concert, and when we tried to haul her into the vehicle, she again pushed us away and grabbed on to the handrail herself, but that was her last try. In the reception ward she gave up for good—she sort of half lay, half sat there on the cold plastic-covered couch under merciless, blinding lamps, her arms hanging feebly down, and didn't even try to pull up the blue tricot, though it had slipped down to her knees—and I didn't turn away. The doors of the room were wide open, women in white coats came and went, it was impossible to tell who was a nurse and who was a doctor; there was a cold draft from the hallway, and we stood in a corner of the room with our coats still on, vaguely hoping that all this toing and froing had something to do with Maria Yakovlevna, and when, finally, a woman in a white coat with a sour, rumpled face came, and, ignoring Maria Yakovlevna, asked us: "Is she yours?" we rushed to her like sprinters from the start line. Interrupting one another, we took to recounting in detail how it all happened, but apparently all these details were superfluous, because the doctor, without even listening to us, ran her eyes over the referral and then called the male nurse in the conductor's uniform, who hadn't yet left for some reason, and began to admonish him for bringing the patient to them—don't the dispatchers over there know we're filled up?—and apparently the whole scenario was nothing new for either of them, because he just shrugged his shoulders placidly and she calmed down quickly and another woman in a white coat—probably a nurse—ran past Maria Yakovlevna, sticking a thermometer under her armpit as she passed, and the doctor, sitting down at a little table and placing a patient history form in front of her, asked her name, and I blurted out Maria Yakovlevna's last name like someone revealing a trump card, a long held secret, but it didn't make any impression at all; the doctor probably never went to concerts, or perhaps she just forgot. Maria Yakovlevna continued to lie there, her eyes closed, her legs tucked under the fallen tricot, with her huge, pregnant-looking stomach jiggling and breathing heavily—just another of the old ladies who arrive at the emergency room each night, creating a lot of fuss and bother for the doctors and employees, and increasing the average yearly mortality for the hospital.

The choir fell silent, the priests had moved away—a cloud of incense that looked like smoke from the explosion of an anti-aircraft gun now floated in the place where they had just been standing; another priest appeared before the ambo as well, only it wasn't a regular sort of priest, like the ones who had just read the requiem prayer, he was an ecclesiastical dignitary—a metropolitan or archbishop—in a shimmering gold vestment and a miter strewn with sparkling jewels—I'd only seen headgear like that in museums, under glass—it was a real crown, like Monomakh's Cap, and in the tension-filled silence, unusual even for a church, I realized that this was Maria Yakovlevna's spiritual leader, Father Nikon, whose name she was even afraid to pronounce aloud, and that he was going to speak now. He began to talk and I understood for the first time what church acoustics mean, although perhaps that was just the way he talked, and although he spoke about abstract things, it seemed to me that I grasped the secret meaning of his words, and everyone else also understood, and once again I felt I was just a part of them—I now imagined the road we had traveled together in the form of a triangle: the base of it lay somewhere in the depths of the centuries, then, as history progressed, it narrowed, until now only the summit remained, the sharp tip, and we were this pointed tip—an island in the middle of the raging sea, which had by some miracle survived world catastrophe, but with every passing day this island sank further and further, it was already covered by water, the water reached up to our chins, but we were all alive and could move ahead, holding hands, and we had to appreciate this, and when Father Nikon, referring to Dostoevsky, said that "beauty will save the world," I felt a lump rising in my throat again and tears filling my eyes, and I even turned around to cast a withering glance at the alcoholic, about whom I'd forgotten but now remembered for some reason, but he wasn't there anymore—he probably realized finally that this wasn't a soccer game—and Father Nikon, recalling the moral virtues and noble deeds of the departed, said that the path to beauty lies through good, and I suddenly remembered Maria Yakovlevna, standing at the very edge of the stage, pressing a bouquet of flowers she'd just been given to her breast. Clutching the flowers to her breast, she made a dismissive gesture with her hand in order to stop the applause, and when the audience had quieted down, she said, in a quiet, humble voice: "Better to give this money to the poor," and everyone felt uncomfortable, like they did that time when she read the holy book over her sister's coffin, and at the poet's grave on the anniversary of his death, and then I remembered one time when she caught up to me on the landing of her staircase and forcibly pressed two apples into my hands—for her it was a sacrifice, because she never had any money, since she gave almost everything to the church—but I didn't like apples and had even told her once, but it was awkward to refuse; and in the same way she gave pieces of sugar to the church acolytes and beggars outside the church and they also took them and thanked her, and for holidays she gave the concierges handkerchiefs and candy and then said how moved they were by the gifts; though once, when there was some kind of problem about the key to her apartment, she bellowed at everyone in the courtyard; at first I didn't even understand what had happened, but walking over, I saw Maria Yakovlevna sitting on a bench, having taken two bottles of kefir out of her bag, and around her the concierges shuffled guiltily, and she was screaming at them and her voice at that moment was indistinguishable from the voice of a market woman who'd had some beets stolen from her stand; it was impossible to believe that this was the same voice that had read Blok or appealed to her audience with a homily on love and kindness; the concierges shuffled around her, moving further and further back with every step—into the bushes or the shade—so that in the end, she was in the middle of an empty zone. "For the repose of the soul of God's newly deceased servant, Maria. Forgive her her trespasses," the choir sang again; Maria Yakovlevna's spiritual leader wasn't there anymore—he had left the ambo, disappearing behind the Holy Gates, and everyone present crossed themselves again, sloppily touching their three fingers to their shoulders as though they were conjurers who were slapping epaulettes on themselves with a single wave of the hand, but in a disorganized sort of way.

The funeral mass was over. Everyone at the mass for the repose of the soul gradually left the church, passing by Maria Yakovlevna's coffin, which was now quite accessible; those who wished to say farewell to her gathered together—some of the lamps were extinguished, like in an auditorium at the end of a performance, and a humid cold entered through the door. Outside a light autumn rain drizzled.

From the church, the coffin with Maria Yakovlevna's body was moved to the conservatory, where the civil memorial service was to be held. The bust of the great composer in the vestibule had been covered with a black horse blanket; and he looked like an oracle, so much so that you felt like going over and tapping on his head with your finger like we did in childhood when we played Oracle downstairs. The mirrors that curved around half of the vestibule in a horseshoe had been covered with plywood painted with a calming birch grove: both the black cover and the plywood with the birch grove were kept in the basement of the conservatory along with red flags and slogans. The coffin with Maria Yakovlevna's body was arranged in front of the composer's bust; between the bust and the birch grove, a piano and several chairs could be seen, not so much seen as they appeared to peek out, because the coffin had been placed on a high pedestal, and moreover a huge number of wreaths with red and white ribbons had been set around it; the composer's bust got in the way actually, so you had to stand on tiptoes and choose a particular position because other people's heads also blocked the view. The people who came to say farewell to Maria Yakovlevna were mostly the same ones who had been in the church—though here and there you caught a glimpse of some new figures in dark suits with concerned, businesslike looks on their faces—they were probably members of the administration; but there was a little more light here than in the church, and everyone was divided in two by a carpet runner that ran like a part in the middle of someone's head, all the way from the very entrance to the vestibule, all the way to Maria Yakovlevna's coffin; ushers patrolled its long edge, jealously protecting its inviolability, because it was brand new and outside it was quite muddy. Many of the people present, rising on tiptoe and craning their necks, looked toward the entrance, too, as though cosmonauts or some other kind of important guests were about to arrive, and from somewhere on the side, two groups of four young people wearing mourning bands on their sleeves were to be let out like athletes at the starting line—they were probably conservatory students. Modestly lowering their eyes, like people carrying string bags full of hard-to-find oranges, and trying to walk in time but continually getting out of step, one of the groups approached the other group of four already standing near the coffin and stood behind them, so for a few seconds there were eight people near the coffin—a double honor guard—and funeral music could be heard from behind the composer's bust, but you couldn't see the musicians. An acquaintance of mine standing nearby, a theater critic, was patting the pockets of his coat, looking for matches. He was almost always looking for matches, even when he didn't plan on smoking: this gesture had become habitual, been perfected, and indicated a state of either anxiety or helplessness, and before beginning to speak he would always cough a lot—like a singer about to perform a ballad— after which he would pause significantly, and, adapting his voice, he'd ask me what I thought about the last flu epidemic, or how tetraborate affected the function of the intestines, underscoring, in his way, that I didn't belong to the lofty and refined world he belonged to. Now he was obviously in a state of anxiety: his spouse had not yet arrived from out of town; they had an apartment in the city, but she had suffered from oxygen insufficiency her whole life and then from an occasional, sudden paralysis of the legs, and once at the special artist's resort where they vacationed, she had suddenly collapsed on a park bench, her earrings and necklace jangling, while he fanned her with a newspaper so as to increase the flow of air; she finally opened her eyes, which were outlined in black circles, and in a helpless and languid voice asked "What time is it?"; for this reason they lived out of town almost year round, in a little lodge near the dacha of the late poet over whose grave Maria Yakovlevna had read the sacred writings; the theater critic's wife had been close to the poet at one time, and although their hut was just a summer dwelling and it was impossible to be there without a coat in the fall and winter, none of this was important, because there was a lot of oxygen, and, besides which, the late poet loved to visit that hut and had even celebrated it in one of his poems. The critic searched nervously for matches, although of course no one was allowed to smoke during the memorial service, and the invisible musicians performed Massenet's "Elegy," Schubert's "Ave Maria," the third part of Shostakovich's Seventh Symphony, and other pieces that were appropriate for the occasion, and all of them were musicians with whom Maria Yakovlevna had no doubt performed more than once, though that was all in the past, since in recent years she had been forbidden to perform because of her love of preaching. Honor-guard groups of four continued to replace one another, but each time the individuals in the groups became more and more imposing—they were probably now representatives of the conservatory administration, or maybe even of the party organization—they didn't even try to walk in step, because they felt that they were the center of attention, and on approaching the group they were replacing, they didn't stand behind, but pushed them gently out of the way, though there was nothing especially offensive about this because each succeeding quartet was one level higher on the administrative ladder. When the memorial service proper started and the speakers began to talk, one group of four young people was sent out again, because you couldn't have the honor guard changing during the service—in order to hide their exhaustion and boredom, the young people gazed at the deceased with an exaggeratedly mournful expression, as though they wanted to imprint every feature of her face on their memory—and when the civil service was coming to a close, from the side, where the honor guard had first come in—a famous tenor appeared and stood in the first row—everyone standing there respectfully made room for him—he was very cautious with what remained of his voice and appeared for just a few minutes, so he wouldn't catch a cold; on the top of his head his thinning hair was turning gray, but his face was crimson, as though he'd just sung a high A or was exerting himself on the john.

It was already growing dark when we arrived at the cemetery. The rain had stopped; there was a slight frost in the air. It was an old cemetery, almost no one was buried there anymore, but for Maria Yakovlevna, people had managed to get permission. However, the place allotted to her was far away, and the burial procession stretched out along a narrow, winding pathway amid graves and the cemetery fence. I didn't make it up to the coffin—there were a lot of people who wanted to, and they all surrounded it and lifted it with an expression that made it immediately clear to me that they had a much greater right to this than I did, and next to them was the relief shift also wearing an expression of rightful ownership; ahead of me the coffin wobbled on someone else's shoulder, but I didn't get upset, because it wouldn't be very pleasant to walk with such a burden over this uneven ground, especially trying to walk in step, and in a new coat, for that matter—it would inevitably get frayed somewhere and there'd be wood splinters—a wreath fell to my lot and I carried it with a partner. I never did make out his face because it was on the other side of the wreath, which had a lot of fir branches woven into it, and its needles scratched my hands and face, and some bare branches of the cemetery trees also whipped my face, and my feet kept slipping on the freezing ground, and moreover, somewhere in the cemetery—where exactly I couldn't see, because of the wreath partitioning me off from the rest of the world—somewhere in the cemetery people were singing quietly. For a moment I caught a glimpse from behind the fir needles—there were only empty graves with crosses, monuments, and little fences—and then I looked back and saw that it was members of the funeral procession. They sang very strangely, almost without opening their mouths, so it was impossible to distinguish the words, or possibly there weren't any words at all. The song came out something like "mmmmm," so they weren't exactly singing but just sort of humming something to themselves, and this humming in some way vaguely recalled a lullaby; gradually they began to sing louder and words emerged, but I still couldn't make them out, and then I suddenly realized that they were singing something religious, spiritual—perhaps a mass or something, or maybe a special burial song.

The coffin with Maria Yakovlevna's body was set up on a sort of plinth, and those attending the burial settled around it, some getting a better view from the mounds of freshly dug earth, the gravestones, and even on the fences; I scrambled onto some little mound, but it had completely iced over, and was uncomfortable to stand on; in order to retain this little hill for myself I grabbed a tree branch, and others also held on to different things, and sometimes leaned on a neighbor's shoulder, and I remembered that, when they buried the poet—at whose grave she later read the sacred book on the anniversary of his death—Maria Yakovlevna kept trying to get closer to his grave, and people were standing and even hanging on the trees in a dense wall, and she couldn't get through, because she was always plump and even then suffered from shortness of breath, though in the end she managed to get up on some little rise, but the rise was so small that everyone else had ignored it and it didn't help her at all—she still couldn't hear anything, and the sweat ran down her face, because this all took place in the summer under a hot sun.

Those standing immediately around Maria Yakovlevna's coffin, especially at the head of it, began singing again, just as quietly and wordlessly, as if only for themselves; others, standing farther away, were silent, but then some of them joined in, too, also as if singing just for themselves, and far off, beyond the cemetery fence you could see some old, barracks-like buildings, and in this concentrated, quiet singing of people bunched together in a small space there was something recalling a silent public meeting, and next to the pit where they were supposed to lower the coffin, the workers smoked, leaning calmly on their shovels, like wardens waiting for a rendezvous to come to an end.

The singing had become louder, and you could now hear words, though it was still impossible to make them out, now again the only ones singing were standing at the head of the grave, but the melody no longer recalled a lullaby—these were notes of rejoicing, even what might be called rollicking or devil-may-care notes, and the faces of the singers were directed not at the deceased, but at one another, as if this were a group that had been singing together a long time, and had just been waiting for a chance to demonstrate its art, and now this opportunity had arisen, and they joyously took up the call and were trying with all their might, and their faces glowed with exultation and mischief. Trying especially hard were a young woman in a black suede cap with a visor and a bald, red-cheeked old man—his head was tied with a wool scarf, not the way it's normally done, but with the ends erect, and these ends stuck up like horns, recalling either a devil or a jester, and he himself was practically dancing. I remembered seeing him in the church either in the choir or among the priests reading the prayer for the repose of the soul—he and the woman in the suede cap kept glancing at one another, as though egging each other on, and the other singers also exchanged glances of encouragement, and they were almost ready to break into a dance—it seemed that just a bit longer and they would get so worked up that they'd grab Maria Yakovlevna's coffin, swing it back and forth, and toss it in the grave.

It was almost dark; only far away, just above the roofs of the buildings, the frosty sky was still pink, and the bare branches of the cemetery trees stood out in clear relief against it, just like a lithograph. The singing stopped unexpectedly. Pushing their way through to the coffin, the workers placed the lid on, and while they were arranging it on the coffin, someone standing nearby managed to straighten the flowers lying on Maria Yakovlevna's breast, and then at opposite ends of the coffin, almost simultaneously, the hammers began to strike, as though they were boarding up a dacha for the winter. Grunting, the workers picked up the coffin together with an exclamation that sounded like "Hey, move aside!" dragged it to the grave, and everyone immediately parted to make way for them; and someone tried to help them carry the coffin, but that was as unnecessary as pushing a moving train. Having placed the closed coffin on a pile of earth near the very edge of the grave, the workers ran thick ropes under it, and, grasping them, pulled the coffin to the pit, then, grunting, lifted it again and, shouting something to each other like "Hey, ease up!" or "Heave ho!" like sailors do; they began to lower the coffin into the hole on the ropes, and everyone else stood around looking like tourists watching the mooring of a ship. They were lowering the coffin, but either the hole was too narrow, or the coffin was disproportionately large, and it got stuck somewhere halfway down and the workers began shouting something to each other again, mixing professional terms with foul language, and the mourners stood there pretending they didn't hear anything or didn't understand the meaning of these words, and just tried not to look at one another. A few even went up to the workers and, imitating their language and intonation, tried to give them advice as to which side of the rope to pull on in order to turn the coffin the necessary angle, drawing some geometrical figures in the air the better to explain, and one of the workers, giving in to this advice, went ahead and pulled on the rope, after which the coffin was inextricably stuck—now it could neither be pushed further down, nor pulled to the surface.

It was completely dark now, only a little piece of sky remained pink, and against that background the workers' figures could be seen—leaning over the grave, as though over a fishing hole in the ice; they were trying to do something, but because of the darkness they couldn't make anything out. Then, in the crowd of friends and well-wishers, a flame flared and flickered, and then another, a third, fourth, and soon dozens of people held lighted church candles over their heads, lifting them high, like torches, and the light from them fell on the plot where the workers were toiling. One of them, standing on a little rise at the very edge of the hole, began to gouge the earth with a pick. His movements, slow at first, became more sweeping and more confident, the pick worked rhythmically and implacably, breaking through the hard rock, striking sparks from it, and the other workers also took up their picks and shovels; the moment of confusion brought on by the unsuccessful mooring had passed, and now this was again a well-coordinated team, working under the leadership of its captain—although the little hummock on which he stood wasn't high, his figure seemed to reign over everything—he worked and broke through the earth, and the others only imitated him or lighted the way, and his figure, illuminated by the flickering tongues of the candles, cast a gigantic, dancing shadow. A dull, heavy thud was heard—and the coffin with Maria Yakovlevna's body fell to the bottom of the grave; everyone surrounding the grave immediately began to throw dirt in—some as though they were sowing seeds, others like they were playing in a sandbox, and the workers, leaning on their shovels, froze in indulgent anticipation: the ship's crew, watching the tourists board their pleasure boats.

As I left, I saw the critic and his wife—they were still there. He was smoking, patting his pockets, looking for matches, and she was standing on a gravestone, looking at someone in the crowd. She offered me her hand, barely touching mine, looking all the while somewhere over my head, and he, coughing, after a significant pause asked me how many times exhumation is allowed.

April 21, 1972

THE LAST FEW KILOMETERS

He had just finished lovemaking, rather indifferently, and now he was returning home on the train. Outside the window, in the murky film of the fading autumn day, Moscow's former suburbs swam past—clusters of identical white high-rises with laundry hanging on the balconies—which weren't suburbs anymore, but inside the city now. Closer to the railroad huddled earthbound two-story structures, blackened with soot; plots of land fenced off with solid walls stretched along the rails, their terrain cluttered with car bodies, stacks of logs, or rusted constructions of unknown purpose.

As was her custom, she had greeted him all dressed up, wearing a little brooch, her hair teased, as if they were going to the theater. He put his lips to her cheek, and then to her neck, in order to demonstrate his passion. Of course, he should have kissed her on the lips, but, as usual, they were covered in a thick layer of lipstick.

"What's our plan?" she asked.

Theoretically, drinking and eating were supposed to come first, but this could lead to excessive palpitations during the hour of love. On the other hand, drinking and eating were pointless afterward, when he just wanted to have a smoke and get home as quickly as possible. And yet entirely refusing the repast she'd spent so long preparing would mean offending her.

"Why don't we have a bite first," he said. He'd reached a compromise decision: he would eat a little, have a drink, and leave the rest for later—he could figure it out then.

She rushed joyfully back and forth between the kitchen and the dining table in her one room, setting out plates, placing forks and napkins, while he reclined on the sofa. It was pleasant to watch how she fussed, pleasant to be in a clean, cozy, room: the sideboard, wardrobe, and gramophone were so highly polished you could use them as mirrors, and a large, fluffy rug lay on the floor. He had a real mistress and she received him the way mistresses generally do only in the movies.

"Oy, don't look, please, the place is so awful," she said, setting a dish of steaming chicken and rice on the table; it was more or less the same thing she said when he undressed her.

She settled opposite him on a low chair; on the table between them were the hors d'oeuvres. He poured wine into the crystal goblets—he had always called them "wineglasses," but she referred to them as "goblets," and now he, too, thought of them that way. The wine was transparent, golden, light—exactly as it was supposed to be in such situations. She sat with her back to the window, facing him.

"It'd be nice to spend a day or two here," he told her.

"Would you like some meat blini?" she suddenly remembered. "Only they're just terrible. Is the chicken dry? It is, isn't it?"

She ran into the kitchen and brought out the blini; as she started to serve him, he cleared some space on his plate, and dropped a drumstick on the floor. Embarrassed, he picked it up, and wanted to put it on the table, but she waved her hands in horror and took the drumstick back into the kitchen.

The blini were tasty—best of all, you didn't have to chew them much. He'd left his removable denture at home so that it wouldn't interfere with the moment of pleasure.

The high-rise buildings were fewer and farther between now. Outside the train window were the neighborhoods that had been built up in the fifties, with extruding cornices, bas-reliefs, and sculptural ensembles designed to depict bounty and the joy of labor. On the roof of one such building, a green neon sign read, "Dawn—A Specialized Shop for the Blind." An oncoming train zipped past like a blast of wind; through the flickering of its cars and windows, the sign could still be seen distinctly.

"You've hurt my feelings," she said when they lay side by side. He was staring up at the ceiling—he wanted to have a smoke and go home.

"Now, now, what's all this? Everything was so delicious, and you are too . . ."

He didn't finish his sentence so as not to say anything trite.

"A day or two, you said. It would have been better if you hadn't said anything at all."

He turned toward her, and thought that her eyes were moist, but perhaps it was just her wide, dark pupils—afterward, her pupils were always enlarged, and sometimes he even stared into her eyes just to check.

The train stopped, although they weren't at a station. There were several rows of rails, with freight cars and an entire train of restaurant cars, a brick water tower with broken windows, and farther on some buildings—tall and short ones, stone and wood, old and new, a mixture of eras and styles piled up randomly, like cliffs. The lights were already on in some of them. There were factory smokestacks, with immobile puffs of bluish-gray smoke above them, and beyond, through the smoke, he could just make out the contours of Moscow's skyscrapers, with red warning lights on the tips of their spires, and these lights seemed to float in the sky. Probably the traffic signal was red, and Moscow wasn't taking trains. A strange silence reigned in the car. There were a fair number of passengers, although no one was standing, but they were all quiet, and the only thing that could be heard was music—it might have been the shake or the twist. He began to look around to determine the source of the music. Diagonally across from him, next to the window, was a young man in a nylon jacket. Although he was sitting quietly like everyone else, it was obvious that the music was coming from his lap—he must have had a portable tape recorder. The voices singing the twist or the shake were going wild, though the tape recorder was set considerately at minimum volume, so the music wasn't bothersome—you could listen to it or not. The train started to move, and the sound of the music was immediately drowned out by the clacking of the wheels. The stacked cliffs of buildings began to turn slowly with the train, unexpectedly revealing narrow cracks between them, through which trams and trucks could he glimpsed speeding along.

She pulled on her black slip, her whole body writhing like a snake, as though she were performing some Indian dance—she always put it on that way. He had finally lit a cigarette, and, watching her, was trying to figure out whether he'd make the train.

When he walked into the kitchen just before he left, he saw a chicken leg lying on a plate in the white enamelled sink, the very drumstick that he had dropped on the floor—she was probably planning to wash it and reheat it—and it seemed to him that he had foreseen all of this from the very beginning.

The train stopped once more—the rail line was probably still busy—and then he heard the music again, the same shake or twist or something of the sort, the same voices, alien, incomprehensible, ranting and raging, but unobtrusive. The singers would be shaking their shoulders, as if teasing someone, their bodies bent and gyrating, their wrists flapping, striking the strings of electric guitars in a frenzied tempo, as though whipping up shaving cream, but at the same time they'd remain in place, as if each of them were delineated by an invisible circle, so that all this ecstasy seemed fake, deliberately put on. Everyone in the train car continued to sit silently: a woman in a headscarf with a tired face; a girl holding a tattered book in her red, probably frostbitten hands; middle-aged men and women in somber-colored, heavy coats.

He could no longer hear the music. The train was now crossing a bridge above a dark river with cement embankments; an
ancient monastery on a hill above the river had once been on the
outskirts but was now in the center of town. When the train
stopped again, in the middle of the bridge, an unnatural, oppres-
sive silence dominated the car. The young man had probably
turned his tape recorder off; no one talked. In the early twilight,
the dark, immobile figures around him were like symbols of
people, and for a moment he thought that, if by some supernatural
act he were removed from the car right that very second,
nothing would change: the people would sit just as silently, continuing to resemble symbols of themselves; far below them
would be the same river with cars streaming along its embankment road; and to the left would be the monastery with its
white fortified walls and its empty, dingy courtyard. Ahead, the
station's traffic signals could already be seen—their green,
yellow, and red lights, partly covered by visors, were dim, but
when he turned a certain way they sparkled like rippling
columns seen through a veil of rain or tears.

December 16, 1972.

THE COCKROACHES

They appeared in the Fedorkins' apartment quite suddenly, in the dead of winter. The first to see a cockroach was Fedorkin himself. It was crawling along the bottom of the bathtub, actually not crawling, but running, and meanwhile Fedorkin was shaving.

"Ruta! Come here right away!" he yelled to his wife who was busy in the kitchen. "We have something here, could be a spiderus, or maybe a cockroachus."

The Fedorkins had been married twenty years, but whenever there was peace between them they still liked to add endings to words to make them sound lovey-dovey, or itsy-bitsy, or Latinate, or just plain murdered, and besides that, Fedorkin wasn't in fact sure what this was—spider or cockroach—and he was even pleased the insect had appeared, since he knew a spider meant if not letters then maybe pleasant news, though he didn't exactly remember if it was the spider that meant letters and news or the cockroach.

Ruta Mikhailovna ran to the bathroom with a pot in her hand, since she had a pathological hatred of all insects, just as she adored all dogs, elephants, tigers, and all animals of prey—even cats— and despite her shyness, she could start a conversation with the first person she met on the street, provided he was accompanied by a dog.

"That's an honest-to-God cockroach!" Ruta shouted in horror, smacking it with her palm, so that instead of a cockroach on the white enamel there was a sort of dirty lump with a smear, like a squashed bedbug at night, only here there was no blood—in summer she swatted flies mercilessly with a special flyswatter that had a wire handle and a plastic spatula with a sieve to squash the fly-bodies better, and maybe diminish air resistance, but traces of the flies still remained on the wall and ceiling. Ruta didn't mind, but Fedorkin thought, better a living fly than a spot like that on the walls or on the ceiling. On summer evenings in their summer cabin, Ruta Mikhailovna was constantly listening for something and insisted it was mosquitoes buzzing or even one mosquito, though Fedorkin heard nothing; then she started listening for mosquitoes back in the city, in bed, with the lights off—"Are you telling me you don't hear them?" she'd ask Fedorkin bitterly— she would turn on the light and start hunting for the invisible mosquito—though she had started complaining that her hearing was getting bad, especially in the kitchen with the water going, when Fedorkin, sitting in a far room reading the newspaper, would shout out some piece of political news. Furious, he would run to the kitchen, waving the newspaper, and hold it to his wife's eyes, only without her glasses, she couldn't see, just like him, and getting even more worked up, he would run to get her glasses, only he couldn't find them, while she couldn't leave the stove because her soup was coming to a boil.

"An honest-to-God cockroach," Ruta repeated, surveying the bathroom walls suspiciously and even checking behind the shelves nailed to the tiled wall. "It's coming from the old woman," she said, motioning to the corridor with her head, and for a second Fedorkin's heart skipped a beat because off the corridor was his mother's room, where she sat confined to her chair for many months now, but Ruta, after all, never called his mama "the old woman"—these days she mostly didn't call her anything— the jerk of her head referred to the neighboring apartment where Nadezhda Pavlovna, "the old woman," lived by herself, lonely, and suffering from incontinence.

Nadezhda Pavlovna had moved into the building long ago, many years back, at the same time as the Fedorkins, and at first, there had been three of them: she, that is, Nadezhda Pavlovna herself, her sister, and her brother. The first to die had been her brother—both summer and winter he used to wear a shabby, between-season coat that smelled of urine—he was almost bald, in no way noteworthy, with high cheekbones, and a sallow, gray face; in the evenings, he would sit on the balcony right next to the Fedorkins' balcony, on a decrepit chair with its springs sticking out, his head back and his mouth slightly open, looking like a corpse, probably asleep. His death passed unnoticed. After that, Nadezhda Pavlovna's sister began sitting out on the balcony in good weather—back then the Fedorkins called *her* the old woman, since Nadezhda Pavlovna was still going out to work— she lectured at some institute or other on botany, or it might have been agronomy; the institute being very far away, she would call a taxi, but she never left the house on time and the taxi would have to wait by the entrance for a long time—the meter would tick off a considerable fare, but that didn't bother Nadezhda Pavlovna. The driver would get out and ring up to her apartment, and sometimes the Fedorkins' apartment, and Ruta Mikhailovna or Fedorkin's mother, who could still walk by herself then, would show the driver Nadezhda Pavlovna's door— the future old woman—she would wear an old-fashioned hat stuck, it seemed, with an artificial flower, and lipstick, and rouge on her cheeks as if she had rubbed her cheeks for a long time before going out—obviously, she put on makeup clumsily—and with the smell of urine that always accompanied her; maybe that was the very reason she took taxis, though it wasn't clear how taxi drivers and auditoriums full of students could put up with all this—anyhow, it was possible the Fedorkins exaggerated slightly, since what was certain was only that it came from her apartment, the smell of urine actually blowing right out the keyhole—no, the hat was stuck not with a flower but with artificial cherries on a green branch. Nadezhda Pavlovna was sometimes visited by a suitor, as the Fedorkins called him, an elderly man of rather fine appearance—evenings they would go out onto the balcony, and almost touching shoulders, they would talk quietly about something. Fedorkin, by the way, didn't rule out the possibility that this was her brother—not the one who had died but some other brother, since she had a great many brothers and sisters scattered all over town. She sometimes called them from the Fedorkins' apartment because her own telephone was always breaking down—she and the sister who lived with her were both on the deaf side and didn't put the receiver down right, and their telephone would go dead, and then Nadezhda Pavlovna would come to the Fedorkins and start trying to get the repair office or her sisters and brothers, or sometimes they couldn't get through to her and in that event they would call the Fedorkins, and Fedorkin's mother, Sofia Dmitrievna, would ring Nadezhda Pavlovna's bell and call her to the telephone; Ruta Mikhailovna and Fedorkin, in turn, would be scandalized by Nadezhda Pavlovna's sloppiness, but Sofia Dmitrievna was on unwaveringly good terms with Nadezhda Pavlovna, as she was with all the other tenants in the building, though she herself liked things neat (it was possible she liked Nadezhda Pavlovna just to annoy her daughter-in-law, but maybe she showed it unconsciously). Nadezhda Pavlovna sometimes came over to Sofia Dmitrievna's to check her blood pressure—Sofia Dmitrievna used to be a nurse but had stopped working long ago—and two or three times Nadezhda Pavlovna had even brought Sofia Dmitrievna a box of candy as a present. Once someone had rung the Fedorkins' doorbell—both Ruta Mikhailovna and Fedorkin took turns looking out the peephole, the stairwell was menacingly empty, and the Fedorkins' hearts pounded like mad—Ruta Mikhailovna fastened the chain and cautiously opened the door a crack and gasped "Ah!": there on the tile floor, right in front of their door, lay Nadezhda Pavlovna. She had apparently started feeling unwell and tried to go to the Fedorkins and managed to ring, but then had fallen down—this was already after her sister's death. Fedorkin and Ruta Mikhailovna carried Nadezhda Pavlovna to her apartment—the door, fortunately, hadn't slammed shut— and Nadezhda Pavlovna was muttering something; she was wearing an old flannelette bathrobe that gave off the smell of urine, with some blue nylon material showing underneath, and they put her on the couch, which was old, with springs sticking out like the chair her late brother used to sit on—in the middle of the room was a heap of something, maybe old clothes, maybe a pile of old rags mixed up with newspapers, on the ceiling and walls were dark spots, the door to the toilet was wide open. Fedorkin expected to see a chamberpot in there, and was somehow suprised not to find it—he pushed Nadezhda Pavlovna nearer to the wall as if she were already not alive, so she wouldn't fall down. She muttered that she'd gotten food poisoning the night before from something she had eaten, but Fedorkin and Sofia Dmitrievna, who usually didn't leave her room for fear of catching cold, thought it must be her heart—Nadezhda Pavlovna suffered from some serious heart ailment and in spite of this still went to work or traveled to serve as a doctoral defense examiner in some far-off cities. Ruta Mikhailovna would sing Nadezhda Pavlovna's praises loudly on purpose, in order to annoy her mother-in-law who used to study the barometer for a long time before leaving the house—Nadezhda Pavlovna had some students and graduate students who telephoned her and she visited them sometimes, though by then she had already stopped teaching. Fedorkin went to wash his hands immediately, while Ruta Mikhailovna began to telephone for an ambulance. The Fedorkins left her apartment door open and their own too and looked in on Nadezhda Pavlovna a few times—she lay on the sofa in the same position they had left her in and groaned softly; when the ambulance arrived, Fedorkin went over to the doctor and tried to explain something to him, but the doctor wouldn't listen and went to get the instrument for measuring blood pressure out of his bag and a syringe; feeling he was in the way, Fedorkin left, and the next day, as if nothing had happened, Nadezhda Pavlovna rang the Fedorkins' bell and began to apologize for causing them any unpleasantness and frightening them, and after another day she brought them a box of candy that was certainly intended for Ruta Mikhailovna and Fedorkin, but it seemed to them that the box smelled of urine, and they gave it away to someone. All this happened well after the death of her sister, whose name the Fedorkins had already managed to forget. Like her late brother, her sister had sat on the balcony on summer evenings in the old chair with the springs sticking out, her head thrown back, just like her brother, her face a sallow gray, her sagging mouth slightly open; sometimes she sat in an old wicker chair by the front entrance, also leaning back—and she walked with a cane because one leg was shorter than the other—she probably died like that, sitting in the chair. At any rate, her death went unnoticed, just like her brother's—after her death, Nadezhda Pavlovna's suitor continued to visit her and even began coming more often, it seemed, and when her admirer was there, Fedorkin was filled with all sorts of indecent thoughts, but he tried to push them away, and Nadezhda Pavlovna would go out in her hat with the cherries, with painted lips and rouged cheeks, and the urine smell would blend with the smell of perfume.

A few days after the first cockroach was seen, some more were found, mostly in the bathroom and kitchen. Ruta Mikhailovna squashed them without mercy, leaving traces on the walls and even the ceiling, while Fedorkin would coo, "They're sort of nicey-dicey, they don't give bitesies, they're not like licies, they like to live." "That's all I need, them giving bitesies," Ruta would say, smashing the next in line. "I'd give 'em such a bitesie back," she continued, suspiciously eyeing the space between the bathtub and the sink.

And yet Fedorkin didn't quite believe that the cockroaches came from Nadezhda Pavlovna's, because once when they were still living in a communal apartment and had bedbugs, Ruta had assured Fedorkin the bedbugs came from some people they shared the apartment with, though Fedorkin was firmly convinced they had crept over from Ruta's parents, who lived there too, through the thin partition, and besides that, Ruta's mother was always imagining that the neighbors were stealing her silver spoons in the kitchen, so maybe Ruta's suspiciousness was hereditary, but once, coming home from work early, Fedorkin noticed the smell of something burning as he was coming upstairs—in general, he had an unnaturally keen sense of smell, and just starting up the stairs he knew what soup and main course were awaiting him—only this time he didn't attach any importance to the smell of burning and even forgot about it until Ruta, who had just taken out the garbage, said there was a funny smell of burning outside.

"Yes, yes, I noticed it when I was coming home," Fedorkin said. "I noticed it right away," he added—he was a little ashamed to have yielded first place in the odors department to Ruta.

"And you know," Ruta said, "the smell comes from her apartment?" Fedorkin went out on the landing and put his nose to the keyhole-side of the crack where the door met the doorpost of the old woman's apartment. From the crack and from the keyhole, instead of the usual smell of urine, there was the unmistakable smell of something burning.

"Yes, it seems to be from here," Fedorkin said.

"By the way," said Ruta, "our Finnish breakfront stands next to the wall we share with her," and Fedorkin's heart turned over and fluttered and sank—he could already see a blaze devouring their new lacquered Finnish breakfront that he had only recently obtained through knowing someone with pull, and now they wouldn't be able to get it out of the apartment, and then again there was his mother who wasn't portable—how were they going to get her down the stairs?

"Maybe we should call the fire department," he suggested.

"And what if she's home?" Ruta asked.

By this time, both Fedorkins were standing by Nadezhda Pavlovna's door and taking turns sniffing, pressing their noses to the crack and at the same time listening for any sounds inside the apartment.

"Let's ring," Ruta said.

Fedorkin rang, at first cautiously and briefly, one time, then again and again until he was no longer letting go of the buzzer, so the bell rang continuously, as if it had been short-circuited.

"But she is deaf," Fedorkin said to his wife as if to justify not letting go of the buzzer.

"As always, she's not home," Ruta said decisively, "and something's burning in there. Do you hear?"

Fedorkin let go of the buzzer and put his ear to the door-crack.

Through the crack you could hear a distant droning sound, strong and even like a fire in a wood stove with a good draft.

"Take a look, it's lit up in there," Ruta said.

Yes, it was light behind the door though it was already evening. The blaze hummed madly, devouring the old lady's things, illuminating the whole apartment with its sinister light, and maybe by now it had broken out and was nearing the Fedorkins' wall where the Finnish breakfront stood.

Fedorkin began to pound the door with his fist, and then to kick it with his foot till the sole hurt—the heavy blows resounded up and down the stairwell.

"On second thought, it must be just the light on in there, and the drone is from an open window vent," Ruta said.

"But what about the smell of burning?"

"Maybe she's at her sister's. Go ask, maybe she has the telephone number," and Ruta motioned with her head in the direction of her mother-in-law's room.

Fedorkin ran to his mother's room. Sofia Dmitrievna, as always, sat in her armchair and stared at something without moving—maybe it was the clock on the dresser, or maybe the window with the curtain drawn over it—as soon as it began to get dark outside, Fedorkin would always turn on the lights in his mother's room and pull the curtain shut; for some reason it seemed to him that people on the street could see everything, and he hurried to draw the curtain. He gave Sofia Dmitrievna her eyeglasses which were in their black case, as if they were made for mourning, and her brown address book in which she had carefully written down telephone numbers, in alphabetical order—Sofia Dmitrievna's handwriting had once been beautiful, almost like calligraphy, but with the progress of her illness the notations had become increasingly uneven, the lines of each letter full of zigzags, and the recent notations actually resembled Chinese hieroglyphics, so that you could trace the whole course of Sofia Dmitrievna's disease by her address book and even determine its onset, the way you can figure out the age of a tree by the number of rings in a cross section of its trunk. She put on her eyeglasses and, with her hands trembling, began to leaf through her notebook—her hands were emaciated and blue like the chickens they sometimes sell at the local food store—before going to sleep, when Fedorkin gave his mother her medicine, she sometimes remarked that her hands were blue, and he had always thought that her perception was distorted because of her illness, but now he suddenly noticed that her hands were blue. She couldn't find Nadezhda Pavlovna's sister's telephone number, or maybe it simply wasn't in her book—probably it was the sister who was always telephoning the Fedorkins when she couldn't reach Nadezhda Pavlovna, or perhaps it was some other sister, since she had a lot of brothers and sisters, some of them were still living in her native city—maybe it was Perm, or Vyatka. From the crack of Nadezhda Pavlovna's door, the smell of burning came as before and something droned, like a fire drawn by a good draft, and a light burned within the apartment—Fedorkin began pounding on the door again, but now more for show since it was clear no one was home.

"Still, we ought to call someone in," Ruta said, and Fedorkin ran out into the courtyard.

"Something's on fire in Apartment 65 next to us," he said to the woman who worked the elevator and who was strolling back and forth on the cleared sidewalk. "The building manager should be notified. Something is always going on in there." He wanted to say something unpleasant about the old lady's apartment.

"The building manager just went home," the elevator operator said. "Maybe ask Yuri Adrianovich to look in."

Yuri Adrianovich was the local handyman, enormously tall and unusually fat, who spoke in a deep bass that shook window-panes and who monopolized all the plumbing work in the house, and not only plumbing work—he had been given an apartment here, it seemed, and all the elevator operators spoke of him with respect, and always called him by his name and patronymic, and were even ready, it seemed, to speak of him not as "he" but "they." Once, he came to the Fedorkins to put up some kitchen cabinets, and from two blows of his hammer that struck some piece of iron in the wall, a crack appeared clear across from the kitchen to the bathroom—from then on Ruta hated him and would never speak of him except as "that fat brute," though perhaps she had other reasons for doing this that were all her own.

Fedorkin stood shifting from foot to foot, then decided to let everything go its own way and ran back to the house.

Ruta was standing beside the old woman's door, straining to hear something. "You know, it seems to me I hear her voice—here, you listen too."

Fedorkin bent close to the doorpost—besides the same unceasing drone behind the door, the old lady's voice could be distinctly heard as if she were talking on the telephone, which made sense since her telephone was located in the foyer by the door—she was going on and on, without pausing in her expressionless, monotonous, o-ing way of speaking, as if she were reading a lecture.

"Well, this is turning into God knows what," Fedorkin exclaimed and threw himself at the door again with renewed force till his hands and feet hurt.

"If she's home, breaking down the door is out of the question," Ruta said. "That idea has to be forgotten."

Fedorkin once again ran downstairs. As he stepped into the courtyard, there was a whole procession moving toward his building entrance, headed by Yuri Adrianovich. Catching sight of Fedorkin, the procession stopped; Yuri Adrianovich with a crowbar in his hand, in the pose of an inquisitor, stood out in all his hugeness against the snowy slope behind him, while on either side and in back of him, like guardian angels, the elevator ladies from all seven building entrances stood dumb with reverence.

"You know it turns out she's home," Fedorkin said, "but for some reason she's not opening the door."

"No mistaking it," Yuri Adrianovich rumbled as he looked down at Fedorkin, who was beginning to go bald. "No mistaking it, she breaks the rules and now she won't open up."

"The things she's gone and done," the voices of the elevator ladies sounded, echoing in counterpoint to Yuri Adrianovich's booming bass, like voices in a church choir, though it might have just seemed so to Fedorkin.

He ran upstairs again. Ruta was standing by the old lady's door, which was shut as before, in conversation with the woman from the neighboring apartment; she had come out because of Fedorkin's knocking. This lady, tall, plump, and middle-aged, had moved in quite recently and for some reason Ruta had disliked her at once. Little by little, Fedorkin had come to think poorly of her, too, though there was no reason whatsoever to find fault with her: she always greeted them pleasantly, was even the first to say hello, and she took the letters out of her mailbox in a noiseless and delicate way, her box being beside the Fedorkins', and now here was Ruta chatting with this lady not just politely but even giggling, though, of course, that could have been out of shyness—in his surprise Fedorkin didn't even say hello.

"We could have all gone up in smoke," Ruta was saying, as though to justify all the noise they had made and laughing for no reason, "and we have a Finnish breakfront right next to the wall."

"But if she's home," the lady was saying.

"Yes, of course, now there's nothing to worry about," Ruta said. "It's likely she's talking so loud on purpose just to show everybody she's home, so it's no use knocking. And she's opened the window vent on purpose to let the smoke out—I can imagine what it's like in there! You were never inside her apartment?" Ruta's opinion was in complete accord with the handyman's, what the elevator operators had seized upon, and what this lady was also corroborating in her own way—strange how Fedorkin himself hadn't thought of it before, but now it suddenly occurred to him for some reason that maybe she was sick, and had crawled toward the door, and had lost consciousness, and was muttering something senselessly, and for an instant the thought even frightened him, and a chill ran down his spine.

"You know, we've started having cockroaches in our apartment," the lady said delicately.

"Not in your apartment too?" Ruta breathed out in delight. "And you just had your apartment redone, and you keep things so clean. They're all from there," Ruta motioned with her head to Nadezhda Pavlovna's door. "Well, now they'll spread through the whole house. How are you getting rid of them?"

One of the elevator operators, a small woman, almost a dwarf, who cleaned for a number of apartments, appeared on the landing.

"No, now she won't open," she said, sniffing the air.

"Well, now you see where the cockroaches are coming from," Ruta said to her husband when they had returned to their own apartment. "If they could show up at our new neighbor's! She keeps things so clean and neat. By the way, have you noticed, there's less of the urine smell from there lately?"

"Damned old woman!" Fedorkin said loudly so that Sofia Dmitrievna could hear, since she had such a strangely neutral attitude to what was going on in the old lady's apartment and to this whole business of the cockroaches, as though she didn't believe it and was expressing mute protest through her silence. It irritated Fedorkin, especially since his mother adored order and cleanliness; her silent solidarity with Nadezhda Pavlovna had to be in blatant opposition to Ruta and himself, and besides that, Fedorkin wanted to make his mother feel that she was a burden to them, that because of her they hadn't been able to take a vacation for two years in a row, and not only could they not go away somewhere, they couldn't even leave the house—Ruta had gone over this with Fedorkin many times, and whenever she spoke of it he would become irritated and protest, but Sofia Dmitrievna considered that everything was as it should be and that they were obliged to take care of her, and walking her to the toilet room Fedorkin would sometimes squeeze her arm above the elbow with hatred, feeling the hard bone through the flimsy softness of her muscle. She walked, leaning on a cane, while he held her up by the arm and steadied her from behind so that she didn't fall backward—her spine had become as bony and sharp as a fish's backbone; seating her on the toilet seat, it was an effort for him to push and lift her so she sat the right way—exactly as he had had to push Nadezhda Pavlovna back on the sofa so she wouldn't fall off—and his mother looked at him with her faded, once gray, eyes. Fedorkin had the same eyes as his mother, only he could never look anyone in the eyes for long and would shift his gaze to the side; his mother followed him with her eyes in silence whenever he came into her room to bring her something to eat or give her medicine—the irises of both eyes were ringed with opaque whitish circles. She almost couldn't read at all anymore and only very rarely asked Fedorkin for the newspaper, and then she only looked at the headlines. And yet, in his heart of hearts, Fedorkin still had secret doubts about the cockroaches.

Five or six days went by. Ruta smashed the cockroaches without mercy as they appeared, not only in the kitchen and bathroom, but even in the room where the Finnish breakfront stood, and Ruta didn't rule out the possibility that they were crawling under the wall from Nadezhda Pavlovna's apartment, under the baseboards, and were building nests behind the Finnish breakfront. Fedorkin learned to his astonishment that cockroaches run exceedingly fast and that catching them isn't so very easy. Their instinct for survival is extraordinarily developed, and maybe their perceptiveness too, because the moment Fedorkin would enter the bathroom, a cockroach who had been sitting there quietly took off at top speed, even before Fedorkin had made up his mind to chase it. Besides the manual method of cockroach elimination, Ruta used some kinds of sprays, while Fedorkin, at his office, learned the name of the powder the exterminators used on each of their monthly visits, and one of his co-workers told him that boric acid was good for getting rid of cockroaches, but Fedorkin told no one that cockroaches had appeared in his apartment, and made all his inquiries in a roundabout way.

Once, toward evening, the Fedorkins' doorbell rang. Ruta went to open the door, and after a moment Fedorkin heard Ruta's voice and another woman's—the woman's voice was expressionless and *o*-accented so at first Fedorkin thought it was Nadezhda Pavlovna. He looked down the hall. Standing in the doorway, Ruta was conversing with a woman—high-cheek-boned, carelessly dressed, much like Nadezhda Pavlovna, only younger.

"You're her sister?" Ruta asked—this had to be the sister whose telephone number Fedorkin had tried to get the day the burning smell came from Nadezhda Pavlovna's apartment. "You know, we haven't seen her for quite a few days now, and, look, her newspapers have been piling up"—Fedorkin now remembered noticing all these days that Nadezhda Pavlovna's mailbox was stuffed full, and a few newspapers and even some magazines were piled against her door because there was no room for them in the mailbox—however, it wouldn't be the first time, because she sometimes disappeared for days or even a couple of weeks while the mail continued coming. "Do please come in," Ruta said hospitably. "But to be honest, we thought she was staying with you. Anyway, the best thing to do is ask one of the elevator operators."

"A strange business," Ruta said when Nadezhda Pavlovna's sister had gone. "Her sister rang the doorbell and nobody opened it, but when she tried to open it with her key—she has a key to the apartment—it wouldn't go in, as if the keyhole were blocked from the inside."

"Yes, strange," Fedorkin agreed, and chills ran down his spine.

A moment later, the sister rang their bell again—the elevator operators didn't know anything, they hadn't seen Nadezhda Pavlovna that day, and there was nobody there from yesterday's shift.

"Permit me to try," Fedorkin said. He took the key from Nadezhda Pavlovna's sister and tried to put it in the keyhole—the key bumped against something hard and wouldn't go in further. Ruta and Nadezhda Pavlovna's sister stood beside him, and the sister was *o*-ing something—she was heavier than Nadezhda Pavlovna and had a short haircut, while Nadezhda Pavlovna had some sort of braids sticking out of her hat that looked like rats' tails.

"Still, most likely she's not home," Ruta said, for it was more comfortable to think so. "Maybe she's staying with one of her graduate students, or someone else. Come in and use our telephone."

"No, no, there's nowhere else she could be, if she stays over somewhere it's only at my place," Nadezhda Pavlovna's sister said with her strong "o"s, but she came in anyway and began making calls.

"Petya, was Nadezhda Pavlovna there? She didn't call? Call Zakhar Ivanovich and ask him if she called?"

No one knew anything, she hadn't called anyone.

"Perhaps I'll go fetch the handyman to break the lock," Nadezhda Pavlovna's sister said.

"But take this into consideration: if it turns out no one's there, you'll have to stay the night in the apartment," Ruta said, who knew how to be categorical at critical moments. "You can't leave an apartment unlocked for the night."

Nadezhda Pavlovna's sister started to fuss, say her funny *o*'s, and write a note.

"So then what, you'll stay?" Ruta asked point-blank.

"No, I couldn't possibly, my husband's expecting me, our apartment is on the other side of the city, we just moved in and don't have a telephone yet, and I don't know anyone in the building to call. Here, I've written her to call her nephew as soon as she gets in."

She tacked the note to Nadezhda Pavlovna's door and left.

The next day was a Sunday, and the Fedorkins got up late. When Fedorkin went to put on his showercap, so as not to spoil the way his hair was combed under the shower, a cockroach fell from the cap. It took off quickly across the tiled floor, but Fedorkin still managed to crush it with his foot.

"Damned old woman! Breeding cockroaches!" he said loudly so his mother would hear—as before, she didn't accept Ruta's version of where the cockroaches came from and maybe didn't believe in them altogether, and, besides, Ruta believed you should die when your time had come and not be a burden to anyone, while his mother didn't see it that way, and yesterday, when the old lady's sister had come in to telephone, Sofia Dmitrievna had been silent and not given any opinion on the subject of Nadezhda Pavlovna, though very likely she had one, but she was stubbornly silent, and Fedorkin regarded this silence of hers as the latest form of protest against Ruta and himself, though it was possible she had turned away from all that or simply didn't hear. When Fedorkin had gone into her room after Nadezhda Pavlovna's sister left, she was sitting in her chair with her blue, emaciated hands on her knees and staring at something, if it wasn't the curtain covering the window, then maybe the clock on the dresser, but she couldn't make out the clockface well and for that reason she asked Fedorkin, as she always did when he came into her room, "What time is it?"

After his shower and Sunday breakfast, which concluded with a cup of strong coffee, Fedorkin sat down to do the cross-word puzzle. After coffee, his mind worked especially well: the white squares seemed to fill themselves with letters, the words formed effortlessly in the spaces designed for them, like well-made parts in the assembly of a machine. At that moment, there was a short ring at the door. Fedorkin's heart clenched; he knew this would happen.

"Look through the peephole," he shouted to Ruta.

"Some people are standing outside the apartment next door," Ruta said in a voice hoarse with anxiety. "You go out."

"The judge will come, you must answer his questions. Hand me my coat and I'll be off," Fedorkin said in a voice of forced courage, and he walked out the door.

Enormous Yuri Adrianovich stood by the door, while behind him, squeezed on the landing, were Nadezhda Pavlovna's sister, the tiny elevator lady, and the tall, plump lady from the next apartment.

"You should go in, y'know, for a minute, just to verify," Yuri Adrianovich said in a voice unusually low for him, and he motioned cautiously with his head in the direction of Nadezhda Pavlovna's door.

The door of Nadezhda Pavlovna's apartment stood wide open, a small crowbar leaning against it.

His heart pounding, Fedorkin walked into the foyer. He wanted to go deep into the apartment, expecting to see the whole of it there, but then he nearly stumbled. There in the foyer, on the floor, lay Nadezhda Pavlovna, with a blue-black face and the same color wrists, in the old flannelette bathrobe, with her hair in unbraided, ratty plaits, her stockings coming down on her legs, bent as if she were sleeping or in the middle of another step when she was interrupted.

"Maybe she's still alive!" Nadezhda Pavlovna's sister exclaimed, following right behind Fedorkin, but staying in the doorway, hugging her arms to her chest and wringing her hands.

Fedorkin wanted to bend down and reach his hand out to touch Nadezhda Pavlovna, but even without doing so, he felt the deathly cold, the heaviness and inflexibility of her body—he could have touched her with his foot, in order to make sure, but it didn't seem proper to do that in her sister's presence.

"Nadya! Nadyusha!" her sister called, as though Nadezhda Pavlovna could waken from her sleep—in childhood she had shouted to her just that way when they played I Spy or catch in the big neglected garden by their house, where their father, a sales-tax collector, had settled the family with his wife and many children in one of the district cities near the Urals, and Nadya with two long russet braids, in a white dress, would appear from somewhere behind a tree or the toolshed and, seeing her sister, would wave to her, and they would run across to some other place, while their other brothers and sisters, a few of them already *gymnasium* students too, would be noisily and merrily chasing each other, and someone came out of the neighboring house that also had a big neglected garden, an upperclassman in the *gymnasium*—he already smoked, though of course on the sly—only Nadya's sister couldn't figure out if he came over to see her or Nadya. Sometimes he caught Nadya, squeezed her arm tight, and once, having caught her, he clumsily kissed her cheek— Nadya's sister saw it, because just then she was running away from someone, too, and stopping to hide, she had seen all of it from behind a lilac bush . . .

"Maybe she was still alive yesterday," Nadezhda Pavlovna's sister was saying, wringing her hands. "If only we had broken in yesterday . . ."

"No, by the look of things, it happened two days ago at least," Fedorkin said, though he wasn't so sure himself.

He walked out of Nadezhda Pavlovna's apartment and began trying to convince the tall plump lady to go inside, too, if only for a moment, so she might verify it; otherwise, "the judge will come, you must answer his questions," Fedorkin thought again—he was afraid they would drag him off to the police station or some other judicial organ; but the lady wouldn't go inside for anything—she was dressed in a blue-silk quilted bathrobe, as if she'd just come out of the bath, and she stood between Nadezhda Pavlovna's door and her own, which stood half open. The more Fedorkin tried to talk her into entering, the further she moved away from the late Nadezhda Pavlovna's door and closer to her own.

"No, no, I cannot, please," she kept saying, standing by then in her own doorway.

The little elevator operator had also slinked down the stairs, with no sign of coming back.

"Maybe you should go inside," Fedorkin said to his wife, who was also peeking out of their half-open door.

"No, not for anything," she said, "you know very well I'm afraid"—anyhow, he and his wife were one family, so if this matter ever reached the courts, it would be taken as a family conspiracy.

Yuri Adrianovich, crowbar in hand, started down the stairs in a dignified manner. Fedorkin also returned to his apartment and shut the door. From Nadezhda Pavlovna's apartment came the sound of her sister sobbing.

Then steps and voices were heard again behind the door. The Fedorkins looked out through their peephole: the building manager and his bookkeeper and someone else had come up.

"The police have to be called," the building manager said, and Fedorkin's heart sank again—it was just what he thought would happen—now he'd be dragged into it; the building manager wasn't very tall, he was heavy, with practically no neck—he always carried a bulging briefcase under his arm, which made one of his shoulders look higher, and he usually looked like the caricature of the bureaucrat in satirical plays, only now he was without his briefcase.

"It's my opinion we should call an ambulance for the death certificate," said the bookkeeper, a blonde woman with blue eyes and the face of a fox.

"Then we might as well call in the forensic specialists," the building manager said.

Fedorkin fastened himself to the peephole, crowding out Ruta—the building manager, the bookkeeper, and someone else, maybe an elevator lady, only not the tiny one, went inside the old lady's apartment; this already made things better, because in case of anything, they would be witnesses, too, though still it was he, Fedorkin, who had been the first, and for that reason the main indictment would lay with him.

In order to distract himself, Fedorkin sat down again to do the crossword puzzle, but this time not a single word appeared in its assigned location, and to make matters worse, Ruta was crashing her pots in the kitchen so much that Fedorkin felt the noise was interfering with his crossword.

"Can't you be quieter!" he shouted to his wife, but just then the doorbell rang again, and both Fedorkins, their hearts pounding, went to open it.

The building manager himself stood outside the door—without his briefcase he had a sort of domestic look, and all his self-importance had evaporated.

"Please come in," Ruta said, fussing—most of the time she suspected the building manager and the bookkeeper of being part of a secret conspiracy and carrying out all sorts of sinister schemes—but the building manager wouldn't step inside and stood in the doorway, his back against the doorjamb, as though he were prepared to have a nice long chat. Voices could be heard coming from Nadezhda Pavlovna's apartment—maybe it was the police who had come, or maybe the ambulance or the forensic specialists.

"You were there, after all, you saw her," the building manager said, motioning with his head in the direction of Nadezhda Pavlovna's apartment and addressing Fedorkin. "What do you think, did it happen some time ago?"

"Well, I can't say for sure," Fedorkin mumbled, "maybe a day, maybe two—in general, it's hard to say"—he positioned himself so as to block from the building manager's view the door of his mother's room—the thought suddenly came to him that his mother might complain to the building manager that she was being mistreated.

Ruta went back to the kitchen, Fedorkin remained face to face with the building manager.

"We've already had two apartments vacated this way, this is the third," the building manager said, and it wasn't clear if he was saddened by this turn of events or put in a difficult position by it.

"Yes, it's no use," Fedorkin said in order to say something. "Quite a contingent of 'em we've got in our house," he muttered.

"Yes, yes," the building manager said vaguely.

Ruta excused herself, invited the building manager in again and squeezed past them, with her coat on—she had to go buy some groceries.

"It's full of cockroaches in there," the building manager said in his vague way, as though there was nothing to say after that.

"You saw?" Ruta gasped, not yet down the stairs and turning back to the administrator. "Now they'll spread through the whole house, I've already seen one myself on the stairs, and we have lots of them, and they've shown up in our neighbor's apartment; it's enough already," she said in a tone that implied that all of this had been known for a long time, but she was letting the authorities know once and for all, and Fedorkin along with them, and her eyes even lit up in triumph . . .

After dinner, she struck without mercy at every cockroach she saw with the flyswatter, and in each of her blows you could feel the modest exaltation of a victor.

"Damned old woman, breeding cockroaches!" Fedorkin said in time to his wife's blows and going after them himself—it was entirely possible that these very cockroaches had been crawling over the dead old lady's body yesterday, and now were running around their apartment, and probably even getting into the food.

He got so carried away killing cockroaches that he even forgot to draw the curtain across his mother's window, and Sofia Dmitrievna, seated in her chair, looked out at the sloping hillside—white with snow on which children were sledding—at the lights going on in neighboring houses, and at the snow-covered roofs, and saw herself as a schoolgirl again skating in tightly laced boots and remembered how she would come home on frosty days, and her mother would push back her hood and kiss her on both cheeks, and the water in the samovar on the table was already boiling, and her father, a railway engineer, came out of his study to have tea, neat as always in his uniform, small and wiry, with a prickly mustache that tickled Sonya when he kissed her; her mother poured his tea first, and then Sonya's next, and then she remembered that when her son was born the first thing she thought and said was that he would have to go to war, but when the war started, Dima was only ten years old, but her husband was killed in the war, a professional soldier, a colonel, and they gave her a big pension for him and gave her an apartment in this house, and when Dima married, in the beginning her daughter-in-law used to kiss her cheek and even call her "pussycat" and stroked her head, but gradually everything changed, and now Ruta mostly didn't call her anything, and would bring her food in silence and leave it on a little table in front of her chair, but for some reason with no napkin, and the tea all cold, and from the kitchen she would hear more and more often the words "hospital" and "nursing home," and then her son's shout breaking into a high decibel and a similar shout and her daughter-in-law's weeping, and then something in there fell and broke, and after that, her son came to her room with an especially hostile look on his face, while now she could hear the flick of a flyswatter and her son exclaiming "Damned old woman!" and it seemed to her it was meant for her. Outside it was almost dark by now—"What time is it, Dima?" she asked her son when he came into her room to draw the curtains and turn on the lights—"Twenty to seven, can't you see?" he said with irritation, though he knew she couldn't see, while out there beyond the window life went on— children came home for supper, lights went on in windows, and again she saw herself as a schoolgirl on a skating rink, circling easily to the tune of "The Blue Danube" . . .

When Fedorkin returned from his evening stroll, the note Nadezhda Pavlovna's sister had written was still tacked to the old woman's door: "Nadya, when you come home, call Petya. Polina," and the mailbox was still stuffed, but there were no longer any newspapers by the door. He put his nose close to the crack where the door met the doorframe and sniffed—it smelled less of urine.

Next day, the note was no longer there, and a white paper tape appeared across the door sealing the doorjamb, bearing the red stamps of the house management office. The mail, though, continued coming, and newspapers and magazines were now sticking out of the mailbox at every possible angle, and some mail lay strewn on the floor.

"Damned mailmen, don't they see," Fedorkin grumbled, and he took a quarter-sheet of paper and wrote on it in big letters: "ADDRESSEE DEAD, APARTMENT SEALED," and fastened it to Nadezhda Pavlovna's mailbox.

March 1, 1978
Translated by Anne Frydman

Afterword
by Jamey Gambrell

Leonid Tsypkin's work is grounded in a specific historical context that has almost faded from memory, not only in the west, but in post-Soviet Russia: the "era of stagnation" under Leonid Brezhnev, and the beginning of a huge Jewish emigration that began in the mid-seventies.

By this time, Soviet citizens were no longer in the fearsome grip of Stalinist terror. Khrushchev's 1956 "secret speech" to the Politburo, denouncing Stalin, had brought about a political and cultural "Thaw": there was a mass exodus from the Gulag as political prisoners were released and "rehabilitated"; artists and writers ventured bravely into territory that would have landed them in Siberia just a few years earlier; and the Iron Curtain was opened a crack—just enough for a peek at the economies and culture of the west.

In 1964, Khrushchev was removed from power and Leonid Brezhnev became general secretary of the Communist Party. A freezing blast of ideology hit the country, resealing the surface cracks in the political and cultural climate. The Thaw was stopped in its tracks.

The Thaw had a lasting impact on the Russian intelligentsia, mostly in Moscow and St. Petersburg: it lit the spark of unofficial (underground or non-conformist) art and literature. However, the apparatus of the Soviet state remained intact (as indeed a good deal of it still is today). The press, the arts, and publishing of any sort—from vodka labels, match boxes, and restaurant menus to novels, cartoons, and museum exhibitions—had to pass through a vast, rigid network of state censorship before reaching the public. Many of Russia's greatest twentieth-century poets, like Boris Pasternak and Anna Akhmatova, and Osip Mandelshtam and Marina Tsvetaeva, were either very selectively published or almost not at all.

The poet Joseph Brodsky—a Jew—was tried in the early seventies for being a "parasite" or "slacker," i.e., having no job. The real issue of course was the nature and content of his poetry. His reply to the court, that his job was being a poet, was deemed absurd: how could he be a poet if he didn't belong to the Writers Union? Brodsky was sent into exile for a time, but after an international outcry on his behalf the authorities thought it more expedient to "banish" him to the west, and he left for the United States.

Despite the regime's crackdowns, writers like Brodsky were "published" and circulated in samizdat (in manuscripts that were usually typed in carbon paper triplicate). Possession of works such as Alexander Solzhenitsyn's *Gulag Archipelago* had extremely serious consequences, from losing your job to imprisonment. Nonetheless, samizdat flourished. The thirst for culture, Russian and foreign, only grew: the first translations of Tolkien's work circulated in samizdat; and though rock and roll and jazz were not often heard on the radio, ever resourceful Russians figured out how to record the music they loved—on x-ray film, an inventive use of technology that was eventually replaced by the tape recorder.

This was the world in which Leonid Tsypkin wrote and his characters lived. Though neither he nor they belonged to this alternative culture, it was there, part and parcel of the Soviet world. Other classic features of Brezhnev's "stagnation" pop up everywhere in Tsypkin's work. The Soviet citizen of the seventies was a modern forager—you could never be sure where you would find what necessary item. Cultural and consumer goods usually had to be "obtained," which often entailed standing on endless lines to acquire some "shortage item," whether oranges, bananas, blue jeans, or perhaps a subscription to the complete works of a great writer. With a stagnant economy and privileged political elite, the country functioned through a meta-barter system known as *blat*. *Blat* meant connections to power and access at whatever level, from the power a shop assistant held because she had access to desirable consumer goods, to that wielded by a high-placed political official who shopped at "special" stores, and could travel abroad, bringing Chanel N°5 home for his wife—which she in turn might barter for something else she wanted or needed more.

Blat could get you sought-after concert tickets, or a prime cut of beef. If you wanted a dignified vacation, in a hotel, rather than at the overcrowded, dirty, uncomfortable resorts run by industries or organizations for their workers, where megaphones announced activities and meal times for the "comrade vacationers"—you needed blat, as Boris Lvovich, the protagonist of *Norartakir* knows all too well.

These everyday realities comprised a demeaning paradox for people who knew they lived in a superpower that sent men and satellites into space and was a treasure chest of natural resources. As books, movies, parades, songs, paintings and the press constantly reminded the populace, the USSR had conquered fascism, against terrible odds and despite terrible losses. Though the people's heroism in crushing the fascist war machine exceeded even the Revolution in the popular mind, the fate of Jews in that conflict was rarely if ever mentioned.

This was another defining feature of the 1970s: rising, state-sponsored anti-Semitism, and the emigration of an enormous part of the Soviet Jewish population. Resurgent anti-Semitism plays a key role in many of Tsypkin's works. As his narrator is aware, the Nazis had not only gassed millions of Jews in concentration camps; they had shot tens of thousands on Soviet territory and dumped them in ditches. But the people who later gathered in silence to commemorate the unmentioned massacre at Babi Yar—in the ancient city known for its churches, as Tsypkin puts it—were themselves arrested and taken away.

The protagonist of Tsypkin's work—always one and the same individual—feels these paradoxes acutely. He wants to be an upright Soviet citizen, but as a Jew he knows that he doesn't really belong, that others see him as a potentially traitorous foreigner. In *The Bridge over the Neroch*, he recalls his family's flight from advancing German troops at the beginning of WWII, and remembers the stories he heard of what happened to Jews who didn't manage to escape in time. Fresh in his mind as well is the memory of his father's Russian colleague, director of the institute where his father worked, who decided to rid himself of "unreliable" (i.e. Jewish) personnel not long before Stalin's death in 1953, during the anti-Semitic campaign known as the "Doctors' Plot."

Many of this character's apparently incomprehensible actions and obsessions originate here: his fear of walking up the little lane where Moscow's main synagogue is located; his constant references to people who "look like him," and to his wife's broad cheekbones (a Russian, rather than Jewish trait) and the fact that his son has inherited this facial feature—though broad cheekbones don't prevent the boy from being recognized as a Jew.

Tsypkin's narrator doesn't live in the era of Kristallnacht and Auschwitz, but that history is imprinted on him like a genetic code. It dwells in an easily accessible, eternal present inside him. It's there when his son is the victim of a random, vicious beating by a group of "friends," because he is a Jew. It is right at his side when he remembers how his son was bullied and threatened at school by Russian boys who taunted him by calling him "Sarah," an Old Testament name that would identify him as Jewish—and a girl's name at that, which only added insult to injury. (Old

Testament names, particularly for women, are instant markers of being a Jew in Russia; naming children Sarah, Rebecca, Judith, David, or Mark is tantamount to tattooing a six-pointed yellow star on their forehead.)

That genetic code, however, only takes him as far as detection, it hasn't programmed him for action; all the efforts that Boris Lvovich, the boy's father, makes to seek justice for his son come to naught. Nor could he defend his son against the boys on the playground. His helplessness is a recipe for guilt, indignation, helplessness, and paranoia. Ironically, when transferred into literature, these characteristics ally him closely with Russian literature, specifically Dostoevsky's "underground man," who is the anti-hero of Tsypkin's novel *Summer in Baden-Baden*.

Every aspect of the narrator's persona is in one way or another related to his being a Jew: his unrelenting self-consciousness about his physical appearance; his heightened sensitivity, which feeds an extreme, at times cruel, narcissism—as is evident in the incident with the hotel directress in *Norartakir*. These character traits in turn engender a particular narrative structure: a hyper-vigilant, self-protective stream-of-consciousness that verges on, and sometimes plunges into, fantasy and paranoia. All history is alive in him simultaneously, so in one sequence Tsypkin may take the reader from the ark of the Old Testament that came to rest on Mount Ararat (which he can see out his hotel window), to the rise of the New Testament Christ and the crucifixion of Jesus, the Jew; through Babi Yar and the Holocaust, to the Soviet military planes he hears flying out of Yerevan at night to supply Egypt and its allies with tanks to use against Israeli Jews during the Yom Kippur war in 1973. He may enter the metro in 1972 but he might just as easily emerge in 1952 as in 1936.

At work throughout these novellas and stories are silences and omissions—what remained unsaid in the seventies—that function as code for concepts too freighted with meaning to pronounce out loud. In *Norartakir*, when the couple is in their hotel room, Tanya gestures meaningfully at the wall with her eyes: watch what you say, the walls have ears; in the seventies, everyone assumed that everything was bugged. When the plane circles to land in Yerevan, Boris Lvovich and his wife realize they are probably flying over Turkish territory; his wife asks him in a whisper whether he would stay; the train heading back to Moscow runs so close to the border that Boris Lvovich can see the barbed wire, and he sticks his hand out the window to let it touch the Turkish air. Both acts have the thrill of the illicit because they put the narrator in close proximity with the forbidden space *over there*.

Over there is the promised land, the origin of the letters the son reads voraciously: that is, the west—Europe, Israel, and the United States. *Over there* is an empty land with no place on the Soviet map; its contours and content are in the eye of the beholder. The narrator's son reads the letters given him by anonymous sources and they confirm his desire to *leave*. His parents read them and ultimately condone his decision, though they have a lifetime of ties and obligations from which they cannot imagine breaking free; the grandmother, having come of age at the turn of the century and lived through pogroms and the Revolution which brought unprecedented equality for Jews, is true to the Party line and her generation: she sees the letters as "provocations," and claims to have never experienced the anti-Semitism her son and grandson talk about.

If *over there* meant beyond the border, *to leave* was certainly not to go on vacation. It meant to step over the state border into that mythical, featureless blank land on the map—and never to return. When Soviet citizens emigrated in the 1970s, they were stripped of their citizenship; they were not allowed back into the country, nor were their relatives allowed to visit them in the west. The decision *to stay*, therefore, was just as fateful as the one *to leave*.

In a literature where anti-Semitism and the narrator's identity as a Jew are so often the lynchpin of the story, it may seem strange that the word Jew is almost never used. The adjective "Jewish" appears only a couple of times: when the narrator remembers his grandfather speaking "the Jewish language" to his old friends, and when the grandfather calls the grandmother affectionate nicknames "in the Jewish manner." Ironically, perhaps, one of the threads most beautifully woven through *Norartakir*, is that of the crucifixion. The narrator's Jesus sees everything from his vantage point on the cross: the gas chambers and the ditches full of bodies, Noah and his sons after the ark has come to rest and the waters have subsided, the cruelty of the Roman soldiers, the scribes of the Old Testament, and the planes taking off to the sun-parched land of the Middle East. Again, however, the word, the name is missing, as if too terrible to speak; Christ is referred to as "the man with the sunken eyes." The narrator cannot understand why the world has forgotten that Jesus himself was a Jew. Why should Boris Lvovich feel so alien in the 1970s, when his people were those of the man with the sunken eyes, when he looks like Jesus and Jesus' friends and family?

The desire to belong to Russia is intense, and so he flirts with the Orthodox Church—and in fact it was very common in the seventies for urban Jews to be baptized in the Russian Orthodox Church, while also affirming their identity as Jews. But the flirtation isn't comfortable for Tsypkin's narrator—if his son openly wears a cross at one point, in "Ave Maria," he crosses himself self-consciously during the funeral service, as though brushing a fly off his shoulders or scratching his nose.

Tsypkin's work is informed by an excruciating fidelity to the truths of biography—the facts are not all that important. For Tsypkin's narrator, history is a tightrope to be walked every minute of every day, in both his internal and external life. On one side is the USSR and Mother Russia, to which he desperately wishes to belong, but feels he never really can; on the other is an abyss, the alluring unknown of "over there," an empty white space like that on the tourist map he carries with him in *Norartakir*. The line he has to negotiate is as thin and as treacherous as the barbed wire running alongside the train tracks, separating his homeland from "the real Turkey."